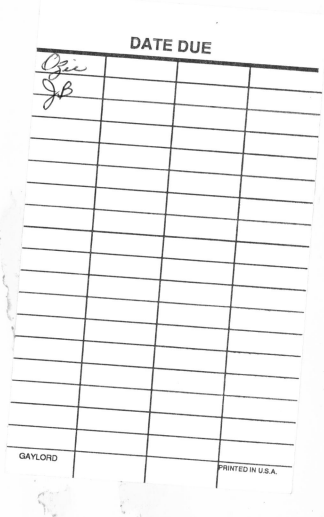

SHOW
OF
EVIL

SHOW
OF
EVIL

WILLIAM DIEHL

BALLANTINE BOOKS • NEW YORK

To my goddaughter Shana, for a wonderful character,
To Shakes, Uncle Don, the two Michaels, Buddy and Brett,
Constant and treasured friends all,
And always and forever—for Virginia

Library of Congress Cataloging-in-Publication Data
Diehl, William.
  Show of evil / by William Diehl—1st ed.
    p. cm.
  ISBN 0-345-37535-1
  I. Title.
PS3554.I345S48   1995
813'.54—dc20   94-24112
                CIP

Manufactured in the United States of America

First Edition: June 1995

10 9 8 7 6 5 4 3 2 1

In law, what plea so tainted and corrupt
But, being season'd with a gracious voice,
Obscures the show of evil?

—THE MERCHANT OF VENICE,
ACT 3, SCENE 2

SHOW
OF
EVIL

PROLOGUE

The town of Gideon, Illinois, biblical of name and temperament, squats near the juncture of Kentucky and Indiana at the edge of the Blue Ridge Mountains. A trickle of a river called the Wahoo forms the western boundary of the town, while Appalachian foothills etch its southern and eastern parameters. It was founded in the mid 1800s by a handful of farmers driven south by encroaching midwestern cities, by railroads, and by brutal winters. They were followed soon afterward by a fire-eyed reader of the Church of Latter-Day Saints named Abraham Gideon, who had split from Brigham Young and led a small troop of followers toward the southern mountains. They had blundered onto the fledgling village, liked what they'd seen, and settled down there. It was Gideon who gave the town its name and a strict moral code that has persisted for nearly one hundred and fifty years.

Inhabited by two thousand and some citizens, most of them hardworking conservatives and many of Mormon descent, it is a town that takes care of itself and minds its own business. Its architecture is stern and simple; its streets paved only when necessity demands; its town core a collection of indispensable businesses without frills or fancies; its town meetings held at the Baptist church, the largest building in town.

The only car dealer sells Fords and farm equipment. A foreign car in Gideon is as improbable as Grandma Moses rising from the grave and running naked through the streets on Sunday morning.

The city council, a collection of dour curmudgeons, runs the town with a kind of evangelical fervor, enduring its handful of bars and taverns but drawing the line at sex, having chased away Gideon's one topless bar during the late eighties and railing against R-rated movies so vociferously that most of the citizens watch them on cable rather than venture forth to the town's twin theaters and thereby risk the scorn of the five old men who set both the tone and moral temper of the town. The young people, who silently revolt against its anachronisms, usually spend their weekends driving to nearby towns that have shopping malls and multiplex theaters, where they can buy a six-pack of beer without being recognized.

For the most part, Gideons are friendly, concerned, protective people who help their townsfolk when they are in trouble and who practice a kind of archaic combination of do-unto-others and love-thy-neighbor. And as long as its citizens sequester their more shocking vices behind closed doors and shuttered windows, nobody really gives a hoot. In short, it is a place that time, distance, and desire have cloistered from the rest of the world.

Gideons like it that way. They do not take kindly to others snooping in their business and they solve their problems without the intrusion of outsiders like state politicians or federal people or snoopy, big-time newspaper reporters.

On a Tuesday morning in October 1993, a few days before Halloween, a single shocking act of violence was to change all that.

Suddenly, trust was replaced by suspicion, ennui by fear, complacency by scorn. People began to lock their doors and windows during the daytime and porch lights glowed all night. And casual neighbors, who once waved friendly hellos in passing, were suddenly as cautious as strangers.

Yet like a protective family, Gideon kept this scandal behind locked doors and whispered of it only in rumors. The horrifying act itself was kept from the rest of the world—for a while, at least.

On that fall morning, Linda Balfour prepared her husband's customary lunch: tuna fish sandwiches with mayo on white bread, a wedge of the apple pie she had made the night before, potato chips, orange juice in his thermos. She had also polished his bright orange hard hat before fixing a breakfast of poached eggs, crisp bacon, well-done toast, and strong black coffee, and the hat and lunch box were sitting beside his plate with the morning edition of the *St. Louis Post-Dispatch* when he came down.

George Balfour was a bulky man in his early forties with a cherubic smile that hinted of a gentle and appreciative nature. A lifelong resident of Gideon, he had married Linda late in his thirties after a brief courtship and regarded both his twenty-six-year-old wife and their year-old son, Adam, as gifts from God, having lived a solitary and somewhat lonely life before meeting her at a company seminar in Decatur three years earlier.

Their two-story house was seventy years old, a spartan, white-frame place near the center of town with a wraparound porch and a large front lawn and an old-fashioned kitchen with both a wood-burning stove and a gas range. It was George Balfour's only legacy. He had lived in the house all his life, both of his parents having died in the bedroom that Balfour now shared with his wife.

He loved coming down in the morning to those smells he remembered from his youth: coffee and burned oak slivers from the wood-burning stove, and bacon and, in the summer, the luscious odor of freshly cut cantaloupe. The TV would be set on the *Today* show. His paper would be waiting.

He was wearing what he always wore: khaki pants, starched and pressed with a razor crease, a white T-shirt smelling of Downy, heavy, polished brogans, his cherished orange windbreaker with SOUTHERN ILLINOIS POWER AND LIGHT COMPANY stenciled across the back and the word SUPERINTENDENT printed where the left breast pocket would normally be. Everything about his dress, his home, and his family bespoke a man who lived by order and routine. Balfour was not a man who liked surprises or change.

He kissed his son good morning, wiping a trace of pabulum from the boy's chin before giving Linda a loving peck on the back of her neck. She smiled up at him, a slightly plump woman with premature wrinkles around her eyes and mouth and auburn hair pulled back and tied in a bun. The wrinkles, George often said, were because his wife laughed a lot.

Nothing about George Balfour's life was inchoate.

"Saints finally got beat yesterday," she said as he sat down.

"'Bout time," he answered, scanning the front page of the paper. "By the way, I gotta run up to Carbondale after lunch. They got a main transformer out. May be a little late for dinner."

"Okay. Six-thirty? Seven?"

"Oh, I should be home by six-thirty."

At seven-fifteen, he was standing on the porch when Lewis Holliwell pulled up in the pickup. He kissed Linda and Adam goodbye, then waved at them from the truck as Lewis drove away from the white-frame house. They turned the corner and suddenly the street was empty except for old Mrs. Aiken, who waved good morning as she scampered in robe and slippers off her porch to pick up the paper, and a solitary utility man carrying a toolbox who was trudging down the alley behind the house. A bright sun was just peeking over the hills to the east, promising a day of cloudless splendor.

Thirty minutes later the Balfours' next-door neighbor, Miriam Perrone, noticed that the Balfours' back door was standing open. *Odd*, she thought, *it's a bit chilly this morning.* A little later she looked out her dining room window and the door was still open. She went out the back door and walked across her yard to the Balfours'.

"Linda?" she called out.

No answer. She walked to the door.

"Linda?" Still no answer. She rapped on the door frame. "Linda, it's Miriam. Did you know your back door's open?"

No answer. A feeling of uneasiness swept over her as she cautiously entered the kitchen, for she did not wish to intrude.

"Linda?"

Suddenly, she was seized with an inexplicable sense of dread. It choked her and her mouth went dry. She could hear the television, but neither Linda nor the baby was making a sound. She walked toward the door to the living room. As she approached the door, she saw the empty playpen and a second later Adam lying on his side on the carpet with his back toward her.

And then, as she stepped through the doorway, she stopped. Her lips trembled for what seemed like eternity before a low moan rose to a horrified shriek.

A few feet from the crib, Linda Balfour's butchered body was crumpled against the wall, her glazed eyes frozen in terror, her mouth gaping, a widening pond of her own blood spreading around her, while Katie Couric and Willard Scott joked about the weather on the bloodstained television set nearby.

That was how it started.

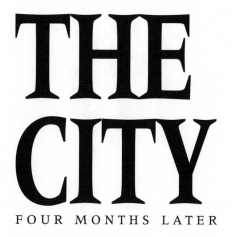

THE CITY

FOUR MONTHS LATER

1

Fog swirled around powerful spotlights in the darkest hours before dawn. Perched atop tall steel poles, they cast harsh beams out across a rancid, steaming wasteland, etching in shadow and light the buttes, knolls, and slopes of trash and refuse, of abandoned plastic bottles, Styrofoam dishes, cardboard fast-food wrappers, old newspapers, abandoned clothing, and maggot-ridden mounds of uneaten food. Like fetid foothills pointing toward the glittering skyscrapers miles away, the city's garbage formed a stunted mountain range of waste. Stinking vapors swirled up from the bacteria-generated heat of the vast landfill, while small, gray scavengers zigzagged frantically ahead of a growling bulldozer that pushed and shoved the heaps of filth into a manageably level plain.

The dozer operator, huddled deep inside layers of clothing, looked like an interplanetary alien: long johns, a flannel shirt, a thick wool sweater, a bulky jacket that might have challenged the Arctic wastelands, a wool cap pulled down over his ears, fur-lined leather and canvas gloves, a surgical mask protecting his mouth from the freezing cold and his nose from the choking odors, skier's goggles covering his eyes. Gloria Estefan's *Mi Tierra* thundered through the earphones of the Walkman in his pocket, drowning out the grinding din of the big machine.

Another hour, Jesus Suarino, who was known as Gaucho on his block, was thinking. *One more hour and I'm outta here.*

He worked the controls. Twisting the dozer in place, he lowered the blade and attacked a fresh mound of waste. The dozer tracks ground under him, spewing refuse behind the tractor as they gripped the soggy base and lurched forward. Through his misted goggles, Suarino watched the blade slice into the top of the mound, showering it into a shallow chasm just beyond. Suarino backed the machine up, dropped the blade a little lower, took off another layer of rubble. As it chopped into the pile, Suarino saw something through his smeared goggles.

He snatched the throttle back, heard the lumbering giant of a machine choke back as it slowed down and its exhaust gasp in the cold wind that swept across the range of rubble. He squinted his eyes and leaned forward, then wiped one lens with the palm of his glove.

What he saw jarred him upright. A figure rose up out of the clutter as the blade cut under it. Suarino stared at a skeletal head with eyeless sockets and strings of blond hair streaked with grease and dirt hanging from an almost skinless skull. The head of the corpse wobbled back and forth, then toppled forward until its jaw rested on an exposed rib cage.

"Yeeeeoowww!" he shrieked, his scream of terror trapped by the mask. He tore the goggles off and leaned forward, looking out over the engine. The corpse fell sideways, exposing an arm that swung out and then fell across the torso, the fleshless fingers of the hand pointing at him.

Suarino cut off the engine and swung out of the driver's seat, dropping into the sludge and sinking almost to his knees. Ripping off the mask, he was still screaming as he struggled toward the office at the edge of the dump.

—

Martin Vail hated telephones. Telephones represented intrusions. Invasions of his privacy. Interruptions. But duty dictated that the city's chief prosecutor and assistant D.A. never be without one.

They were everywhere: three different lines in his apartment—one a hotline, the number known only to his top aide, Abel Stenner, and his executive secretary, Naomi Chance—all with portable handsets and answering machines attached; a cellular phone in his briefcase; two more lines in his car. The only place he could escape from the dreaded devices was in the shower. He particularly hated the phone in the dead of night, and although he had all the ringers set so they rang softly and with a pleasant melodic tone, they were persistent and ultimately would drag him from the deepest sleep.

When the hotline rang, it was never good news, and the hotline had been ringing for a full minute when Vail finally rolled over onto his back and groped in the dark until he located the right instrument.

"What time is it," he growled into the mouthpiece.

"Almost five," Stenner's calm voice answered.

"What's that mean?"

"Four-twenty."

"You're a sadist, Major Stenner. I'll bet you put toothpicks under the fingernails of small children and light them. I bet you laugh at them when they scream."

"Better wear old clothes."

"Where are we going?"

"Twenty minutes?"

"What's going on, Abel?"

"I'll ring you from the car."

And he hung up.

Vail verbally assaulted the phone for half a minute, then turned on the night light so he would not fall back to sleep. He stretched, kicked off the covers, and lay flat on his back in the cold room, arms outstretched, until he was fully awake.

Four-twenty in the damn morning. He got up, threw on a robe, and went to the kitchen, then ground up some Jamaican blue, poured cold water into the coffee machine, and headed for the shower. Fifteen minutes later he was dressed in corduroy pants, a wool sweater, and hiking boots. He doctored two large

mugs of coffee, dumped several files from his desk into his briefcase, and when the phone rang he was ready to roll.

He snatched up the phone and said, "This better be good," and
hung up. Throwing on a thick sheepskin car coat, he headed for
the lobby ten floors below.

Major Abel Stenner sat ramrod straight behind the wheel. He
was impeccably dressed in a gray pin-striped suit. When Stenner
had accepted the job of Vail's chief investigator, Vail had promoted
him to major, a rank rarely used except in the state police. It was
a diabolical act on Vail's part—Stenner now outranked everyone
in the city police but the chief. Vail handed him a mug of coffee.

"Thanks," Stenner said.

"I thought you said to wear old clothes. You look like you're on
your way to deliver a eulogy."

"I was already dressed," he answered as he pulled away from
the curb.

Stenner, a precise and deliberate man whose stoic expression
and hard brown eyes shielded even a hint of emotion, was not
only the best cop the city had ever produced, he was the most pe-
nurious with words, a man who rarely smiled and who spoke in
short, direct, unflourished sentences.

"Where the hell are we going?"

"You'll see."

Vail crunched down in the seat and sipped his coffee.

"Don't you ever sleep, Abel?"

"You ask me that once a week."

"You never answer."

"Why start?"

More silence. That they had become close friends was a miracle.
Ten years ago, when Vail had been the top defense attorney in the
state and had worked against the state instead of for it, they had
been deadly adversaries. Stenner was the one cop who always had
it right, who knew what it took to make a good case, who
wouldn't bite at the trick question and could see through the
setup, and who had only been broken on the stand once—by Vail

during the Aaron Stampler trial. When Vail took the job of chief prosecutor, one of his first official duties was to steal Stenner away from Police Chief Eric Eckling. He had fully expected Stenner to turn him down, their animosity had been that profound, and he had been shocked when Stenner accepted the job.

"You're on my side now," Stenner had explained with a shrug. "Besides, Eckling is incompetent."

Ten years. In those years, Stenner had actually begun to loosen up. He had been known to smile on occasion and there was a myth around the D.A.'s office, unconfirmed, that he had once cracked a joke—although it was impossible to find anyone who actually had heard it.

Vail was half asleep, his coffee mug clutched between both hands to keep it from spilling, when Stenner turned off the high-way and headed down the back tar road leading to the sprawling county landfill. His head wobbled back and forth. Then he was aware of a kaleidoscope of lights dancing on his eyelids.

He opened them, sat up in his seat, and saw, against a small mountain of refuse, flashing yellow, red, and blue reflections against the dark, steamy night. A moment later Stenner rounded the mound and the entire scene was suddenly spread out be-fore them. There were a dozen cars of various descriptions—ambulances, police cars, the forensics van—all parked hard against the edge of the landfill. Beyond them, like men on the moon, yellow-garbed cops and firemen struggled over the steamy land-scape, piercing the looming piles of garbage with long poles. The acrid smell of the burning garbage, rotten food, and wet paper permeated the air. For a moment it reminded Vail of the last time he had gone home, to a place ironically called Rainbow Flats, which had been savaged by polluters who repaid the community for enduring them by poisoning the land, water, and air. First one came, then another, attracted to the place like hyenas to carrion, until it was a vast island of death surrounded by forests they had yet to destroy. He had gone home to bury his grandmother thir-teen years earlier and never returned. A momentary flash of the

Rainbow Flats Industrial Park supplanted the scene before him. It streaked through his mind and was gone. It had always angered him that they had had the gall to call it a park.

Three tall poles with yellow flags snapping in the harsh wind seemed to establish the parameters of the search. They were bunched in a cluster, a circle perhaps fifty yards in circumference. The sickening sour-sweet odor of death intruded on the wind and occasionally overpowered the smell of decay. Four men came over a ridge of the dump hefting a green body bag among them.

"That's three," Stenner said.

"Bodies?"

"Where the flags are." He nodded.

"Jesus!"

"First one was over there, in that cluster. A woman. They tumbled on the second one when I called you."

A freezing blast of cold air swept the car as Stenner got out. Vail turned up his collar and stepped out into the predawn. He jammed his hands deep in his coat pockets and hunched his shoulders against the wind. He could feel his lips chapping as his warm breath turned to steam and blew back into his face.

Two cops, an old-timer and a rookie, were standing guard beside the yellow crime-scene ribbons as Vail and Stenner stepped over them. The wind whipped Stenner's tie out and it flapped around his face for a moment before he tucked it back under his jacket as they walked toward the landfill.

"Jesus, don't he have a coat? Gotta be ten degrees out," said the rookie.

"He don't need a coat," the older cop said. "He ain't got any blood. That's Stenner. Know what they used to call him when he was with the PD? The Icicle."

Twenty feet away Stenner stopped and turned slowly as the cop said it and stared at him for a full ten seconds, then turned back to the crime scene.

"See what I mean," the older cop whispered. "Nobody ever called him that to his face."

"Must have ears in the back of his head."

"It's eyes."

"Huh?"

"It's eyes. He's got eyes in the back of his head."

"He didn't see you, he heard you," the young cop said.

"Huh?"

"You said—"

"Jesus, Sanders, forget it. Just forget it. Coldest night of the year, I'm in the city dump, and I draw a fuckin' moron for a partner."

"There's Shock," Stenner said to Vail.

He nodded toward a tall, beefy uniformed cop bundled in his blue wool coat, standing at the edge of the fill. Capt. Shock Johnson was ebony black and bald, with enormous, scarred hands that were cupped in front of his mouth and shoulders like a Green Bay lineman. When he saw Vail and Stenner, he shook his head and chuckled.

"I don't believe it," he said. "You guys don't even have to be here."

"What the hell's going on?" Vail asked.

"The dozer operator turned over the first one, so I decided we ought to punch around a little and, bingo, now we got three."

"What killed them?"

"Better ask Okimoto that, he's the expert. They're a mess. Been in there awhile. Maggots have had Thanksgiving dinner on all of 'em."

Vail groaned at the image. "So we don't know anything yet, that it?" he asked.

"Know we got three stiffos been cooking down in that gunk for God knows how long."

"May be hard to determine when these happened," Stenner offered. "Location will be very important."

Johnson nodded. "We're taking stills and video, doing measurements. If the weather's okay later I've ordered a chopper flyover. We'll get some pictures from up top."

"Good."

Johnson had once been Stenner's sergeant and had made lieutenant when Stenner quit. Johnson was now captain of the night watch, a man beholden to Stenner for years of education and for fostering in him a strong sense of intuition. He was Stenner's pipeline to a very unfriendly police department.

"Eckling here yet?" Vail asked.

"Oh yeah. He's down there in the thick of it, looking important for channel 7. They were the first ones to get a whiff of it."

"Nicely put," said Vail.

"Any ideas?" Stenner asked.

"Not really. My guess is, these three here were dumped about the same time, but we can't be sure. You couldn't hardly find the same spot twice, the tractors keep moving this shit around so much." He looked off at the ragged landscape. "Excuse me, I gotta check that bag just came up. Besides, Eckling sees you." He chuckled again. "And I've had enough fun for one night." He left.

"I'll wait in the car," Stenner said. He had not spoken a word to his former boss since the day he quit.

The chief of police huffed up the small hill with a camera crew and a reporter trailing out behind him. He was waving his arms as he spoke and his words came out in little bursts of steam.

"I see the D.A.'s man is here," he sneered. "Everybody loves a circus."

Eckling always referred to Vail as "the D.A.'s man," putting an edge to the words so that it sounded like an insult. The three-man crew, having got everything they could out of Eckling, turned their camera on Vail. "Any comment, Mr. Vail?" asked the reporter, a small, slender man in his twenties named Billy Pearce, who peered out from the depths of a hooded parka.

"I'm just an interested spectator," he answered.

"Care to speculate on what happened here?"

"I don't care to speculate at all, Billy. Thanks."

Vail turned away from them and walked toward Eckling as the crew, grateful for his brevity, fled toward their van. Eckling was a tall man with the beginnings of a beer belly and eyes that glared from behind tinted spectacles.

"What's the matter, Martin, couldn't wait?" he snapped.

"You know why I'm here, Eric, we've had that discussion too many times."

"Can't even wait until the bodies're cold," he growled.

"That shouldn't take long in this weather."

"Just want to get your face on the six o'clock news," he said nastily.

"Isn't that what got you out here?" Vail said cheerily.

"Look, you can't butt in for seven days. How about leaving me and mine alone and letting us do our job?"

"I wish you could, Chief," Vail said pleasantly.

"Go to hell," Eckling said, and stomped away.

Vail returned to the car and shook off the cold as he got into the warm interior.

"Damn, it's bitter out there."

"You and Eckling have your usual cordial exchange?"

"Yeah, things are improving. We didn't bite each other."

2

Stenner pulled around in a tight circle and headed back toward the city.

"Go to Butterfly's," Vail said. "I'm starving."

"Not open yet."

"Go to the back door."

Vail laid his head back against the headrest and closed his eyes, thinking about Stenner, so stingy with language. Soon after Stenner had joined the bunch, he and Vail had driven to a small town to take a deposition. An hour and a half up and an hour and a half back. As he had gotten out, Vail had leaned back through the car window and said, "Abel, we just drove for three hours and you said exactly twelve words, two of which were 'hello' and 'goodbye,' " to which Stenner had replied, "I'm sorry. Next time I'll be more succinct." He had said it without a smile or a trace of humor. Later, Vail had realized he was serious.

They drove for fifteen minutes in silence, then: "We're going to end up with this one," Stenner said as they neared the city.

"Always do," Vail said without opening his eyes.

"Very messy."

"Most homicides are."

Not another word was spoken until Stenner turned down the alley behind Butterfly's and stopped. While he propped the OFFI-

CIAL CAR, DISTRICT ATTORNEY'S OFFICE placard against the inside of the
windshield, Vail rapped on the door. It opened a crack and a
scruffy-looking stranger, who was about six-three with machine-
molded muscles, peered out.

"We ain't open yet."

"It's Martin Vail. We'll wait inside."

"Vail?"

"New in town?" Stenner said from behind Vail.

"Yeah."

"This man is the D.A. We'll wait inside."

"Oh. Righto. You betcha."

"Assistant D.A.," Vail corrected as they entered the steamy
kitchen.

"I'm the new bartender," the stranger said.

"What's your name?"

"Louis. But you can call me Lou."

"Glad to meet you, Lou," Vail said, and shook his hand. Vail
and Stenner walked through the kitchen. It was a fairly large
room with stainless-steel stoves and ovens and a large walk-in
refrigerator with a thermal glass door. Bobby Wo, the Chinese
cook, was slicing an onion so quickly, his hand was a blur. *Chock,
chock, chock, chock, chock.* Vail stopped to check the "Special of the
Day" pot.

"Shit on a shingle," Wo said without slowing down.

"That's three times this week," Vail complained.

"Tell the lady." *Chock, chock, chock, chock, chock.*

"Quit bellyachin'," a growl for a voice said from across the
room. Butterfly, who was anything but at five-four and two hundred and fifty pounds, entered the kitchen. "There was a special
on chipped beef, okay?"

"Know what I've been thinking about, Butterfly? Crepes."

"Crepes?"

"You know, those little French pancakes, thin with—"

"A short stack," she yelled to Bobby. "How about you,
General?"

"Major," Stenner said. "The usual."

"Two soft-boiled, three and a half minutes, dry toast, burned bacon," she yelled.

"Coffee ready?" Vail asked.

"If it wasn't, I wouldn't be this damn pleasant," she snarled, and shuffled away on flat feet encased in ancient men's leather slippers.

Vail and Stenner drew their own coffee and sat at their usual round table in the rear of the place. The morning papers were already stacked on the table.

"I'm thinking about this," Stenner said.

Vail smiled. Of course he was. Stenner was *always* thinking.

"You mean, Why the dump?" Vail asked without looking up from the paper.

"No, I mean, Who are these people? How long have they been in there? Doesn't somebody *miss* them?"

"Disposing of them in the city dump, that's rather ironic."

"Obvious when you think about it."

"At least they're biodegradable," Vail said, continuing to sip his coffee and read the paper.

Stenner stared down into his coffee cup for several seconds, then said, "I don't think it's a pattern job. It doesn't feel right."

"We know *anything* about these people?"

"We have two men and a woman. All ages, sizes, and shapes. A redhead, a blonde, a bald man with a glass eye."

"Maybe it is a pattern kill. Maybe . . . they're all from the same neighborhood, work in the same building, eat at the same restaurant . . ." Vail shrugged. He turned to the editorial pages.

"My intuition tells me this is not a pattern kill."

"A hunch, huh?"

"A hunch is a wild guess. Intuition comes from experience."

"Oh."

Stenner stared at Vail for a moment, took a sip of coffee, and went on: "They usually don't hide bodies. They leave them out where they can be found. Part of the thing."

Vail ignored him.

"So what are the options?" Stenner went on. "Three people in the landfill. Can we assume they're not there by accident?"

Vail did not look up from the paper. "I'll give you that."

"A burial ground?"

"For whom?"

"People who have been disposed of."

"Murder for pay?"

"In the thirties, Murder Incorporated buried their leftovers in a swamp in New Jersey. Dozens of them."

Breakfast came and the conversation ended abruptly for fifteen minutes. Stenner carefully crunched up his bacon and sprinkled it into the eggs and stirred them together, then spooned the mixture onto his toast before attacking the meal with knife and fork. When he was finished, he wiped his lips with a paper napkin and finished his coffee.

"Eckling will screw it up as usual. He's looking for a quick break."

Vail laughed. "Sure he is. The heat's on him. This thing is going to make the national news. It's too bizarre not to."

He finished and leaned back in his chair. "Maybe it's a disposal service," he ventured. "You know? You kill your mother-in-law, make a phone call, they come pick up the baggage and dump it for you."

"You seem to be taking this very lightly," said Stenner. "Maybe these are people caught up in some kind of gang war—maybe up-scale gangs—the ones who go to church, wear ties." He paused for a moment and added, "Contribute to politicians."

"Now there's a discomforting thought," Vail said.

"It's a discomforting thing."

"Abel, we have a lot on our plate. Eckling has a week before we get involved. Let's give him the week."

"I just want to be ready."

"I'm sure you will be," Vail said.

Stenner thought a moment more, then said, "Wonder what the Judge would've thought?"

For a few moments, Vail was lost in time, waiting for the Judge to stroll jauntily through the door with the *New York Times* under his arm, dressed in tweeds with a carnation in his lapel, greeting the gang sardonically before settling in for breakfast, reading, and talking law.

The Judge had had four loves: his wife, Jenny, Martin Vail, the law, and horse racing. But he had nearly been destroyed by two tragedies. His beloved Jenny, a demure Southern lady to whom he had been married for thirty-seven years, had been terminally injured in a car accident, lingering in a coma for a month before dying. The second tragedy was of his own design. To allay his grief, he had turned to a lifelong love of the ponies and had lost thirty thousand dollars to the bookies in a single month. His reputation on the bench literally lay in the palms of bookmakers. He had been saved by the devotion and respect of defense counsels, prosecutors, cops, newspaper reporters, law clerks, librarians, and politicians, all of whom respected his fairness and wisdom on the bench. They had contributed everything from dollar bills to four-figure donations and settled his debts. The Judge had quit cold turkey.

When he retired, he spent his days either as Vail's devil's advocate on cases or in the back of Wall Eye McGinty's horse parlor, which looked like the office of an uptown brokerage with a traveling neon board quoting changing odds, scratches, and those other bits of information that would be a foreign language to most humans. He always sat at the back of the room in the easy chair he himself had provided, legs crossed, his legendary black book in his lap, twirling his Montblanc pen in his fingers and studying McGinty's electronic tote board as he considered his next play.

That book! The Judge placed imaginary bets each day, keeping elaborate records on every race, track, jockey, and horse in the game, using wisdom, insight, and a staggering knowledge of statistics to run a ten-year winning streak that was recorded in the thick leather journal, a book so feared by the bookmakers that they had once banded together and offered him six figures if he would burn it. He refused but never gave tips or shared his vast knowledge of the game to anyone else. The Judge had amassed an imaginary fortune of over two million dollars, all of it on paper.

So he would spend his mornings at Butterfly's, challenging young lawyers, and his afternoons at Wall Eye McGinty's lush emporium for horse players.

His third joy was matching wits with Marty Vail. It was more than a challenge, it was a test of his forty-five years on both sides of the bar. His forays and collaborations with Vail provided an excitement unmatched by his horse playing. They would bet silver dollars arguing points of law, sliding the coins back and forth across the table as each scored a victory. After almost fifteen years, the Judge was exactly twenty-two cartwheels ahead of Vail.

A gangster client of Vail's, HeyHey Pinero, had once called the Judge swanky. "A most swanky guy," he had said, and it was the perfect way to describe the Judge.

A most swanky guy.

And then age and the turbulent past caught up with the old jurist. At eighty-one, a series of strokes felled him. He had survived his third stroke, but it left him arthritic and frail, unable to cook for himself or even scrounge up a snack. Ravaged by insomnia and elusive memories and trapped in his memory-drenched house, he stared out the windows at passing traffic or dozed in front of the TV set every day until one of the regulars came by, helped him get dressed, and carried his frail bone-flesh body to the car and from there to Wall Eye McGinty's horse parlor, where the players greeted him with almost reverential solicitude. McGinty, charitable bookie that he was, always drove the Judge home when the parlor closed.

Someone came every day. Vail, his paralegal executive secretary, the incomparable Naomi, Stenner, or one of Vail's young staff lawyers. And on days when everyone seemed bogged down with other things, Vail would send a cop over to perform the duty. On those days, McGinty met the officer at the door so as not to make him uncomfortable, no questions asked. After all, McGinty's betting parlor had existed in the same place for more than twenty years. The cops would hardly have been surprised had they gotten to peek through the door.

Six days a week the Judge doped the horses and entered his picks in the now encyclopedia-size black book.

On the seventh day, the Judge rested. Collapsed in his wheelchair, his atrophied legs tucked under a blanket, dressed as nattily as his palsied hands and weakened eyes would permit in a tweed jacket and gray flannels, he sat in his garden, facing the sun, his eyes shielded behind black sunglasses, and tanned the gray tint of old age from paper-thin flesh.

Age had robbed him of everything but pride.

So, on a warm Sunday morning in June two years before, dressed in his nattiest outfit, the Judge sat in the garden, spoke softly to the long-gone Jenny about their life together and his life without her, and told her he could no longer go on. Then he put the business end of a .38 special in his mouth and pulled the trigger.

He left behind a simple note for Vail, who had watched as the detectives did their work, then rode the ambulance to the morgue with the man who was as much a father to him as anyone had ever been. When he had overseen the cruel journey, he walked out behind the hospital, sat on a bench, and wept uncontrollably for more than an hour. Stenner had stood a hundred yards away, watching over, but not wanting to impose on, his boss. Finally Vail had opened the note.

Dear Martin:
   I liked you better on defense, but you're a great prosecutor.
   I love you as a son. You always made me proud to know you.
   My mind is slipping away. We all know it, right? Haven't picked a winner in weeks. Can't even eat a bagel anymore.
   Need I say more, my brash and brilliant friend?
   I won't ask for your forgiveness—nothing to forgive.
   Invest in Disaway, third race at Del Mar tomorrow. Buy a round for the gang on me with the proceeds.
                                        Farewell, dear friend,
                                                The Judge

Twenty-two silver dollars had weighted down the note. The tip had parlayed the twenty-two cartwheels into nine hundred and seventy-four dollars.

It had been one hell of a party.

"He's not coming, Martin," Stenner said, breaking his reverie. Vail snapped around toward him, aware that he had been staring at the door revisiting the past.

"Mind reader," Vail said.

"I sometimes have a moment . . ." Stenner started but never finished the sentence.

"I'm sure we all do from time to time," Vail said, turning back to his paper.

To Vail, on that chilly morning, the landfill case was a curiosity, an annoyance, something else to clutter up the already crowded agenda of the district attorney's office. In fact, the landfill mystery would lead to something much bigger. Something far more terrifying than the decomposed bodies in the city dump. Something that would force Martin Vail to come to terms with his past.

A name that had haunted Vail for ten years would soon creep back into his mind.

The name was Aaron Stampler.

3

Shana Parver rushed through the frigid morning air and climbed the steps of the county criminal courthouse. Overly sentimental and idealistic by nature, although she shielded it with a tough, aggressive facade, Parver always got a rush when she saw the front of the hulking building. "The law is the only thing that separates us from animals," Vail had once said. Of course he had added his own cynical postscript: "Although, these days, you'd never know it." But looking up at the Doric columns soaring above the entrance, each surmounted by allegorical figures representing Law, Justice, Wisdom, Truth, Might, Love, Liberty, and Peace, reassured her faith in the sanctity of the law and reaffirmed her belief in the profession she had chosen while still in grammar school.

She was early this morning. In forty-five minutes she would be face-to-face with James Wayne Darby, and while it wasn't a courtroom, the interrogation was the next best thing, a chance to match wits with the flabby, smart-aleck chauvinist. She would take a few last minutes to prepare herself mentally for the meeting.

Naomi Chance had beat her there as usual. The coffee was made in Vail's giant urn, and she was at her desk ready to do battle when Parver burst in at eight-fifteen. Naomi was always the first to arrive, walking through the sprawling office, flicking on lights before making Vail's coffee. Her look was regal and intimidating. She was a stunning, ramrod-straight woman, the color of milk chocolate, almost Egyptian-looking with high cheekbones and wide brown eyes, her black hair cut fashionably short and just beginning to show a little gray. A widow at fifty, she had the wisdom of an eighty-year-old with the body of a thirty-year-old. She was a quick learner and a voracious digger. Give her a name and she'd come back with a biography. Ask for a date and she'd produce a calendar. Ask for a report and she'd generate a file. She could type 80 words a minute, take shorthand, and had earned her law degree at the age of forty-six. Her devotion to Vail superseded any notion of practicing law. She had taken care of him from the beginning, knew his every whim; his taste in clothes, movies, food, women, and wine; and was, without title, his partner rather than his associate prosecutor, a title he had invented for her because it was nebulous enough to cover everything and sounded a lot more important than executive secretary.

Naomi gnawed through red tape as voraciously as a beaver gnaws through a tree bole, had no use for bureaucratic dawdling, knew where to find every public record in the city, and acted as a surrogate mother and a friendly crying shoulder for the youthful staff Vail had assembled.

If Vail was the chief of staff, Naomi Chance was the commanding general of this army.

Parver was the youngest and newest member of what Vail called the Special Incident Staff—better known around town as the Wild Bunch—all of whom were in their late twenties and early thirties, all of whom had been "discovered" by Naomi, whose vast authority included acting as a legal talent scout for the man they all called boss.

Shana Parver was the perfect complement to Naomi Chance. She was not quite five-two but had a breathtaking figure, jet-black hair that hung well below her shoulders, and skin the color of sand. Her brown eyes seemed misty under hooded lids that gave her an almost Oriental look. She wore little makeup—she didn't need it—and she had perfect legs, having been brought up near the beaches of Rhode Island and Connecticut, where she had been a championship swimmer and basketball player in high school. She was wearing a black suit with a skirt just above the knee, a white blouse, and a string of matched pink pearls. Her hair was pulled back and tied with a white bow. Dressed as conservatively as she could get, she was still a distracting presence in any gathering, a real traffic stopper, which had almost prevented Vail from hiring her until Naomi pointed out that he was practicing a kind of reverse discrimination. She had graduated summa cum laude from Columbia Law School and had made a name for herself as assistant prosecutor for a small Rhode Island county D.A. when she applied for a job on the S.I.S. Naomi had done the background check.

A rebellious kid who had made straight A's without ever cracking a book, Parver had raised almighty hell and flunked out of the upscale New England prep school her parents had sent her to. Accepted in a tough, strict institution for problem kids, she had made straight A's and from then on had been an honor student all the way through college and law school.

"What happened?" Naomi had asked in their first face-to-face interview.

"I decided I wanted to be a lawyer instead of a big pain in the ass," Parver had answered.

"Why did you apply for this job?"

"Because I wrote a graduate piece on Martin Vail. I know all his cases, from back when he was a defense advocate. He's the best prosecutor alive. Why wouldn't I want to work for him?"

She had had all the right answers. Naomi's reaction had been immediate.

"Dynamite."

Vail had expected anything but the diminutive, smart, sophisticated, and aggressive legal wunderkind.

"I want a lawyer, I don't want to give some old man on the jury a heart attack," he had said when he saw her picture.

"You want her to get a face drop?" Naomi had snapped.

When Parver stepped out of the elevator and walked resolutely toward his office for her first interview, Vail had groaned.

"I was hoping the pictures flattered her."

"There's no way to unflatter her," Naomi had offered. "Are you still going to hold her looks against her?"

"It's not just looks. This child has . . . has . . ."

"Magnetism?" Naomi had suggested.

"*Animal* magnetism. She is a definite coronary threat to anyone over forty. I speak from personal experience."

"You going to hold her looks against her?" Naomi had asked. "That's discrimination. Marty, this girl is the best young lawyer I've ever interviewed. She's a little too aggressive, probably self-protective, but in six months she'll be ready to take on any lawyer in the city. She has an absolute instinct for the jugular. And she wants to be a prosecutor. She doesn't give a damn about money."

"She's rich."

"She's well off."

"Her old man's worth a couple million dollars—*fluid*. I call that rich."

"Marty, this young lady reminds me so much of you when we met, it's scary."

"She's a woman, she's rich, and she's gorgeous. The only thing we have in common is that we inhabit the same planet."

"You better be nice to her," Naomi had warned, leaving the office to greet her.

Six months earlier, Parver had tried two cases and blown one. Vail had told her later that she was too tough, too relentless.

"The jury likes tough, they don't like a killer," he had said. "You have to tone down, pull back. Study juries, juries are what it's all about. I had a friend we called the Judge who used to say that murder one is the ultimate duel. Two lawyers going at it in mortal combat—and the mortal is the defendant. Excellent analogy. Two sides completely polarized. One of them's right, the other one's wrong. One of them has to perform magic, turn black into white in the minds of the jurors. In the end, the defendant's life depends on which lawyer can convince the jury that his or her perception of the facts is reality. That's what it's all about, Shana, the jury."

Toning it down hadn't come easily.

"You ready, Miss Parver?" Naomi asked, shaking her back to the present.

Parver scowled at her. "It's not like it's the first time I ever questioned a murder suspect, Noam."

Parver was the primary prosecutor on the Darby case but had been in court and missed Darby's first interrogation. Now it was her turn to have a shot at him.

"This Darby is a nasty little bastard. Don't let him push you around."

Parver smiled. "Be nice if the creepy little slime puppy tries," she said sweetly.

"You haven't met Rainey yet. Be careful, he's a killer. A good, honest lawyer, but a killer. Don't let that smile of his fool you."

Parver drew herself a cup of coffee, sprinkled in half a spoonful of sugar, stirred it with her finger then sucked the coffee off it.

"Somebody said he's as good as Martin was in the old days," she said casually, and waited for the explosion.

"Ha!" Naomi snorted. "Who the hell told you that?"

"I don't know. Somebody."

"Don't let *somebody* kid you, nobody's that good—or is ever likely to be."

"You never talk about those days, Naomi. How long have you been with Marty?"

"Eighteen years," Naomi said, tracing a long black finger down Vail's calendar for the day. "When I started with Martin, he charged fifty dollars an hour and was glad to get it. And all I knew about the law was that it was a three-letter word." She paused for a moment, then: "My God, wait'll I run this by him. A luncheon and a cocktail party, both on the same day. The State Lawyers Association. I'll wait to tell him, he's liable to go berserk and kill Darby if I tell him before the inquiry."

A moment later Vail stepped out of the elevator, threading his way through the crowded jungle of glass partitions, desks, file cabinets, computers, blackboards, telephones, and TV screens toward his office. It was in a rear corner of the sprawling operation, as far away from D.A. Jack Yancey's office as it was possible to get and still be on the same floor.

God, Naomi thought, *he must've dressed in the dark.* Vail was wearing an old gray flannel suit, unshined loafers, and an ancient blue knit tie that looked like it had been used as a garrote by stranglers from Bombay.

"Christ, Martin," Naomi said, "you look like an unmade bed."

"I am an unmade bed," he growled, and stomped into his office. "How old's this coffee?"

"Fifteen minutes."

"Good." He went to the old-fashioned brass and chrome urn he had taken as part payment for handling a restaurant bankruptcy years ago and poured himself a mug of coffee. Parver and Naomi stood in the doorway.

His cluttered, unkempt office was a throwback to what Naomi sometimes referred to as the "early years." It was dominated by an enormous, hulking oak table that Vail used as a desk. Stacks of letters, case files, and books littered the tabletop, confining him to a small working area in the center of the table. There were eight hardback chairs around the perimeter of the table. He flopped down in his high-backed leather chair, which was on wheels so he could spin around the room—to overrun bookshelves or stuffed file cabinets—without getting up. An enormous exhaust fan filled the bottom half of one window. Vail was the only smoker left on the staff and no one would come into his office unless he sat in front of the fan when he smoked.

"Stenner had me up before five taking a nature walk in the city dump," Vail muttered, and sipped his coffee. "Good morning, Shana."

"You were out there?" Parver said with a look of awe. "Is it true they found three bodies in the landfill?"

"What?" Naomi said.

"Three corpora delicti," said Vail. "And they were in there a looong time. Wonderful way to start the day. You don't want to hear any details."

"Do you think it's murder?" Naomi asked.

"Okie'll let us know. Ready to take on James Wayne Darby and Paul Rainey?" Vail replied.

"Yes." Emphatically.

"Want to talk about it? We have fifteen minutes before we go down."

"If you do," Parver said with confidence.

"Ah, the audacity of youth," Naomi said, rolling her eyes. "Oh, to be thirty again."

"I'm twenty-eight," Parver said in a half-whisper.

"Twenty-eight," Naomi said, shaking her head. "I don't even want to *think* about my twenties. I'm not sure, but I think twenty-eight was one of my bad years."

Vail casually studied the young lawyer. She was cool and steady, very self-assured for a twenty-eight-year-old. He had assembled his group of young turks carefully during the past six years, moving the assistant prosecutors from Yancey's old staff—mostly bureaucratic burnouts and unimaginative lawyers who preferred plea bargains to trails—into routine cases: drive-by gang shootings, local dope busts, assaults, robberies, burglaries, and family disputes, many of which ended in homicide. Gradually he had phased out several of them, replacing them with younger, more aggressive, yet unspectacular lawyers who preferred the long-term advantages of security to making a name for themselves before moving out into the private sector. Under Vail's careful guidance, they handled the bulk of the 2,600 murders, robberies, rapes, aggravated assaults, burglaries, car heists, child molestations, and white-collar felonies the D.A.'s office handled every year.

The Wild Bunch was something else. Young, aggressive, litigious, and brilliant, they took on the complex, multifarious cases acting as a team. Although they were extremely competitive, they were bonded by mutual respect, arduous hours, meager pay, and the chance to learn from the master. Some, like Parver, had applied for the job. Others had been tracked down by the tenacious

Naomi Chance. Through the four or five years they had been together, each had become a specialist in a certain area and had learned to depend on the others. They were backed up by Stenner and his investigators, seasoned cops who were experts at walking the tightrope between statutory compliance and forbidden procedures. They were all cunning, adroit, resourceful. They questioned legal theory and were not above taking tolerable risks if the payoff was high enough, and on those rare occasions when they screwed up, they did it so spectacularly that Vail, an outrageous risk taker himself, was usually sympathetic.

The young lawyers had one thing in common: they all loved the courtroom. It was why Naomi and Vail had picked them, a prerequisite. Like it was for Vail, the law was both a religion and a contest for them; the courtroom was their church, their Roman Coliseum, the arena where all their competitive juices, their legal knowledge, their resourcefulness and cunning were adrenalized. Vail had also instilled in each an inner demand to challenge the law, to attack its canons, traditions, statutes, its very structure, while they coaxed and maneuvered and seduced juries to accept their perception of the truth. It was his fervent belief that this legal domain had to be defied and challenged constantly if it was to endure. He insisted that they spend two or three days a month in court, studying juries and lawyers, their timing, their tricks, their opening and closing statements, and he watched with satisfaction as each developed his or her own individual style, his or her own way of dealing with this, the most intriguing of all blood sports.

The whole team disliked James Wayne Darby intensely. He was brash, arrogant, swaggering, and flirtatious toward the women on the team and surly toward the men. His lawyer, Paul Rainey, was just the opposite, a gentleman, but a hardcase, with a strong moral streak. He believed passionately in his clients. So far, no charges had been brought against Darby.

Parver was hungry to try another case to get over her recent defeat. Darby could be it—if they could break his story. But Vail was aware that Parver's eagerness could also be her undoing.

"This is our last shot at Darby," he told Parver. "Just remember,

Paul Rainey can kill you with a dirty look. If he gets pushy, ignore him. You know the playing field; if he gets offside, I'll jump on him. You stay focused on Darby. Just keep doing what you do best."

"I know," she said.

"Do you have anything new?"

"Not really. There's one thing. The phone number?"

"Phone number?"

"The slip of paper with Poppy Palmer's phone number."

Parver went through a thick dossier of police data, coroner's reports, evidence files, and interviews, finally pulling out a copy of the slip of paper, which she laid before Vail.

"This is the note that Darby claims he found beside the phone," she said. It was a ragged piece of notepaper with the entry: Pammer, 555-3667.

"He says Ramona Darby must have written the note because he didn't—and also Palmer's name is misspelled. Two handwriting analysts have failed to come up with a conclusive ID."

"So . . . ?"

"So suppose he wrote it and left it there for Ramona to find. Or . . . suppose he left it there *after* the fact. Supposing Ramona never called Poppy Palmer at all and there were no threats? If we can prove Ramona Darby never called Palmer and never threatened to kill Darby, we raise reasonable doubt about his whole case."

"Only if we get him into court. There isn't any case at this point. We don't have a damn thing to take to a grand jury."

"There's some strong evidence here," she said defensively.

"All circumstantial," he argued. "You can call it whatever you want: evidence, conjecture, guesswork, insinuation, circumstance, lies, whatever, it's all for one purpose. Define the crime and lure the jury into separating your fact from the opposition's fiction—and right now we don't have one, single hard fact to nail this guy with."

"True. But suppose we could panic Palmer? She backed up his story. If she's looking at perjury and accessory before the fact . . ."

"So you're looking to shake *her* up, not him."

"Eventually. Start with him, then take another shot at her."

"It's some long shot," Vail said.

"We're busted anyway. What've we got to lose?"

"Okay, let's see how good you are."

4

The office where prosecutors conducted interrogations and depositions was on the third floor of the courthouse, a floor below the D.A.'s headquarters. It was sparsely furnished: a table, six wooden chairs, an old leather sofa and a chair in one corner with a coffee table separating them. There was a small refrigerator near a window. A Mr. Coffee, packets of sugar and dry cream, and a half-dozen mugs were neatly arranged on its top. The view was nothing special. No telephone. It was a pleasant room without being too comfortable. The room was also bugged and had a video camera mounted in one corner that was focused on the table.

Vail and Parver were waiting when Paul Rainey and James Wayne Darby arrived. Rainey was a deceptively pleasant man. Tall, slender, his dark hair streaked with gray, he wore gold-rimmed glasses and an expensive dark blue suit and could have passed for a rich, Texas businessman. Darby was his antithesis, an ex–high school baseball player gone to seed: six feet tall, thirty pounds overweight, and sloppily dressed in jeans, heavy hiking boots, a flannel shirt, and a camouflage hunting jacket. Cheap aviator sunglasses hid his dull brown eyes. His dishwater-blond hair was cropped too close and he had a beer drinker's complexion, a beer drinker's stomach, and a beer drinker's attitude. He was

thirty-eight but could easily have passed for a man in his late forties. A farmer from Sandytown, a small farming community of
four thousand people on the north end of the county, he had shot
his wife to death with a shotgun after claiming she first tried to
kill him.

Everyone on the team believed he had murdered his wife, but
they could not prove his story was phony. There were some dam-
aging circumstances, but that was all they were: circumstances. He
was having a fling with a stripper named Poppy Palmer. He had
insured both himself and his wife for $250,000 six months before
the shooting. And the previous two years had been a disaster.
Darby, on the verge of bankruptcy, was about to lose his farm.

But there were no witnesses, so there was no way to challenge
him. His story, supported by the bovine Miss Palmer, was that a
hysterical Ramona Darby had called Palmer an hour or so before
the shooting and threatened to kill both Darby and Palmer. A slip
of paper with Palmer's number had been found near the Darbys'
phone.

Vail did the introductions, which were cordial enough. Vail and
Parver sat with their backs to the camcorder and Darby sat across
from them, slouching down in his chair and crossing his arms
over his chest. He kept the hunting jacket on. Rainey laid a slender briefcase on the table and stood behind his client, leaning on
the back of his chair.

"Okay," he said. "Let's get this over with."

Vail smiled. "What's the rush, Paul? Plenty of coffee. You can
smoke. Nice view."

"Martin, I've advised my client to cooperate with you people
this one, last time. He's been interrogated twice by the police—
once for six hours—and previously by your department for three.
He's not accused of a thing. This is beginning to feel a little like
harassment. I want an agreement that this is a voluntary interrogation and that all formal requirements in connection with such
are waived. Also that this statement, or series of statements, by
my client does not constitute a formal deposition or a sworn
statement."

"Are you implying that he can lie to us with complete immunity?" Parver asked.

"I am saying that Mr. Darby has agreed to cooperate with you in this matter. You can take his statement at face value."

"Do you have any objections if we videotape the inquiry?"

Rainey thought for a moment. "Only if we get a complete copy of the tape and you agree that it will not be used as evidence in a court case and will not be released to the public."

Parver nodded. "Acceptable."

"Then it's acceptable to my client. We haven't got a thing to hide."

Vail pressed a button under the table and started the camcorder.

John Wayne Darby said nothing. He stared across the table at Vail and Parver, his lips curled in a smirk.

Parver opened a file folder and took out a pencil. "Are we ready?" she asked, trying to smile.

"Any time, little lady."

She glared at him but did not respond. "Please state your full name and address."

"Sheee . . . you know my name and address."

"Just do it, Jim," Rainey said.

"James Wayne Darby. RFD Three, Sandytown."

"How long have you lived at that address?"

"Uh, eight years. My daddy left it to me."

"Age?"

"Twenty-nine." He laughed and then said, "Just kiddin'. I'm thirty-eight and holding."

"Are you married?"

"I was. My wife is dead."

"Was your wife Ramona Smith Darby?"

"That's right."

"How long were you married?"

"Ten years."

"Did you graduate from high school, Mr. Darby?"

"Yep."

"Did you attend college?"

"Yes, I did, on a baseball scholarship."

"And did you graduate from college?"

"No. Got my leg broke in a car wreck when I was starting my third year. Couldn't play ball anymore and lost my scholarship, so I had to drop out."

"Then what did you do?"

"Went to work on my daddy's farm."

"Were you married at the time?"

"Yes. Ramona and I married just after I dropped out."

"That's when you went to live at RFD Three, Sandytown?"

"Right. My daddy's farm. He built a garage apartment for us."

"Do you have any children?"

"No."

"Is your father still living?"

"He got a stroke four years ago."

"And died?"

"Yeah, he died."

"How about your mother?"

"She died when I was in college. Cancer."

"I will ask you if you will now agree to a polygraph test."

"Objection," Rainey said. "We've been over this. I've advised my client against the polygraph. It's not admissible in court and there's no advantage whatsoever to Mr. Darby taking a polygraph since it cannot benefit him in any way. And let's not make an issue of this with the press, okay, Martin?"

"I assume that's a 'no,' " Parver said.

"That's right, little lady, it's a no," said Darby.

Vail leaned across the table, but Parver moved a foot over his and stopped him. She stared straight at Darby and said, "Mr. Darby, I'm nobody's little lady, especially yours. Now, you agreed to this interrogation. We can do this quickly or we can spend the day here. It's up to you."

Darby's face turned a deep shade of vermilion. He started to get up, but Rainey put a hand on his arm and nodded toward his chair. Darby sneered, then shrugged, sat back down, and fell quiet.

Parver took a diagram out of the folder and laid it before him. It showed the first floor of the Darby farmhouse. The front door led from a wide porch into a small entrance hall. An archway opened on the left into the living room. Facing the archway was the sketch of a chair and a distance line between the arch and the chair that measured twelve feet, four inches. There were two *X*'s marked on the chair, two on the hallway wall opposite the chair, one on the wall next to the arch, and one that measured eight feet, seven inches marked "floor to ceiling."

"I show you this sketch, Mr. Darby," Parver said. "Is this an accurate sketch of the scene of the crime?"

"Strike the word *crime*," said Rainey wearily. "There isn't any crime. Nobody's been accused of a crime."

"Would *homicide* suit you?" Parver asked.

"*Event.* I think scene of the event would be an accurate description."

"Mr. Darby, is this an accurate sketch of the scene of the event?"

Darby studied it for a minute and nodded. "Yeah. There's some other furniture in the room."

"It's inconsequential, is it not?"

"You mean did it enter into the shootout? No."

"Now, Mr. Darby, will you please describe for us what happened on January 7, 1993?"

"You mean getting out of bed, taking a shower . . ."

"You were going hunting . . ."

"Charlie Waters, Barney Thompson, and me went duck hunting. We go once or twice a week in the season."

"Where did you go hunting?"

"Big Marsh."

"What time did you get there?"

"We were in the blind by, I don't know, four-thirty, five."

"Did you speak to your wife before you left?"

"She was asleep. I never woke her up. She made the sandwiches and stuff the night before."

"Did you two have a fight or a disagreement the previous night?"

"Not really."

"What do you mean, 'not really'?"

"We weren't getting along. I told you that before. Things were not exactly peaches and cream around the place, but we weren't yelling at each other, nothing like that. It was just kind of cool between us. Hell, she made my lunch."

"How long were you hunting?"

"We left Big Marsh about three P.M. We always stop on the way home and have a couple beers, brag about who bagged the most birds, like that."

"And it was on the way home from one of these hunting trips that you first met Poppy Palmer at the Skin Game Club, isn't that right?"

"Sure, I told you all that before." He looked at Rainey and held his hands out and shrugged.

"Do you have anything new to ask?" Rainey said with irritation.

"There are several points we need to clear up," Parver said quietly. Vail was impressed by her control. "How soon after you met Poppy Palmer did you first have sexual relations with her?"

"In minutes or hours?" Darby smirked.

"Hours will be fine," Parver answered coolly.

"Like I told you, we went into the Skin Game and she was workin' that day and we had a couple of beers and then Charlie asked her to have a beer with us only she wanted a champagne cocktail. That's the way it works, they put Coca-Cola in a glass or something and you pay five bucks for it and that's what they call champagne. So we fooled around talking until about seven and she was getting off work, so I said, How about it? You want to stop somewhere, have a real drink? One thing led to another and we finally went to the Bavarian Inn and got a room." He leaned across the table toward Parver and said, "You want all the details?"

"That won't be necessary." She looked down at her notes. "Not now, anyway."

Nice shot, thought Vail. *Let him think this isn't going to be the end of it. Throw him off.*

"Did you have sexual intercourse with Miss Palmer on that occasion?" Parver continued.

Darby looked at Rainey, who waved off his concern.

"Sure."

"How many times after that did you and Miss Palmer meet?"

"I dunno, four or five. I don't remember exactly."

She checked her notes. "Miss Palmer says she met you at the Bavarian Inn six times. You have said five. Then six. And this time four or five. Which is it?"

"Look, what's the dif? I had a fling with her. I never tried to say I didn't. I told the cops that the first night they talked to me."

"So was it four, five, or six?" she asked calmly.

"I just told you, I don't remember. Okay, six. Hell, it was six if Poppy says so. I don't mark my calendar, maybe she does."

"But you always had sex with her?"

"Yeah. Why, does it turn you on hearing about it?"

"That's enough of that, Darby," Vail snapped.

"Look, what I did was in self-defense. How many goddamn times do I have to repeat it to you people? Why don't you go out and bust some drug dealers, do something for the community?"

Vail turned to Rainey. "This can go on forever if that's what he wants," he said.

"Just answer the questions yes or no," Rainey said, still staring at Vail.

"Let's get back to the day you shot your wife," Parver said. "Did you go to the Skin Game Club that day?"

"No. We stopped in a beer joint out on 78. I don't know if it's got a name. The sign in front says cocktails."

"Did you see Poppy Palmer at all that day?"

"Nope."

"Talk to her?"

"Not before the shooting."

"At any time?"

"I called after the police came and I found the paper with her number on it by the phone."

"Why did you call her?"

"I wanted to tell her what happened and I wanted to know about the phone number. Where Ramona got it because Poppy's number isn't in the book and she told me Ramona had called her about four-thirty, five o'clock and went crazy on the phone. Said she was gonna fix me. You know all that, you talked to Poppy."

"What did she tell you exactly?"

"Just that. Ramona called her and was all outta shape. And, like, blamed Poppy for what happened. And Poppy couldn't get a word in edgewise, Ramona was crying and screaming so. Said she was gonna fix my wagon. That's exactly what Poppy told me, that Ramona said she was gonna fix my goddamn wagon."

"What time did you leave the bar on 78?"

"I don't know, about five-thirty. I wasn't watching the clock." He chuckled. "Usually my old lady didn't take a shot at me when I came home late."

"Roughly what time was it?"

"It takes about a half hour to drive home and the news was coming on when I got there. I could hear Dan Rather talking on the TV when I walked in. It was just starting."

"Show us on the diagram exactly what happened when you entered the house."

"Damn!" He grabbed a pencil and traced his steps into the house on the diagram. As he told the story, he began talking faster. "I come in the house here and I walk to the doorway to the living room that's, I don't know, five feet maybe, and as I look into the living room, she's . . . Ramona's . . . sitting in the easy chair here and she's aiming my .38 target pistol at me and she cuts loose! Just starts shooting! So I dive straight ahead to the other side of the arch and I'm against the wall here and she puts a shot here where this X is, and another one here, and I panic and I shove two shells in my shotgun and just then she shoots again and the bullet goes through the wall here and misses my head by a gnat's ass and I just thought, She's gonna kill me! So I charge around the corner and fire once and it kind of knocks her back in the chair and her arm flung up and she put another shot into the ceiling and I was charging right at her and I shot again. It all happened in, like, less than a minute."

"What did you think after all the shooting was over?"

"What did I *think*? I was out of breath. I was scared. She almost killed me."

"But what did you think while this was happening? Did you call to her, try to reason with her?"

"Hell, no, it all happened just like that. Bang, bang, bang, bang. Bullets flying through the wall. I wasn't thinking. I was trying to stay alive."

"Did you warn her?"

"A bullet just flew that damn close to my head. Warn her about what? 'Hey, Ramona, here I come, ready or not'? I just panicked and I figured it's her or me and ran into the room shooting."

"So now it's over. Your wife is lying there with two wounds, one in her head. What went through your mind?"

"At first I got choked up. I almost puked, I never shot a human being before. And she was bleeding. And I dropped the gun down and felt for a pulse in her wrist, but I, y'know, I was confused and upset, so I went in and called 911. That's when I saw where she broke into my gun cabinet and that's when I found the phone number beside the phone."

"Was the phone number in your wife's handwriting?"

"Hell, I dunno, you think I was analyzing handwriting? The cops talked to me for three, four hours that night. They took the note and I haven't seen it since."

"But you didn't write it?"

Vail sat back in his chair and concentrated on Parver. She was doing a superb job. The handwriting of the note had not occurred to Vail—or to anyone that he was aware of. She was cool, quiet but not soft, very direct, and she was beginning to rattle Darby. She was totally focused. For a moment, she reminded Vail of Jane Venable, the prosecutor who had preceded him as chief prosecutor.

"Hell, no," Darby snapped. "I told you, she wasn't listed, you think I wanted my wife to call her up?"

"Do you have any idea where she might have found that number?"

"No."

"Who else knew the number?"

"How the hell would I know?"

"Is it possible that you wrote the number down and forgot it and she found it? In a drawer or something like that?"

"I . . . didn't . . . write . . . the goddamn number. Is that clear?"

He turned to Rainey and said plaintively, "It's the same damn questions as last time. They know the answers, what the hell is this?" He turned back to Parver. "I killed my wife, okay? She shot at me, I shot at her. That's it. I got nothing more to say."

"He's right," said Rainey. "It's the same ground you plowed last time."

"I just want to make it clear to you, Mr. Darby, that we have two strong motives for murder here," Shana Parver said. She counted items off on her fingers. "Money—a $250,000 insurance policy, and you're about to go into bankruptcy—and infidelity. They're the biggies, Mr. Darby. It's also a hard story to come to terms with, this shootout scenario. Your wife wasn't a violent woman from everything we've been told. And she also hated guns. Isn't it true that you wanted her to take shooting lessons and she refused to touch a gun?"

"Yeah. Maybe that's why she missed me," he said with a sneer.

"The point is, Mr. Darby, if we need to talk to you again, we will. We'll keep talking to you until we decide for sure whether or not this homicide was justifiable."

He stood up angrily and leaned toward her with both hands on the table. "It happened just the way I said it happened. Ramona and me are the only two people that were there, and she's dead. Try to prove otherwise or leave me alone, *little* lady."

He spun around and slammed out of the room.

Rainey stood and put his papers in his briefcase. He looked at Vail and shook his head.

"I object to this whole meeting, Miss Parver. The note is moot. It was there. It substantiates Miss Palmer's statement and both you and the cops have had rounds with her. Stop trying to make chicken salad out of chickenshit. You know this could just as easily have gone the other way. Jimmy could be underground and you could be going after Ramona Darby for blowing him away." He shook his head. "You two are whistling 'Dixie' on this one."

He followed Darby out of the room.

"Damn!" Parver said, and slammed down her pencil.

"Darby's hanging tough," Vail said. "He doesn't have any choice."

"You think Rainey really believes him?"

"I have no doubt he believes Darby's innocent. We haven't given him anything to change that. He knows we don't have a case."

"Darby killed her in cold blood," Shana Parver said. "I know it, we *all* know it."

"Let me tell you a little story," Vail said as they started back to the fourth floor. "A few years ago an elderly man named Shuman was found in a northside apartment dead of a gunshot wound to the head. The windows and doors were all locked, but there was no weapon anywhere on the premises. The last man to see him alive was a friend of his named Turk Loudon, a junkie who had served time for robbery and assault. He had the victim's ring and fifty-seven dollars and a key to the apartment. And no alibi. He claimed the old man had told him he was sick of living and had given him the money and the ring earlier in the day. He had the key because he was homeless and Shuman let him sleep on the floor at night. He was arrested and charged with murder one.

"His pro bono lawyer wanted to go for a deal. Problem was, the gunshot wound to the head was a contact shot, which suggested extreme malice. A bigger problem was Loudon. He absolutely refused to plea. He claimed he was innocent, period. Nobody believed him, particularly his own lawyer.

"Then about two weeks after Loudon was arrested, some painters went to redo the apartment. They found an army .45-caliber pistol lodged behind the radiator. Shuman's prints were all over it and the bullets. Ballistics matched the gun and the bullet in

Shuman's head. Shuman had shot himself, and when he did, his arm jerked out, the gun flew out of his hand and dropped behind the radiator. The cops missed it when they searched the place because they didn't think a gun would fit behind it and it was hot. So they looked under the radiator but not behind it."

"Were you the prosecutor?"

"No, I was the lawyer. I didn't believe my client—and I was wrong. I damn near plea-bargained him into Joliet for the rest of his life."

"So you're saying give Darby the benefit of the doubt?"

"I'm saying if you're going to defend someone, particularly for first-degree murder, you can't afford to doubt their innocence. Paul Rainey believes Darby's innocent because he doesn't have any choice. If we can crack Darby's story, if Paul begins to doubt him? It'll gnaw on him until he finds out what the truth is. The trouble is, we can't make a dent in Darby's version of what happened."

"So Darby sticks to his guns . . ."

"And we're out of luck," Vail answered. "He got lucky. Usually amateurs like that, some little thing trips them up. Something they overlooked, a witness pops out of the cake, a fingerprint shows up where they least expect it. We've been working on this guy for a month and right now we don't have a case."

"Let me go back to Sandytown," she said. "Take one more crack at it, just to make sure we haven't missed something."

Vail sighed. He knew the frustration Shana Parver was feeling— they all were feeling—but he also had seen more than one felon walk for lack of evidence and he had to balance the time of his prosecutors and investigators against the odds of breaking Darby. The odds were in Darby's favor.

"You know, maybe it happened the way he says it did, Shana. Maybe we all dislike this guy so much we *want* him to be guilty."

"No!" she snapped back. "He planned it and he did her."

"Are you ready to go up against Rainey in the courtroom?" Vail asked her.

"I can hardly wait," she answered confidently.

"With this case?"

She thought about his question for several moments. Then her shoulders sagged. "No," she said finally, but her momentary depression was gone a second later. "That's why I want to go over all the ground once more, and question Poppy Palmer again, before we shut it down," she pleaded.

"Okay." Vail sighed. "One more day. Take Abel with you. But unless you come up with something significant by tomorrow night, this case is dead."

5

Harvey St. Claire was on to something.

Vail could tell the minute he and Parver got off the elevator. The heavyset man was sitting on the edge of a chair beside the main computer, leaning forward with his forearms on his thighs. And his left leg was jiggling. That was the tip-off, that nervous leg.

Sitting beside St. Claire was Ben Meyer, who was as tall and lean as St. Claire was short and stubby. Meyer had a long, intense face and a shock of black hair, and he was dressed, as was his custom, in a pinstriped suit, white shirt, and somber tie. St. Claire, as was *his* custom, wore a blue and yellow flannel shirt, red suspenders, sloppy blue jeans, heavy brogans, and a White Sox windbreaker.

Meyer, at thirty-two, was the resident computer expert and had designed the elaborate system that hooked the D.A.'s office with HITS, the Homicide Investigation and Tracking System that linked police departments all over the country. St. Claire, who was fifty-two, had, during his twenty-eight years in law enforcement, tracked moonshiners in Georgia and Tennessee, wetbacks along the Texican border, illegal gun smugglers out of Canada, illegal aliens in the barrios of Los Angeles and San Diego, and some of the meanest wanted crooks in the country when he was with the U.S. Marshal's Service.

Meyer was a specialist in fraud. It was Meyer who had first detected discrepancies that had brought down two city councilmen
for misappropriating funds and accepting kickbacks. Later, in his
dramatic closing argument, Meyer had won the case with an impassioned plea for the rights of the taxpayers. St. Claire was a
hunch player, a man who had a natural instinct for link analysis—
putting together seemingly disparate facts and projecting them
into a single conclusion. Most criminal investigators plotted the
links on paper and in computers, connecting bits and pieces of information until they began to form patterns or relationships. St.
Claire did it in his head, as if he could close his eyes and see the
entire graph plotted out on the backs of his eyelids. He also had a
phenomenal memory for crime facts. Once he heard, read, or saw
a crime item he never forgot it.

When Meyer and St. Claire got together, it meant trouble. Vail
ignored Naomi, who was motioning for him to come to his office,
and stood behind Meyer and St. Claire.

"Here's what I got in mind," St. Claire said. "I wanna cross-
match missing people and unsolved homicides, then see if we
have any overlap in dates. Can we do that?"

"State level?"

"Yeah, to start with. Exclude this county for the time being."

"Nothing to it," Meyer said, his fingers clicking on the computer
keyboard.

"What the hell're you two up to?" Vail asked.

"Hunch," St. Claire said, still watching the screen. His blue eyes
glittered behind wire-rimmed glasses that kept sliding down to the
end of his nose.

"Everybody's got a hunch. I had to listen to Abel's hunches all
the way through breakfast. A hunch about what?"

"About this new thing," St. Claire said.

"What new thing?"

St. Claire's upper lip bulged with a wad of snuff. Without taking
his eyes off the big screen of the computer, he spat delicately into
a silver baby cup he carried at all times for just that purpose.

"The landfill murders," he said. "We're trying to get a leg up on it."

"Well, Eckling's got seven days before we officially enter the case."

"Cold trail by then."

"Let's wait until Okimoto tells us something," Vail said.

"That could be a couple days," St. Claire said. "I just wanna run some ideas through the computer network. No big thing."

"Who says they were murdered, anyway?" Meyer said.

"Hell," said St. Claire, dropping another dollop of snuff into his baby cup and smiling, "it's too good not to be murder."

"What's your caseload, Ben?" Vail asked.

"Four."

"And you're playing with this thing?"

"I don't know how to run this gadget," St. Claire complained.

Vail decided to humor him. "You can have the whiz kid here until after lunch," he said. "Then Meyer's back on his cases."

"Can't do much in three hours," St. Claire groaned.

"Then you better hurry."

Naomi finally walked across the office and grabbed Vail by the arm. She pointed across the room to Yancey's office.

"He called ten minutes ago. I told him . . ."

"No. N-o," Vail said, entering his office. He stopped short inside the door. Hanging on the coat tree behind the door were his dark blue suit and his tuxedo.

"What's this?"

"I had your stuff picked up for you. Didn't think you'd have time to get home and change."

"Change for what?" he growled.

"You have to accompany Yancey to the opening luncheon of the State Lawyers Convention. He's the keynote speaker. High noon—"

"Oh, for Christ sake!"

"And the opening-night cocktail party is at the Marina Convention Center at six."

"God*damn* it! Why didn't you tell me earlier?"

"I may as well give you all the bad news. Yancey wants to see you in his office. He wanted me to go down and get you."

"Out of an interrogation?"

"I explained that to him—again."

"Tell him I'm tied up until lunchtime."

"I don't think he'll buy it. Raymond Firestone's in there with him. Came in unannounced."

Vail looked at her with a sickened expression. "Saved the worst until last, huh? Just stood there and sandbagged me."

"No, no, I'm not taking the rap for this one. You agreed to both the lunch and the cocktail party last summer."

"And you're just reminding me now?"

"What did you want me to do, Marty, give you daily time ticks? Three days to go until the lawyers convention, two days, eighteen hours. Call you at home and wake you up. Nine hours to go!"

"Wake me up? I haven't been to *bed*!"

"I did not drag you out to the city dump. Parver set up the interrogation with Darby, not me. And I had nothing to do with Councilman Firestone's visit."

Vail stared angrily across the broad expanse of the office at D.A. Jack Yancey's door. He knew what to expect before he walked into Yancey's office. Raymond Firestone had arrived in the city twenty years earlier with a battered suitcase, eighty dollars in his pocket, and a slick tongue. Walking door to door selling funeral insurance to the poor, he had parlayed the nickel-dime policy game into the beginnings of an insurance empire that now had offices all over the state. A bellicose and unsophisticated bully, he had, during seven years as a city councilman, perfected perfidity and patronage to a dubious art. As Abel Stenner had once observed, "Firestone's unscrupulous enough to be twins."

Firestone, who was supported openly by Eckling and the police union, had let it be known soon after his first election that he was going to "put Vail in his place." It was a shallow threat but a constant annoyance.

Firestone was seated opposite Yancey with his back to the office door and he looked back over his shoulder as Vail entered, staring at him through narrowed dubious eyes that seemed frozen in a perpetual squint. Firestone was a man of average stature with lackluster brown hair, which he combed forward to hide a receding hairline, a small, thin-lipped mouth that was slow to smile, and the ruby, mottled complexion of a heavy drinker.

"Hello, Raymond," Vail said, and, ignoring the chair beside Firestone, sat down in an easy chair against the wall several feet from the desk.

Firestone merely nodded.

Yancey sat behind his desk. He was a chubby, unctuous, smooth-talking con man with wavy white hair and a perpetual smile. A dark-horse candidate for D.A. years before, Yancey had turned out to be the ultimate bureaucrat, capitalizing on his oily charm and a natural talent for mediation and compromise, surrounding himself with bright young lawyers to do the dirty work since he had no stomach for the vigor of courtroom battles.

"We seem to have a little problem here," Yancey started off. "But I see no reason why we can't work it out amicably."

Vail didn't say a word.

Like Jane Venable before him, Vail had little respect for Yancey as a litigator but liked him personally. Abandoned ten years earlier by Venable, Yancey had eagerly accepted Vail—his deadliest opponent in court—as his chief prosecutor. Their deal was simple. Yancey handled politics. Vail handled business.

"It's about this thing between you and Chief Eckling," Yancey continued.

Vail stared at him pleasantly. The "thing" between Vail and Eckling had been going on since long before Vail had become a prosecutor.

"It's time to bury the goddamn hatchet," Firestone interjected.

"Oh? In whose back?" Vail asked quietly, breaking his silence.

Firestone glared at Yancey, who sighed and smiled and leaned back in his chair, making a little steeple of his fingertips and staring at the ceiling.

"That's what we want to avoid, Martin," he said.

"Uh-huh."

"What we're suggesting is that you back off a little bit," Firestone said.

"That's a compromise?"

"I thought it had been agreed that the D.A.'s office would keep out of the chief's hair for seven days after a crime. That's the deal, he gets the week. Am I right? Did we agree to that?" Firestone looked at Yancey when he said it.

"Uh-huh," Vail answered.

Firestone turned on him and snapped, "Then why don't you do it?"

"We do," Vail said flatly.

"Bullshit! You and your people show up every time a felon farts in this town," Firestone growled.

"Now, now, Raymond," Yancey said, "it's not uncommon for the D.A. to go to the scene of a crime. Usually the police appreciate the help."

"He ain't the goddamn D.A."

"No, but he is my chief prosecutor. It's well within his jurisdiction."

"We're talking about cooperation here," snapped Firestone, his face turning crimson.

"Why don't I go back to my office?" Vail suggested with a smile. "You guys are talking like I'm not even in the room. I feel like I'm eavesdropping."

Firestone whirled on him. "You go out of your way to make Eckling look bad," he said, his voice beginning to rise.

"I don't have to," Vail said. "He does that all by himself."

"See what I mean!" Firestone said to Yancey. "How can Eric do his job with this smartass needling him all the time?"

"You'll excuse me," Vail said calmly, and stood up.

"Take it easy, Marty, take it easy," Yancey said, waving him back to his seat.

"You got a beef with me, tell me, not him," Vail said to Firestone, his voice still calm and controlled.

"He's your boss, that's why."

"Not in this area," Vail said. He knew the best way to get to Firestone was to stay calm. The hint of a smile toyed with his lips. "You know, frankly, I don't give a damn whether it pleases you or not, Raymond. You're a city boy. The county runs this office. You don't have any more clout over here than the janitor, so why don't you mind your own business and stay out of ours?"

"Jesus, Marty . . ." Yancey stammered.

"C'mon, Jack, I'm not going to listen to this windbag yell insults at me."

"Goddamn it, I told you this was a waste of time, Jack," Firestone said angrily. "Vail isn't capable of cooperating with anybody."

"Did you say that, Jack? Did you say I'd *cooperate* with them?"

"What I said was, maybe everybody could kind of stand back and cool off. What I mean is, try a little cooperation between your two departments."

"I'm quite cool," Vail said. "And as far as cooperating goes, I wouldn't share my dirty socks with Eckling. He's incompetent, he's on the take, and he wouldn't know a clue if it was sitting on the end of his nose."

"Listen here—"

"No, you listen, Councilman. I'm an officer of the court. I'm charged with the responsibility of prosecuting the cases that come before me to the best of my ability. I can't do that if I rely on Eric Eckling. Two years ago he was ready to drop the case against your two buddies on the council. We took it away from him and they're both doing hard time in Rock Island for malfeasance." Vail stopped for a moment, then added, "Maybe that's the problem. Maybe you're just getting jumpy, Raymond."

Firestone began to shake with anger. His face now turned bright red. He started to speak, but the words stuck in his throat.

"Tell you what," Vail went on. "You throw Eckling out on his ass where he belongs and put a police chief instead of a pimp in the job and you won't have a problem."

"God*damn* you!" Firestone screamed, and stomped out of the office.

Yancey watched him leave. He blew a breath out. A line of sweat formed on his forehead. "Jesus, Marty, you gotta be such a hard-ass?" he said.

"You and I have a deal, Jack. I run the prosecutor's office and you do the politicking. I don't ask for your help, don't ask for mine, okay?"

"He throws a lot of weight in the party."

Yancey had, within his grasp, the thing he had yearned for all his life, an appointment to the bench. But he needed the support of every Democrat in the county, so at this moment his chief concern was keeping peace in the family. Vail knew the scenario.

"So throw just as much weight around as Firestone does. Stop acting like the Pillsbury Doughboy and kick his ass back."

"I didn't mean for you to—"

"Sure you did. We've been through this song and dance before. You don't need Firestone anyway, his whole district's union and blue collar. Solid Democrats. They wouldn't go Republican if Jimmy Hoffa rose up from the dead and ran on the GOP ticket."

"I just hate to look for trouble."

"You know, the trouble with you, Jack, is you want everybody to love you. Life ain't like that, as Huckleberry Finn would say. Hell, when you're a judge you can piss everybody off and they'll smile and thank you."

Vail started out the door.

"Marty?"

"Yeah?"

"Uh . . . are you gonna wear that suit to the luncheon?"

"Sweet Jesus," Vail said, and left the office.

—

St. Claire and Meyer were scatter-shooting, feeding information into the computer and looking for links, bits of information that St. Claire eventually would try to connect together into patterns. Meyer was caught up in the game. It was like Dungeons and Dragons, where the players are lured through a maze of puzzles to the eventual solution.

Some of the unsolved homicides that HITS turned up were interesting, but nothing seemed to relate to the city landfill case and Meyer was getting tired. He and St. Claire had been at this cross-matching game for three hours and his stomach was telling him it was lunchtime. The office was empty except for the two of them. They had developed a list of seventy-six missing persons and nineteen unsolved homicides throughout the state, but neither of the figures appeared to correlate.

"What're you after, Harvey?" Meyer asked. "None of these cases could possibly relate to the landfill."

"The three bodies have to be connected in some way. They were almost side by side, so they had to have been dumped at the same time, don't you agree?"

"That makes sense."

"Well, think about it. Three people show up in the same area of the city landfill. If they were dropped at the same time, in all probability they knew each other. They had something in common."

"Yeah, they're all dead," Meyer said.

"Also they've been in there awhile. What I'm gettin' at, son, is that if the three of them knew each other and were involved with each other in some way, and they all disappeared at the same time, don't you think *somebody* would have reported that? First thing I did this morning, I called Missing Persons and asked them one question. 'You looking for three people who knew each other and were reported missing at the same time?' The answer was no."

"Maybe—"

"Folks who are missing friends or relatives will come forward to see if they can identify these bodies. Hell, if your kid was missing, and you picked up the paper and read that three unidentified bodies were found in the city landfill, wouldn't you be curious to see if he might be one of those three? There's a lotta missing persons out there, cowboy. And at least one person looking for every one that's missing."

"What the hell's your point, Harve?"

"Let's say we don't get an ID on these people—at least for a while. Doesn't that raise the possibility that maybe they're from someplace else?"

Meyer looked away from the screen for a moment. "You think they're out-of-towners?"

"Maybe tourists. Conventioneers. Or assume for a minute that they were killed out of town and brought here."

"You're reaching on this one, Harve."

"Humor me, son. I know it's a long shot. What if they ain't local? Think about it. What if they were involved in something outside the city? A bank heist, a dope deal, some cult thing. And suppose it went sour and these John and Jane Does were killed because of this deal and they got dropped in the dump. Hell, *somebody* dumped those people out there, they didn't fall out of the sky."

"It's a wild-goose chase."

"Maybe," the old-timer said, throwing his empty coffee cup into a wastebasket. He leaned back in his chair, tucked a fresh pinch of snuff in his cheek, and interlocked his pudgy fingers over his stomach. "I'm remembering a time five, six years ago. The Seattle police turned up two white males in a common grave just outside the city. They couldn't ID the victims. Six months go by, they've about written the case off, and one day they get a call from a police chief in Arizona. A thousand miles away! Turns out the Arizona cops nabbed a guy for passing a hot fifty-dollar bill that was lifted six months before in a bank heist. The guy breaks down and not only confesses to the bank job, he says there were three of them involved and they drove up to Seattle to hide out and started squabbling and he takes them both down and buries them out in the woods and drifts back down to Phoenix. The story checks out. The Seattle police solves its case. The Arizona PD solves its bank robbery."

"And everybody's smilin' but the guy that did the trick," said Meyer.

"Right. The *last* place the Seattle PD would've expected to get a line on their John Does was in Arizona. So you never know. We're looking to see if anything strikes our fancy, okay?"

Meyer was back staring at the big computer screen, watching it scroll through case descriptions. Suddenly he stopped it.

"How about Satanism, Harve? Does that strike your fancy?"

"Satanism?"

"Here's a little town called Gideon down in the southern corner of the state, probably hasn't had a major homicide in twenty years. The local PD thinks Satanists killed a housewife down there."

"Gideon? There's a nice biblical name," St. Claire said. "Seems an unlikely place for Satanists to rear their ugly heads."

"The chief of police refused to supply any crime reports. Didn't even call in the state forensics lab—which is required by law in a case like this. According to the cover sheet, it's a small, religious community. They think it involves Satanism and they don't want any publicity about it."

He ripped a computer printout of the cover report from the printer and read it aloud:

"UNREPORTED HOMICIDE, 12/7/93: Murder of Gideon, Ill., Housewife. Gideon is a religious community of Mormons. The population is approximately 2,000. Al Braselton, an agent with the state Bureau of Investigation, learned of the event while on an unrelated investigation in Shelby, 12 miles north of Gideon. The Gideon police chief, Hiram Young, reluctantly turned over to Agent Braselton some photographs and the sketchy homicide report. This is all the information the Bureau has on this crime at this time. According to Chief Young, the town didn't want a lot of outsiders coming there . . ."

Meyer exclaimed, "And this is in quotes, Harve, 'Because of the Satanism angle'! The homicide is still unresolved."

"There's an angle I never thought about," said St. Claire. "Satanism." He laughed at the thought.

"My God, look at these photos," Meyer said.

Six photographs had popped up on the computer monitor. Like all graphic police studies of violence, they depicted the stark climate of the crime without art or composition. Pornographic in detail, they appeared on the fifty-inch TV screen in two rows, three photos in each row. The three on the top were full, medium, and close-up shots of a once pleasant-looking, slightly overweight woman in her mid to late twenties. She had been stabbed and cut dozens of times. The long, establishing shot captured the nauseating milieu of the crime scene. The victim lay in a corner of the room, her head cocked crazily against the wall. Her mouth bulged open. Her eyes were frozen in a horrified stare. Blood had splattered the walls, the TV set, the floors, everything.

The medium shot was even more graphic. The woman's nipples had been cut off and her throat was slit to the bone.

But the close-up of her head was the most chilling of all.

The woman's nipples were stuffed in her mouth.

"Good lord," St. Claire said with revulsion.

"I'm glad we haven't had lunch yet," Meyer said, swallowing hard.

The lower row of photographs were from the same perspective but were shots of her back, where the butchery had been just as vicious.

"I can see why the police chief thinks Satanists were involved," Meyer said. "This is obscene."

St. Claire leaned over Meyer's shoulder and together they read the homicide report filed by Chief Hiram Young:

On October 27, 1993, at approximately 8 A.M, I answered a call to the home of George Balfour, local, which was called in by a neighbor, Mrs. Miriam Peronne, who resides next door. I found a white female, which I personally identified as Linda Balfour, 26, wife of George, on the floor of the living room. Mrs. Balfour was D.O.A. The coroner, Bert Fields, attributes death to multiple stab wounds. Her son, age 1, was five feet away and unharmed. Her husband was several miles from town when the crime occurred. There are no suspects.

Meyer turned to St. Claire. "Not much there," he said. But St. Claire did not answer. He stood up and walked close to the screen. He was looking at the close-up of the back of the woman's head.

"What's that?" he asked.

"What?"

"There, on the back of her head." St. Claire pointed to what appeared to be markings under the woman's hair.

"I'll zoom in," Meyer said.

He isolated the photograph, then blew it up four times before it began to fall apart. Beneath the blood-mottled hair on the back of her head were what appeared to be a row of marks, but the blown-up photo was too fuzzy to define them.

"Maybe just scratches," Meyer suggested.

"Can you clear it up any?" St. Claire asked.

Meyer digitally enhanced the picture several times, the photo blinking and becoming a little more distinct each time he hit the key combinations.

"That's as far as I can take it," Meyer said.

"Looks like numbers," St. Claire said, adjusting his glasses and squinting at the image. "Numbers and a letter . . ."

"Looks like it was written with her blood," Meyer said with disgust.

A familiar worm nibbled at St. Claire's gut. Nothing he could put his finger on, but it was nibbling nevertheless.

"Ben, let's give this Chief Young a call. He's got to know more about this case than the network's got."

"Harvey, I've got four cases on my desk . . ."

"I got a nudge on this, Ben. Don't argue with me."

"A nudge? What's a nudge?"

"It's when your gut nudges your brain," the old-timer answered.

6

In the lobby of the Ritz Hotel, the city's three hundred most powerful men preened like gamecocks as they headed for the dining room. They strutted into the room, pompous, jaws set, warily eyeing their peers and enforcing their standing in the power structure by flaunting condescending demeanors. The State Lawyers Association Board of Directors luncheon was the city's most prestigious assembly of the year and it was—for the most powerful—a contest of attitudes. Three hundred invitations went out; invitations harder to acquire than tickets to the final game of a World Series because they could not be bought, traded, or used by anyone else. The most exclusive—and snobbish—ex officio "club" in town established who the most powerful men in the city were. To be on the invitation list connoted acceptance by the city's self-appointed leaders. To be dropped was construed as a devastating insult.

Yancey's invitation to be the keynote speaker was a sign that he was recognized as one of the city's most valued movers and shakers. For years, he had secretly yearned to be accepted into the supercilious boys' club and he was reveling in the attention he was getting. Vail followed him into the dining room, smiling tepidly in the wake of the pandering D.A. as he glad-handed his way to the head table. This was Yancey's day and Vail was happy for him, even though he regarded the proceedings with disdain.

His seat was directly in front of the lectern at a table with three members of the state supreme court and the four most influential members of the legislature, an elderly, dour, and boring lot, impressed with their own importance and more interested in food and drink than intelligent conversation. Vail suffered through the lunch.

Yancey got a big hand when he was introduced. And why not? Speaking was his forte and he was renowned for spicing his speeches with off-color jokes and supplicating plaudits for the biggest of the big shots. As he was being introduced, Yancey felt an annoying pain in the back of his head. He rubbed it away. But as he stood up to speak, it became a searing pain at the base of his skull. He shook his head sharply and then it hit again like a needle jabbing into his head. The room seemed to go out of focus; the applause became hollow. He reached for the lectern to steady himself.

Vail saw Yancey falter and shakily steady himself by gripping the lectern with one hand. With the other, he rubbed the base of his neck, twisting his head as if an imaginary bee was attacking him. He smiled, now grabbing the edge of the speaker's platform with both hands. From below him, Vail could see his hands shaking.

Yancey took all the applause, taking deep breaths to calm himself down.

"Before I begin, I'd like to take this opportunity to introduce, uh . . . my . . . m-m-my right *and* left, uh, left . . ." His speech was slurred and he was stuttering.

Vail leaned forward in his chair. *What the hell was wrong with Yancey?* he wondered.

". . . one of this . . . this, uh . . . th-th-this country's great p-p-prosecutors and the m-m-man who . . . uh . . ."

Yancey stopped, staring around the room helplessly, blinking his eyes. Vail got up and rushed toward the end of the head table, but even as he did, Yancey cried out, "Oh!", pitched forward over the lectern, arms flailing, and dropped straight to the floor.

———

Vail rode in the ambulance with the stricken D.A., after first calling St. Claire and sending him to find Yancey's wife, Beryl. Yancey was gray and barely breathing. The paramedics worked over him feverishly, barking orders to each other while the driver called ahead to alert the trauma unit and summon Yancey's personal physician to the emergency room. When they arrived, they pushed Yancey's stretcher on the run into the operating room and Vail was left alone in the wash-up room.

Almost an hour passed before Yancey's doctor came out of the OR. Dr. Gary Ziegler was a tall, lean man with a craggy, portentous face studded with sorrowful eyes. He looked perpetually worried and was not a man who exuded hope to those waiting to get news of a stricken loved one. He wearily pulled off his latex gloves and swept off his cap and face mask, then pinched the bridge of his nose with a thumb and a forefinger and sighed.

"That bad, Gary?" Vail asked.

Ziegler looked over at him and shook his head.

"I hope you have a lot of energy, Martin."

"What the hell does that mean?"

"It means you're going to be a busy man. It's going to be a long time before Jack goes back to work—if he ever does."

"Heart attack?"

"Massive cerebral thrombosis."

"Which is what, exactly?"

"Blockage of a main artery to the brain by a thrombus—a blood clot. Specifically, it means the cerebellum of the brain has been deprived of blood and oxygen."

"In other words, a stroke."

"In other words, a *massive* stroke. He's suffering severe *hemoplegia*—we can already determine that, his reflexes are nil. And I suspect he's suffering *aphasia*, although I can't tell how bad it is yet."

"Translate that into simple English for me," Vail asked.

Ziegler walked to the sink and began scrubbing his hands. "Paralysis down his entire left side caused by damage to the right cerebral hemisphere. A speech deficiency caused by damage to the left hemisphere. It could have been brought on by a brain tumor, atherosclerosis, hypertension, I can't be sure at this point. Right now we've got him stabilized, but his condition is poor and he's unconscious."

"My God."

"The fact that he survived the first two hours is encouraging," Ziegler said. "If he holds on for another week or ten days, the outlook will be greatly improved. But at this point there's no way of predicting the long-term effects."

"What I hear you saying is, Jack could be a vegetable."

"That's pretty rash," Ziegler said, annoyed by Vail's description.

"It sounds pretty rash!"

"Well, nothing good can be said about a stroke of this magnitude, but until we can do an ECG, blood tests, CAT scans, an angiography, hell, I couldn't even guess at the prognosis."

"Can I see him?"

Ziegler pointed to the door of the Intensive Care Unit.

"I'm going to clean up. If Beryl gets here before I come out, talk to her, will you? I won't be long."

Vail looked through the window of the ICU. Yancey lay perfectly still with tubes and IV bottles attached to arms and legs, his face covered with an oxygen mask, machines beeping behind his bed. He was as still as a rock and his skin was the color of oatmeal.

What irony, Vail thought. *One of the biggest days of his life and his brain blows out on him.*

A few moments later the elevator doors opened and Beryl Yancey and her 30-year-old daughter, Joanna, accompanied by a uniformed policeman, stepped out. They looked dazed and confused and stood at the door, their hands interlocked, looking fearfully up and down the hallway. When Beryl saw Vail, she rushed to him, clutching him desperately, and chattering almost incoherently. He put his arms around her and Joanna. Beryl Yancey knew there were frequent skirmishes between her husband and Vail, but she and Jack Yancey both liked the tough prosecutor and were well aware that his stunning record had helped keep Yancey the district attorney for the past ten years.

"I was at the beauty parlor," Beryl babbled. "Can you imagine, the beauty parlor? Is he alive, Martin? Oh, God, don't tell me if he's gone. I can't imagine, I won't—"

"He's hanging on, Beryl."

"Oh, thank God, thank you, Marty . . ."

"I didn't—"

"Is he awake? Can we see him? Oh, my God, my hair must be a mess. I was right in the middle of . . ." The sentence died in her mouth as she primped her incomplete hairdo.

"Gary Ziegler's just inside the emergency room. He'll be right out. He can give you all the details."

"They came and got me in a police car. The whole beauty parlor got hysterical when that nice man . . . Who was that man, Martin?"

"His name's Harvey. Harvey St. Claire."

"He said he would wait for you in the car."

"Fine."

"You're not going to leave us, are you? Nobody would say anything, you know. Mr. St. Claire wouldn't tell me anything! I thought . . . Oh, God, I thought everything."

"He doesn't know anything, Beryl. Harvey doesn't know any more than you do."

"How bad does my hair look?"

"Your hair looks fine, Mom," her daughter said, patting her on the arm.

"You know if you need anything, anything at all, just call me. At the office, at home . . ."

"I know that, Martin. But Jack's going to be all right. I know he'll be all right. He never gets sick. Do you know, he never even gets the flu?"

A minute or two later Ziegler came out wearing a fresh gown and the two Yancey women fled immediately to him. Vail took the elevator to the first floor, but as he stepped out he saw a half-dozen reporters and a television crew clustered around the front door. He jumped back inside the elevator and rode it to the basement. He took out his portable phone and punched out the car's number. It rang once and St. Claire answered.

"Where are you?" he asked.

"The basement. There's press all around the front door."

"I know. I'm looking at them as we speak."

"I'm not ready to talk to the press."

"Follow the arrows to the loading dock on the back side. I'll pick you up there."

"Right," Vail answered, following an arrow down a long, dreary tunnel. Empty dollies with bloody sheets wadded up on them lined the walls. Several of the overhead lights were burned out. The narrow, depressing shaft smelled of alcohol and dried blood. He reached the service entrance and bolted through it, raced to the loading platform, and jumped to the ground as St. Claire pulled up beside him. He got in the car and St. Claire pulled out into the hospital driveway, then sped off toward the courthouse.

"What was it, heart attack?" St. Claire asked.

"Stroke. He can't walk, he can't talk, he's living on canned air, his brain has been deprived of oxygen and blood, and he's unconscious. When I suggested he might end up a mashed potato, Ziegler got edgy."

"Wasn't a very professional diagnosis," St. Claire said. He spat out of the window.

"I'm not a doctor."

"No." St. Claire chuckled. "You're the new D.A."

"I don't have time to be D.A.," Vail answered sharply. "This is going to sound weird, but ever since this happened I keep thinking about the day Kennedy was killed, that picture of Johnson in the airplane taking the oath of office."

"Passing of the mantle, Marty."

"I'm not a hand squeezer and I'm too blunt in social gatherings. I don't want the mantle."

"No, cowboy, but you sure got it."

—

Chief Hiram Young sat behind his gray metal desk and drummed his fingers, staring at the phone message lying in front of him. Rose, his impressionable secretary, always responded to long-distance phone calls, especially those from big-city police departments, as if each was an omen of impending national disaster. Young even found her careful, impeccable, Palmer-method handwriting annoying, but she was the mayor's sister, so he couldn't complain. Even worse, she underlined words she felt required emphasis.

> You had an urgent phone call from the District Attorney in Chicago (!!) at 1:30 P.M. I tried to reach you in several places. You must call Mr. Ben Meyer as soon as you get in. I took Charlotte to the dentist. Back at 3. Call ASAP. I promised!!!

The phone number was written double-size across the bottom of the memo pad.

Warily, he dialed the number and asked for Meyer.

"This is Ben Meyer," the deep voice answered.

"Chief Hiram Young returning your call, sir," Young replied.

"Yes, sir!" Meyer responded enthusiastically. "Thanks for getting back to me so promptly."

"My pleasure," Young answered. He cradled the phone between his jaw and shoulder and leafed through the mail as they spoke.

"I hate to bother you," Meyer said, "but we're working a case up here you may be able to assist us with."

"Glad to help," Young said, opening the phone bill.

"It's in regard to the Balfour murder case."

There was a long pause. A *long* pause.

Finally, "Yes . . . ?"

"We think it may relate to a case here."

"Uh-huh."

"Uh, would it be possible to get some additional information from your department, Chief? We have the I.B.I. report, but it's pretty skimpy."

"Our information is pretty skimpy."

"Have you had any further developments? Suspects, new information . . ."

"Not a thing."

"As I understand it, you suspect Satanists may have—"

"That was speculation," Young said tersely.

"I see. Was there anything specific . . ."

"You seen the pictures we sent over to the I.B.I.?"

"Yes, sir."

"Self-explanatory, wouldn't you say?"

"So it was the nature of the crime that led you to that conclusion?"

"I said it was speculation. Some of the city fathers and local ministers came up with that idea."

"You don't agree then?"

"Didn't say that. What's your case about?"

"Some unidentified bodies. There are some similarities. Did Mrs. Balfour have any enemies? Any—"

"Nothing like that. I knew Linda since she married George up in Carbondale and came here. Three, four years ago. Nice lady. No problems. George is the salt of the earth. Bringing up that little boy all by himself. He's had enough trouble."

"Do you have any background on Linda Balfour—you know, from before she moved to—"

"I didn't feel it was necessary to snoop into her business. Like I said, she was a nice lady. No problems."

Meyer was floundering, trying to strike a nerve, something that would open the chief up.

Meyer said, "And there were no suspects to speak of?"

"There was a utility man near the house that morning, but we never could locate him."

"A utility man? What company—"

"Lady across the street saw him walking down the road. Fact is, we never ascertained who he worked for."

"And that was your *only* suspect?"

"Told you, Mr. Meyer, she didn't have any enemies. Nothing

was stolen. Some nut comin' through town, most likely. We worked on that case for about a month."

"Fingerprints?"

"Nothin' didn't match up with the family and their friends."

"We're interested in the condition of the body, Chief. Can you—"

"I'm not at liberty to talk about that, sir. You might talk to Dr. Fields at the clinic—if he'll talk to you. He's also the coroner."

"Thanks, Chief. Do you have that number?"

Young gave him the number and hung up. He sat and stared at the phone for several moments, started to call Fields, and then changed his mind. Doc Fields was a grown man. He could tell this Meyer fellow whatever he wanted to tell him. Young turned his attention back to the mail.

———

Doc Fields was staring across a tongue depressor at the most inflamed and swollen throat he had seen in recent years. He threw the wooden stick in the wastebasket and looked sternly down at the six-year-old.

"You been smoking, Mose?" he asked.

The boy's eyes bulged and his mother gasped, and then Fields laughed.

"Just jokin', young fella. Got us some baaad tonsils here. Lessee, you're Baptist, aren't you, Beth?"

The mother nodded.

"Those tonsils have to come out. Sooner the better."

The boy's eyes teared up and his lips began to tremble.

"Oh, nothin' to it, son. Besides, for a couple days you can have all the ice cream you want to eat. How 'bout that?"

The promise of mountains of ice cream seemed to allay young Moses's fears.

"Check with Sally and see when's the best time for both of us," Fields said. But before the woman and her son could get up to leave, Fields's secretary peeked in the door.

"You got a long-distance call, Doctor," she said. "It's Chicago."

"You don't say," said Fields. "Probably the university school of medicine seeking my consultation." He snatched up the phone.

"This is Dr. Bert Fields. What can I do for you?" he said gruffly.

"Doctor, this is Ben Meyer. I'm a prosecutor with the D.A.'s office. You may be able to help me."

"You ailing?" Fields said sardonically.

Meyer laughed. "No, sir. We have a case in progress that may relate to a homicide you had down there."

"The Balfour murder?"

"How'd you guess?"

"Only homicide we've had hereabouts in a dozen years. In fact, the worst I ever saw and I been the town doctor since '61."

"I understand you're the coroner."

"Coroner, family doctor, surgeon, you name it."

"And you performed an autopsy?"

"Of course."

"Do you remember any of the particulars?"

"Sir, I remember every inch of that child's corpse. Not likely to forget it."

"Would it be possible to get a copy of your report?"

Fields hesitated.

"I can assure you, we'll treat it confidentially," Meyer hurriedly added. "We may have a similar case up here. If this is a serial killer, it would help us greatly to stop the perp before he goes any further."

"Perp?"

"Perpetrator."

"Ah. Perp." He laughed. "I'll have to use that. It'll throw Hiram for a loop."

"Yes, sir. I was wondering, do you have a fax machine?"

Fields got another hearty laugh out of that. "Just got me an answer machine last year," he said. "Can't think of any reason why I'd need a fax machine."

Meyer sounded depressed by the news. "It sure would help me right now," he said.

"Why don't I just get the report out and read it to you? Isn't that long."

"That would be great!" Meyer answered. He reached over to the telerecorder attached to his phone and pressed the record button. "Mind if I tape it?"

"Just like that?"

"Yes, sir, just like that. We're big-timers up here." And they both laughed.

Fields left the phone for a minute and Meyer could hear a metal file drawer open and shut.

"This is exactly what I reported, Mr. Meyer. Ready?"

"Yes."

"The victim, Linda Balfour, is a white female, age 26. The body is 53.5 inches in length and weighs 134 pounds and has blue eyes and light brown hair. She was dead upon my arrival at her home on Poplar Street, this city. The victim was stabbed, cut, and incised 56 times. There was evidence of cadaver spasm, trauma, and aero-embolism. There was significant exsanguination from stab wounds. The throat wound, which nearly decapitated Balfour, caused aero-embolism, which usually results in instantaneous death. Wounds in her hands and arms indicate a struggle before she was killed. There was also evidence of mutilation. Both of the victim's nipples and the clitoris were amputated and placed in the victim's mouth. It appears that the wounds were accomplished by a person or persons with some surgical knowledge. Also the inscription C13.489 was printed with the victim's blood on the rear of the skull, 4.6 centimeters above the base of the skull and under the hairline. The weapon was determined to be a common carving knife with an eight-inch blade found on the premises and belonging to the victim. A routine autopsy revealed no alcohol, controlled substances, or poisons in the bloodstream. The victim was nine weeks pregnant. Signed, Edward Fields, M.D. Date, 10/6/93."

"That help any?" Fields asked.

"Yes, sir," Meyer said, his pulse racing. "Can you repeat the inscription on the back of the head so I'm sure I have it right?"

"C13.489. Any idea what that means?"

"Not the slightest," Meyer said. "But if we figure it out, I'll let you know."

"Hope I've been some help, Mr. Meyer."

"Thank you, sir. Thank you very much. If you're ever in town give me a call. I'll buy lunch."

"My kind of fella."

Meyer cradled the phone and sat for a long time staring down at the scrap of paper in front of him.

C13.489. What the *hell* could that mean?

Maybe the old-timer would know.

7

Vail braced himself and pushed open the doors to the main salon, knowing exactly what to expect. A tidal surge of noise and heat assaulted him. He faced a thousand lawyers and their wives, all babbling at once with a calypso band somewhere on the other side of the room trying to compete with them, all enveloped in an enormous ballroom with eight food tables, each with its own towering ice sculpture, a dozen or more bars, nobody to talk to but lawyers, lobbyists, and politicians—and no place to sit. The world's biggest cocktail party. Vail, a man who despised cocktail parties, was about to take a stroll through Hades.

Vail was the most feared man in the room, for he represented a potential danger to every lawyer at the party: a loose-cannon prosecutor, unpredictable, unbuyable, unbeatable, who had spent nine years on their side of the fence before switching sides and becoming their worst nightmare, a prosecutor who knew all the tricks and was better at the game than they were. In ten years he had successfully prosecuted two city councilmen, a vice mayor, and a senator for everything from bribery to malfeasance in office and had wasted a local bank for money washing. They would treat him cordially but at a distance as he worked his way through the room, subtly letting him know that he was not one of them.

It was the only part of the ordeal Vail enjoyed, for he reveled in the role of the untouchable outsider.

Otherwise, he despised the annual ritual dance of the state's legal power players and their fawning associates. The corporate partners used these occasions to study the young sycophants and their wives and to reaffirm their choices. How did they handle themselves in this social bullring? Did they have the proper social graces? Did the women dress properly? Did the young lawyers drink too much? Express unacceptable political views? Hold their own in social debate with their peers? And perhaps most important of all, did they discuss the business of the company? Like pledges at a fraternity party, the young bootlickers performed for their bosses, fully aware that their performances would be discussed later and in harsh detail in the halls of the kings. Divorce had even been suggested after these forays.

They drank too much and they bragged too much and it was business. Big business. They talked about lobbying for this bill or that; which PACS they contributed to because they "got the job done"; which congressmen and state legislators were "spinners," those whose opinions could be influenced with a free dinner at a four-star restaurant or a hunting trip to some exclusive lodge in Wisconsin or Minnesota; which were "bottom feeders," cheap sellouts who could be bought for a bottle of good, hearty scotch and a box of cigars; and which were "chicken hawk" neophytes who could be lured into the fold with flattery and attention. They scorned the "UCs," uncooperatives whose votes were not available at any price and subtly shunned them until they were "seasoned" and learned the first rule of the game: compromise. These conversations were not about the law, they were about business and politics, enterprises that had little use for the law or ethics or integrity.

As Vail entered the room, he passed a group of five lawyers, all performing for a tall, white-haired potentate with smooth pink skin who was obviously enjoying the playlet.

"It'll be tacked on House Bill 2641," said one. "Furley will take care of it, he's already spun. It'll glide right through."

"How about Perdue and that new joker, what's his name, Eagle?" suggested another.

"Harold Eggle," another intoned. "A chicken hawk, nobody pays any attention to him."

"And Perdue's a bottom feeder," said still another. "Send him a bottle of Chivas and forget him."

"It's a done deal. Nobody will buck Tim Furley except the usual UCs and they'll be laughed out of the chamber," the imperious senior partner sneered, ending the conversation.

Vail sighed as he passed them, knowing he would drift aimlessly from one group to the next, nodding hello, smiling, and moving around the room until he was close enough to a side exit to slip out and flee the event.

But tonight was different. As he walked into the room, he was deluged with handshakes, smiles, pats on the back. He was overwhelmed with goodwill. It took a few moments for it to sink in, for him to realize what was happening.

Across the room, he was being observed as he made his way through the swarms of people. Jane Venable watched with a smile. Tall, distant, untouchable, classy, arrogant, self-confident, Venable had it all. From the tip of her long, equine nose to her long, slender neck, she created a mystique that was part of her haughty allure. She was almost six feet tall and, on normal business days, disguised a stunning figure in bulky sweaters and loose-fitting jackets. But in court, the perfect showcase for her brains, beauty, and élan, she was truly in her element. There she put it all to work at once, performing in outrageously expensive tailor-made suits designed to show off the perfection of her body. From her broad shoulders to her tight buttocks, her hair pulled back into a tight bun, her tinted contact lenses accentuating her flashing green eyes, she was a tiger shark. Immaculately prepared, she was a predator waiting to slam in for the kill: the ultimate jugular artist. There was no margin for error when doing battle with her.

Like Vail, she had one rule: Take no prisoners.

On this night Venable had thrown out the rule book. She flaunted it all. Devastatingly packaged, she was encased in a dark green strapless sheath accented with spangles that embellished both her perfect figure and the flaming-red hair that cascaded down around her shoulders. She was wearing green high heels that pushed her to over six feet. In the otherwise stifling milieu of the room, she was a beacon of sex, standing half a head taller than most of the men in the room. There was no denying her; no way to ignore this brilliant amazon. Jane Venable knew exactly what buttons to push to claim the night and she was pushing them all.

The day before Venable had wrapped up one of the biggest corporate buyouts in years. It was no longer a secret that Venable had spent six months studying Japanese culture and learning the language before going to Tokyo and masterminding Mitsushi's buyout of Midland Dynamics. Her strategy had pulled the rug from under four other law firms, one of them a Washington group that everyone had assumed had the inside track. It had earned her a $250,000 bonus and moved her name to number three on the corporate letterhead.

She had been watching Vail since he entered the big room, watching the minglers part like water before him, congratulate him, pat him on the back, then swirl back to continue their conversations in his wake. And at the moment she was thinking, not about her latest legal coup, she was remembering a day ten years earlier when she had suffered one of the worst defeats in her career.

Although they occasionally traded glances from across a theater lobby or a restaurant, it had been ten years since Venable and Vail had exchanged even a hello. It had been her last case as a prosecutor before moving to a full partnership in one of the city's platinum law firms—and it was one of the most sensational cases in the city's history. A young Appalachian kid named Aaron Stampler had been accused of viciously stabbing to death one of Chicago's most revered citizens, Archbishop Richard Rushman. An open-and-shut case—except that Vail had been the defense attorney.

In a bruising trial presided over by the city's most conservative and bigoted judge, Harry Shoat—Hangin' Harry, as he was known in the profession—Vail and Venable had provided plenty of fireworks for the media. Then Vail had ambushed her. Stampler suffered from a split personality, a fact Vail had not introduced into evidence and had kept from the public. He had tricked Venable into bringing out Stampler's alter ego on the stand, and instead of the chair, Venable had had to settle for far less. Stampler was sent to the state mental institution "until deemed cured" and she had left office a loser, at least in her own eyes.

But the case had preyed heavily on Vail's mind. After winning his points in court, Vail had had second thoughts. The outcome had troubled him, and in an ironic twist, Vail, the state's deadliest defense lawyer, had replaced Venable as chief prosecutor. Even as a prosecutor he did not get along any better with Judge Shoat. They had continued to clash in the courtroom until Hangin' Harry had been appointed to the state supreme court.

Forgiveness came hard for Venable, but she had held a grudge long enough. Vail had always attracted her, although it was years before she had admitted it to herself. Like her, he was a predator with an instinct for the jugular. In court, he was mercurial, changing moods and tactics on the whim of the moment, dazzling juries and confounding his opponents. And she was also drawn to his dark Irish good looks and those gray eyes that seemed to look right through her. Now he was not only the most dangerous prosecutor in the state, he was also *the* district attorney, and proper respect was being paid. Impetuously, she decided to end the feud.

She moved resolutely through the crowd, charting a collision course with him but staying slightly behind him so that he would not see her. Then an arm protruded through the mass of people. Massive fingers locked on Vail's elbow, steering him toward the perimeter of the ballroom and a small anteroom.

Shaughnessey, the old-timer who had carved a career from city councilman to D.A. to attorney general to state senator, losing only one political race in thirty years, was claiming Vail for the moment. Two years ago he had made his bid for the governor's seat only to be turned away in the primary. But it had not damaged his power. Shaughnessey was the state's high priest who with a nod could bring disaster down on the shoulders of anyone who challenged the political powers of the state house. Compared to him, most of the other state politicos were gandy dancers. The burly man, his bulk wrapped in a fifteen-hundred-dollar silk tuxedo with a trademark splash of colored silk in its breast pocket, his fleshy face deeply tanned under a thick, white mane, his thick lips curled almost contemptuously in what the unsuspecting might have mistaken for a smile, was obviously wooing the new D.A.

Her curiosity piqued, she decided to wait.

Inside a small, barren room, Shaughnessey fixed his keen and deadly hooded eyes on Vail and smacked him on the arm.

"How do you like being D.A.?" he asked.

"I told you ten years ago, Roy, I don't want to be D.A. I wanted to be chief prosecutor then and that's what I am now."

"Not anymore, my friend. You are the acting D.A., you need to start acting like one."

Vail had a sudden surge of déjà vu. Ten years ago. A snowy afternoon in the backseat of Shaughnessey's limo, sipping thirty-year-old brandy. The moment it had all started.

———

"You're the best lawyer in the state. Nobody wants to go up against you."

"Is this some kind of an offer?"

"Let's just say it's part of your continuing education. You've got to slick up a little."

Vail laughed. "You mean go legit?"

"Exactly, go legit. Get a haircut, get your pants pressed, stop kickin' everybody's ass."

"Why bother? I'm having a good time."

"Because you want to move to the other side of town. You want what everybody wants, bow and scrape, tip their hat, call you mister and mean it. You don't want to cop pleas for gunsels the rest of your life. Yancey needs you, son. Venable's left him. He's lost all his gunslingers. His balls're hanging out. Hell, he never did have the stones for that job. He's a politician in a job that calls for an iceman. What he wants is to make

judge—eight, nine years down the line—and live off the sleeve for the rest
of his time. To do that, he needs to rebuild his reputation because you've
been makin' him look like Little Orphan Annie. Twice in one year on
headline cases—and you burned up his two best prosecutors to boot.
Silverman's still in a coma from the Pinero case and Venable's on her
way to Platinum City. He needs you, son."

"Is that why you dumped this Rushman case on me?"

"Ah, you need a little humility, Martin. Besides, they want a monkey
show out of that trial and you'll give it to them."

"So that's what it's all about, getting a good show and teaching me a
little humility?"

Shaughnessey just smiled.

———

Now, ten years later, nothing seemed to have changed.

"Now what the hell's that mean, I got to start acting like one?"
Vail responded.

"This thing between you and Eric—"

"He's an incompetent ass-kissser."

"He's chief of police. You two got to work together—"

"Listen, Roy, in my first nine months in office, I lost more cases
than in the entire nine years I'd practiced law. Know why? Eric
Eckling."

"Just work with him instead of going out of your way to make
him look like a schmuck."

"Eckling's cops reflect his own incompetence. They lose evidence, lie, fall apart on the witness stand, put together paper
cases, violate civil rights . . ."

"Maybe that's because you stole his best cop."

"I caught him on the way out the door. He couldn't stand
Eckling, either. The only thing these guys are competent at is
screwing up. We do our own investigating now. And we don't lose
cases anymore."

"Why not practice a little discretion, would that hurt anything?"

"What are you, Mr. Fixit, the jolly negotiator?"

"It doesn't help anybody—this friction."

"Hell, you're getting mellow in your old age. You used to tell, not ask."

"Everybody else I tell. You I ask. Hell, I'm just trying to keep a little peace in the family, yuh mind?"

"Family! I'm not in any goddamn family. What is it, you been talking to Firestone?"

"He bellyaches to a mutual friend, it works its way back to me, I get a call or two. You really pissed him off, you know. What'd you do, tell him to kiss your ass?"

"No, I told him I wasn't there to kiss his."

"He's vice chairman of the city council, for Christ sake. Do you have to *not* get along with him? It's like you and Yancey used to be."

"Yancey and I get along fine. We have an understanding. The only time we have problems is when he forgets it."

"Firestone is very friendly with the police and firemen. And he's not a big booster of that kindergarten of yours."

"It's the senior high."

"Okay, okay . . . yeah. I'm just saying—"

"You're just feeding me the same old line, Roy. Con Firestone into thinking I like him. Get along with Eckling. It's an open sore, the thing with Eckling. It's not gonna go away. Tell Firestone to butt out. It's none of his damn business. I don't work for the city, I represent the whole county."

"Christ," Shaughnessey said, shaking his head. "You still hustling around trying to put all the town's big shots in jail?"

"Where'd you hear that?"

"Come ooon," Shaughnessey answered, peeling the wrapper off a cigar the size of the Goodyear blimp.

"Maybe one of these days you'll be one of them. I warned you about that when you conned me into this job ten years ago."

"Not a chance," Shaughnessey said, and laughed. "I'm out of your league now. It would take the attorney general"—he leaned forward and said softly—"and I put him in office, too. And he's a helluva lot more grateful than you are."

Venable was standing with her back to the anteroom door when

Vail and Shaughnessey reappeared. She watched them shake hands, then Vail started back through the crowd, heading for the side entrance. She fell in behind him. When he stopped suddenly and turned to shake hands with someone, he saw her. Their eyes locked, green on gray, and this time neither of them broke the stare. Finally she thought, *What the hell*, and raised her champagne glass in a toast to him. He smiled and threaded his way through the crowd to her.

"How you doing, Janie?" he asked.

"I think we're both doing just great," she said, and offered him a sip of her champagne. He took it, signaled to one of the floating waiters, and got them two fresh glasses. They headed for a corner of the room, away from the crowd and the band.

"I just read about your international coup," Vail said. "Congratulations."

"Thank you, Mr. District Attorney."

"Don't jump the gun," Vail said.

"Oh, you've got the power now, Martin. Can't you tell?" She swept her arm around the crowd.

"Tomorrow'll be just another day."

"No, it'll never be the same. You're the man they have to deal with now. And everybody knows you don't give two hoots in hell about playing politics."

"You're a very smart lady, Janie." He took a step backward and stared at her for several moments. "And more handsome now than you were ten years ago, if that's possible."

She caught her breath for just an instant but covered herself well.

"Why, Martin," she said, "I didn't think you noticed."

"I'm not dead. I just overlooked it in the courtroom."

"You certainly did."

"Does this mean we're declaring a truce? Putting all that business behind us? Are we going to be civil to each other again?"

"We were never civil to each other." She laughed.

"Well"—he shrugged—"we could try."

Her green eyes narrowed slightly. *Is he up to something?* she wondered, not yet willing to trust this apparent truce.

She's wondering what the hell I'm up to, he thought. And quickly moved to put her mind at ease. "We'll probably never face each other in a courtroom again," he said.

"What a shame."

He knew exactly what she meant. Going at it before a jury one more time would be exciting. They played the staring game for a few moments longer, then she abruptly changed the subject.

"What's the real prognosis?"

Vail shrugged. "You know doctors. He's got half a dozen specialists hovering over him and none of them'll give us a straight answer. One thing's for sure, he's got a tough road ahead of him."

"I always liked Jack," she said, thinking back over a decade to the obsequious, smooth-talking grifter with wavy white hair and a perpetual smile. What wasn't there to like? Yancey was not a litigator and never had been. He was a talker not a fighter, the ultimate bureaucrat who surrounded himself with smart, young lawyers to do the dirty work.

"Yancey's the ultimate ass-kisser, but he's never made any bones about it," said Vail.

"Yes," she agreed. "He'd kiss *anything* to stay in grace." Venable took a long sip of champagne. "I only let him down twice, you know. You were the reason both times."

"Hell, that was a long time ago. Water under the dam as a friend of mine used to say."

"Shit, you were a monster, Martin. Hell, I guess you still are. You've been prosecutor what, ten years now?"

He nodded. "Ten years next month."

"Long time to wait. That was the promise, wasn't it? Jack would move up to judge and you'd step in."

"I was never promised anything except a free hand to run the prosecutor's office my way. Besides, promises aren't worth a damn in politics. You know how to tell when a politician's lying? His lips are moving."

She laughed a throaty laugh. "Okay," she said, "you know what they'd call it if all the lawyers in this room were on the bottom of a lake?"

"No, tell me."

"A good beginning," she said, and laughed again. "Well, if it did happen that way, it was brilliant of them. Taking you out of the game, putting you on their side. I'll bet Jack engineered that whole deal himself."

"Nope. He was just along for the ride."

"Who then? Not Shaughnessey!"

"Shaughnessey made the pitch."

"You're kidding! Now there's a well-kept state secret."

"It wasn't any secret. Shaughnessey made the pitch and Jack slobbered all over himself agreeing. Hell, you were leaving and he didn't have a good prosecutor left."

"Why'd you do it? You were making what? A million a year or more? You gave that up for a hundred and fifty thou?"

Her remark reminded him again about the Stampler case and the others through the years—dope pushers and mobsters, thieves and rogues he'd saved from the proverbial gallows.

"Money was never the consideration," he said simply.

"Then why? Just tired of dealing with the scum of society? You put a lot of bad boys back on the street in your day, Mr. Vail. Bargain-basement justice."

"Justice? One thing I've learned after twenty years in the business: If you want justice, go to a whorehouse; if you want to get fucked go to court. I'm paraphrasing Thomas Jefferson."

"A very cynical attitude for an officer of the court."

"We're all cynics. It's the only way to survive."

"So what's next? Finish out Jack's term as D.A., run for a term to see how good you look at the polls? Then governor?"

"You sound like a campaign manager."

She looked at him and warmth crept into her green eyes. "It's worth a thought," she said quietly.

He decided to take a stab at it. "Why don't we have dinner tonight? Exchange secrets."

"You already know all my secrets, Marty," she said rather dole-fully, but quickly recovering. "But not tonight. Give me a call. It's an interesting thought."

"If you change your mind, I'll be up the street at Avanti! eating dinner."

He started to leave, then walked back and stood close to her and said in her ear, "All by myself." He kissed her on the cheek and was gone.

She turned back to the crowded room and the heat and noise and lawyers and calypso rhythm and her shoulders sagged.

Ah, what the hell, she thought. *Screw pride.*

8

Handsome, debonair, the perfect host, and master of Avanti!, the best Italian kitchen in the state, Guido Signatelli had but one flaw: outrageously tacky taste. Plastic grapes and dusty Chianti bottles dangled from phony grape arbors that crisscrossed the ceiling, and the booths that lined the walls were shaped like giant wine barrels. But Guido and Avanti! had survived on the strength of personality, discretion, and dazzling cuisine. Located three blocks from City Hall, Guido's—the regulars never referred to the place by its name—had become the lunchtime county seat and the legal profession dominated the fake landscape. Guido's personal pecking order was as precise as a genealogical chart. Starting at the bottom were the lobbyists, their mouths dry and their palms damp as they sucked up to everybody. They were followed by young lawyers eager to be seen as they cruised the room, hoping for a handshake; then the assistant prosecutors, huddled over out-of-the-way tables and whispering strategy; and finally the kingmakers, the politicos who greased the wheels of the city from behind closed doors in what was jokingly called "executive session"—to avoid the state's sunshine laws. Many a shady executive decision had been made in the quiet of one of Guido's booths. On the top were the judges, the emperors of justice, each with his or her own preordained table, each patronized by his or her own mewling sycophants and each pandered to by the rest of the room.

Guido, a chunky, little man with a great mop of silver hair and a permanent smile, led Vail to the corner booth. While still the state's most feared defense advocate, Vail had established the booth as his own. There he could eat, read, or talk business in relative seclusion. A few barflies hugged the long oak and marble bar and a half-dozen tables were occupied. Conversation was a low rumble.

Vail ordered a glass of red wine and settled down to read what the *Trib* had to say about Yancey and the bodies in the city dump, both of which were prominently displayed on page one. He didn't see Jane Venable until she appeared beside him at the table. He was genuinely surprised when he looked up and saw her and it was a moment before he reacted. He stood up, throwing the paper aside.

"I don't know what I'm doing here. I must be crazy! I guess I'm as tired of that bunch of hucksters as you are and . . ."

She was babbling to cover her embarrassment, obviously having second thoughts about following the man she had ignored—and who had ignored her—for a decade. Vail held a chair for her.

"You don't have to apologize to me for anything," he said quietly. "Ever."

"I'm not apologizing, I'm . . ."

"Glad to be here?" he suggested.

She glared at him for a moment and then her consternation dissolved into a sheepish grin as she sat down opposite him.

"It has been ten years," she said sheepishly.

"Well, we've been busy," he said casually. "What are you drinking?"

"I'll have a glass of champagne. If I switch to something else, I'll end up on my nose."

"Eddie," Vail called to a nearby waiter. "Champagne for the lady and I'll have the same. Why don't you just bring us a bottle? Taittinger '73 would be nice."

They sat without speaking for half a minute, then both started speaking at the same time and then stopped and laughed.

"Hell, Janie, it's time we started acting like grown-ups. Why not? You've been divorced for what, two years? I'm free as a bird."

She seemed surprised that he knew anything about her personal life. "Been keeping track of me, have you, Lawyer Vail?" she asked.

He did not answer. He was looking across the table, his eyes directly on hers. Their gazes locked for several seconds and she finally broke the stare.

"The one that got away, huh," she said, reaching for a cigarette.

"If I thought about all the ones that got away I wouldn't have time to do anything else."

She laughed. "I suppose we have been acting juvenile, haven't we?"

"Maybe it's just the right time and the right place, Janie."

"I've told you before, Martin, nobody calls me Janie."

"Except me," he said, taunting her. "What're you gonna do, get me arrested? I'm the friggin' D.A."

"Somewhat reluctantly, I assume," she answered.

"Want a job?"

"Why, are you quitting?"

He whistled softly through his teeth. "You haven't lost your edge, I see. So why do you suppose we're sitting here, Janie?"

She shrugged. "We're both forty . . . ?" she suggested.

"Plus," he added ruefully.

"We both hate cocktail parties?"

"We both hate lawyers?"

"Good one," she said. "Or maybe we're both just lonelier than hell."

"I can only speak for myself," he said. "I've missed you. Me and every other male who ever saw you in a courtroom. You really turned it all on. You were a real dazzler—the Hope diamond of the Cook County Courthouse. Don't you miss it? The roar of the courtroom, the smell of the crowd?"

"I still have my days in court."

"Not like the old days. Defending polluters in civil cases really ain't the same."

"Come on, Vail, I did one."

"And won, unfortunately."

"Hey . . ." she started, anger creeping into her tone.

"Sorry," he said hurriedly. "I'll get off the soapbox."

She shrugged. "Maybe I'm a little too touchy on the subject. I've always been curious about something I heard. Did they really clean your tank back when you were starting out? Is that true?"

"Oh, yeah," he said, "they whipped my ass good. The Chamber of Commerce sold everyone down the river, the newspaper lied to them, the bigshots bought off the judges, they brought in the heaviest, ball-busting lawyers they could find from the big town, and they turned a paradise into a killing ground. All I got out of it was a good lesson."

"What was that?"

"It's dangerous to be blinded by idealism. The minute the hyenas find out you have integrity, they bring on their assassins in silk suits."

"You haven't done badly. Blowing off one of the most respected banks in the city for money laundering, shutting down two chemical companies, busting half the city council for being on the sleeve. I call that getting even."

"It's a start," he said, and changed the subject, focusing the conversation back on them. "What I miss are our old skirmishes, even after ten years."

"There's something to be said for good, old-fashioned cutthroat competition."

"You ought to know."

"Look who's talking."

She raised her glass and offered a toast to cutthroat competition. Their eyes locked again and this time she didn't break the stare.

"Janie," he said, "just how hungry are you?"

She slouched back in the booth and looked at the ceiling and closed her eyes and shook her head ever so slightly, sighed, and peered down her long nose at him.

"Cocktail parties always did ruin my appetite," she said.

———

She was seeing a side of Vail he had never revealed to her before, a vulnerability, a romantic flair. He had brought home the bottle of chilled Taittinger after informing Guido that they had changed their mind about dinner. She had always been attracted to Vail, even in the old days, but had never admitted it to herself, dispelling her feelings as a combination of admiration and fear of his talent. Now, standing in his living room, watching him light the fire, she realized how much she wanted him and began to wonder if she had made a mistake. Was she rushing into something? A one-night stand? Would it turn into one of those awkward mistakes where she would awaken in the morning with a sexual hangover? But when he stood up and faced her, her fears vanished, washed away in another rush of desire. He took off her coat and tossed it over the sofa and went into the kitchen to get wineglasses.

She looked around the apartment. It was a large two-bedroom, high enough to have a nice view of the city but not ostentatious. One of the bedrooms had been converted into an office, a cluttered room of books filled with paper place markers, files stacked in the corners, magazines piled up, most of them with their wrappers still on them, scraps of notes, and newspaper clippings. A blue light glowed from the bathroom and she peered in.

It had been converted into a minigreenhouse. A six-foot-long zinc-lined sink ran along one wall, with faucets and tubes running from the bathroom sink. Pots of flowers crowded the bathtub. A row of grow lights plugged into an automatic timer created the illusion of daylight twelve hours a day. Beneath the lights were bunches of small, delicate blue flowers surrounded by fernlike leaves. On the other side of the narrow room was a small plastic-covered cubicle, its sides misty with manmade dew. Through its opaque sides, she could see splashes of color from other flowers.

She looked around the small room. "What do you know, a closet horticulturist," she said, half aloud.

"They're called bluebells," he said from behind her.

She whirled around, startled, and caught her breath. "I'm sorry. I was snooping."

He handed her a tulip glass bubbling with champagne.

"Belles as in beautiful young ladies. They're winter flowers. Grew wild along the banks of the river where I grew up. I used to pick them and take them home to my mom and she'd put them on the piano and sometimes I'd hear her talking to them. 'This is Chopin,' she'd say and then play for them."

"She sounds lovely."

"She was. She died when I was in the eighth grade."

"I'm sorry."

"Long time ago."

Her anxiety was slowly transforming back to desire. Her mouth got a little drier and she took another sip of champagne. Oddly, there was only one photograph in the bedroom, a grim, dark, foreboding picture of a murky colony of industrial plants, partially obscured by a manmade fog of steam and dirty smoke. They appeared as one long, gray mass with stacks spewing black smoke that rose to an ominous tumor of low-lying, polluted clouds hovering over the disgusting spectacle. In the foreground a scummy river with steam lurking around its edges vaguely reflected the despondent scene.

"Welcome to Rainbow Flats. Believe it or not, I used to swim in that river when I was a kid."

"So that's where they got you," she said.

"Yeah. Ironic, isn't it? The Chamber of Commerce calls that an industrial park. I used to think a park was a cheerful place where kids play. The spin doctors destroyed that illusion."

"Why keep a picture of it?"

"So I never get complacent."

"I can't imagine you being complacent about anything." She flipped off her shoes as they walked back into the living room. "Hope you don't mind, my feet are killing me."

"Sit down. I give great foot."

"Foot?"

"Best foot massage this side of Sweden."

She sat down on the sofa and leaned back against soft, down pillows. He took one foot in both hands, first rubbing it gently, then squeezing harder, kneading his fingers into her instep. The massage was like electricity being transmitted up between her legs along the silken strands of her panty hose. She closed her eyes. Her breath was growing shorter, her pulse quickening. The champagne kicked in.

"Very good foot," she whispered.

He slid his hand along her silken leg slowly, moving up to her calf, then to the edge of her thigh. She sat up suddenly, realizing she was completely out of breath.

"Need to stand up for a minute," she said. She got up and walked to the fireplace. He followed her.

"Marty . . ." she started to say, but he turned her to him, took her face in both hands, and kissed her. She surrendered, responding hungrily, her mouth linked to his, their lips and tongues frantically exploring, their bodies crushed together. The allure of each to the other was hypnotic. His hands moved down her sides, around to her back, caressed her tight buttocks, then slid tentatively down the outside of her legs, urging her against him. One hand moved to the inside of her thigh, his forearm pressed between her legs, then he moved his hand higher, caressed the smooth lip of her panty hose, his fingers barely touching her. She whimpered softly, moved against his exploring fingertips and pressed against his hand, and he began to stroke her. He kissed her ears, the small place in her throat, and she responded by putting her hand behind his head and moving it slowly down to her breasts. Pent-up denial exploded. They began frantically undressing each other without ever losing the cadence of the mutual seduction, his hand moving in slight, wet circles, exploring every pore of her. He gasped for breath as she laid her hand over his exploring fingertips, guiding them. He reached behind her with his other hand and unzipped her dress. She pressed against him, taunting him, keeping the dress from falling, then pressed the flat of her hand to his stomach, slid it across the hard muscles, her thumb encircling his navel. She slid her fingers under his belt, slid her hand down until she felt him rising to meet it.

She leaned back. The dress slipped slowly down, hung for a moment on her hard nipples, then slipped over her breasts and down to her hips. They kept kissing, their eyes closed, as their hands explored each other. Their lips still locked together, she pressed his hand with hers, moved it slowly to her stomach and then down until it was between her legs, and then she pressed it hard against her and began moving it up and down, then she turned her hand, pressing the back of it against the back of his until they were stroking each other in perfect rhythm. She could feel him growing and she let her free hand glide down his back, caressing his buttocks. The tips of their nipples touched and she moved closer, felt him growing hard against her, moving her body under his fingers, tracing his hard muscle with a featherlike touch.

She ground her head into his shoulder, her muscles trembling as he continued to massage her faster and faster, and she arched her back slightly and for several minutes they stood together, moving slowly to the rhythm of her sighs.

"My God," he whispered into her mouth, "slow down."

"I can't," she whispered. "C-*cant!*" She began to grind against his hand, began stroking him faster, and he began to move with her hand. She was trembling now; she sucked in her breath and rose on her toes and he could feel her trigger getting harder and wetter under his fingers until she cried out, thrusting herself against his hand, her legs trembling with spasms.

He lowered her to the floor and lay down beside her. Her arms fell away. He was on top of her, leaning over her, his eyes closed, his biceps twitching, and she guided him into her. He took in a breath and held it, then began thrusting into her. She reached up with both arms, wrapped them around his neck, and rolled him over so that she was on top of him, sliding her hard nipples up and down his chest, straddling him, then, rising slightly, she guided him back into her and leaning forward trapped his cries with her mouth. Hypnotized, they made love, stopped, held back, trembling, until they could not resist the demand any longer, until the tension was no longer bearable. He felt her wet muscles close around him. He slid his hand down between their stomachs, felt her grow even harder as he stroked her. She stiffened, stopped breathing for several seconds, then she thrust herself down on him and cried out and began to shudder, and her response was so overwhelming that all his senses spun crazily out of control. He felt a spasm, then another, and another, and still another, before he exploded.

She felt electrified, lost in time and space, and the waves began to build again.

"Oh God," she cried, falling down across him and stretching out her long legs, tightening them and keeping him trapped while they kissed until, finally, she came again.

"Ooooh," she slowly mumbled several times.

He lay under her, arms enfolding her, lightly scratching her back as they regained their breath, and then in a frenzied reprise, she felt him slide deeper inside her and then out, slipping against her, and she began to tighten again. Her hair fell across his face as she twisted her head from side to side, both moaning in unison as their dance built and built, until she cried out, sitting up on him, moving up and down, then she fell back across his chest.

They lay quietly for a moment while her muscles tightened and loosened with his own contractions. Her mouth was against his ear and he listened as she slowly regained her breath and finally she slid first one leg, then the other, down until she was stretched out full above him.

She lifted her head until they were almost nose to nose and she swept the tip of her tongue across his upper lip.

"God," she whispered, still breathless, "why did we wait so long?"

She slid off him, lying beside him with one leg over his. He put his arm around her and they lay there for several minutes watching the fire.

"Whatever happened to that gorgeous woman who worked for you," she said, breaking the silence.

"Naomi Chance?"

"Was that her name? That's a lovely name."

"She still works for me. You've gotten out of touch."

"People used to talk about you two."

She rolled over on her back, raised one leg up, and moved slightly so that he had a taunting view of her naked body.

"Did you two ever have a thing?" she asked.

He held up a single finger.

"Once? You did it *once*?"

He nodded. "One night a very long time ago. She said she didn't want to keep it up, that it would ruin our professional relationship."

Jane leaned over and bit his big toe, very lightly. "She was nuts," she said.

"Are you getting hungry?" he asked.

She stroked her saliva off his toe with her palm and fingers. "I could eat a little something."

"Will champagne and cheese do?"

"For starters. Any candles?"

"If they haven't turned to dust by now."

"Candles, wine, and cheese. How elegant."

"Got your appetite back, huh?"

"Oh yes," she said softly.

She watched him as he walked to the kitchen. He had a tight, hard, rather lean body. She liked that. Not an ounce of fat, but no steroid muscles either, and a very attentive lover who knew all the buttons to push and all the doors to open. But she had suspected as much. Vail did everything with passion.

He came back in a minute or two with fresh wineglasses dangling between his fingers, a box of stone-wheat thins, and a wedge of Brie cheese in one hand and two candles in the other. He dumped the burned-out cigarette butts out of a large ashtray, lit a candle, and dripped wax into a hot pool in the ashtray's center. She watched intently as he twisted the candle into the pool, holding it while the wax hardened around its smooth base. He opened the package of Brie and, with his little finger, scooped out a mound from under the hard crust and held it out to her. She put his whole finger in her mouth and sucked off the cheese.

The phone rang.

"Oh sweet Jesus," he moaned.

He tried to ignore it, but after five rings he knew Stenner was not to be denied. The man knew he was home and why.

"Shit, shit, shit," he growled, and finally snatched up the receiver. "Major, I'm not home at this time. If you'll leave a—"

"John Farrell Delaney."

A pause. "What about him?"

"He's lying in the middle of a penthouse on Lake View Drive wearing two .38-caliber slugs and nothing else. Either shot would have killed him."

"You son of a bitch."

"Ten minutes? Or do you need to take a shower?"

Vail thought he heard a snicker in Stenner's voice. He ignored the remark.

"Been over there yet?"

"Shock called me. What I just told you is all I know."

"Ten minutes," Vail said in surrender.

"I'm down front waiting."

"I should've known."

He hung up. She stared at him, still admiring his naked body as he started to dress. "You don't have to go home," she purred. "Why don't you spend the night?"

"Very funny," he muttered. "It's a homicide."

"Not very flattering."

"What?"

"Screwing my brains out and then leaving me for a corpse."

He pulled up his pants and angrily jerked up the zipper. "Midnight forays in the human jungle."

"As I recall, there were about two thousand homicides last year. Did you get out of bed for *all* of them?"

"They didn't all happen at night," he said, looking for one of his shoes.

She sat up and groped for a cigarette.

"Shall I wait up for you?" she asked, flapping her eyelids at him like a silent-screen vamp.

"Didn't this ever happen when you were a prosecutor?" he asked.

She shook her head very slowly. "I only had one phone and I unplugged it."

"Suppose it was something big?" he said, putting on his socks and loafers.

She blew out a slow stream of smoke. Curiosity crept into her voice. "How big?"

"Veeery, veeeery big."

"Where are you going?" she asked suspiciously.

He waved her off. "It was a rhetorical question, Janie."

"No, no, you're not getting away with that, Vail. What happened? Where are you going at . . ."—she looked at the clock—"eleven-thirty at night?"

"John Farrell Delaney pique your interest?"

She straightened up when he said the name, surprise rounding her eyes. "What about him?"

He looked at her, smiled, and held a finger over his lips.

"He did something! Did he do . . . No! Something was done to him."

A brief vision from the past flashed through Vail's mind. *The Judge and Vail, facing each other across his big desk, fingers on silver dollars, as they played mind games.*

"It's classified at this point, Jane. You know I can't—"

"Don't give me that shit, Martin Vail. Ever hear of date rape? Speak up or I'll start screaming."

"You wouldn't dare."

"He's dead, isn't he?" She leaned over until she was an inch from his face. "Is he dead, Marty?"

Vail nodded. "Somebody popped two shots in his ugly, old heart."

"Wooow!" she said slowly. "Somebody hit *Delaney*? Oh, you do have a problem, Mr. D.A. We may be the only two people in the city that don't have a good reason to kill the bastard. You don't, do you?"

"No, I always get his pimp, Firestone," Vail said. He stood up, dressed in his tuxedo but without the tie, and put on his coat. "I never had much to do with Mr. Delaney."

"You're lucky. Well, I'll forgive you for abandoning me, but only if you promise to give me all the gory details when you get back. This is going to be the hottest gossip in town tomorrow."

He leaned over and kissed her on the lips.

"If I'm not here when you leave, lock the door behind you."

"Don't turn this into something cheap," she whispered with a smile, and kissed him back.

9

"**W**as Delaney alone when they found him?" Vail asked as he got in the car. "I mean, do they have a suspect?"

"Told you all I know," Stenner said. He drove the few blocks from Vail's Dearborn Park town house to the Loft Apartments, pulling up in front of a tall, glass shaft of a building. Behind it, a hundred yards away and beyond the Hilton, the lake shimmered in the light of a half-moon. There were four police cars, an ambulance, and Okimoto's omnipresent van parked all over the street in front of the place. A small crowd weathered the cold and pressed against the crime-scene ribbons waiting for something dramatic to happen. Vail and Stenner took the elevator to the thirtieth floor.

The elevator opened onto a small hallway with only two doors. One was propped open with a chair and a uniformed cop stood beside it, looking back over his shoulder at the action inside.

As they entered the apartment they saw Shock Johnson, standing at the end of a long hallway, which was carpeted in white and softly illuminated with indirect lights. The big cop smiled, sauntered over to them, and stuck out a hand the size of a catcher's mitt.

"Hi, boys," he said, leading them down the hallway toward

the living room. "We seem to be seeing a lot of each other these days."

"Yeah, people'll think we're going steady," said Vail.

"You're not my type," Shock said. "I like blondes."

"I'll wear a wig."

"It ain't the same."

They reached the end of the hall and looked into a large living room with picture windows overlooking the lake. A lab man, who was on his hands and knees vacuuming the rug with a small hand machine, stood up and left as they entered. Another was dusting lamps, tables, chairs, and anything else in the room that might have gathered fingerprints. A pebbled old-fashioned glass was sitting on one of the tables, powder still clinging to it.

Except for the panoramic view of the lake, the room was cold and sterile. Black, ultramodern furniture contrasted harshly with white carpeting and walls. The three large paintings on one wall were abstracts in various configurations of black and white. The place appeared to be spotless. Spotless except for City Council Chairman Delaney, who lay flat on his back, stark naked, staring blandly at the ceiling. There was a hole in his chest and another over his right eye. A lot of blood had collected under the body and dried in a large, brown stain on the carpet.

"Where's Okie?" Vail asked.

"Other room. He's guessing he got it between seven and eight-thirty."

"Who found him?" Stenner asked.

"Delaney was the key speaker at a banquet tonight. When he didn't show up or answer his phone by the end of dinner, somebody called the office. The doorman answered, told them he hadn't seen Delaney leave the place. He checked the parking deck to make sure Delaney's car was there—you can get to it without going through the lobby. It was. There was a lot of hemming and hawing until the meeting was over. A couple of the dignitaries came over, the night manager used a passkey, and they came in. Welcome to Goodbye City."

"What time was that?" Stenner asked.

"Eleven-oh-five."

Stenner walked a little closer, leaned over, and looked down at the corpse. The right side of Delaney's face was scorched and his right eyebrow was singed off. Still leaning over, he looked back over his shoulder at Vail and Shock.

"Almost a contact shot, I'd say," he remarked.

Shock nodded. "Burned his eyebrow off and fried half his face. Couple inches at best. Probably wasn't necessary. They're both insurance shots."

"Anything happening in the bedroom?" Stenner asked.

Shock shrugged. "Take a look."

"Delaney doesn't look very surprised," Vail said as Stenner walked into the other room.

"Maybe he was blinking when he got it," Shock said.

"Probably knew who did him, wouldn't you say?"

"I'd say that's a pretty safe assumption. I mean, what the hell was he doing, anyway, traipsing around the living room with his unit hanging out?"

"Maybe his wife did him."

"Or girlfriend?"

"Or boyfriend."

"That, too."

"I have a friend who says she's the only person in town that didn't have a reason to kill him."

"You ever have a run-in with him, Marty?"

"Nah. He always sent Firestone to do his dirty work."

"He's another one."

"Maybe we can pin it on him."

Shock laughed. "I like that idea."

"Eckling have a lot of boys working on this?"

"Half the force."

"I'll bet he does," Vail said. "He can feel the heat already. This is going to give every politico in the city an enema."

"Like maybe one of them'll be next?" Shock said, and snickered.

"Guilty conscience," said Vail, and they both started to laugh.

"You two don't have much respect for the dead. After all, he *was* chairman of the city council, head of the finance committee, head of the city's Democratic Party . . ."

A short, dignified Japanese American with black, closely cut hair and tortoiseshell glasses entered from the bedroom. Oichi Okimoto, wearing a surgeon's paper robe and plastic boots and gloves, strode back into the living room. "How're you, Martin?" he asked as he walked past.

"I'm not getting enough sleep lately," Vail said.

"At least it's more comfortable than the landfill."

Okimoto, at thirty-six one of the best forensic scientists in the business, walked across the room, carefully moved a straight-back chair to a corner, and sat down on it backward, folding his arms over its back and leaning his chin on them. He perused the room without saying a word. Vail took out his cigarette pack and Okimoto said, without turning his head, "Don't light that, please."

"You taking samples of the air, Okie?" Vail asked.

"It annoys me."

Vail put the cigarettes away and everybody stood around waiting for Okimoto to finish thinking. Three minutes crept by. Finally Okimoto got up and returned the chair.

"We're through, so you may as well go home," he said to Vail. "Except for that mess over there, the place is immaculate. Here's what I can tell you. There's no sign of forcible entry. Wet towels on the bathroom floor. Tuxedo's laid out on the bed. He's wearing a gold, waterproofed Rolex—not a knockoff—worth about ten K, and his wallet, credit cards, et cetera, plus three hundred and eighteen dollars in cash, are on the dresser."

He looked back at the body.

"I think—*think, okay*—somebody he knew, somebody with a key, entered the apartment while he was in the shower. Delaney finishes, gets out, towels off, comes in here to get a drink from the wet bar over there in the corner. He thinks he's alone, so he doesn't bother to put anything on—if he had answered the door or heard somebody come in, he would have put on a robe or something. He gets his drink, turns around, and our mystery guest is standing about here, in the entrance to the living room. He gets in a conversation with this somebody—or maybe he realizes he's in trouble and he's pleading for his life—anyway, he puts the drink on the table, and as he turns around, the mystery guest plugs him twice. I'm fairly certain the first shot was the torso shot; we found a spent shell casing right here. Then our somebody walked over, probably straddled him, leaned down, and popped him in the forehead. There was another shell beside the head. Robbery obviously was not the motive. And I think the culprit was a woman."

"Why?" Vail asked.

"Imprints in the carpet. High heel, not a spike. I would say a medium heel from the configuration. We've got plenty of photos and a wax cast of the heel prints. I don't think there'll be any surprises from the autopsy. Maybe some drugs in his blood, but I doubt it, no indication of illegal substances anywhere in the place. And his stomach's probably fairly empty; he was on his way to dinner."

"Whoever shot him came here for that purpose," Stenner said.

"How do you figure that?" Okimoto asked.

"Because he was naked, right?" Shock offered. "If there had been any kind of conversation, he would have gone in the bedroom and put something on."

"That's very good," Okimoto said.

"If it went down the way you see it, Okie," said Vail, "the lady really must've hated his guts. Abel's right, she came here to do him."

"It'll all be in the autopsy," Okimoto said. "By the way, I won't have anything on the landfill case until tomorrow, maybe the day after. The bodies are a real mess."

He went down the hall toward the kitchen.

"Hell, Shock," Vail said, "all you have to do is find someone who hates him. According to my friend, that could be anybody in the county."

"I have a thought," Shock said, looking back at the body. "He's running for reelection in the fall. Maybe he was getting some campaign photos made."

"There you go, that's it," Vail said. "Hell, he's hung like a bull moose. Probably wanted to wrap up the women's vote."

They both started to laugh.

"How about taxidermists, he could probably get them, too."

"Yeah." Vail stopped laughing long enough to agree. "They could stuff it and name it after him."

"Right. The Big Prick," Shock said.

They were laughing hard when Eckling came into the apartment. He stalked down the hall and entered the death room.

"What's so goddamn funny?" he snapped. "One of the city's leaders is lying dead on the floor and you two think it's funny? I'm surprised at you, Captain."

"Aw, c'mon, Eric, lay off him," Vail said. "You know how it is around a murder scene, it's nervous laughter."

"I already know what you think of our councilmen," Eckling said haughtily. "I'll remind you they represent the people. They deserve respect."

"Why don't we bag the small talk, Eckling," Vail said with disgust. "It's a murder investigation. Investigate."

"Throwing yer new weight around, Vail?" Eckling snarled.

"If I do, you'll know it. You won't have to ask."

Eckling was distracted by Stenner as he entered from the bedroom. Stenner stopped when he saw Eckling and stood in the doorway with his arms crossed. They did not speak.

Eckling said, "About through in here, Captain?"

"Soon as the lab boys are wrapped up," Shock answered.

"I have people working the entire neighborhood," Eckling said to him. "We'll be doing the people at City Hall and at his business first thing in the morning. I'm going to run this investigation myself, Captain Johnson. You're first in command."

"Yes, sir."

"His wife is on the way down now," Eckling went on. "Would you believe it, she didn't know he had this place. A fucking penthouse, his old lady doesn't even know it exists. She thought he was visiting somebody when I told her where he was."

"She knows he's dead, doesn't she?" Shock asked.

"Uh, we told her there was an accident. I think Councilman Firestone was going over to tell her. They were very close."

The elevator doors shushed open behind them and Shock looked back to see Raymond Firestone enter the hallway, step back, and usher Ada Delaney into the apartment. She was a tall, stern-looking woman in her fifties, with arched eyebrows and confused eyes. Her face, stretched smooth by cosmetic surgery, still showed the sorrowful lines of a sad woman trapped in an un-satisfying life. She was dressed in a knee-length black cocktail dress and wore no makeup. She stood inside the door, looking around, then walked down the hall toward the living room.

"Jesus," Shock said, "somebody get a sheet. Cover that up."

"No!" Ada Delaney demanded, standing in the entrance to the living room and looking across the room at the remains of John Farrell Delaney. "Leave it just the way it is."

Shock looked at Eckling and he nodded. She walked slowly into the room, stopping five or six feet from the corpse.

"He was like that?" Ada Delaney asked.

"Yes, ma'am," Shock said.

She almost sneered down at the corpse. "Typical," she said.

There was a quick exchange of glances. Nobody said a word.

"I didn't even know about this apartment," she said, staring out the window. She seemed transfixed by the scene of death. Her voice began to climb, not louder, but higher-pitched, and she spoke in a rush, as if she had memorized a monologue and was afraid she would forget something. Vail thought she was perhaps in some stage of shock, traumatized by the sight of her husband's corpse.

"It's quite lovely. A little severe, but quite lovely. Pretty good for a man who made a fortune running slaughterhouses." She peered at one of the paintings. "I never did like his taste in art. Abstracts leave me cold." She turned to face Firestone. "Doesn't seem quite fair, does it, Raymond? To have a beautiful place like this and not share it with the woman you supposedly love, who bore your children, shared your bed?" She paused for a moment and then added nonchalantly, "Put up with all those lies."

She stepped closer to the corpse until she was almost looking straight down at it.

"I married him right out of college, you know. Thirty-one years. I never knew another man—intimately, I mean. It was always just Farrell. Farrell, Farrell, Farrell. He was such an attentive suitor . . . and I did love him so . . . thirty-one years ago. He bought me an orchid for our senior prom. I don't know where he got the money. I'd never seen a real orchid before. He used to give me five orchids every anniversary. Until a few years ago." She put her hand to her mouth. "Oh, my, I would love to cry. But I can't even do that, I just can't seem to find my tears. You know how I feel, Raymond? I feel relieved. I'm relieved that it's over." She looked back down at her dead husband. "I was really growing to hate you, Farrell. And to think I didn't have to do anything. I didn't have to divorce you or go on being humiliated by you. It was done for me. What a nice . . . unexpected . . . surprise."

She turned away from her dead husband and strolled out of the room.

"You can take me home now, Raymond," she said.

As Vail watched her leave, he thought about Beryl Yancey, panicky with fear that her husband was dead or dying, in contrast with Ada Delaney, who couldn't even shed a tear over hers.

"Phew!" he said as they watched the elevator doors close behind her.

"Definitely a suspect," Stenner answered.

"Oh yeah," said Shock Johnson. "This may turn out to be an easy one, Marty."

"They're never easy."

—

When Vail got home, there was a paper towel on the floor inside the door. On it was a lipstick print and below it Jane Venable's unlisted phone number.

No other message.

10

The Delaney house was in Rogers Park on Greenleaf just off Ridge Avenue, an old, columned, Italianate mansion with tall windows and bracketed eaves, which from the outside had a gloomy nineteenth-century look. Eckling left his aide in the car. The maid led him through a house that had been gutted and re-modeled with large, high-ceilinged rooms decorated in bright pastel colors, to a radiant atrium at the rear of the house with French doors opening onto a large garden protected by high hedgerows. Outside, a bluejay fluttered and splashed in a concrete birdbath.

Ada Delaney, dressed appropriately in black, was seated on a bright green flowered sofa with a tall, slender man with shiny gray-black hair, olive skin, and severe, hawklike features. He was dressed in dark blue. Her confused look of the night before had been replaced with a mien of cold, controlled calm and she greeted Eckling with the attitude to go with it. Antagonism permeated the room.

"Eric." She nodded curtly. "Do you know Gary Angelo?"

"We've met," Eckling said, shaking his hand.

"Mr. Angelo is the family attorney," she said. "He's going to handle things for me. I'm sure you don't mind if he joins us."

"Not at all," the chief of police answered, as if he had a choice.

"Would you like coffee?" she asked, motioning toward an ornate silver service. "Or perhaps a drink?"

"Nothing, thank you. I hope I'm not comin' at a bad time."

"Not at all," she said with a grim smile. "We were just discussing how well off Farrell left me and the children. At least he did something thoughtful."

"I'm sorry, Ada—"

"Forget the compulsory grief," she said brusquely, cutting him off. "The fact is, you were one of his friends, Eric. You knew what was going on."

"Uh, it wasn't my business to—"

"To what? Raymond Firestone told me all about it. Parties, poker games, weekend *retreats*, as Farrell called them, for his in-crowd. You were one of them. Now you come here implying—"

"I'm not implyin' anything," Eckling said with chagrin. "I'm just doin' my job. These things have to be addressed."

"Well, at least you came yourself, you didn't send one of your flunkies."

"Please," Eckling said, obviously ill at ease. "I want to make this as pleasant as possible."

"I'm sure. What is it you want to know?"

"Do you know of anyone who might have had a motive to do this to John?"

She sneered at the question. "Don't ask stupid questions, Eric. It was very easy to hate Farrell Delaney."

"How about, uh . . ." Eckling started, letting the sentence dangle.

"Women? Are you usually this diplomatic when you grill suspects?"

"Please, Ada."

"Don't *please* me. That's why you're here and we both know it. I'm sure my comments last night put me at the top of the suspect list."

"There's no list as yet."

"Well, why don't you just get out the phone book and start with *A*," she said with a sardonic smile.

Eckling looked helplessly at Angelo, who ignored him. He sat with his legs crossed, appraising freshly manicured fingernails.

"So you can't provide any leads?"

"You might start with his business partners. He was famous for screwing his friends. Or perhaps *infamous* would be a better word. Frankly, I don't really care who shot him. I hope whoever did the world that favor doesn't suffer too much for it."

"Christ, Ada!"

"Oh, stop it. Don't be such a hypocrite, ask me what you really came here to ask."

"Yes," Angelo said, appraising Eckling with a cool stare. "Why don't we cut through the felicities and get on with it. I'm sure we've all got better things to do."

"All right, where were you between seven-thirty and nine P.M. last night?" Eckling asked bluntly.

"I was having dinner at Les Chambres with my daughter and son-in-law," she answered with a smug smile. "They picked me up here about seven-thirty. I had been home about thirty minutes when Raymond Firestone called me."

Eckling mentally calculated how long it would take to get from the Delaney house in Rogers Park to the restaurant located in the Gold Coast. Thirty minutes at least. Les Chambres was ten, fifteen minutes from Delaney's penthouse. Five or ten minutes to do the trick . . .

"We arrived at the restaurant at eight," she said. "We were there until nearly ten-thirty. We saw several people we know."

"You can relax, Chief," Angelo said. "She's airtight."

"I see."

"Was there anything else?" Ada Delaney said coldly.

"I guess . . . No, unless you can think of—"

"I can't, Eric. And I doubt that I will. Please don't come back here again." She got up and left the room.

"Christ," Eckling said to the lawyer, "we gotta *ask* her. She oughtta realize we gotta ask her, y'know, clear her up right off the bat."

"She has an alibi," the lawyer said curtly. "Check it out. I'll advise her to be as cooperative as you need her to be—*after* you're satisfied she's not involved."

"Thanks," Eckling said.

———

Across town, the Wild Bunch was gathering for a staff meeting called by Shana Parver. Parver and Stenner were in her cubbyhole office talking on the phone while the rest of the bunch gathered in Vail's office, where doughnuts and coffee were waiting: Meyer; Stenner; Naomi; Hazel Fleishman, the daughter of an abusive, hard-drinking army sergeant, who, at thirty-four, was a specialist in sexual and physical abuse cases and rape and was a ferocious litigator; and Dermott Flaherty, a black Irish, streetwise, former petty thief with a gallows sense of humor. Flaherty had escaped dismal beginnings in the east and was graduated cum laude from the University of Chicago, where he had won a four-year scholarship to law school.

Missing were Bobby Hartford, the son of a black ACLU lawyer, who had spent his first ten years as a lawyer fighting civil rights cases in Mississippi and, at thirty-seven, was the oldest of the Wild Bunch; Bucky Winslow, a brilliant negotiator, whose father had lost both legs in Vietnam and died in a veterans' hospital; and St. Claire.

"Where are Hartford and Winslow?" Vail asked Naomi.

"Both in court this morning."

"St. Claire?" Vail looked at Ben Meyer.

"He's checking on something over at the records building," Meyer said.

"About that hunch of his?" Vail asked. "Anything to it?"

"Well, uh, nothing yet," Meyer said, not wishing to comment until St. Claire was in the room.

The conversation quickly centered on Yancey's stroke and the murder of John Delaney, the landfill trio taking a backseat to these two new developments. Vail filled them in on the Delaney homicide and assured them that he had no intention of wasting a lot of time playing D.A.

"This is where the action is, and this is where I intend to stay," he insisted as Stenner and Parver finished their phone call and entered his office, she wearing a Cheshire cat grin.

"Okay, Shana," said Vail. "What're you so proud of?"

"I think we've got Darby," Parver said, rather proudly. "We can blow his story off the planet."

"Oh?" Vail said. He walked around the desk and sat down. He leaned back in his chair and rolled a cigarette between two fingers. "Let's hear it from the top," he said to her. They all knew the facts of the crime, but this was the usual drill: taking it from the top so the rest of the bunch could get the whole run in perspective.

Parver gave a quick summary of the facts: that Darby was having trouble at home with his wife, Ramona, had three bad years on his farm, had lost a subsidy contract with the government, had gone through all his family's money and a fifty-thousand-dollar inheritance Ramona got a year before, and was shacking up with a nude dancer named Poppy Palmer who performed at a strip club called the Skin Game. There was also the insurance policy.

"Darby said last summer he had an accident with a harvesting machine," she said. "It rolled back and almost killed him, so he took out a $250,000 insurance policy on himself—and one on Ramona while he was at it.

"Now it's January third, six o'clock in the afternoon. Darby has been hunting with two of his buddies since before dawn. They stop for a couple of beers on the way home."

Parver stood up, acting out the event as she spoke, substituting a steel ruler for the shotgun. Parver was an actress. She loved visual impact. She leaned with her back against an imaginary wall, the steel ruler pressed against her chest.

Parver: "He gets home and walks in the house. The CBS news is just coming on. His wife, Ramona, is sitting in the living room. Before he can even say hello, she comes up with his .38 target gun and starts shooting at him. He jumps out of the doorway behind the wall of a hallway leading to the kitchen. She sends another shot through the wall. It misses him by inches. He freaks out. He slams two shells in the shotgun and rushes around the corner."

She spun around and aimed the ruler at Fleishman.

Parver: "And shoots her. The shot hits her in the side. Her gun hand goes up, she puts another shot into the ceiling as he charges her."

She rushed up to Fleishman and held the steel ruler an inch away from her forehead.

Parver: "*Boom!* he shoots her right here, just above her right eye. He drops the shotgun and crosses the room to the phone and calls 911. There's a slip of paper beside the phone with Poppy Palmer's unlisted phone number on it. Later he claims he didn't write it, doesn't know where it came from. Then he goes outside and sits on the porch steps until the police arrive. That's his story. No witnesses, nobody to argue with him."

Fleishman: "Gunfight at the O.K. Corral, right?"

Parver: "Right. Later Darby claims he called Poppy Palmer to tell her what happened and to find out where Ramona got the unlisted number. Palmer tells him that Ramona Darby called her about five and went crazy on the phone, threatening them both."

Vail: "Them being . . . ?"

Parver: "Palmer and Darby."

Vail: "Go on."

Parver: "Given the motives and the nature of the individual, I don't think any of us believed it happened this way, but we don't have anything to take to the grand jury. The insurance company is about to pay off the policy. Martin and I conducted an interrogation with Darby yesterday and he froze us out. So Abel and I went back out to Sandytown. We decided to take one more crack at everybody out there who might know something, *anything.*

"There's this elderly lady—she's seventy-six—lives on the opposite side of the road from Darby, about eighty yards—actually it's eighty-three—from Darby's house. It's a field that separates these two houses, a corn field in the summer—some trees line the dirt driveway leading to the Darby place, but basically it's wide open between Darby's house and hers. Her name's Shunderson, Mabel Shunderson, a widow. She's lived there more than thirty years, has known the Darbys for the entire time they lived across the road, which is . . . uh,"—she consulted her notes—"twelve years. Mrs. Shunderson saw Darby come home in his pickup truck. She was in the kitchen looking out her window, which faces the Darby place, and she had the window open because she burned something on the stove and she was shooing out the smoke. She saw Darby come home, saw him get out of the pickup carrying the shotgun, and go into the house. A minute later she heard the shots. She had told us all this before, that she heard the shots, I mean, but we never talked about the *order* of the shots."

Vail: "In her seventies, you say?"

Parver: "Yes, sir. Anyway, she says she heard the shots very clearly. It was a clear night, very cold."

Fleishman: "She's sure it was him?"

Parver: "No question about it."

Meyer: "And she's sure about the time?"

Parver: "Says the news was just coming on the television, which ties in with Darby's story and the phone call to 911, which was at six-oh-six."

Vail: "Okay, go on."

Parver: "Well, we were doing what you might call a courtesy call just to make sure we covered everything and I said to her, Did you hear all six shots, and she said yes. She knows about guns because Gus—that's her husband, her late husband, he's been dead about six years now—did a lot of hunting and she could tell there were two guns going off. And then she said . . ."

She stopped a moment and read very carefully from her notes.

". . . said, 'I know the difference between a shotgun and a pistol, my Gus spent half his life either hunting or practicing to hunt, and when I heard that shotgun, then all those pistol shots, I knew there was something goin' on down there and I thought it was maybe a burglar in the house.' "

Parver looked at Vail and then around at the group. She repeated her remark.

Parver: " 'I heard that shotgun, then all those pistol shots,' that's exactly what she said."

Vail stared at her as she went on.

Parver: "So I said to her, 'You mean you heard the pistol, then the shotgun,' and she said, 'Young lady, I know the difference between a shotgun and a pistol. I heard the shotgun, then four pistol shots, then the shotgun again.' "

Vail: "She's saying Darby fired the first shot?"

Parver: "Exactly."

Flaherty: "She's seventy-five?"

Parver: "Six. Seventy-six."

Flaherty: "And the house is eighty yards from Darby's place?"

Parver: "Eighty-three, but she knows what she heard. I don't think there's any doubt about that. But just to make sure, Abel and I did a test."

Vail: "A test?"

He looked at Stenner.

Stenner: "We set up a tape recorder in her kitchen beside the open window. I went down to Darby's place and went in the barn and fired two sets of shots into some sacks of grain."

Vails: "Where was Darby?"

Stenner. "He wasn't there."

Vail: "Uh-huh. Trespassing."

He scribbled some notes on a legal pad.

Stenner: "We can go back and do it legal. I just wanted to make sure we had a live one here."

Vail: "I know."

Stenner: "First I did it the way Darby says it happened. I fired three shots from the pistol, one from the shotgun, another pistol shot, and the final shotgun blast. Then I did it the way Mrs. Shunderson says she heard it: the shotgun first, four pistol shots, and the final shotgun. Shana stood beside Mrs. Shunderson exactly where she was standing when the event took place and taped both sets of shots."

Parver: "She was adamant. She says it was BOOM, bang, bang,

bang, bang . . . BOOM. *Not* bang, bang, bang, BOOM, bang, BOOM. Here's the tape."

She put a small tape recorder on the desk and pressed the play button. There was silence except for the room tone. Then there were the shots, echoing very clearly in the night air.

Bang, bang, bang . . . BOOM . . . bang . . . BOOM.

"No, no. Not the way it was 'tall" came an elderly woman's firm, very positive voice. "As I told you . . ."

Shana's voice interrupted her. "Just a minute," she said. "Listen."

BOOM . . . bang, bang, bang, bang . . . BOOM.

"Yes! That's the way it was. 'Cept there was a little more time between that last pistol shot and the shotgun."

"You're absolutely positive?" Parver asked.

"I told you, child, I know the difference between a shotgun and a pistol."

"And you're sure of the sequence?"

"The shotgun was first. And there was that little pause between the last pistol shot and then the shotgun again."

Parver turned off the tape recorder.

Hazel Fleishman said, "Wow!" The rest of the group started to talk all at once. Vail knocked on the table with his knuckles and calmed them down.

"Is she a good witness, Abel?" Vail asked.

"A crusty old lady." Stenner nodded with a smile. "I think she'll hold up."

"A woman that age—" Meyer started.

"She's positive about what she heard. And there's not a thing wrong with her hearing," Stenner assured him.

"You think we can bring a first-degree murder case against Darby on this boom-bang testimony?" Flaherty said.

"This woman knows what she heard," Stenner insisted.

"This is what I think happened," Parver said. She acted out her theory again, walking to the middle of the room with her hand down at her side holding the ruler-shotgun.

"He comes home, has the shotgun loaded, walks into the house. His wife is sitting in the living room. . . ."

Parver approached Flaherty. When she was two feet away from him, she swung her arm up, aiming the imaginary gun at his forehead.

"BOOM! He walks right up to her and shoots her in the head point-blank, just like that. Then he takes the .38—he's still got his gloves on—and he puts it in her hand and *bang, bang, bang, bang*—he puts the two shots in the hall, one in the wall, and one in the ceiling—then he backs off a few feet and hits her with the second shotgun blast. I mean, he thought of everything. Powder burns on her hand, the long shot that he claims he shot *first* after she cut loose at him. He covered everything *but* the sound."

"It's not just the order of the shots," Stenner said in his under-played, quiet manner. "It's the pauses in between them. Or lack of same. Mrs. Shunderson says there was no pause between the four pistol shots. She says it was BOOM . . . bang bang bang bang . . . BOOM. Ramona Darby was dead when he put the gun in her hand and fired the pistol."

Vail leaned back in his chair and stared at the ceiling for a moment, then chuckled. "Nice job, you two," he said.

"The problem is proving premeditation," Flaherty offered. "We'll have to give up Shunderson in discovery so they'll know what we have. Darby'll change his story."

"That won't hold up," Stenner said. "No jury will believe that he charged into her while she was shooting at him and got close enough to pop her point-blank in the head without getting hit himself. It's that point-blank head shot he has to live with."

"He could plead sudden impulse," Dermott Flaherty offered. "He came in. She had the gun. She threatened him, he shot her. Then he panicked and jimmied up the rest of the story because he was afraid he couldn't prove self-defense."

"So how do we trap him?" Vail asked.

Silence fell over the room.

Vail went on. "Unless we have some corroborative evidence, Darby will be dancing all over the room. And Paul Rainey will jump on the strongest scenario they can come up with and stick with it."

"Which will probably be Dermott's take on it," Hazel Fleishman said.

Vail nodded. "Namely that he came in, she had the gun, he freaked out and shot her but didn't kill her, blah, blah, blah."

"Doesn't work," Parver said. "He can't get around the fact that for his story to work, his first shot had to hit her in the side. That shot in the face was from twelve inches, maybe less. It was cold-blooded. That shot put her away instantly."

"Heat of the moment?" Fleishman suggested. "The woman throws down on him, he fires in a panic—"

"And runs twelve feet across the room before he shoots again?" Stenner asked. "No jury'll buy that. If the farm lady's testimony holds up—if Rainey doesn't dissect her on the stand—Darby's stuck with the sequence, he'll have to change his story."

"He's in a panic. He's exhausted. He's been out in a blind for five hours." Flaherty lowered his head, miming Darby: "I was cold and tired. I came in and suddenly this crazy woman's blazing away at me. I duck behind the hall wall. She keeps shooting. Finally I just charged into the room and fired. It all happened so fast. I don't remember firing that last shot. All I remember is the noise and the smoke, one of those shots coming so close to my cheek that I could feel the heat. It was over just like that." He snapped his fingers.

Vail said, "Very good, Dermott. You ought to be defending him." The group laughed except for Shana Parver, who glared at Flaherty. He smiled at her and shrugged. "Just doin' my job, Counselor," he said. "I think nailing that witness was a stroke of genius."

"No question about it," Vail said. "The questions we have to decide are: One, do we arrest him yet? And two, do we go for murder in the first or second?"

Shana Parver said, "It's cold-blooded murder. We can prove premeditation. He did it the minute he walked in the door."

"So do we arrest him?" Stenner asked. A hint of a smile played at the corners of his mouth. He watched Vail go to the urn and draw another cup of coffee. The old master, playing all the angles in his head.

Vail walked over to Shana and toyed with the ruler and said, "How about Betty Boop? Did you talk to her about the phone call?"

Parver smiled. "She flew the coop."

"She did *what*?"

"We went by the club and her boss told us she left town yesterday afternoon," Stenner said. "Told him her sister in Texarkana is dying of cancer. We checked it out this morning, that's what we were doing on the phone. Her sister lives in San Diego. In perfect health. Last time she heard from Poppy Palmer was five years ago."

"What do you know," Vail said to Parver. "Your ploy may have worked. The questions you asked Darby about the phone number could have spooked her."

"Something did," Stenner said.

"You want to go for an indictment now?" Vail asked Parver.

She nodded.

"Fleishman?" Vail said.

"Yeah, we bust him. It'll hold up the insurance payoff and that could shake him up. And maybe Rainey, too."

"Good point. Meyer? Indict him?"

"Pretty risky. Our whole case hangs on Shunderson's testimony. Maybe we need something more."

"There's plenty of strong circumstantial evidence to go with it," Parver countered.

"Abel?"

"If it gets that far."

Vail smiled. The young lawyers looked at one another. "What's that mean?" Parver said.

Vail stood up and circled the desk slowly. He finally lit a cigarette, then returned to the corner near the exhaust fan and blew the smoke into it. "What we're after here is justice, right? Here's a man who killed his wife in cold blood for greed and another woman. He planned it, even down to putting the gun in her dead hand and using gloves to fire it so she'd have powder burns on her fingers. That's planning. No way around it, he didn't even have time to think about it if we believe Mrs. Shunderson's testimony. He knew exactly what he was going to do when he walked into the house. That's what we have to prove to get a first-degree conviction. Flaherty's right, the whole case will hinge on whether the jury believes Shunderson *and* the time element involved. If they don't, he could walk off into the sunset with his jiggly girlfriend and two hundred and fifty thousand bucks. So, do we go to the wall with this guy? Or maybe try an end run?"

"You mean a *deal*?" Parver said with disbelief.

"Not a deal," Vail said. "*The* deal."

"And what's that?" she demanded. She was getting angry.

"Twenty years, no parole."

"Part of our case is that he premeditated this," Parver said, defending her plea for a murder-one indictment. "Twenty years, that's a second-degree sentence."

"*No*, it's a first-degree sentence with mercy. Think about it, Shana. If we go to trial and get a conviction, but the jury brings in second-degree instead of first, he could get twenty years to life and be back on the street in eight."

"You think you can maneuver Rainey into twenty, no parole?" asked Flaherty.

"If we can shake his faith in Darby. Right now, he's sold on his client. Look, most defense advocates don't give a damn whether their client is guilty or innocent. It's can the state make its case and will the jury buy it. Rainey's a little different. If he finds out he's been lied to, then it comes down to whether he thinks we can prove our case. It's really not about guilt or innocence, it's about winning. If he thinks we've got him, he'll make the best deal he can for his client."

"You think the tape will do that?"

"I don't know," Vail said. "But I don't know whether we can win a trial with this evidence, either. If we put the S.O.B. away for a flat twenty, he'll be fifty-six and dead broke by the time he's back on the street."

The room fell silent for a few moments. Vail put his feet on the edge of his table and leaned back in his chair. Stenner could almost hear his brain clicking.

"Shana," Vail said finally, "get an arrest warrant on James Wayne Darby. Murder one. Tell the sheriff's department we'll serve it. Naomi, set up lunch with Rainey as soon as possible. Flaherty, check with your pals in the audio business, see if you can get the sound on that tape enhanced a little."

"Ah, the art of the deal . . ." Stenner said softly, and smiled.

11

The section known as Back of the Yards sprawled for a dozen square blocks, shouldering the stockyards for space. Its buildings, most of which were a century old, were square, muscular structures of concrete, brick, and timber behind facades of terra-cotta. The warehouses and old manufacturing plants were once headquarters for some of the country's great industrial powers: Goodyear and Montgomery Ward, Swift and Libby. Developers had resurrected the structures, renovating them and turning the once onerous area of canals, railroad tracks, and braying animal pens into a nostalgic and historic office park.

The Delaney building was six stories tall and occupied a quarter of a block near Ashland. The brass plaque beside the entrance read simply: DELANEY ENTERPRISES, INC., FOUNDED 1961.

The executive offices were on the sixth floor and were reminiscent of the offices that had been there a hundred years before. As Shock Johnson stepped off the elevator, he looked out on a vast open space sectioned off into mahogany and glass squares. With the exception of Delaney's office suite and the three vice presidents' offices that adjoined it, which occupied one full side of the large rectangle, all the other offices lacked both privacy and personality. Johnson thought for a moment of Dickens: He could almost see the ghost of Uriah Heep sitting atop a high stool in the corner, appraising the room to make sure everyone kept busy. The executive secretary, Edith Stoddard, was dressed to mourn in a stern, shin-length black dress. She wore very little makeup; her hair was cut in a bob reminiscent of the thirties and was streaked with gray. She was a pleasant though harsh-looking woman; her face was drawn and she looked tired.

"I've arranged for you to use three V.P. suites," she said, motioning to them with her hand. "You got the list of employees?"

"Yes, ma'am, thank you," Johnson answered.

"We have very hurriedly called a board of directors meeting," she said. "I'll be tied up for an hour or two."

"Are you on the board?" Johnson asked.

"I'm the secretary," she said.

Three teams of detectives were assigned to the V.P. offices. The forty-two secretaries, sales managers, and superintendents had been divided into three lists. Each of the interrogation teams had its list of fourteen subjects. Johnson and his partner for the day, an acerbic and misanthropic homicide detective named Si Irving, took the middle office. Irving was a box of a man, half a foot shorter than his boss, with wisps of black hair streaking an otherwise bald head. He was an excellent detective but was from the old school. As he had once told Johnson, "Catch 'em, gut 'em, and fry 'em, that's my motto."

They suffered through a half-dozen dull men and women, none of whom would say an unkind word about "Mr. D." and none of whom knew anything. Shock Johnson was leaning back in a swivel chair, his feet propped up on an open desk drawer, when Miranda Stewart entered the room. She was a striking woman, zaftig and blond, wearing a smartly tailored red business suit and a black silk shirt. Her hair was tied back with a white ribbon. Johnson perked up. Irving appraised her through doleful eyes.

"Miss Miranda Stewart?" Johnson said, putting his feet back on the floor and sitting up at the desk.

"Yes," she said.

"Please have a seat. I'm Captain Johnson of the Chicago PD and this is Simon Irving, a member of the homicide division."

She smiled and sat down, a composed, friendly woman in her mid-thirties who seemed self-assured and perfectly at ease. She crossed her legs demurely and pulled her skirt down. It almost covered her knees.

"I want to point out that this is an informal interview," Johnson said. "By that I mean you will not be sworn and this session will not be transcribed, although we will be taking notes. However, if at some point in this interview we feel the necessity of reading you your rights, we will give you the opportunity to contact an attorney. This is standard operating procedure in a situation like this and we tell everyone the same thing before we start, so I don't want you to feel that bringing that up, about reading you your rights, is in any way a threat. Okay?"

"Okay," she said in a sultry voice. She seemed to be looking forward to the experience or perhaps the attention.

"What is your full name?"

"Miranda Duff Stewart."

"Where do you live?"

"At 3212 Wabash. Apartment 3A."

"Are you married, Ms. Stewart?"

"No. Divorced, 1990."

"How long have you lived at that address?"

"Since 1990. Three years."

"And how long have you worked at Delaney Enterprises?"

"Eighteen months."

"What did you do before you came here?"

"I was the secretary to Don Weber, the vice president of Trumbell and Sloan."

"The advertising agency?"

"Yes, in Riverfront."

"And what is your job here at Delaney Enterprises?"

"I was recently appointed Mr. Delaney's new executive secretary. Edith Stoddard—she has the job now—is getting ready to retire."

"So you haven't started in that job yet?"

"Well, I've had some meetings with Mr. Delaney. You know,

about what he expects of me, my responsibilities. Things like that. I know what I'll be doing."

"Have you been working with Mrs. . . . Is it Mrs. Stoddard?"

"Yes, she's married and has a daughter going to U.C."

"What's her husband do?"

"He's crippled, I understand."

"And have you been working with Mrs. Stoddard during this period?"

"No. Mr. Delaney said he wanted me to start off fresh." She smiled. "Said he didn't want me carrying over any of her bad habits, but I think he was kidding about Edith. I mean, everybody knows how efficient she is. I think he was just, you know, looking for a change?"

"Do you know how long she's had the job?" Johnson asked.

"Not really. She's been here forever. Maybe fifteen years?"

"What we're lookin' for here, Ms. Stewart, is if any bad blood might've existed between Delaney and people on his staff or maybe his business associates. Know what I mean?" Irving's voice was a raspy growl. "Arguments, disagreements, threats . . . bad blood."

"Well, I don't know about his business associates, you'll have to ask Edith about that. He seemed to get along fine with the people in the office . . . of course . . ." She stopped and let the sentence hang in the air.

"Of course, what?" Irving asked.

"Well, I don't think Edith was real happy about the change."

"Was she bein' demoted, that what you mean?" said Irving.

"She was, uh, she was leaving the company."

"Did she quit?"

"He said, Mr. Delaney said, that she was taking early retirement, but I got the impression that it was an either-or kind of thing."

"Either-or?" Johnson asked.

"Either retire or, you know, you're out on your . . ." She jerked a thumb over her shoulder.

"So Mrs. Stoddard wasn't happy about it?"

"I got that impression."

Johnson said, "Did Delaney discuss this with you?"

"No, it was just . . . just office gossip, you know how people talk. See, it wasn't really announced yet, about me taking that job."

"So you're the only one that knew officially?"

"That I know of."

"Did his wife know?"

"I never met his wife. She never came up here. I've seen her picture in the society pages, at charity things and stuff, but I never saw her face-to-face."

"That wasn't the question," Irving said bluntly. His tone was brusque and formal compared with that of Johnson, who was warmer and tended to put people at ease.

"Oh. Uh, I'm sorry, what was the question again?"

"Did his wife know you were taking Mrs. Stoddard's place? That was the specific question," Johnson said.

"Oh. I don't know." She shrugged.

"When did he first approach you about takin' over Stoddard's position?" Irving asked.

"This was about two months ago."

"Was it mentioned when you first came to work here? I mean, was it kinda, you know, in the works?" Irving asked.

"It was mentioned that if I lived up to my résumé, I could move up rapidly."

"Specifically to be Delaney's exec?"

"That was mentioned. He didn't dwell on it."

"So it was kinda like a carrot on a string for you, right? You do good, you could nail the top job? That's what it is, ain't it, the top woman's job here?"

"There are some women in sales, but you know how it is, working that closely to the boss and all, it's a very personal thing. A very good job. For a person with my qualifications, it was one of the best jobs in town."

"So then, two months ago, Delaney offered you the position, that it?" said Irving.

"Yes."

"Let me ask you something, Ms. Stewart," said Johnson. "Are you under the impression that Mrs. Stoddard was upset by all this?"

"I never talked to her about it. I worked on the first floor, she's up here on six."

"But you said earlier, when you were talking about Mrs. Stoddard leaving . . . uh, you implied it was 'an either-or kind of thing,' " Johnson said, checking his notes.

"That was what Mr. Delaney said," she said.

"Well, lemme put it this way," Irving said. "Did you ever see anything in Mrs. Stoddard's attitude toward you that would indicate she was upset with *you* about the change?"

"I told you, I was at pains to keep out of her way," she said. Annoyance was creeping into her tone.

"Whose idea was that?"

"What?"

"Whose idea to keep outta her way, yours or Delaney's?"

"His. Joh—Mr. Delaney's."

"Call him by his first name, didja?" Irving said.

"So does . . . did . . . Edith. That was his idea, to call him John." She sighed. "Look . . . can I smoke? Thanks. When this first came up, about Edith retiring? He took me to lunch because he didn't want people around the office to know what he had in mind. So I never really saw much of him around the office. Sometimes just walking through the first floor, that was about it."

"So he picks you. I mean, there was obviously a lot of other women who'd been working here longer . . ." Irving let the sentence die before it became a question.

"Am I under suspicion or something?" she asked, her forehead wrinkling with apprehension.

"Not at all, Ms. Stewart," Johnson interjected. "There's been a homicide and we're just trying to get a fix on this man, you know, the people who work around him."

"I'm a computer expert, among other things, Captain," she said. "I took courses two years ago. I knew sooner or later I'd have to be an electronics whiz to get along in the world. That's one of the things that attracted him to me. On the résumé, I mean. Also that I was familiar with advertising. That appealed to him, too."

"Okay, just to catch up," Irving said. "You was workin' as a V.P.'s secretary at Trumbell and Sloan and you took courses to become computer . . . computerized . . ."

"Computer literate," Johnson suggested.

"Computer literate, yeah. And Delaney saw that and offered you a job and mentioned the top slot might come open. Then you and Delaney slipped out to lunch and he offered you the job and implied that Edith Stoddard was given an 'either-or' option, which I assume means either retire or get canned. Is that generally the way things went?"

"Yes."

"How did he get your résumé?" Johnson asked.

"What is this?" she snapped suddenly. Blood rose to her face and her cheeks reddened. "Why are you asking me all these personal questions? I didn't have anything to do with this. I lost a damn good job when . . . uh, when Mr. Delaney was, uh, was . . ."

"Nobody's accusing you of anything," Johnson said reassuringly. "We're just trying to get a feel for office politics and how Delaney operated. For instance, have you ever been to Delaney's penthouse apartment over on the Gold Coast?"

"Not really . . ."

" 'Not really'?" said Irving. "I mean, either you was or you wasn't. It ain't a 'not really' kinda question."

"I don't want anybody to get the wrong impression."

"We're not doin' impressions today, we're listenin'," Irving shot back.

"Just level with us," Johnson said softly, with a broad, friendly, "trust me" smile. "Did you have a key to the penthouse apartment?"

"No!" she said, as if insulted. "Edith was the only one I know who had a key."

"Edith Stoddard had a key? How do you know that?"

"The time I went over there, I took a cab over at lunch. He had a desk in his bedroom and he had spreadsheets all over it. He said he worked there a lot because he never could get anything done at the office. He had some sandwiches brought in and we talked about the job. That's when he told me that Edith had a key because he was thinking of having the lock changed when she left. I mean, that's not uncommon, you know? When somebody leaves—to change the lock."

"Did he say why she had a key?" Johnson asked.

"He told me there were times when I might have to go over there to pick something up or to sit in on meetings outside the office. He also said I was never to mention the apartment. That it was a very private place for him and he wanted to keep it that way."

"Do you own a gun, Miss Stewart?" Irving asked suddenly.

"No!" she said, surprised. "I hate the things."

"You know does the Stoddard woman own a weapon?"

"I have no idea."

"Did Delaney have any problems with Edith Stoddard recently? Over this thing, I mean?" said Johnson.

"I don't know."

"When's the last time you saw him?" Johnson asked.

"Uh, this is Thursday? Monday. Monday or Tuesday. I was coming back from lunch as he was leaving the office. We just said hello. I told you, I didn't see him that often."

"And when was Stoddard due to leave?"

"Today was her last day."

———

When they had dismissed Miranda Stewart, Irving snatched up a phone, punched one of a dozen buttons, and tapped out a number. Johnson was going back over his notes.

"Who's this?" Irving asked. "Hey, Cabrilla, this is Irving. No, Si Irving, not Irving whoever. Yeah, down in Homicide. I need a check on a gun purchase. Well, how often do they turn 'em in? Okay, if it was the last week I'm shit outta luck. The name is Edith Stoddard. S-t-o-d-d-a-r-d. I don't know her address, how many Edith Stoddards could there be? Yeah." He cupped the mouthpiece with his hand. "They turn in the gun purchases every week. He says with the new law, they're behind entering them in the comp— Yeah? Oh, hold on a minute." He snapped on the point of his ballpoint pen and started scratching down notes. "That it? Thanks, Cabrilla, I owe ya one." He hung up the phone, punched out another number, spoke for a minute or two, then hung up.

"Mrs. Stoddard purchased an S&W .38 police special, four-inch barrel, on January twenty-two, at Sergeant York's on Wabash. I called Sergeant York's, talked to the manager. He remembers her, says she asked who could give her shootin' lessons, and he recommended the Shootin' Club. That's that indoor range over in Canaryville, mile or so down Pershing. Wanna take a break? Tool over there?"

———

The Shooting Club occupied the corner building of a shopping strip a mile or so from Delaney's office. Inside, glass-enclosed islands displayed the latest in friendly firepower: pistols, automatics, shotguns, assault weapons, Russian night-vision goggles, laser scopes, zoom eyes, robo lights. Patches from U.S. and foreign armed forces lined the top of the wall. At the rear, a steel door led to the shooting range. Viewed through tinted glass, thirty slots offered target shooters the opportunity to shoot human silhouette targets to bits. The range was soundproofed. There were three or four customers in the showroom and a half-dozen people were firing away behind the glass.

The owner was a ramrod-straight man in his forties with bad skin, wearing a tactical black camouflage parka and trousers and heavy Special Forces boots with thick lug soles. His black cap was pulled down to just above his eyes. Johnson showed his badge. The man in black introduced himself as Roy Bennett.

"No problem, is there?" he asked in a hard voice he tried to make friendly.

"We're interested in talking to whoever teaches on the range."

"We take turns," Bennett said. "All our personnel are ex-military and qualified expert."

"We're checking on a woman, probably come over either at lunch or right after work," Irving said. "The name Edith Stoddard wake ya up?"

"Older lady? Maybe fifty, fifty-five, 'bout yaa high?" He held his hand even with his shoulder.

"Yeah," Irving said. "She purchased a .38 Smith & Wesson from Sergeant York's. They sent her over here to learn how to use it."

"That's the lady." Bennett reached under the counter and brought out an appointment book, then flipped back through it a few pages.

"Yeah, here you are. She started coming on the twenty-second of last month . . ." He flipped through the pages, running his finger down the list of names each day. "And stopped last Monday. Fifteen days in a row. I remember her pretty good now. Didn't say a whole lot. You could tell she was uncomfortable with her weapon. Personally, I would've sold her a .25, certainly nothing heavier than a .32. That .38 was a lot of gun for her."

"How'd she do?" Johnson asked.

"I can teach a Dodge pickup to shoot straight in two weeks," Bennett said with a smile.

"So she done good, that what you're sayin'?" said Irving.

"She was really interested in becoming proficient at short ranges. Twenty-five yards. Yeah, she could blow the heart outta the target at twenty-five. Something happen to her?"

"Not her," Irving said. "But I'll tell you this, you taught her real good."

———

Johnson and Irving got into the police car and headed back toward Back of the Yards.

"You wanna good-guy, bad-guy her, Shock?"

"Christ, we're not talking about Roger Touhy here, Irving, it's a fifty-year-old-woman, for God's sake."

Irving shrugged. "One in the pump, one in the noggin," he said.

"So she owns a .38 and took shooting lessons. Do you know

how many women in this town fit that bill? A lot of scared ladies out there."

"A lotta scared everybody out there. But they don't all have a key to Delaney's place and they all ain't been kicked out on their ass to make room for Little Annie Fanny. It's lookin' awful good to me, Cap'n."

"We'll talk to her, Si."

"One in the pump, one in—"

"Yeah, yeah, yeah."

"Do we read her her rights?"

"Damn it, Si, we're just talking at this point!"

"Okay, okay. I just don't want that fuckin' Vail pissin' in my ear over this. If we're gonna get into the gun, I say give her her Miranda."

"Let me worry about Vail."

—

What Johnson had first thought was fatigue in Edith Stoddard's face took on different connotations as she sat across the desk from the two officers. Her eyes were flat and expressionless. The lines in her face seemed to be lines of defeat. It was the face of a woman who had been dealt badly by life; a woman tied to a crippled husband, trying to get her daughter through college, and suddenly thrown out of a prestigious job that was absolutely essential to the welfare of her family. What Shock Johnson saw in Edith Stoddard's face was humiliation, betrayal, anxiety, frustration—everything but wrath. Her anger, if she was angry, had been satisfied, if not by her, by someone.

Irving saw guilt.

He was tapping his pen nervously on the table, waiting to get past the amenities to go in for the kill. Johnson reached over without looking at him and laid his hand gently over the pen. Mrs. Stoddard sat stiffly at the desk with her hands folded in front of her. Johnson repeated the same instructions he had given to the other interview subjects earlier in the day.

"You understand," he said, "if, at some point in this interview—see, we could stop and read you your rights, ma'am, but I don't say that as any kind of a threat. By that I mean we aren't planning to do that at this point, we tell everyone the same thing when we start, so I don't want you to feel that bringing it up now means we're going to go that far. Okay?"

She nodded.

"Please state your name."

"Edith Stoddard."

"Age?"

"Fifty-three in May."

"Are you married?"

"Yes."

"Where does your husband work?"

"He's disabled. He has a small pension."

"Disabled in what way?" Johnson asked.

"He's a quadriplegic. Crippled from the neck down."

"I'm sorry," Johnson said.

"Charley loved to work around the house. He was fixing some shingles on the roof and slipped and landed flat on his back on the concrete walk. Broke his back in two places."

"When was that?"

"In 1982."

"He's been bedridden ever since?"

She nodded.

"And you have a daughter?"

"Angelica. She's twenty-one, a junior at U.C. Studying physics."

"Mrs. Stoddard, how long did you work for Delaney? Delaney Enterprises?"

"Seventeen years."

"And how long were you Delaney's executive secretary?"

"Nine."

"Were you happy in that job?"

At first she looked a little confused by the question. Then finally she said, "Yes. It was a wonderful position. Mr. Delaney was . . . very helpful, sympathetic, when we had the accident."

"You say 'was,' Mrs. Stoddard," Irving said. "Is that because Delaney is, uh, deceased?"

"I was . . . Yes."

"You was about to say . . . ?"

"Nothing."

"Ain't it true, Mrs. Stoddard, that you were about to retire? That today was to be your last day here?"

She hesitated for a moment. "Yes."

"So when you say 'was,' you really meant you don't work here no more, is that correct?"

"I don't see that . . . I mean . . ."

"I think what Detective Irving is driving at here is that you were leaving the firm," Johnson said softly.

"Yes, that's true."

"And were you satisfied with the arrangement? Retiring, I mean?"

She did not answer. She fiddled with her fingers and her lips trembled. Irving could see her beginning to crumble and decided to go for the throat.

"Mrs. Stoddard, you had a key to Delaney's penthouse on Astor, didn't you?"

"Yes."

"Go there often, did you?"

"It was part of my job. Mr. Delaney didn't like to work here in the office. Too many disruptions."

"So you were familiar with the surroundings there, at the penthouse, I mean?"

"Yes, of course."

"And you could more or less come and go as you please, right?"

"I only went when I was told to go there."

"Uh-huh. Point is, ma'am, you had free access, din'cha?"

"Well, I guess you might say that."

"And how many other people do you know had keys and access to the apartment?"

"I don't know, I wouldn't know that."

"So what you're sayin', what you're tellin' us is, as far as you know, nobody else had that kind of access to the premises? As far as you know?" said Irving.

"As far as I know."

"Did Mrs. Delaney have a key, as far as you know?"

"I wouldn't know . . . I mean, I assume . . . uh . . ."

"Ain't it a fact, Mrs. Stoddard, that you know she don't have a key, didn't even know the place existed? Isn't that right?"

"That really wasn't any of my business."

"Uh-huh. Well, ain't it a fact you were told not to talk about that apartment? That it was kinda a secret place for him?"

"Sir, I was privy to a lot of information that was confidential. Mr. Delaney never mentioned Mrs. Delaney specifically."

"But it was a confidential kinda place, right?"

"Yes."

"Now, did you ever go over to Mr. Delaney's penthouse on Astor when you weren't specifically invited?"

"Of course not!"

"Never kinda busted in on the place, y'know, looking for records or files or somthin' like that, and Mr. Delaney wasn't expectin' you?"

"No. I don't understand what your point to all this is," she said, becoming passively defensive.

"Will you excuse us for just a minute, please," Irving said, and motioned Johnson to step outside the office. He leaned close to the captain and whispered, "We're gettin' close to the skinny, here, Cap'n. I think it's time we Miranda her."

"Not yet," Johnson whispered back. "She brings in a lawyer and we're in for a long haul. We'll find out as much as we can before we start that."

"Yeah, if she starts takin' the fifth, we got problems. I just get nervous, gettin' too far into this without lettin' her know her rights. I'm goin' for the gun here any minute now, okay? Then we're into it."

"I'll let you know when I think it's time to Miranda her," Johnson said, his voice edgy and harsh.

"I just don't wanna fuck up at this stage."

"I'll say when, Si."

"Yes, sir."

They returned to the room.

Edith Stoddard was slumped in her seat, her hands now in her lap, staring at the wall. Johnson thought to himself, *This lady is verging on shock.* Johnson and Irving sat down.

"Now, Mrs. Stoddard," Johnson said, "we were talking about your access to the apartment. Did you ever go over at night?"

"Sometimes," she said numbly. "If he wanted me to."

"So this was kind of like a second workplace for you, is that correct?"

She nodded. She was still staring past them at the wall.

"And it was natural for you to spend a lot of time there?"

"I suppose you could say that."

"Let's move on," Irving said. "Mrs. Stoddard, do you own a gun?"

She looked at him sharply, as if suddenly drawn out of her daze by his question.

"A gun?"

"Yeah, a gun." He pulled back his jacket and showed her his weapon. "A gun."

"I . . ."

Johnson stepped in. "Mrs. Stoddard, we know you purchased a .38-caliber handgun at Sergeant York's on January twenty-second of this year. Where is that gun now?"

"Oh, yes, the gun."

"What about it?" Irving asked.

"It was stolen."

"Stolen?" Irving said, turning to Johnson and raising his eyebrows.

"From my purse."

"You were carryin' it in your purse?" Irving said.

"There's been a lot of crime, you know, muggings and the like, and I—"

"Do you know how to use a handgun, Mrs. Stoddard?" Johnson asked.

"I thought . . . I thought it would scare them."

"Who?"

"People who steal from people."

"So you didn't know anything about this weapon, you just wanted it as a scare card, that it?" said Irving.

"Yes. To scare them."

"But you were not familiar with the weapon, is that what you're saying?"

"Yes. Or no. I mean, I don't know much about guns, that's what I mean."

Johnson looked down at his fingers for a moment and then finally he looked her straight in the eye and said, "Mrs. Stoddard, I have to interrupt these proceedings at this point and advise you that you have the right to remain silent. If you say anything more, it can, and will, be used against you in a court of law. You are entitled to an attorney. If you do not have one or—"

She cut him off. "I killed him," she said without emotion and without changing her expression.

Johnson and Irving were struck dumb by the admission.

"Excuse me?" Johnson said after a few seconds.

"I killed him," she repeated without emotion.

"Christ!" Irving muttered.

"Mrs. Stoddard," Shock Johnson said firmly but quietly, "you understand, don't you, that you are entitled to have a lawyer present now?"

She looked back and forth at them.

"I don't understand anything anymore," she said mournfully.

12

The felony and misdemeanor history of the county was stored in canyons of documents in an enormous warehouse that covered a square block near the criminal courts building. Row after row and tier upon tier of trial transcripts, bound between uniform brown covers, filled the enormous warehouse with faded and fading files. Many more had been misplaced, lost, destroyed, or misfiled; simply transposing the numbers in the index could send a record into file oblivion. Physical evidence was harder to come by. Returned to owners, lost, or destroyed, it was hardly worth the effort to track it down.

St. Claire signed in and quickly found the registration number of the trial transcript: "Case Number 83-45976432, the State Versus Aaron Stampler. Murder in the first degree. Martin Vail for defense. Jane Venable for prosecution." He was pointed down through the narrow passageways. Dust seemed to be suspended in shafts of lights from skylights. It took fifteen minutes before he found a cardboard box with STAMPLER, A. 83-45976432 scrawled on the side with a Magic Marker. He carried the box containing the transcript, three volumes of it, to a steel-frame table in the center of the place and sat down to study Vail's most famous case.

Something had triggered St. Claire's phenomenal memory, but he had yet to finger exactly what was gnawing at him: an abstract memory just beyond his grasp. But in that box St. Claire was certain he would find what he was looking for, just as he now knew it would have nothing to do with the bodies in the landfill.

He started reading through the first volume but realized quickly that he would have to categorize the material in some way. He leafed through the jury selection and the mundane business of preparing the court for the trial; scanned ahead, looking for key words, piecing together bits and pieces of testimony; and made numerous trips to the copy machine. Then he began his own peculiar version of link analysis, categorizing them and working through the trial in logical rather than chronological order.

But St. Claire was also interested in how Vail had conducted a defense that almost everyone believed was hopeless. And also the adversarial cross-examination of Stenner, who was the homicide detective in charge of the investigation. The fireworks began in the opening minutes of the trial.

JUDGE SHOAT: *Mr. Vail, to the charge of murder in the first degree, you have previously entered a plea of not guilty. Do you now wish to change that plea?*

VAIL: *Yes sir.*

JUDGE SHOAT: *And how does the defendant now plead?*

VAIL: *Guilty but insane.*

JUDGE SHOAT: *Mr. Vail, I'm sure you're aware that three professional psychiatrists have concluded that your client is sane.*

VAIL: *. . . they screwed up.*

That started what St. Claire realized was ultimately a battle of titans—Venable versus Vail—both at the top of their game, both keen strategists and intractable jugular artists. Venable's opening statement to the jury was short, to the point, and almost arrogantly confident. Obviously, she figured the case was in the bag.

VENABLE: *Ladies and gentlemen of the jury, I'll be brief. During the course of this trial, you will see pictures and they will shock you. You will see overwhelming physical evidence. You will hear expert witnesses testify that Aaron Stampler—and only Aaron Stampler—could have committed*

this vicious and senselessly brutal murder of a revered community leader.
Aaron Stampler is guilty of coldly, premeditatedly killing Archbishop
Richard Rushman. In the end, I am sure you will agree with the state
that anything less than the death penalty would be as great a miscarriage
of justice as the murder itself.

Vail, in sharp contrast, set up his entire defense in a complex
and obviously impassioned plea to the jury.

VAIL: *Ladies and gentlemen of the jury, my name is Martin Vail. I have*
been charged by the court to represent the defendant, Aaron Stampler.
Now, we are here to determine whether the defendant who sits before you
is guilty of the loathsome and premeditated murder of one of this
city's most admired and respected citizens, Archbishop Richard Rushman.
In criminal law there are two types of criminals. The worst is known as
malum in se, *which means wrong by the very nature of the crime. Mur-*
der, rape, grievous bodily harm, crippling injuries—purposeful, planned,
premeditated crimes against the person's body, if you will. This is such a
crime. The murder of Bishop Rushman is obviously a case of malum in
se. *The accused does not deny that. You will see photographs of* this *crime*
that will sicken you. And you will be asked to believe that a sane *person*
committed that crime. And you will be asked to render judgment on what
is known as mens rea, *which means did the accused intend to cause*
bodily harm—in other words, did Aaron Stampler intentionally commit
the murder of Archbishop Rushman? Aaron Stampler does *deny that he*
is guilty of mens rea *in this murder case. . . . The extenuating circum-*
stances in the case of the State versus Aaron Stampler are of an unusual
nature because they involve mental disorders. And so you will be made
privy to a great deal of psychological information during the course of this
trial. We ask only that you listen carefully so that you can make a fair
judgment on mens rea, *for in order to make that judgment you will be*
asked to judge his conduct. Did Aaron Stampler suffer a defect of reason?
Did he act on an irresistible impulse? . . . These and many more questions
will hinge on the state of Aaron Stampler's mental health at the time the
crime was committed. And as you make these judgments, I would ask also
that you keep one important fact in the back of your mind at all times:
If Aaron Stampler was in full command of his faculties at the time of this
crime, why did he do it? What was his motivation for committing such a

desperate and horrifying act? And if he did, was he mentally responsible at the time? In the final analysis, that may be the most important question of all. And so, ladies and gentlemen, your responsibility will be to rule on the believability of the evidence the prosecutor and I present to you. Whom do you believe? What do you believe? And most important of all, do you accept the evidence as truth "beyond a reasonable doubt"? . . . In the end, when you have heard all the evidence, I sincerely believe that you will find on behalf of my client, Aaron Stampler.

St. Claire had spent hours copying parts of the testimony and inventing his own chronology of the trial. The method would eventually guide him to the elusive clues he was pursuing. The initial skirmishes came quickly, during the first cross by Vail. The witness was the state's psychiatric expert, Dr. Harcourt D. Bascott.

VAIL: Are you familiar with Aaron Stampler's hometown: Crikside, Kentucky?
BASCOTT: It has been described to me, sir.
VAIL: You haven't been there?
BASCOTT: No, I have not.
VAIL: From what you understand, Doctor, is it possible that environmental factors in Crikside might contribute to schizophrenia?
VENABLE: Objection, Your Honor. Hearsay. And what is the relevance of this testimony?
VAIL: Your Honor, we're dealing with a homicide which we contend is the result of a specific mental disorder. I'm simply laying groundwork here.
VENABLE: Are we going to get a course in psychiatry, too?
VAIL: Is that an objection?
VENABLE: If you like.
JUDGE SHOAT: Excuse me. Would you like a recess so you can carry on this private discussion, or would you two like to address the court?

So, in the opening interrogation, the tone and pace of the game was set. Stampler, St. Claire learned from several witnesses, had been a physically abused, religiously disoriented, twenty-year-old Appalachian kid with a genius IQ and illiterate parents. He had been stifled in a narrow niche of a village in the Kentucky mountains, forced into the coal mines where the future was a slow death by black lung or a quick demise by explosion or poisonous gases. The thing he had feared the most was the hole, a deep mine shaft that, in his words, "was worse than all my nightmares. I didn't know a hole could be that deep. At the bottom, the shaft was only four feet high. We had to work on our knees. The darkness swallowed up our lights."

Forced on his ninth birthday to begin working in the hole, he had finally escaped the confines of Crikside, Kentucky, when he was eighteen, urged by Miss Rebecca, the town's one-room-school teacher, who had nurtured his thirst for knowledge since his first day in school. In Chicago, he had been rescued by Archbishop Richard Rushman, founder of a home for runaways called Savior House. It had been Stampler's home until he and his girlfriend decided to live together. It had turned out to be a disastrous idea. She had left and returned to her home in Ohio. Stampler had ended up in a sordid and lightless hades for the homeless called the Hollows.

VAIL: *Aaron, did you blame Bishop Rushman for that, for having to live in that awful place?*
STAMPLER: *He never said a thing about it, one way or the other.*
VAIL: *Aaron, did you ever have a serious fight with Archbishop Rushman?*
STAMPLER: *No, sir, I never had any kind of fight with the bishop. We talked a lot, mostly about things I read in books, ideas and such. But we were always friends.*
VAIL: *So the bishop did not order you out of Savior House and you were still friends after you left?*
STAMPLER: *Yes, sir.*

St. Claire next studied the testimony relating to the murder itself. There were two versions of what happened: Aaron's, which had no details, and Medical Examiner William Danielson's, which was almost pornographic in its specifics.

VAIL: *Now I want to talk about the night Bishop Rushman was murdered. There was an altar boy meeting scheduled, wasn't there?*

STAMPLER: Yes suh.

VAIL: *Did any of the altar boys show up?*

STAMPLER: No.

VAIL: *Nobody else?*

STAMPLER: No, sir.

VAIL: *Was the bishop upset?*

STAMPLER: No. He were tired anyway and we could meet another time.

VAIL: *What did you do when you left?*

STAMPLER: . . . I decided to go to the bishop's office and borrow a book to read. When I got there, I heard some noise—like people shouting—up in the bishop's bedroom, so I went up to see if everything was all right. When I got to the top of the stairs I took my shoes off and stuck them in my jacket pockets. The bishop was in the bathroom and then I realized what I heard was him singing. Then . . . I felt like there was somebody else there, beside the bishop, and that's when I lost time.

VAIL: *You blacked out?*

STAMPLER: Yes, sir.

VAIL: *You didn't actually see anyone else?*

STAMPLER: No, sir.

VAIL: *Did you see the bishop?*

STAMPLER: No, sir. But I could hear him. He was singing in the bathroom.

VAIL: *You just sensed that somebody else was in the room?*

STAMPLER: Yes, sir.

VAIL: *Then what happened?*

STAMPLER: Next thing I knew, I was outside, at the bottom of the wooden staircase up to the kitchen, and I saw a police car and the . . . there was a flashlight flicking around, then I looked down . . . and uh, there was blood all over . . . my hands . . . and the knife . . . And . . . and then, I just ran . . . don't know why, I just ran into the church and another police car was pulling up front and I ducked into the confessional.

VAIL: *Aaron, did you have any reason to kill Bishop Rushman?*

STAMPLER: No, sir.

VAIL: *Did you plan his murder?*

STAMPLER: No, sir.
VAIL: To your knowledge, did you kill Bishop Rushman?
STAMPLER: No, sir.

Vail had started early in the trial introducing evidence and testimony implying that Stampler was not alone in the room at the time of the murder. He maintained that his client had blacked out and did not know who the mystery guest was, a contention that was hard to prove but even harder to disprove. William Danielson, the M.E., filled in the blanks in his version of the killing, guided by Venable.

VENABLE: Dr. Danielson, based on the physical evidence at the scene of the homicide, what is your assessment of this crime?
DANIELSON: That Stampler entered through the kitchen, took off his shoes, removed the nine-inch carving knife from the tray, leaving fibers from his gloves when he did it, went down the hallway to the bedroom, and attacked the bishop. Bishop Rushman fought for his life, as witness the wounds in his hands. He was stabbed, cut, punctured, and sliced seventy-seven times. He had less than a pint of blood in his body after the attack, which is one-twelfth of the normal blood supply in the body.

The first major battle came when Vail tried to keep photographs of the crime scene out of the testimony as prejudicial. He was overruled. The original photographs, unfortunately, were part of the physical evidence that had been misplaced or lost years before, and the copies of the pictures, which were attached with other documents at the end of the transcript, were of poor quality and told St. Claire nothing. On the witness stand, Danielson went into detail of all the gruesome aspects of the crime, using a combination of photographs, physical evidence, fiber samples, bloodstains, fingerprints, the number of stab wounds and their locations, the results of certain kinds of wounds, the difference between a stab, a puncture, and an incision, and so on. Venable was painting a mural of horror.

VENABLE: So, Dr. Danielson, did you conclude that death can be attributed to several different factors?

DANIELSON: Yes. Body trauma, aeroembolism, cadaveric spasm, several of the stab wounds, exsanguination—that's loss of blood. All could have caused death.

VENABLE: Can you identify which you think was the primary cause?

DANIELSON: I believe it was the throat wound.

VENABLE: Why?

DANIELSON: Because it caused aeroembolism, which is the sudden exit of air from the lungs. This kind of wound is always fatal; in fact, death is usually instantaneous. And this wound was profound. Exsanguination was also a factor.

VENABLE: Loss of blood?

DANIELSON: Yes.

As St. Claire read the description, his mind flashed back to the coroner's description of Linda Balfour's body. ". . . victim was stabbed, cut, and incised 56 times . . . evidence of cadaver spasm, trauma, and aeroembolism . . . significant exsanguination from stab wounds . . . throat wound caused aeroembolism . . . evidence of mutilation . . . accomplished by a person or persons with some surgical knowledge . . ." St. Claire's nudge was really kicking in, promoted further by Vail's clarification.

VAIL: The knife entered here, just under the right ear, slashed to just under the left ear, cut through to the spinal column, severed the jugular, all the arteries and veins in his neck, the windpipe, and all muscle and tissue.

Then Vail attacked Danielson's assertion that this throat wound was the one that killed Rushman, once again pursuing the possibility that someone else was in the room with Stampler when the bishop was killed.

VAIL: So . . . if two of the fatal chest wounds could have been struck by one person and the rest of the wounds by another, it is also possible that one

person actually struck the death wound and someone else then stabbed and cut the bishop after he was dead, right?
DANIELSON: *I suppose . . . yes, that's true . . . but unlikely.*

St. Claire frequently stopped to scribble notes to himself. He wrote, "Was another person in the room? Ask Vail? Stenner?" And why was Vail making this point if Stampler was pleading guilty? Was the insanity plea a ploy of some kind? St. Claire kept plowing through the encyclopedia-sized transcripts, skipping occasional exchanges.

VAIL: *Aaron, are you familiar with the term "fugue" or "fugue state"?*
STAMPLER: *Yes, sir.*
VAIL: *What does it mean?*
STAMPLER: *Means forgetting things for a while.*
VAIL: *Do you have a term for it?*
STAMPLER: *Yes, sir. Call it losing time.*
VAIL: *And did you ever lose time?*
STAMPLER: *Yes, sir.*
VAIL: *Often?*
STAMPLER: *Yes, sir.*
VAIL: *When?*
STAMPLER: *Well, I'm not perfectly sure. At first you don't know it's happening. Then after awhile, you know when you lose time.*
VAIL: *How do you know?*
STAMPLER: *Well, one minute I'd be sitting here, a second later—just a snap of a finger—I'd be sitting over there, or walking outside. Once I was in the movies with a girl and just an instant later we were walking outside the movie. I don't know how the picture ended, I was just outside on the street.*
VAIL: *Did you tell anyone about this?*
STAMPLER: *No, sir.*
VAIL: *Why not?*
STAMPLER: *I didn't think they'd believe me. Thought they'd make fun of me or maybe put me away.*

It was the question of Stampler's blackout and the "fugue state" that stirred the liveliest cross-examination of the trial, ironically between Vail and Stenner, who was then city detective in charge of the investigation.

VAIL: *Are you familiar with the medical term "fugue state" or hysterical amnesia?*
STENNER: *Yes, I discussed it with Dr. Bascott.*
VAIL: *As a matter of fact, you don't believe in the fugue theory, do you, Lieutenant Stenner?*
STENNER: *I have no firm opinion.*
VAIL: *It is a scientific fact, Lieutenant.*
STENNER: *As I said, I have no firm opinion.*
VAIL: *Do you believe that two plus two equals four?*
STENNER: *Of course.*
VAIL: *Do you believe the earth revolves around the sun?*
STENNER: *Yes.*
VAIL: *Are you a Christian, Lieutenant?*
STENNER: *Yes.*
VAIL: *Do you believe in the Resurrection?*

And later . . .

STENNER: *Yes, I do.*
VAIL: *Is the Resurrection a matter of fact or a theory?*
VENABLE: *Objection, Your Honor. Lieutenant Stenner's religious beliefs have nothing to do with this case.*
VAIL: *On the contrary, Your Honor. If I may proceed, I think I can show the relevance.*
JUDGE SHOAT: *Overruled. Read the last question, please, Ms. Blanchard.*
BLANCHARD: *"Is the Resurrection a matter of fact or theory?"*
VAIL: *Lieutenant?*
STENNER: *It is a matter of faith, sir.*
VAIL: *So you believe in scientific fact and you believe in religious faith, but you question the scientific reality of a psychiatric disorder which all psychologists agree exists and which is included in DSM 3, which is the*

standard by which all psychiatric disturbances are identified, isn't that a fact, sir?

STENNER: *It can be faked. You can't fake two plus two, but you could sure fake a fugue state.*

VAIL: *I see. And how many people do you know for a certainty have faked a fugue state?*

STENNER: *None.*

VAIL: *How many people do you know who have had experiences with faked fugue states?*

STENNER: *None.*

VAIL: *Read a lot of examples of faking a fugue state?*

STENNER: *No.*

VAIL: *So you're guessing, right?*

STENNER: *It's logical. If there is such a thing, it could certainly be faked.*

VAIL: *Have you asked a psychiatrist if it's possible?*

STENNER: *No.*

VAIL: *So you're guessing, Lieutenant, yes or no?*

STENNER: *Yes.*

VAIL: *Ah, so your reason for doubting Aaron Stampler's statement is that you guessed he was faking—or lying, right?*

STENNER: *That is correct.*

VAIL: *So you assumed that Aaron was lying and that he killed Bishop Rushman, correct?*

STENNER: *It was a very logical assumption.*

VAIL: *I'm not questioning the logic of your assumption, just that it existed. You assumed Stampler was guilty, right?*

STENNER: *Yes.*

VAIL: *At what point, Lieutenant, were you positive from reviewing the evidence that Aaron Stampler acted alone?*

There it is again, St. Claire thought. Christ, had there been someone else in the room?

STENNER: *From the very beginning.*

VAIL: *... Aaron Stampler tells you that he blacked out when he entered the bishop's room, correct?*

STENNER: *Yes.*

VAIL: *What did you do to disprove his allegation? In other words, sir, what evidence or witnesses can you produce that will verify your contention that he was alone in the room and that he acted alone?*

STENNER: *Forensics evidence, physical evidence, just plain logic . . .*

VAIL: *. . . I have a problem with some of these logical assumptions that have been made during this trial. Do you understand why?*

STENNER: *Most of the time—*

VAIL: *Lieutenant, my client's life is at stake here. "Most of the time" won't do. And so much for logic and a preponderance of evidence. Dr. Danielson says he cannot say for sure that Aaron was alone in the room, cannot say for sure that only one person actually stabbed the bishop, and cannot prove evidentially that Aaron even came in the back door or brought the knife to the murder scene. Yet you assumed Aaron Stampler lied to you because it wasn't logical, right?*

STENNER: *(No response.)*

VAIL: *The fact is, Lieutenant, that you are willing to accept on faith that Christ was crucified and died, that he arose from the dead, and went to heaven. But you don't choose to believe the fact that a person, under extreme stress or shock, can black out and enter a scientifically described limbo called a fugue state. So you never actually tried to prove that Aaron Stampler was lying, did you?*

STENNER: *It's not my job to prove the defendant is innocent, it's yours.*

VAIL: *On the contrary, Lieutenant, it's your job to prove he's guilty.*

Next St. Claire got into the testimony about symbols. His nudge became a reality.

VAIL: *I'd like to go back to symbols for a moment. Doctor, will you explain very simply for the jury the significance of symbols. What they are, for instance?*

BASCOTT: *Symbolic language is the use of drawings, symbols, uh, recognizable signs, to communicate. For instance, the cross is a symbol for Christianity while the numbers 666 are a universal symbol for the devil. Or to be more current, the symbols for something that is prohibited is a red cir-*

cle with a slash through it. That symbol is recognized both here and in Europe. As a sign along the road, for instance.

VAIL: *Could a symbol come in the form of words? A message, for instance?*

BASCOTT: *Possibly. Yes.*

VAIL: *So symbols can come in many forms, not just drawings or pictures?*

BASCOTT: *Yes, that is true.*

VAIL: *Now, Doctor, you have testified that you have seen the photographs of the victim in this case, Bishop Rushman?*

BASCOTT: *Yes, I have.*

VAIL: *Studied them closely?*

BASCOTT: *Yes.*

VAIL: *Were there any symbols on the body?*

BASCOTT: *Uhh . . .*

VAIL: *Let me put it more directly. Do you think the killer left a message in the form of a symbol on the victim's body?*

BASCOTT: *I can't say for sure. It appears that the killer was indicating something but we never figured that out and Stampler was no help.*

VAIL: *Doctor, we are talking about the letter and numbers on the back of the victim's head, correct?*

BASCOTT: *I assumed that is what you meant. Yes.*

VAIL: *Do you recall what the sequence was?*

BASCOTT: *I believe it said "B32.146."*

VAIL: *Actually, "B32.156."*

BASCOTT: *I'm sorry. Correction, 156.*

VAIL: *And do you believe that this was a symbol left by the killer?*

BASCOTT: *Uh. Well, yes, I think we all made that assumption.*

"Yeah!" St. Claire said aloud. There it was. Maybe the folks in Gideon weren't too far from the truth. It was the same combination of letter and numbers that the killer had put on Linda Balfour's head. St. Claire frantically read ahead. *What does it mean?* he wondered. *Did they ever figure it out?*

VAIL: *And that is as far as you took it, correct?*

BASCOTT: *It takes years, sometimes, to break through, to decipher all these subtleties.*

VAIL: *In other words, you really didn't have time to examine all the facets of Mr. Stampler's problems, did you?*

VENABLE: *Objection, Your Honor. Defense is trying to muddle the issue here. The doctor has stated that it might take years to decipher this symbol, as the counselor calls it. We are here to determine this case on the best evidence available. This line of questioning is completely irrelevant. The numbers could mean anything—maybe even an insignificant phone number.*

VAIL: *Then let the doctor say so.*

JUDGE SHOAT: *Rephrase, Counselor.*

VAIL: *Doctor, do you think this symbol is relevant?*

BASCOTT: *Anything is possible.*

But St. Claire found the answer to his question in another skirmish between Stenner and Vail.

VAIL: *. . . I have only one more question, Lieutenant Stenner. You stated a few minutes ago that this crime was premeditated. You said it unequivocally, as a statement of fact. Isn't that just another one of your unsupported allegations, sir?*

STENNER: *No, sir, it is not.*

VAIL: *Well, will you please tell the court upon what evidence you base that supposition?*

STENNER: *Several factors.*

VAIL: *Such as?*

STENNER: *The symbols on the back of the bishop's head.*

VAIL: *And what about the symbols, Lieutenant?*

STENNER: *They refer to a quote from a book in the bishop's library. The passage was marked in the book. We found similar markings in a book retrieved from Stampler's quarters in the Hollows. Same highlighter was used and we can identify the handwriting in both books as Stampler's.*

VAIL: *Lieutenant, why do you believe these markings on the victim's head prove premeditation?*

STENNER: *Because he planned it. He wrote in blood, on the victim's head, the symbol B32.156. B32.156 is the way this book is identified, it's a method for cataloging the books in the bishop's library.*

VAIL: *And what does it mean?*

STENNER: *It is a quote from the novel* The Scarlet Letter *by Nathaniel Hawthorne. "No man, for any considerable period, can wear one face to himself, and another to the multitude, without finally getting bewildered as to which may be the true."*

VAIL: *What is the significance of that quote?*

STENNER: *It is our belief that Stampler felt betrayed by Bishop Rushman, who made him leave Savior House. His girlfriend left him, he was living in a hellhole. He felt the bishop was two-faced. So he put this symbol in blood on the victim's head to add insult to injury.*

VAIL: *I think you're reaching, Lieutenant. . . .*

STENNER: *We proved it to my satisfaction.*

VAIL: *Well, I guess we should thank our lucky stars you're not on the jury, sir. . . .*

St. Claire's pause was doing double time. He wrote on his pad: "What happened to the bishop's books?" But he kept reading until the trial came to its startling conclusion.

VENABLE: *You have quite a memory for quotations and sayings that appeal to you, don't you, Mr. Stampler?*

STAMPLER: *I have a good memory, yes, ma'am.*

VENABLE: *Are you familiar with Nathaniel Hawthorne's book* The Scarlet Letter?

STAMPLER: *Yes, ma'am, I know the book.*

VENABLE: *And does the phrase "B32.156" mean anything to you?*

STAMPLER: *(No response.)*

JUDGE SHOAT: *Mr. Stampler, do you understand the question?*

STAMPLER: *Uh, I believe those are the numbers that were on the back of the bishop's head, in the pictures.*

VENABLE: *Is that the first time you ever saw them?*

STAMPLER: *I reckon.*

VENABLE: *And you don't know what the numbers mean?*

STAMPLER: *I'm not sure.*

VENABLE: *You mark passages in books that appeal to you, do you not?*

STAMPLER: *Sometimes.*

VENABLE: You marked passages in the books in the bishop's library, didn't you?

STAMPLER: Sometimes.

VENABLE: Your Honor, I'd like this marked as state's exhibit thirty-two, please.

State's 32, a copy of Nathaniel Hawthorne's The Scarlet Letter *from Bishop Rushman's library was so marked.*

VAIL: No objection.

VENABLE: Recognize this book, Mr. Stampler?

STAMPLER: I reckon that's from the bishop's library.

VENABLE: Mr. Stampler, I ask you, did you or did you not mark a passage on page 156 of this copy of The Scarlet Letter—*indexed by the number B32?*

STAMPLER: Uh.

VENABLE: I'll be a little more direct, Mr. Stampler. Are you familiar with this quote from Nathaniel Hawthorne's Scarlet Letter: *"No man, for any considerable period, can wear one face to himself, and another to the multitude, without finally getting bewildered as to which may be true"? Do you recognize that, Mr. Stampler?*

STAMPLER: Uh.

VENABLE: Do you recognize it? B32.156. Doesn't that strike a bell, Mr. Stampler?

STAMPLER: I don't.

VENABLE: Mr. Stampler, did you memorize that passage and print those numbers on the back of the bishop's head when you killed him?

VAIL: Objection.

The defendant Stampler suddenly screamed and jumped over the railing separating witness from examiner, attacking Ms. Venable.

STAMPLER: You lying bitch! Try to kill me.

At this point, defendant Stampler had to be overpowered by guards and the bailiff. There was general disorder in the courtroom.

JUDGE SHOAT: Order! Order in this courtroom!

So it was the symbol on the back of Rushman's head that had set Stampler off on the witness stand. The case had obviously been settled in the judge's chambers. When the trial reconvened,

Shoat had announced that an agreement had been reached between the state and Vail. Aaron Stampler was sent to the state mental hospital at Daisyland "until such time as the state rules that he is capable of returning to society."

What was settled in chambers and why? St. Claire wondered as he started to gather up his notes. A methodical man, he arranged them in order, scanning each of the pages as he put them in a file folder. Then he stopped for a moment, staring down at a section from early in the testimony. Suddenly his mouth went dry.

My God, he thought, *how could I have missed* that*!*

And where the hell is Aaron Stampler now?

13

Jane Venable stared south from her thirtieth-floor office window in the glass and steel spire toward the courthouse and thought about Martin Vail. It had been a long time since she had felt such passion or been as comfortable with a man. Throughout the day she kept having flashbacks of the night before, fleeting moments that blocked out everything else for an instant or two. Now, staring into the late-afternoon mist in the direction of the courthouse, she wondered if Vail was having the same kind of day.

God, I'm acting like a high school girl, she thought, and shrugged it off.

But she had a brief to be filed and she decided to take it herself rather than have her secretary do it. Then she would drop in on Vail. Why not? Her memory jumped back to an afternoon ten years earlier when Vail had shown up unannounced, in the same office that was then hers; how she had suddenly realized while they were talking that she was breathing a little faster and paying more attention to him than to what he was saying. Ten years and she still remembered that brief encounter when she had first realized that she was attracted to the rough-and-tumble, sloppy, shaggy-haired courtroom assassin.

He had slicked up a bit since then: the hair was a little shorter and his suits weren't so bagged-out, but the cutting edge was still there, just under the surface. Even as a prosecutor he was a gambler, unlike most of the lawyers she knew, who were more concerned with how close to the corner of the building their office was and what kind of car to move up to next.

What the hell, we started something, I'll be damned if I'm going to let it fizzle.

Then she laughed at herself.

Fizzle! It hasn't even started yet. What's the matter with you?

Aw, screw you, she said to herself.

She stuffed the brief in her attaché case and headed out the door.

———

On the fourth floor of the Criminal Courts Building, Abel Stenner burst out of his office and raced toward Naomi's desk.

"My God, Abel, what set you on fire?" she asked.

"Is he busy?" Stenner asked, ignoring her question.

"He's on the phone with—"

"Won't wait," Stenner cut her off, and entered the office with Naomi trailing close behind. Vail was sitting in his chair with his back to the door, blowing smoke into the exhaust fan. He wheeled around when Stenner entered, took one look at his chief investigator, and knew something was up.

"I'll call you back," he said, and put down the phone.

"They made a bust in the Delaney case," Stenner announced.

"Already? Who?" Naomi asked with surprise.

"His executive secretary. Fifty-three years old. Crippled husband, daughter in college."

"Sweet Jesus. How did they nail her so quickly?" Naomi said.

"Shock must've been on the case," Vail answered.

"You're right. Called me from his car. They had just Mirandized her and she came out with it. Said it twice. 'I killed him.' They're bringing her in now. Murder one."

Vail whistled slowly through his teeth.

"Why'd she do it?" Naomi asked.

"That's all I know. Maybe we ought to head down to Booking."

They breezed out of Vail's office. Shana Parver was deep in a law book as Vail and Stenner passed her cubbyhole. Vail's rap on the glass startled her.

"C'mon," said Vail.

"Where?"

"Downstairs."

———

Edith Stoddard cowered as Shock Johnson and Si Irving led her through the wave of press that swarmed toward her when she got out of the car. They brought her into the booking office just as Stenner, Vail, and Parver got off the elevator, which was directly across the hall from the entrance to Booking. Three TV crews, several photographers, radio interviewers, and reporters crowded through the doorway as they brought Stoddard in. Her hands were cuffed behind her and she seemed terrorized by the media and the police and the grim surroundings. Her eyes flicked from one group to another. Detectives crowded around a railing that separated the desk from the hallway to see who the celebrity was. The press shoved microphones in her face, yelled questions at her, jostled for space, while TV cameras scorched the scene with searing lights.

Shock Johnson led the stunned and frightened woman toward the booking desk as she looked around in bewilderment, flinching every time a strobe flashed, cowering under the blistering TV lights, while the press screamed at her. At that moment, Eckling appeared from a side room and took his place beside the tiny, trembling woman, displaying her like a big-game trophy. Vail watched the feeding frenzy with disgust.

"Whatever happened to innocent until proven guilty?" Shana Parver said.

"That son of a bitch is turning this into a freak show," said Vail, and he charged into the room followed by Parver and Stenner.

In the back of the crowded room, Jane Venable eased her way into the crowd of newshounds. She watched the scene with disgust, then saw Vail charge the crowd and grab Shock Johnson by the arm.

"What the hell's he doing?" Vail demanded.

"I got nothing to do with this circus," Johnson said. It was obvious he was disgusted. "She's a nice little lady, Marty. We were giving her Miranda. She interrupted and says, 'I killed him. I killed him.' "

"You sure this confession is legit, Shock?"

"She said she went in and he was taking a shower. She was standing in the entrance hall and he walked in naked and poured a drink. He saw her. When he saw the gun he put his drink down and she whacked him. Then went over and gave him the clincher."

"What else did she tell you?"

"That's it. What I just told you is it. Marty, she's fifty-three. Got retired out early. Today was her last day. Has a crippled husband, a daughter in college, and Delaney dumped her for a thirty-year-old blond bombshell. She bought a .38 three weeks ago, spent two weeks on a shooting range learning how to use it. She was standing right where Okie said she was when she popped him. And she flat-out confessed right after we Miranda'd her. What the hell more do you want?"

"Do you know what any good criminal attorney'll do with this? Displaying her like this, questioning her without an attorney present? We won't have a damn case left!"

Vail pushed his way to Eckling's side. "Stop this right now," he snarled in Eckling's ear. "You're jeopardizing this case with this stupid stunt."

"Goddamn it . . ." Eckling whispered back, but before he could go any further, Vail took Edith Stoddard gently by the arm and led her back into a sealed-off holding area with the press screaming questions at her as he led her away. The door shut out the sound.

"Oh," she said, and closed her eyes.

Outside, as the press began to disperse, Venable headed toward the processing area. *I know that woman,* she thought.

Four years ago. Venable had settled an injury case for Delaney

Enterprises. Edith Stoddard had been Delaney's private secretary. Venable remembered that she had felt very sorry for the woman. Her husband was a quadriplegic and she had a very bright daughter about to enter college. She had seemed weighed down by her world, almost self-effacing. It was in her face then, and it was worse now.

Venable could sense Stoddard's humiliation and fear.

A lot of people in this town will think she did the world a favor, she thought as she moved toward the security room.

Inside the quiet area, Vail said, "I'm sorry, Mrs. Stoddard, that was uncalled for."

She stared up at him and the fear in her eyes was slowly replaced by stoicism.

"You're the new district attorney," she said.

"Yes. And this is Shana Parver, one of my associates. I want Shana to explain your rights to you."

"They read me my rights."

"Yes, but I think you should understand what all this means."

Eckling burst into the room. "What the hell do you think you're—"

Vail grabbed his arm and shoved him into an empty interrogation room, slamming the door behind them.

"Listen to me, Eckling, this is not some dipshit drug bust, this woman's going to end up with the best pro bono attorney the judge can find and *any* defense advocate worth two cents is going to make hay of that circus you just put on."

"She confessed, fer Chrissakes!"

"So what? Does the name Menendez mean anything to you? If those brothers can walk, this woman can ride out of here on a golden chariot—and you're gonna be pulling it." Vail speared the air with his finger. "This woman is innocent until a jury says she's guilty or until a judge accepts her plea. That's if she doesn't change her mind, which she probably will the minute a good lawyer grabs her ear." He started to leave and then whirled back on the chief. "By the way, this isn't the chief prosecutor talking anymore, Eckling, it's the D.A. Get your head out of your ass."

Vail left the room. Shana Parver walked over to him as two guards led Mrs. Stoddard off to be fingerprinted and processed.

"She wouldn't listen. She insists she did it and she doesn't want a trial."

"Does she know she'll end up doing life without parole?"

"I don't think she cares, Martin."

Behind them, the door opened and Jane Venable entered the security room. Her eyes were ablaze. It was the old Jane Venable, spoiling for a fight.

"What the hell was that all about?" she demanded. "Eckling pilloried that woman!"

"I know, I know," Vail said defensively. "I just chewed his ass about it. Do you know Shana Parver? Shana, this is Jane Venable."

"Hi," Parver said. "I feel like I know you, I've read the transcript of the Stampler trial several times."

"I've had better days than that!" she said, glaring at Vail.

"What are you doing here?" Vail asked, then quickly added, "I mean, I'm glad you're here but I'm, you know, surprised."

"I came down to file a brief and saw the mob scene. I thought maybe they'd arrested the mayor or something."

"Listen, Janie, you need to do that lady a favor," Vail said.

"What do you mean?"

"She's determined to confess to killing Delaney. She doesn't have a lawyer. Judge Pryor will probably appoint one in the morning. In the meantime, Eckling's going to have her on the griddle as soon as they process her. If she makes a confession in there, I won't have any choice. I'll have to max her out."

"Marty, I can't . . ."

"You can go in there and talk to this lady. Explain her options."

Venable scowled at Vail. "Just because I happen to walk in here, I get stuck—"

"You're the best there is and you're a woman. Maybe she'll respond to you."

"Damn!" She blew out a breath, then walked across the room and back.

"Do you know any of the details?"

"That's moot. She needs somebody to hold her hand until she has a full-time lawyer. Give her that at least."

"Christ, Marty, you're talking like a defense advocate."

"Janie, she just lost her job. Her husband's lying in bed helpless from the neck down. Her daughter's in college and she probably can't afford to keep her there. Her whole world is unwinding around her. If she screws up now, she'll end up doing life without parole. That's what we'll ask for and we'll get it."

"You're one weird prosecutor, Marty," Venable said.

"I want all the details before I decide what we're going to do to her. If we let Eckling loose on her, I'll never have that opportunity. Talk to her, Janie." He smiled at her. "Then I'll buy dinner."

"Shit," Venable said, and walked down the hall toward the fingerprint room.

Parver looked at Vail with a smirk.

"I thought you two hated each other."

"We're trying to get over it," Vail said.

———

Harvey St. Claire had made myriad phone calls to the Catholic cathedral, the custodian, two priests, and finally to a nun named Sister Mary Alice before he finally got an answer to his question.

"Sister," St. Claire said, frustration apparent in his tone, "I'm trying to find out what happened to all the books in Bishop Rushman's library. Nobody seems to know."

"Who did you say this was again?" she asked.

"M'name's Harvey St. Claire. I'm with the D.A.'s office."

"You work for Mr. Vail?"

"That's right, he's m'boss. You know him?"

"I met him once, years ago," she said. "I know it's none of my business, but does this have anything to do with Aaron Stampler?"

"That's very incisive of you, Sister. How did you guess?"

"Well, you work for Mr. Vail and he defended Aaron. A book from the bishop's library was an important part of the evidence."

"You remember that?"

"I just remember it had something to do with the murder. That was a long time ago."

"So do you know where those books are now?"

"Do you know the Newberry on Walton Street?"

—

The Newberry Library was an imposing, burly, five-story brick building with a triple-arched entrance that occupied an entire block of West Walton. It had just celebrated its one hundredth anniversary and there was about the formidable old sentinel of a structure a sense of antiquity and conservatism. It had been endowed by businessman William Loomis Newberry to be "an uncommon collection of uncommon collections," and so it was.

A pleasant woman who identified herself as Miss Prichard, the assistant librarian, chatted amiably as she led St. Claire down hallways through arroyos of books, maps, and documents.

"Did you know this was the first electrified building in the city?" she asked, pointing toward the ceiling of the lobby. "That's why the bulbs in that chandelier are pointed downward, so people would know. Gas lamps won't work upside down, of course."

"Is it always this cool in here?"

"We have climate control for twenty-one miles of books and manuscripts, Mr. St. Claire," she said proudly. "We haven't lost a book in one hundred years."

"Quite a feat these days. Some people will steal anything."

"I should hope that our clientele is a bit more singular than that," she said in a very matter-of-fact tone.

The Rushman collection was in one of the rear chambers. It was a small room without windows and, except for the door, lined on all four sides with Bishop Rushman's books. An oak table contained three equally spaced brass table lamps with green shades. It occupied the center of the room, surrounded by heavy, unpadded chairs. The place was as quiet as a mausoleum.

It was a surprisingly diverse collection. Novels by Dostoyevsky and Dante sat beside the works of Rousseau, Hobbes, and Darwin.

Leather-bound codes of canon law shared space with Faulkner, Hammett, and Chandler.

St. Claire eagerly pulled out a book and checked its spine. And his shoulders slumped. Rushman's peculiar method of indexing had been replaced by the Dewey decimal system. He looked around the room at the hundreds of books and realized that there was no way to identify C13 among all the volumes. He stared at the library for several minutes, trying to figure out if there was any correlation between the Dewey numbers and Rushman's old index numbers. He turned abruptly and went back to the office.

"Ms. Prichard, I notice the indexing system has been changed on the books in the Rushman collection."

"Oh yes, we had to go to the Dewey decimal system. All the books must conform, you know. What a mess it would be if we made an exception! But it was done without damage. We have never damaged a book."

"No, you don't understand. Did the Newberry, by any chance, keep a record of the bishop's indexing system?"

"My, my, you are a purist, aren't you, Mr. St. Claire? Well, now, let's just go to the records."

She opened a narrow oak drawer and her nimble fingers danced along the index cards. She pulled one out, looked at it for a moment, and then handed it to him with a smile. It was labeled "Huckleberry Finn." In the corner of the Dewey card was noted: "Rushman index: J03."

"Bless you," St. Claire said with a wide grin. "Now all I have to do is go through all these cards, find C13, turn to page 489, and hope to hell I know what I'm looking for."

———

"I remember you," Edith Stoddard said to Jane Venable. "You handled the Robertson injury case. That was in 1990, as I recall." She had recovered from the booking ordeal and seemed almost relaxed. She was seated at a tattered bridge table in a small holding cell adjacent to the processing station. The room was bare except for the table and a cot in the corner. She had been fingerprinted, strip-searched, and issued a pair of orange county-issue coveralls with the word PRISONER stenciled across the back. The sleeves were rolled back several times. Stoddard would be held there until court convened in the morning. Venable had a momentary flashback, remembering these same surroundings ten years earlier. Nothing seemed to have changed. The same blue-gray paint on the walls, the small barred window in one corner.

"That's right," Jane Venable answered.

"You were a very nice person, but you were a ferocious negotiator," Stoddard said bluntly but unassumingly.

"That's what I get paid for—being a ferocious negotiator, I mean—not for being a nice person. Thank you for that."

"I don't need a lawyer, Miss Venable," the prisoner said firmly.

"Yes, you do. You never needed one more than you do right now," Venable answered.

"I'm guilty, Miss Venable."

"Please call me Jane."

"Jane. I just want to plead guilty and get it over with."

"There's more to it than that," Venable said.

"Not really."

"Listen to me carefully, please. You have to—may I call you Edith? Good. You have to realize that even if you did kill him—"

"I *did* kill him!"

"Okay. But you still must give your lawyer all your help so he or she can deal a proper sentence for you. Even if you don't go to trial, let whoever the judge assigns to the case save you as much time as possible."

"I don't want a trial, I told you that," Stoddard said as firmly as she could.

"It won't be a trial, it will be a plea bargain. It will be worked out between your lawyer and the prosecution."

"Mr. Vail?"

"Yes, or one of his prosecutors."

"Will it be made public, the negotiations?"

"No."

"I don't know. I just . . . I want to get it all over with. My life is ruined anyway."

"Edith, who's going to take care of your husband? What's to become of your daughter?"

"I'll be gone for years, anyway. What's the difference?"

"If we can get this reduced down to, say, first- or possibly second-degree manslaughter, your sentence could be as light as, oh, ten years. You could be out in four or five. That gives both of them hope. It's not like you'd be going away forever."

Stoddard stood up and walked to the window. She stared out at the brightly lit highway in front of the criminal building, watched a semi lumber by, listened to a dog barking somewhere far off in the night. She sighed very deeply and seemed to collapse into herself.

"Will you do it?" she asked, turning back to Venable.

"Do what?"

"Handle it for me?"

"I'll get you to court tomorrow. Then—"

"No. I mean handle it all the way."

"I have—"

"It's just sitting with Mr. Vail and working it out, isn't it? Can that take so much time?"

"It's not time, it's . . . I haven't done this for years. I'm afraid I'm rusty. There are other lawyers out there more qualified than I am."

"Then let me go ahead and tell the police what they want to know."

Venable sighed. She looked at the small woman for a moment. "Will you level with me?" she asked. "Tell me everything I need to know to make the best deal for you?"

"It depends."

"On what?"

"On what you want to know."

—

Corchran's was a run-down mahogany and brass steakhouse that smelled of beer and cigarette smoke. It was located a block from the river near the old *Sun-Times* building and had been a favored hangout of Vail's for years. Two tired middleweights were waltzing each other on the big-screen TV in one corner and there was a noisy dart game in progress near the front of the restaurant. A dozen regulars sat at the bar watching the last round of the fight and yelling at the screen as Vail and Venable entered the tavern.

"You do know all the right places, Vail," she said, looking around the noisy watering hole.

"Best steaks in town," Vail said. "Come on, it's quiet in the back."

They found a booth in a tiny back room that was shielded from the din. A sign over the archway into the niche said LADIES ROOM. It was decorated with facsimiles of old cigarette and beer ads.

"I can see why there's nobody back here." She snorted. "No self-respecting lady would be caught dead in here. They ought to be up front with it and call the place the Chauvinist Pit." She brushed breadcrumbs off the cushions with a napkin before she sat down.

"You didn't tell me you've turned into a snob," Vail joked.

"I like a good Irish bar as much as the next person," she said. "But this place hasn't seen a broom in weeks. Has the health inspector heard about it?"

"He wouldn't dare come in here," Vail said. "They'd throw him in the river. What do you want to drink?"

"What're we eating?"

"Steak, French fries, salad, hard rolls."

"Alka-Seltzer."

Vail laughed. "What'll you wash it down with."

"A Black Jack old-fashioned."

The waiter had a biscuit ear, knuckles the size of pinballs, and a glass eye. His smile was missing three teeth.

"Hey, Mart, how'th the boy, how'th the boy?" he lisped, plopping a brandy bottle with a candle stuck in it on the table and lighting it with a wooden kitchen match. "Atmothphere," he said.

"Steamroller, this is Miss Venable. She may become a regular if you treat her right."

"Yeah?" Steamroller beamed. "That would bring thome clath to the joint."

"Oh, thank you," Venable said, flashing a smile that was almost sincere. "Not that it needs it."

"Steamroller was heavyweight champion of Canada once," Vail told her.

"How wonderful," she replied.

"Yeah, I was on my way t' the top and some dinge knocked my eyeball out. Then the thon of a bitch thtepped on it, kinda ground his heel on it, kin ya believe it?"

"What an engrossing tale," Venable said. "Ever thought about writing your memoirs?"

Steamroller stared off at the corner for a moment, thinking, then said, "Uh . . . I can't remember 'em." Then he shrugged. "Oh, well. Bushmill's thtraight up and a Corona fer the champ. How about chu, Mith . . . what wath it again, Vennie, Vinnie . . ."

"Venable," she said sweetly. "Why don't you just call me Jane. A Black Jack old-fashioned."

"Aw right," he said, flashing his shattered smile. "I like a lady knowth how to drink." He walked away, wiping his hands on a towel stuck in his belt.

"Next time I'm taking you to Aunt Clara's Tea Room," Venable said. "All the waitresses are ninety and speak in old English."

"Cucumber sandwiches and lemonade?"

"Exactly."

"Okay, tell me about Edith Stoddard."

"I can't do that. You're the enemy."

"Oh God, are we back to that?" he answered.

"I'm going to represent her, Marty."

"What! I just wanted you to give her some advice until the judge gives her a . . ." He hesitated.

"A *real* lawyer, is that what you were going to say?"

"No, no. You know, one of the courthouse heavies. This isn't your game anymore."

"It is now, and blame yourself. You sent me in there."

"Just to get her over the rough spots."

"Uh-huh. Well, it didn't work."

"What the hell happened?"

"It was either me or she was going to dump the whole story on Eckling," Venable said.

Steamroller brought the drinks and plopped them down on the table. A little of the old-fashioned slopped over and he left licking his fingers.

Venable leaned across the table and said in a low voice, "There's something not quite kosher about this."

"How so?"

"She's determined *not* to stand trial. She'll max out before she does."

"Why?"

"You tell me."

"All I know is what Shock Johnson told me. She didn't tell you *anything*?"

"If she did, I wouldn't tell you. But she didn't want to talk tonight. I told Eckling to leave her alone until morning. And I intend to make a little hay over that performance of his, you can bet your sweet ass on that, Mr. District Attorney."

"Ahhh, one hour away from that platinum law firm of yours and you're talking like the Jane I remember."

"I'm going to make this as tough as I can," she said.

"Tell it to Shana Parver. It's her case."

"What's the matter, afraid of me?"

"The experience'll do you both good."

"How good is she?"

"Brilliant lawyer. A little too antagonistic. You two should get along fine."

"Well, thanks."

Steamroller wandered back to the table.

"You gonna order or are we juth drinkin' tonight?"

"How do you like your steak?" Vail asked.

"Medium-rare."

"Make it pink," Vail said to Steamroller. "She doesn't want to have to stab it to death before she eats it."

"Do you have baked potatoes?" she asked.

"Of courth! Whaddya think?"

"And house dressing on my salad."

Steamroller looked at Vail and his brow furrowed. "Houth drething?" he said.

"Italian. I'll have the same."

"Gotcha." And he was gone again.

"Look," said Venable, "I haven't even seen the homicide report. All I know is what I read in the papers. And you didn't call with the details, as promised."

"You left early."

"I figured you'd be exhausted when you got home."

"I was exhausted when I left," he said with a smile, then just as quickly turned serious. "Look, from what Shock says, she could be headed for the fryer. She bought a .38 back in January, went to a shooting gallery over in Canaryville every night for two weeks, and learned to use it. She sure as hell can't plead self-defense, he was naked as Adam when he got it. Also she plugged him twice, once here"—he pointed to his heart—"and once here." He placed his finger over his right eye. "That second shot was an after-thought. Delaney was already with the angels when she capped him with the head shot." He held his arms out at his sides. "Now you know all I know."

"Why would she risk life without parole rather than go on trial?" Venable mused.

"Maybe she doesn't trust her lawyer."

"Cute."

"I don't know," Vail said. "You tell me."

Venable shrugged. "Death before dishonor?"

"She can't dishonor Delaney, he took care of that himself a long time ago."

"I wasn't thinking of him."

Vail thought for a moment, then said, "Her husband? You think she had a thing with Delaney? Nah, no way. He goes in for bodies, not brains. She's a nice lady but hardly a raving beauty."

"Maybe he went in for *any*body. I've known men like that."

He thought about it a little longer and shook his head. "I can't see it. Besides, so what? I won't buy the spurned-woman defense."

"It's worked."

"Not with me."

"How about Parver?"

"She's too hungry to buy it. And too smart. You'll have to do better than that for Stoddard to beat murder one."

"You're singing a little different tune than you were two hours ago."

"I said I'd be fair, I didn't say I'd give her any breaks."

"That confession won't hold up. She was stressed out, under duress. . . ."

"Hey, you going to make a thing out of this, Janie?"

"I took the case, didn't I?"

14

The man leaned over his worktable, concentrating on the job of soldering a cobweb-thin piece of wire to a chip smaller than his fingernail. He was a husky man; his shirtsleeves were rolled up over machine-molded biceps. A pair of magnifying goggles was perched on his nose.

"Hey, Raymond, goin' to lunch?" Terry called to him.

"Can't stop now," Raymond answered without taking his eyes off his task.

"Want me to bring you something?"

"Yeah. Cheese crackers and a Coke."

"You got it."

Raymond heard the door slam shut. He finished the soldering job and placed the hot iron in a small, fireproof tray, took off the goggles, and leaned back in his chair. He stared through the window at the office across the way, watching the secretaries as they puttered around, getting ready to go to lunch. *Creatures of habit*, he thought. He could set his watch by their moves. Noon, five days a week, and they were out of there. He watched them until they left the office, then he walked across the small repair room choked with VCRs, TVs, and PCs and picked up a VCR and brought it back to the worktable. He removed the top and took out a small minicomputer and a black box about two inches square. He attached the box to the minicomputer with a short length of phone wire, then turned on the computer. He typed MODEM on the keyboard and a moment later a menu appeared on the screen. He moved the cursor to RECEIVE and hit enter. A moment later, the words ON LINE flashed in the corner of the screen. He watched the empty office across the way while he waited. Five minutes passed and the words INCOMING CALL flashed on the screen and a moment after that:

ARE YOU THERE, FOX?
HERE, HYDRA. ARE YOU PREPARED?
ALWAYS, FOX.
HAVE YOU SEEN THE SUBJECT?
YES, FOX. THREE DAYS AGO.
AND THE REFERENCE?
IN MY HEAD.
EXCELLENT. LEAVE TONIGHT.
OH, THANK YOU, FOX. IT HAS BEEN SO LONG.
THE TIME IS PERFECT.
THANK YOU, THANK YOU. IT IS AN EXCELLENT PLAN.
BE CAREFUL.
ALWAYS.
IN TWO DAYS. SAME TIME.
TWO DAYS.

15

Lex was pissed off. The last trip of the day and he had to drive thirty-five miles down to Hilltown to deliver a stinking package. Thirty-five fucking miles, and he had two ladies lined up that night. Pick-and-choose time. He laughed and slapped the wheel of the minivan. Maybe he could get them both interested. Hell, what a night that would be!

But first things first. Thirty-five miles down to Hilltown. He couldn't speed.

Two tickets down, one more and I'm out.

He couldn't afford to lose his license, the job was too good, except when they dumped a late load on him and he had to drive thirty-five miles down and thirty-five miles back. And drop off the stupid package. Seventy miles. Ten minutes to do the package. Two hours, no more. He'd be back in town by 8 P.M. Then he'd make up his mind.

Toni? Or Jessie? What a choice. Brunette or redhead?

He was thinking so hard he almost missed the turnoff. He wheeled the minivan off the main highway and headed down the last two miles on a two-lane blacktop.

Christ, who the hell would want to live out in this godforsaken place? His headlights led him to the city limits.

What a joke. City limits? A city? Twelve hundred people? The whole

damn town would hardly fill up the old Paramount Theater in St. Louis.
He turned on the dome light and took out the delivery slip.

Calvin Spiers. RFD 2.

Shit, the whole place was one big RFD.

He turned it over. Someone had scribbled instructions on the
back. He slowed down and squinted under the dim dome light.

"Left past public library. One and a half miles to bright red mailbox just past Elmo's SuperStore."

Well, that oughtta be easy enough.

Ten minutes later found him out on a country road on the other
side of Hilltown. Elmo's SuperStore was on the right, a garish, low-
slung cinder-block building with a flashing BUD sign on the roof. He
drifted past it and his headlights picked up the red mailbox.

"Piece a cake," he said aloud.

He pulled down the dirt road, peering into the darkness for
signs of life. Finally he saw the house, off to the left through the
trees. It was a small bungalow set back in the woods with a well-
kept yard. The porch light was out, but he could see a light behind
the curtains of what he assumed was the living room. He turned
into the rutted driveway and beeped the horn twice, then got out,
went to the other side of the van, and slid the door back. The
package was about a foot square and light, no more than one or
two pounds. He checked the name, took his delivery pad, and
went to the front door.

Must not of heard me, he thought as he went up the steps to the
porch. Then he saw the note. It was tucked in the screen door. He
put the package down and pulled out the note.

UPD man: Had to run to the store. Door open. Please put package
on table in den, second door on left. Thank you.

He tried the door and it swung open to reveal a long, dark hallway that led back to an open door. Light from the living room
spilled over into the hall, reflected into the darkness of the hall.

Shit, I oughtta just leave it here. What the hell do they think I am?
"Anybody here?" No answer. "Mr. Spier?"

But he picked up the package and headed down the hall. He saw a light switch and flicked it, but there was no bulb in the overhead socket.

Great. Coulda left me a flashlight at least.

"Anybody here? UPD," he called as he approached the den door.

He peered inside the darkened room, squinting his eyes to try to make out a light or a lamp. He put the box down and, facing the wall, swept his hands over its smooth surface, feeling for the light switch. He did not hear the figure emerge from the darkness behind him, moving slowly, raising its hand high. There was a flash in the light from the living room. Lex started to turn, then felt a searing pain piercing deep into his back and into his chest.

He screamed and stumbled forward, felt the blade slide out of his back as he grabbed the doorjamb. Then he felt it again, this time plunging down through his shoulder. He fell to his knees, reached out in the dark and felt the back of a chair, and grabbed it.

"Oh God," he cried out, "I'm just . . . delivery man. UPD . . . Please!"

The knife struck again. And again. And again. It ripped into his back, his side, his arm as he floundered weakly, trying to escape the deadly blade. He felt his life seeping out of him. He began to shake violently. The room became an echo chamber and he seemed to reverberate within it. He tasted salt. Sweat showered from his face.

Then he felt hot breath beside his ear and a voice whispered, "Billy . . . Peter . . ."

"My . . . God . . ." Lex answered feebly. The last thing he felt was the deadly blade slicing into his throat, slashing through tissue and muscle. Air burst from the gaping wound and showered blood as it hissed from his lungs. With demonic glee, the assassin kept striking over and over and over in the darkness of the room.

When the deadly work was done, the executioner dipped a finger in the widening pool of blood and, lifting the hair on the back of the victim's head, printed, "R41.102."

16

The red rays of dawn filtered through the wooden slats of the shutters, casting long, harsh shadows across the hardwood floors. Vail lay on his back and stared up at the pickled-blond cathedral ceiling, softly crimson in the floor's reflection of morning light. Vail turned his head. Jane lay on her side, her forehead resting against his arm. He pulled the feather comforter up over her naked shoulders and slid out of her bed, gathering up his clothes and shoes from where they were strung out across the floor.

"Whew!" he said to himself, remembering how they had gotten there.

Tudor Manor was one of an ensemble of mansions built in the mid-twenties and modeled after the Tudor mansions of England. From the outside they seemed strangely incongruous with the more midwestern architecture of Rogers Park. Each building (there were four in what was collectively known as Tudor Estates) had sweeping projecting gables decorated with gargoyles and crenellations, a slate roof, ornamental chimney pots, and towering casement windows.

Inside, Venable had turned her apartment into a bright, cheery place. Its walls were painted in soft pastels, the woodwork and cabinets were pickled-white oak. There was a large living room with casement windows facing Indian Bounty Park, fifty yards away. The rear wall of the room faced a hedged courtyard and was divided by a bullet-shaped copper-and-glass atrium, which towered up to the bedroom above. Two tall ficus trees dominated its core and climbing plants adorned its glass walls. Begonias, narcissi, and impatiens wove colorful patterns between and around the two trees. There was a guest bedroom and a formal dining room and a kitchen that looked like a chef's dream.

He found filters and a pound of coffee in the freezer and started the coffee before heading into the guest bath. Thirty minutes later, dressed in the previous night's wrinkled suit and shirt, he poured two cups of coffee and took one back up the stairs to the bedroom.

He placed her cup on the night table, leaned over the bed, and kissed her on the cheek. She stirred for a moment and reached out for him. Her arm fell across the empty sheet. She opened one eye and squinted up at him.

"You're due in court in three hours," said Vail. "Pryor won't be happy if you're late. If you'd like to hustle, you can join me at Butterfly's for breakfast."

She rolled over onto her back.

"I'll be busy for the next three hours," she said sleepily.

"You got something up your sleeve, Lawyer Venable?"

She pulled the comforter slowly down until it was two inches below her navel, held her arms toward the ceiling, and wiggled them slowly.

"No sleeves," she said.

"You're gonna catch cold."

"I always wake up this way," she said. "It's too chilly to fall back to sleep. And I wouldn't dare set foot in Butterfly's this soon. It's your turf. They'd probably lynch me."

"I thought we were putting all that behind us."

"After Stoddard."

"That's Shana's problem."

"We'll see where we stand after the bail hearing."

He leaned over her, supporting himself on both arms, and kissed her on the mouth. "Great," he said.

"See you in court."

On the way out, he picked up the downstairs phone and dialed Stenner's car phone.

Stenner answered on the first ring. "Where are you? I'm parked in front. Been calling you for fifteen minutes."

"Pick me up on the Estes-Rockwell corner of Indian Bounty Park," Vail said.

"What are you doing out there?"

"Jogging. I ran out of breath."

"Damn it, what do you mean standing on a street corner in broad—"

Vail hung up. He'd heard it all before. He headed across the park toward the far side, stopped once, and looked back. The shutters were open on one of the bedroom windows and she was watching him, wrapped only in the down comforter. She didn't wave; she just watched. Vail smiled up at her and walked through the park.

Stenner's concern for Vail went back four years, just after Flaherty had joined the Wild Bunch. Vail leaned over backward to be impartial, but in his heart Shana Parver and Dermott Flaherty were his two favorites, probably because he saw in them his own rebellious spirit. Parver rebeling against her rich parents, Flaherty against the streets where he grew up.

Flaherty had been an angry kid, always in trouble, living on the streets, getting into fistfights, shoplifting, picking pockets, and heading for big trouble. He had one saving grace: he loved school. It was the one place he could rise above his desperate life. When he was busted for picking the pocket of a Red Sox fan and scalping the two tickets from his wallet, a kindly judge, who knew about him and was impressed with his grades, sent him to a halfway house for hardcase juveniles, where they kicked his ass and wore him out with leather belts and tried to whip the anger out of the wrathful orphan. The kid never cried.

One cold night, sitting in a bare, unheated closet that served as solitary, he had a revelation: His only asset was his brain. Intelligence was the only way out of the bleak, dead-end street he was heading down. Back on the street, he scrounged for a living, earned pocket money brawling in illegal backroom bare-knuckle fights, focused his anger on books. He became a voracious, self-motivated, straight-A student. Top of his class.

Once a month he hitched rides three hundred miles to Ossining to spend thirty minutes with the man who was responsible for his dreary existence.

"I'm gonna be a lawyer," he would tell the man. "I'm gonna get ya out."

"Fuck lawyers," the man would answer. "Lawyers is why I'm here."

He changed his name from Flavin to Flaherty, lived on fast-food hamburgers and chocolate bars to keep up his energy, avoided friendships, fearful they would find out who he was. He lived in fear of that. When he graduated from college, he decided to put distance between himself and Rochester and hitchhiked west until he ran out of money in Chicago. He applied for a scholarship, spent hours in the public library studying for the qualification tests. His scores were astronomical. For a kid of twenty-three, he seemed to have more than a passing knowledge of the law. Nobody knew why, nobody asked, but he impressed the review board enough to earn himself a full scholarship for one year, with the future hanging on what he showed during the first four quarters. He got a job as a night janitor in one of the city skyscrapers, slept on a pallet in the utility room. When he wasn't studying, he was in the courtroom, taking notes, watching the big boys in action, always rooting for the defendants and nursing an inbred hatred of prosecutors until he saw Vail in action, read about his young Wild Bunch, and realized, reluctantly, after a year that the assistant D.A. had become his idol. At the end of his first year he was courting a 3.8. Two more years on scholarship and he waltzed out with his law degree and with summa cum laude on his sheepskin.

He was twenty-seven at the time. Streetwise. Tough. Antisocial. Brilliant.

He had offers but chose to work for a broken-down, old warhorse named Sid Bernstein, a once blazing star in the legal world who had turned to alcohol and coke to get through the day. For one year, Flaherty honed his skills studying the old boy's cases; reading law books; and dragging the old drunk out of bed, holding him under ice-cold showers and pumping the blackest coffee into him, dressing him and getting him into the courtroom, then prompting him through each case with notes scratched out on legal pads and law books marked with self-stick notes. One morning when Bernstein failed to show up at the office, he went to Bernstein's apartment and discovered that his boss was in the hospital. Pneumonia. The old guy lasted five days.

Sitting in Bernstein's drab office after the funeral, staring at the battered law books and worn-out cardboard file folders, he looked up and saw a handsome black woman standing in the office doorway.

"Dermott Flaherty?"

"Yes."

"Sorry about Bernstein."

The kid didn't know how to answer that. Bernstein was a cross he had borne for a year and a half. His sympathy for the man was superficial.

"Thanks," he said. "What can I do for you?"

"Are you taking over the practice?"

"Nothing to take over. Just trying to figure out what to do with his stuff. Uh, was there something . . . ?"

"How'd you like a job?"

"Doing what?"

"Law, what else?"

"For who?"

"Ever hear of Martin Vail?"

—

When he came in for his interview with Vail, he was wearing a black turtleneck, a tweed jacket he had bought at a Division Street pawnshop for six bucks, and tennis shoes. He had no expectations.

"We've been watching you in court," said Vail. "You've been dragging old Sid Bernstein through life for a year and a half."

"It was a job."

"You've got quite a transcript, Mr. Flaherty. Probably could have landed a pretty good spot with some of the better law firms around town. How come you picked Sid?"

"Figured I could learn more from him."

"You actually tried most of his cases," Vail said, flipping through papers in a file.

"You been checking up on me?" Belligerently.

"Bother you, does it?"

Flaherty shrugged.

"You're originally from Rochester, New York?"

Flaherty hesitated, stared down at the file. Finally: "I guess so."

"You guess so? You don't know where you're from?" Vail said with a laugh.

"I put that behind me."

"Why? You did pretty well for a homeless kid with no parents. How long were you on your own? When did you lose your mother and father?"

Flaherty stood up suddenly, his fists balled up, his face red with fury. His reaction surprised Vail.

"Forget it," Flaherty said, heading for the door.

"What's your problem, son? You've got the makings of a great lawyer, but you have a chip the size of Mount Rushmore on your shoulder."

"It won't work," Flaherty said.

"What won't work? Sit down, talk to me. You don't want to talk about Rochester, forget it, we won't talk about Rochester."

Flaherty sat down. "Can I smoke?" he asked.

Vail wheeled his chair to the exhaust fan and flicked it on. He lit up, too.

"Sooner or later you'll find out."

"Find out what, son? What kind of load are you carrying?"

"M'mom died when I was nine."

"Okay."

He looked at Vail and sadness seemed to invest itself in his rugged young features.

"Actually . . . actually, she didn't die. Actually what happened . . . See, what happened . . ." And then he said out loud something he had bottled inside himself for years. "Actually my old man killed her. Beat her to death with his bare hands. He's on death row at Sing Sing. Been there . . . twenty years. I used to think . . . I used to think that I'd get to be a lawyer and then . . . then I'd spring him, and then I'd take him out, and then . . ."

"And then what?" Vail asked softly.

"Then I'd beat him the way he beat my mom. Beat him and beat him until . . ."

The young man fell silent and sat puffing on his cigarette.

"When's the last time you saw him?" Vail asked.

"Before I came out here four years ago. I used to go see him once a month. I never even wrote after I left."

"Dermott?"

"Yeah?"

"Your father died two years ago. Heart attack."

"You knew about all that?"

"Naomi—Naomi Chance, the lady that came to see you when Sid died? Naomi knows everything, Dermott. You're one helluva young lawyer. The thing with your father? You put that behind you. It wasn't your fault, anyway. Thing is, we're pretty tight here. What the press calls the Wild Bunch. They're very supportive of each other. They'll expect the same of you. What I'm saying is, it's too heavy a load. Maybe if you share it, maybe if you put it behind you forever, maybe you can forget it. You want a job?"

Stenner had been skeptical about the new kid, who seemed sullen and involuted and dressed in black like a funeral director and who was basically, as Stenner put it, "a street punk." The Shoulders case had changed all that and it put Vail in jeopardy for the first time in his life.

Jake Shoulders, whose felony record prevented him from owning liquor stores, gun shops, restaurants, and bars, kept a low profile, but he was known in the D.A.'s office. His game was blackmail and extortion and city hall was his target. Staff members, department heads, councilmen, anybody who had anything to hide, eventually appeared on Shoulders's list. Then he spread out into the restaurant business, obtained liquor licenses under phony names, even got a piece of the airport action. Obviously he was paying off *somebody* in the city, somebody high up, somebody who raked it off the top and let the health and police inspectors earn their cuts by making sure the licenses were nicely covered up and easily approved.

Vail and his team knew what Shoulders was up to, but they could not make the city connection. Without it, it was just another bust. By tying it to the city hall gang, they could do real damage to a corrupt bunch that had run the city for too long. Vail needed a linchpin, a witness or evidence that would tie Shoulders directly to city hall. The break came when a three-time loser named Bobby Bollinger was arrested for assault with a deadly weapon. Facing life without parole, Bollinger, who was only thirty-three, decided to toot his whistle in exchange for immunity and a ticket out of town. He called Stenner, who had arrested him his third time down. Stenner got him off the street and holed him up in a run-down hotel on Erie Street. Then Bollinger became troublesome.

"Bollinger is waffling," Stenner told Vail one morning.

"What's his problem?"

"Perks."

"We gave him perks."

"He's suffering from the 'more' syndrome."

"What else?"

"Witness protection out of state. A job making one hundred thou a year. Name change and we clear his record. A new car. He says they'll be able to trace his Corvette."

Vail chuckled. "No yacht?"

"He says that's less than he's making now on the docks."

"Does he also say he's guilty of a felony? Has three priors? He goes in for good this time."

"I think he's forgotten about that."

"Remind him."

"How far are you willing to go?"

"I'll go with the witness program and the name change goes with it. We can probably arrange something out of state. His record goes into limbo with his old name, so he gets that. But no hundred grand. We'll support him for three months while he's in a retraining program. After that he's on his own. And he can ride a bicycle."

"What if he still says no?"

"We'll max him out with the judge; he's a three-time loser."

"He came to us, Marty."

"He came to us because if he stays around here, he's a dead man. He's looking for a ticket out and a free ride."

"He says he can give us the link we've been looking for."

"That's what he says. Look, I'm not going to buy a conviction for one hundred grand a year. Tell me I'm wrong on this, Abel."

"I don't know. His way, we bring down the city hall bums, get rid of Bollinger while we're at it. Let some other state put up with him."

Vail stopped and lit a cigarette. He walked around in a tight little circle for a minute or so.

"He'll also stand up in court," said Stenner. "Part of the deal."

"Christ, I never know how you're gonna jump on these things, Abel." Vail leaned against the wall and blew smoke toward the floor. "I don't like Bollinger. I don't like doing business with him. No matter where he ends up, he's always going to be up to something. He wouldn't know how to straighten out. And I'm still skeptical about whether he can link our case up. But . . . okay, give him my proposal first. Scare him with the options. If you have to, twenty-five thou for six months. And no car, that's out. Tell him to dump the Vette and use the take for a down payment."

"Maybe I can sell that."

"Give it a shot then. It gets sticky, we'll good-guy, bad-guy him. He already has you pegged as the negotiator, so you play the hero. Take Flaherty for the bad guy."

"Flaherty?"

"I think he'll surprise you, Abel. Let him play it his way. When he takes over, stand back, let him do it."

Flaherty looked tough enough to play a mean cop. He bordered on handsome with coal-black hair and dark brown eyes, but his rugged, brooding Irish features were marred by a slightly flattened nose and a scar over one eye.

In the fleabag hotel, Stenner sat talking to Bollinger, a grungy redhead with bad teeth and a worse attitude. Flaherty sat in a corner of the room watching the proceedings, wearing a .38 under his arm.

"Shit," Bollinger snapped, "I'm giving up everything, man. Friends, my place, my car, every fuckin' thing, and he's pissin' about one hundred grand a year and a car to replace my Vette!"

"I'll tell you what you're not giving up," said Stenner.

"Oh yeah, what's that?"

"The rest of your life, Bobby. No parole. And when we do nail down this case, you'll be hauled in again for aiding and abetting. You won't see daylight until my son runs for president and my son hasn't been born yet."

"This is great, just fuckin' great, man. I come to you with a reasonable—"

"A hundred grand a year and a new joy wagon is not reasonable. Sell your vehicle. Get something nice with the down payment."

"What are you, my business manager?"

Stenner said, "You could look at it that way."

"I do this, I'm on the dodge the rest of my life."

"Then it's Joliet. They'll pop you there—if not before. You're running. This way, we make the reservations and pick up the tab."

"Well, then, I guess it boils down to how bad you want my information, huh?"

"No, it boils down to how bad you want to stay alive. You want to shoot craps with your life for a damn car?"

Bollinger's lips were getting dry. He licked them nervously. *That fucking D.A. is calling my hand.*

"How long's this gonna take?" he asked.

"As long as it takes. Could be a year before we put the case together and get into court."

"A year! In this fuckin' funeral parlor!"

"Christ, why don't we find him a nice place out in the goddamn country," Flaherty snarled.

Bollinger looked over at Flaherty, who was clipping his fingernails. *Who the hell is this guy?* He looked back at Stenner.

"No pie for a fuckin' year?" he whined.

"Pie?"

"You know . . . the old ying-yang," Bollinger said with a lascivious grin. "I deserve that much."

Flaherty suddenly exploded. He threw the fingernail clippers across the room and charged at Bollinger with such fury that he surprised even Stenner. He shoved past the detective and loomed over Bollinger.

"You don't deserve shit," he snarled.

He slid an easy chair over with his foot and sat down in front of Bollinger, leaning forward with his face an inch from the mobster and spoke in a low, nasty monotone.

"I know all the tricks, Bobby. Know why? Because I've been there. I know what you're thinking right now. I know what you're gonna say before you say it. I'm hip, Bobby. Understand?"

Bollinger's eyes bulged with uncertainty.

"The major, here, tries to treat you like a decent human being, what'd we get? A cheap brand of grift. You been playin' us like a fiddle for two days. Well, I just took your goddamn bow away from you. Forget the fuckin' Corvette and the fuckin' one hundred grand job. You're off the goddamn sleeve. Do you understand? Am I getting through that fat head of yours?"

"I got myself—"

"You got yourself to blame, that's what you got yourself. Now here's what's gonna happen. You're gonna give up *every*thing. Names, dates, times, places, whatever the action was, you're gonna give it up. Try to con us, you lose your ticket. Dodge the questions, you lose your ticket. You tell us one goddamn lie, you lose your fuckin' ticket."

Bollinger turned to Stenner for help. The quiet man ignored him.

"And after we make the bust, you're gonna stand up in court and sing on these guys like the canary you are—"

"Goddamn you, I had a deal working—" Bollinger started to interrupt.

"You didn't have shit. You don't cooperate, you know what we're gonna do? We're gonna drop the charges on you and turn you out on the street, and just before we do?—just before they open up those pearly fuckin' gates?—we're gonna drop dimes all over this town that you jumped on the stoolie wagon. You'll be a dead man. They'll whack you before you get to the corner."

Stenner sat back and watched Flaherty's performance with awe. He knew the Irishman had been a street kid, but he had never seen him in action before, not like this.

Flaherty began jabbing home his points with a forefinger. "So we're gonna start over because right now you don't have a goddamn thing. You made some talk and we made some talk, but *nobody* said 'yea,' and *nobody* said 'nay.' Nobody said *bullshit.* Now what's it gonna be, Bobby? Do I turn on the tape recorder, or do you take a trip to the icebox?"

Bollinger looked pleadingly at Stenner.

"Man's got a point," Stenner said casually.

"Let's hear your story," Flaherty said. "Now."

Bollinger looked back and forth between his two captors and then said, "I was the bagman."

"For who?"

"Shoulders."

"And who?"

Bollinger hesitated for a moment, then said, "Roznick."

"Vic Roznick? The city manager?" Stenner said with surprise.

"How many Roznicks you know?"

"How did you make the delivery?"

"I get a call. I go to the Shamrock Club on West Erie. Shoulders has a office on the second floor. He gives me a briefcase fulla twenties and fifties. I take it to a parking lot on Illinois near the *Trib*. The trunk's unlocked. I put the case in, that's it."

"How do you know what was in the case?" Stenner asked.

"Christ, Jake counted it out right in fronta me. Tells me there's a fuckin' dollar missin' it's my ass."

"And it was Roznick's car?"

"Sometimes. I sat in my car half a dozen times and watched him come out, dip into the trunk, and split with the case. Other times it was Glen Scott, Eddie Malone, Pete Yankovitch."

"City staff?"

"Yeah. Different places for them. Shoulders had 'em all over a barrel. Stuff they did years ago. Videotape. Audio. Photos. Get 'em on a hook, then make the deal. They cooperate, he pays off and lets 'em off the spike."

"Once they're in, they never get out," Stenner said.

"I even shot some photos."

"Why?" Stenner asked.

"To cover my ass, y'know, just in case."

"You mean to do a little blackmailing of your own, don't you?" Flaherty suggested.

Bollinger shrugged but did not answer.

"You got pictures of these pickups?" Flaherty asked.

"Yeah. They oughta be worth a little extra."

"Part of the deal," Flaherty snapped back.

"I, uh . . . I got sompin' else maybe worth a new Vette."

"It better be good," said Flaherty.

"There's paper out on your boss."

Stenner stood up, his eyes narrowed. "Who you talking about, Yancey?"

"No, man. The piranha."

"Piranha?" Flaherty asked.

"Vail. They're scared shitless of him. Can't be bought. Never know where he's gonna jump next."

"You saying there's a contract out on Martin Vail?" Flaherty said fiercely. "Who?"

"Do we have a deal on the Vette?" Bollinger asked with a smile.

With a growl, Flaherty pulled the .38 out of its shoulder holster. He jammed it under Bollinger's nose.

"Don't fuck with us. Who put out the contract and who's doing the job? You say it now or I swear to God I'll throw you out the damn window."

"Hey, hey . . ." Bollinger said, turning pale.

Stenner reached out and laid his hand over the gun. "Answer those two questions right now, Bobby," he said sternly.

"Shoulders. It's like two hundred K."

"Shoulders ordered the hit?"

"Yeah, but I think maybe they're all in on it. You know, the whole gang chipped in."

"Who's the shooter?" Flaherty said. His voice had gone dead.

"You better cover me on this."

"Who's the fuckin' shooter?"

Bollinger sighed. He was beginning to sweat. "It's a cop, does Shoulders's tricks."

"A cop?" Stenner said. "What cop?"

"Look I . . . I . . ." Bollinger stammered.

"What cop?" Flaherty demanded.

"His name's Heintz," Bollinger babbled.

"Lou Heintz? A sergeant?" Stenner said.

"That's the one."

"You know him, Major?" Flaherty asked.

"Oh yes, Lou Heintz. Doesn't surprise me a bit. When is this supposed to go down?"

Bollinger shrugged. "Whenever. It's paid for."

"My God," Stenner said, and headed for the phone.

"This better be the McCoy," said Flaherty.

"Who the hell *are* you, anyways?" Bollinger whimpered.

Flaherty smiled for the first time. "I'm the guy who's gonna make you the greatest song-and-dance man since Fred Astaire," he said.

And he had. It had taken eighteen months, but Flaherty had successfully prosecuted Shoulders, two of his henchmen, three department heads, the city manager, and an assistant city attorney and set in motion Meyer's successful cases against the two city councilmen. All of them were still in prison.

Bollinger was in Oregon with orders never to set foot east of the Mississippi River.

Lou Heintz, the killer motorcycle cop, had vanished. And Stenner had immediately become Vail's bodyguard, picking him up every morning, delivering him to meetings, watching his back constantly, usually delivering him home at night.

About a year later, Heintz was found dead in an abandoned car in Pittsburgh with four .22s in the back of his head. It was written off as a gang hit. Nobody would ever know whether it involved the contract on Martin Vail or not.

But Stenner never stopped his surveillance. He had been Vail's constant companion ever since, except at those times when Vail managed to shake him. Like the night before.

—

Vail was still deep in reminiscence when Stenner pulled up in the car. He glared up at his boss and shook his head.

"Right out in the open," he said as Vail got into the car. "Alone. Perfect target."

"Please, Abel. That's over. Heintz is dead, Shoulders is doing ten years."

"Once warned . . ."

"Okay. You know I appreciate your concern. I just need a little privacy every once in a while. Kinda like sneaking out when you were a kid."

"I never sneaked out when I was a kid."

"I think I knew that, Abel."

Stenner looked at Vail's wrinkled suit and twisted tie. "You want to go home and change?" he asked.

"Hell with it," Vail said.

"You're in court this morning and Naomi says you have a lunch with Paul Rainey."

"Butterfly's, Major. I want breakfast. Anyway, it's not my case, it's Parver's. I'm just going to sit in the back of the courtroom and spectate."

"How about the lunch with Rainey?"

"I'll pick up the check. He won't care what I'm wearing."

17

When Vail and Stenner arrived at Butterfly's, Naomi Chance and Dermott Flaherty were already there, immersed in the morning papers. Naomi looked disapprovingly at Vail as he sat down.

"Didn't get too close to your razor this morning," she commented.

He couldn't think of an appropriate answer, so he said nothing. Instead he turned to Butterfly, who loomed over the table staring down at him.

"Two poached, sausage, white toast," he said.

"Poached," she snarled. "God!" And slouched away.

"And that suit—" Naomi began.

"I don't want to hear about my suit or shaving or anything else," Vail said.

"You can grab a quick shave in your private bath," Naomi said.

"Screw my private bath. It's not a bathroom, it's an afterthought. They put a sink and a shower in a broom closet and called it a bathroom."

"It's convenient."

"It's the size of the can in an airliner."

"There's a clean shirt and a tie in one of your file cabinets and your gray pinstripe is in the closet, take you fifteen minutes before you go down to court," Naomi said, scanning the front page of *USA Today.*

"What is it with everybody today?" Vail grumbled. "I'm not posing for *GQ,* you know. Why don't you pick on Flaherty? He wears that same black suit every day."

"I have four black suits," Flaherty said without looking up from his paper. "I don't wear the same one every day."

"Don't you find it a little bizarre that he dresses like Johnny Cash *every day*?" Vail said. "Why don't you pick on him?"

Stenner said, "I think some variety might be in order."

"I'm comfortable in black," Flaherty said, ending the conversation.

Further discussion was cut short by the arrival of Okie Okimoto, who looked smug and important as he approached the table. He was carrying his briefcase.

Butterfly frowned at him. "We don't serve sushi in here," she growled.

"I have no desire to eat here, Madame Butterfly. Hopefully I can survive a cup of coffee."

"Smartass," she muttered, and dragged her feet into the kitchen.

Okimoto sat down at the round table, opened his case, and took out a file folder.

"I have here the report on the famous landfill kill," he said, almost with a snicker. "Or perhaps I should say *infamous* landfill kill."

"What's so funny?" Stenner asked.

"All the fuss," he said. "Where's Harvey? I want him to hear this from my own two lips."

"Must've overslept," Naomi said.

"Hmm. Perhaps I should wait."

"I don't think so," said Vail. "You've gone this far, you better finish."

"Okay. I'll skip the anatomical details and the long medical terms for now and just give you the essence," Okimoto said, opening the folder. "By the way, Eckling doesn't have this yet. I assume you will be discreet with the information for at least an hour."

"Sure. Just get on with it," Vail answered.

"They froze to death," Okimoto said with a smile.

"What!" Flaherty said, finally looking up from his paper.

A deadly quiet fell over the table as Stenner, Vail, Flaherty, and Naomi stared at Okimoto, waiting for the details of his surprising announcement.

"Well, the two males froze to death and the woman suffocated," he said to the stunned group.

"Froze to death?" Stenner repeated.

"You want my expert opinion?" said Okimoto. "I think what happened was, they crawled into a Dempsey Dumpster somewhere, probably burrowed under the junk to keep warm—this was several weeks ago, early to mid January, we had a helluva freeze for about two weeks right after New Year's if you'll remember—and by morning two of them were dead and the woman was too weak to move. They pick up the Dumpster, haul it out to the landfill, and unload it. The woman suffocated in the garbage, probably after she was in the dump."

"Good God!" Flaherty said.

"So we don't have a homicide, we have a homeless tragedy?" said Vail.

"Yeah," Okimoto said, snickering. "So much for Harvey's murder theory."

Then he leaned his elbows on the table. "Know what I think? I think maybe this happens a lot. Probably other bodies out there, but I'm not going to mention it to anybody. They'll be out there digging up the whole damn landfill."

"They froze to death," Stenner said half aloud and shaking his head. "Harvey's going to be crushed."

"I hear he was on the computer network tracking down missing persons from all over the state," Okimoto said, and started to laugh. He finished his coffee. "Tell you what, tell Harvey the murder weapon was a refrigerator." Then he left, still chuckling to himself.

"Harvey finally blew one," Flaherty said, turning back to his paper. "Him and his intuition."

"He's usually right," said Naomi. "Give the devil his due."

"Yeah, but he kind of rubs it in, don't you think?" Flaherty said. "Anybody else notice that, that he kind of rubs our noses in it because we don't remember some oddball bit of information like the day John Dillinger was killed, something like that. Hell, John Dillinger was killed thirty years before I was born."

"July twenty-second, 1934," said Naomi. "In front of the old Biograph Theater. Actually, it's not too far from here." She smiled at Flaherty's surprised look and added with a wink, "It's part of our local history, darling, don't feel bad."

When they got to the office, Parver was already there, pacing back and forth at the rear of the big room, drinking a cup of coffee and psyching herself up.

"Ready for battle?" Vail called to her as he entered his office and peeled off his jacket and tie.

She nodded and kept pacing.

"What's your plan?"

"No bail. Go to the grand jury as soon as possible."

"She's gonna fight you," Vail said.

"Well, we'll just have to kick ass," Parver answered, still pacing.

Vail smiled. "That's my girl," he said.

Naomi took a clean shirt out of a drawer and handed it and his suit to Vail.

"There isn't room in here for me and my clothes," he griped, and pulled the door shut behind him.

"Twenty minutes," Naomi called out, and went to her desk.

Fifteen minutes later Parver and Vail bumped into Harvey St. Claire, who was getting off the elevator as they were leaving. He seemed either tired or deep in thought.

"Missed you at breakfast, Harve," Vail said.

"May I talk to you for a minute?" St. Claire answered, his tone more serious than usual.

"I have to go down to the Stoddard bail hearing with Shana. Then lunch with Rainey. Can it wait until this afternoon?"

"Uh, yeah, sure."

"Incidentally, Okie was at Butterfly's this morning acting the fool. The bodies in the landfill? Three homeless people got in a Dumpster and froze to death. Well, actually one of them suffocated. Anyway, you can forget working the network and get back to business."

He and Parver headed for the elevators.

"Ohhhh, I don't think so," St. Claire drawled half aloud as he watched them leave.

—

Two guards led Edith Stoddard down a long, dismal hallway toward the back stairs to courtroom 3 on the second floor. Her hands were shackled behind her, but Venable had convinced the jailers not to shackle her legs by embarrassing them.

"This is a fifty-three-year-old woman," she said. "You think she's going to outrun you two and make a dash for the border?"

As they approached the door to the stairwell, a TV team from channel 7 burst through the back door with lights blazing and microphone ready. Edith Stoddard cried out and lowered her face in alarm.

"Damn them," Venable snapped, and glowered at the two jailers. It was an old media trick, slipping the security men ten bucks apiece to tell them where and when they could get a shot at the defendant. She rushed Stoddard along, but the TV crew caught them at the door. Venable opened it and urged Stoddard through, followed by the guards. Then she stood in the doorway. Questions came at her in a jumble.

"When did you take on the case?"

"Did Edith Stoddard call you?"

"Are you going for reduced bail?"

"Is it true that she's already confessed?"

And on and on. Venable finally held up a hand, and when that didn't quiet them, she raised her voice and bellowed, "Listen!" She waited until they shut up. "I will answer no questions. This is a bail hearing. If you want to know what's going on, go upstairs to the court like everyone else. Other than that, no comment. And I'll have no comment after the hearing, either. Is that clear?"

She stepped inside the stairwell and slammed the door in their faces. The stairwell smelled of Lysol, an odor that sickened Venable. *Why is it all of the nastier public buildings smell of Lysol? Perhaps my reaction to it is psychosomatic.*

"Please, please . . ." Edith Stoddard said. Tears welled in her eyes.

"This will take about five minutes," Venable said. "Just hang in there and trust me." She held her breath until they got to the security room at the top of stairs.

Parver was already at the prosecutor's desk. There were a thin file folder, a large yellow legal tablet, and a handful of freshly sharpened pencils on the desk in front of her. She watched as the guards led Edith Stoddard and Jane Venable to the defense desk. They sat down and Venable leaned over and spoke to her in a whisper. She did not acknowledge Shana.

In the back of the room, Vail settled back to watch the first brief skirmish between the two lawyers. Venable's objective would be to get bail as low as possible—perhaps even have her client released on her own recognizance—without giving away any of her case. Parver's objective: No bail, period.

Vail looked at Edith Stoddard. One day had beaten her down. Her shoulders were rounder, her head down. He thought for a moment about the irony of the Darby and Delaney cases. In both murders, a shot to the head was key. In Darby's case, it came first and proved premeditation; in Delaney's case, the head shot was second and proved malice.

Judge Ione Pryor, a tall, hawk-faced woman in her forties with a no-nonsense air and a steely glare behind gold-rimmed glasses, entered the courtroom and took her chair behind the bench.

"First case," she said to the bailiff.

"The state versus Edith Stoddard. A bail hearing. Defendant was arrested yesterday on a charge of murder in the first degree."

"Who's representing the state?" Judge Pryor asked.

Parver stood up. "I am, Your Honor. Shana Parver, assistant prosecutor, D.A.'s office."

Judge Pryor looked over the top of her glasses toward the defendant's desk, settled her gaze on Venable.

"Are you representing the defendant?" she asked with surprise.

"Yes, Your Honor. Jane Venable for the defense."

"Been a while since we've seen you in criminal courts," the judge said.

"Yes, Your Honor."

"Ms. Parver?"

"Your Honor," she said, standing behind her desk. "The state has sufficient evidence to obtain a first-degree murder indictment from the grand jury against Mrs. Stoddard for the slaying of John Farrell Delaney. We move that Mrs. Stoddard be held without bail until the trial. This is premeditated murder, Your Honor."

Venable stood up.

"Objection, Judge," she said. "The state's case consists of a statement made by my client to two police officers who were interrogating her concerning the death of her boss, John Delaney. She never mentioned Delaney by name. She said 'I killed him.' That's all she said."

"If the court please," Parver countered, "the entire interrogation concerned Mrs. Stoddard's relationship with the deceased, John Delaney. It is obvious the 'him' in her confession was John Delaney. I seriously doubt she was talking about John Kennedy or Abe Lincoln."

Pryor squinted over her glasses at Parver, considered admonishing her for a fleeting moment, then changed her mind. The young prosecutor had a strong point. She looked back at Venable.

"I would have to agree with that, Ms. Venable."

"It's moot anyway, Your Honor. The statement made by my client is inadmissible. She was under great stress at the time. She was scared to death. She had no legal representation—"

"She was given an opportunity to call a lawyer in her Miranda," the judge said.

"I really don't think she was rational at that point. There are a great many extenuating circumstances in this matter, Judge. As far as bail goes, Mrs. Stoddard has a husband who is a quadriplegic. My client is fifty-three years old and takes care of him. I don't believe she poses a danger or threat to society and, I can assure you, she's not going anywhere."

"Excuse me, Judge Pryor," Parver said. "If counsel is suggesting that Mrs. Stoddard be released on recognizance, the state strongly objects. I say again, this is a murder-one case. As far as Mrs. Stoddard's husband is concerned, she has a twenty-one-year-old daughter who will have to take on that responsibility. And Mrs. Stoddard's age is immaterial."

The judge looked at Stoddard for a minute or two, then took off her spectacles and tapped them lightly against her jaw.

"Where is her daughter?" the judge asked. "Is she in court today?"

"No," Venable said.

Parver moved quickly to quell any further discussion of the specific issues of the case. "We have a motion before the court, Judge. I suggest the counselor wait until the trial to plead her case."

Pow, right in the kisser, thought Venable. *Vail's taught his young lawyers well.*

The judge smothered a smile. "Please read the motion," she said to the court reporter, who checked the stereotape, found the motion made by Parver, and said: " 'We move that Mrs. Stoddard be held without bail until the trial.' "

The judge leaned back in her chair. "When do you plan to go to the grand jury, Ms. Parver?"

"As soon as possible. Hopefully, this week sometime."

"Okay. I'm going to deny bail at this time. I agree with Ms. Parver, Ms. Venable. This is first-degree murder. As for the confession, the trial judge can deal with it, if and when it comes to that."

"One more point, if it please the court," said Venable. "Defense would like to request that Mrs. Stoddard be kept in the holding cell here in district two until the grand jury rules rather than moving her into the general prison population at this time."

Pryor looked at Parver. Shana thought for a moment and said, "The state has no objection."

"Good, then that's all settled."

Pryor rapped her gavel and called for the next case.

Venable walked across to the prosecutor's table. "Nicely done," she said to Parver. "Looks like you took round one."

"Thanks," Parver answered.

"See you next time."

Venable returned to Edith Stoddard as the guards prepared to handcuff her and lead her out.

"Do you boys mind cuffing her in front?" she asked. "She isn't going to turn rabbit on you."

The two guards exchanged glances and one of them shrugged.

"Sure, Miss Venable," he said.

"Why did you do that?" Stoddard asked as they were leading her out of the courtroom. There was emotion in her voice for the first time, a sense of betrayal and anger. "I told you, I want to plead guilty. I can't stand these photographers and reporters screaming at me. The pictures—"

"Edith, please trust me. Let me do this my way," Jane Venable said. "They will most certainly indict you for murder one. Then I'll move to throw out the confession. They don't have the gun, so they can't prove yours was even the murder weapon. That gives me good ammunition when I go to Vail to strike a deal."

"I just want it over with," Stoddard said mournfully.

"And it will be soon," Venable said with sympathy as they led Edith Stoddard out of the room.

Parver worked her way back through the reporters, who had now descended on her. Vail slipped out the door and walked across the hall to wait for her.

Parver stopped just outside the courtroom doors.

"We will seek a murder-one indictment of Mrs. Stoddard as soon as possible, hopefully before the end of the week. That's all I can tell you now."

"Will you ask for the death penalty?" a female TV reporter asked.

Parver stared at her for several seconds. The impact of the question threw her. "I'm not going to try this case in the media," she said. "I've told you all I can tell you at this time. Thank you."

She walked away. The press swarmed off down the hall, looking for Jane Venable. Vail fell in beside Parver and they threaded their way through the crowded hall.

"I don't understand why Edith Stoddard is so determined to plead guilty," Parver said.

"A lot of reasons," Vail said. "She's scared, she's depressed, she knows she's guilty. Doesn't want her family hurt any more than necessary. My guess is, she's being protective of her husband and daughter. And it's a humiliating experience, very traumatic."

"I don't believe it's sunk in yet that she blew this man away in cold blood and she's going to pay heavily for it," Parver said. "She's facing life."

"I'm sure Jane's drumming that into her, but I really don't believe that's a reality to her at this point."

"I feel a little sorry for her," Parver admitted, half aloud.

"You don't have that luxury," Vail said, then added: "There is one thing—"

"Find the gun," Parver said.

"You're one step ahead of me."

"Abel's working on it," she said. "When do I get a crack at Mrs. Stoddard?"

"Let's wait until after the grand jury," Vail said. "Once she's indicted, when the reality of what she's up against sets in, she may begin to break down a little."

"I don't think so," Parver answered. "I think she's determined to enter a plea."

"And Venable's determined to fight it. Let's wait and see how that one plays out. Ready to take on Paul Rainey?"

"Yes, sir."

"Have the paper?"

"Right here." She took out the arrest warrant and gave it to Vail, who put it in the inside pocket of his jacket.

"Let's go rattle his cage," Vail said.

18

They were at Sundance, a two-story-high atrium covered with skylights to give the illusion of being outside when the weather was inclement or just too damn cold, as it was on this blustery February day. The glass partitions covering the large plaza could be opened with the press of a button in the manager's office, weather permitting. It was a popular lunchtime place for downtown workers, serving the best hot dogs east of the Mississippi and mountainous salads for vegetarians. It was located behind one of the city's largest bookstores, and its old-fashioned wrought-iron tables were usually filled by noon with bookworms who bought novels or periodicals and read through lunch in the sunlit piazza.

"You really know how to entertain, Marty," Paul Rainey said as he doctored two hot dogs with sauerkraut, relish, mustard, ketchup, and onions. He looked down at Parver. "Does he always entertain this lavishly, Shana?"

"It's all I can afford on the assistant D.A.'s salary," Vail answered.

"Who're you kidding?" Rainey said. "You made enough before you took that job to live on the tenderloin forever. I'll bet you've got the first dime you ever made. Hell, you don't own a car and you dress like a damn ragamuffin. Did you know the Lawyers Club was thinking of taking up a collection to buy you a new suit?"

"This *is* a new suit," Vail answered a bit firmly.

"Cotton and wool. Off the rack. Two hundred tops. You know how much this outfit cost me? Two thou. Barneys."

Vail bit into his frankfurter and chewed in silence for a minute, then said casually, "That's more than you're going to make off James Darby."

Rainey looked up and rolled his eyes. "Oh, hell, not even gonna wait until we finish this elaborate spread, are ya?" He sighed. "Okay, Counselors, what're we doing here?"

"You and I go back almost twenty years, right, Paul?"

"I've never counted."

"I've seen it from both sides of the street."

"Forget the endorsements and make your point," Rainey said.

"Your boy Darby is guilty as sin."

"Uh-huh. You gonna take that to the grand jury? That Darby is guilty as sin? I don't think so. And that's all you've got. Look, I don't like him any more than you do, but that doesn't make him a wife killer. So he's a putz. Half the world is a putz."

"Paul, I'm telling you this guy carefully planned and killed his wife in cold blood. And he did it for the two worst reasons: money and a stripper with a fancy ass and a 40-D cup."

"C'mon, Marty, you fried everybody who screws around on his wife they'd only be ten men left on the planet."

"The jury'll be back in an hour on this one."

"What's the matter, you can't wait for the trial?" Rainey said with a laugh. "You want to try him here over lunch? Maybe we should call over a waiter to act as judge."

"I'm here in the interest of justice and saving the taxpayers' money," Vail said calmly.

"Of course you are."

"Listen a minute. Where we stand in this investigation, we have Darby saying he came in the house, his wife popped three shots at him, he shot her with a shotgun, she knocked one in the ceiling, and he finished the job with the head shot. Isn't that Darby's story?"

"It's what happened."

"Well, think about that for a minute. Three shots from a .38, a shotgun blast, another .38, another shotgun blast."

Vail opened his briefcase and took out a small tape recorder. It contained an enhanced reproduction just of Stenner's replay of the shots as Mrs. Shunderson said they occurred, with the shotgun blast first. He plugged a set of headphones into the machine and handed it to Rainey.

"Listen to this," Vail said. He waited until Rainey had the headphones adjusted and then pressed the play button. They watched as Rainey listened. He took off the 'phones and handed it back to Vail.

"So? Somebody shooting a gun."

"It's clear that the first shot came from the shotgun," Vail said.

"Is that what we're here about? This dummied-up tape. What kinda scam are you trying to pull, Martin?"

"I'll tell you right now, Paul, I have an unimpeachable witness who'll testify that the tape is accurate," said Vail.

"So what," Rainey said, obviously getting annoyed.

"So your guy's been lying to you, which is understandable, considering he killed his wife in cold blood. Point is, he hasn't been level with you. You're flying blind at this point and he's navigating you right into a mountain."

"Where are you going with this, Marty?"

"I'm offering you a deal, Paul. We'll let him plead to second-degree murder. He gets twenty years without parole. I'm offering you twenty years and he's out. He'll be fiftysomething and broke, but he'll be out. I think society will be happy with that arrangement."

"You're crazier than a Christmas mouse, you know that?"

"I know you, Paul. I know you believe that Darby's innocent and it happened the way he said it happened. But I hate to see you get conned by your own client. Listen to the tape again."

"I don't have to listen to the tape again. I heard the tape. It doesn't mean a damn thing."

"It means Darby came into his house, walked over to his wife, who was watching TV, and shot her in the head. Then he put the .38 in her hand, fired four shots—one into the ceiling—and then backed off and shot her in the side with the shotgun. And it also means it was premeditated. Malice aforethought. The whole magilla."

"If you're so damn sure you got him, you wouldn't be offering me a deal. I know you. You'd take me to the limit."

"Look, I don't have the staff or the time for depositions and tracking down witnesses and pretrial and trial and then your appeal and on and on. I've got a desk full of cases and now I have to handle Jack's business, too. We settle this, I save the taxpayers a couple hundred thousand bucks, I save myself a lot of aggravation, you save face, and your client stays alive."

Vail turned to Parver and held out his hand. She took out the warrant and handed it to him. He laid it on the table and slid it in front of Paul Rainey.

"I'll serve this on you if you'll accept it. You can bring him in by, say, eight tonight?" he said.

Rainey opened the warrant for first-degree murder on Darby. He looked up at Vail with surprise, then looked back down at the warrant. His jaw began to spasm as his anger rose.

"I can't believe you're pulling this stunt," he said finally.

"There's another thing," Vail said. "He's dead broke. I talked to Tom Smoot at New York Life last night. They're freezing the insurance funds pending the resolution of this case."

"Never miss a trick, do you?" Rainey said, and there was ire in every word. "Know what I think? I think you're giving up an awful lot of information, that's what I think."

"There's a lot more," Parver said softly.

"Oh?"

"Well, there's the slip with the phone number on it. We think the phone number beside the phone was written by Darby to make it appear as though his wife called Palmer. I don't think Poppy Palmer ever talked to Ramona Darby."

"You've had more than one shot at the Palmer woman," said Rainey. "You can't prove any of this. It's all conjecture. You want to talk to her again? Go ahead, be my guest."

"We'd like to, Paul, if we could find her," Shana Parver said in a matter-of-fact tone.

"What the hell're you talking about?"

"Poppy Palmer flew the coop," Vail said.

Rainey's gaze jumped back and forth between Vail and Parver.

"She called her boss yesterday, about two hours after Shana questioned Darby about the slip with her phone number on it. She told him her sister was dying down in Texarkana and she had to go immediately. Her sister lives in California and is in perfect health. She hasn't heard from Poppy Palmer in five years."

Rainey, a very shrewd lawyer, leaned back in his chair and studied Vail's face, then he looked at Parver. His eyes narrowed, but he kept quiet. At this point, he knew he would learn more by keeping his mouth shut.

"We are going to issue a subpoena on Palmer and I'm seriously considering taking out a warrant against her for perjury," Vail said. "She made the statement about her phone call from Ramona Darby under oath. We contend she's lying—there never was a phone call. Then I intend to go to the FBI and swear out a warrant against her for unlawful flight to avoid prosecution."

Rainey fell deep into thought. He drummed his fingertips on the table but still maintained his silence.

"You're already in, Paul. You want to go *pro bono* from here on, representing a killer in a case you can't win? You owe it to yourself, your peace of mind, to get the truth out of him. Explain the options. Either he takes twenty years, no parole, or he goes to death row and gets fried—or spends the rest of his life staring down the hall at the chair, waiting to."

"You want me to sell out my client because he can't pay," Rainey said with an edge.

"Not at all. What I'm saying, Paul, is you need to satisfy yourself about this. Then consider all the angles and do the best thing for you *and* your client. Either he pleads to second-degree and takes his medicine or he goes down for murder one. It's up to you. In your hands. Just one thing—if he turns rabbit, he'll never make the county line."

Rainey slumped back in the chair. He stared at Vail, at the warrant, then back at Vail.

"He'll say he was confused," Rainey said. "He walked in, she was aiming the gun at him, he cut loose with the shotgun—"

Parver cut him off. "It's the head shot," she said. "That's what's going to get him in the end. Do you really think any jury's going to believe she kept blazing away at him with a hole the size of Rhode Island in her side? The head shot *had* to be the first shot. Listen to the tape."

"The hell with the goddamn tape. The tape doesn't mean shit and you know it!"

"You're an old hand at getting to the truth, Paul," said Vail. "If he sticks to his story"—he tapped the tape recorder—"he's lying to you."

Rainey took a sip of water, tapped his lips with his napkin, and dropped it on the table. He toyed with the warrant, sliding it around on the tabletop with his fingertips.

"We're playing straight up with you, Paul," said Vail. "I could've had the sheriff pick him up last night and he'd be sitting in the cooler right now."

Rainey pocketed the warrant and got up.

"I'll be in touch," he said. Then he leaned over the table and, with a smile, said very softly in Vail's ear, "I've been in this game ten years longer than you and this is the first time a D.A. ever offered me a deal before he even arrested my client."

"It's the times," Vail said, smiling back. "Everybody's in a hurry these days."

"There's something not right about this," Rainey said with a scowl.

"Yeah, your client, that's what's not right about it," Parver said.

"I was having a pretty good day until now. You two're a real item. Buy a guy lunch, then do your best to make him lose it."

Rainey left the table. Parver didn't say anything. She looked down at the tablecloth, moved her water glass around on it.

"Okay, what's bothering you?" Vail asked.

"Nothing."

"Uh-huh. C'mon, spit it out."

"Why let Darby off the hook? I mean, why even offer a plea bargain? We can take this guy, Martin. We can take him all the way, I know we can."

"All you have is an elderly woman who heard the shots. Paul Rainey'll chew her up and spit her out. We have no backup on Mrs. Shunderson and Poppy Palmer powdered on us and we haven't a clue where she is. Suppose you get a soft jury? Darby could walk. Or maybe get voluntary manslaughter, in which case he'd be back on the street in three, four years. This way, if Rainey bites, we take Darby out for twenty years."

"I still think I can win this case."

"You did win, Shana. Putting Darby away for twenty years without parole, that's as sweet a deal as we can ask for. Look, you just came off a case, you've got the Stoddard thing to deal with, and by tomorrow you'll probably have two more on your desk. Forget Darby, we've got him. Let's hope Rainey sees through him."

"We just gave Rainey our whole case!" she said. "And why didn't we let the sheriff arrest that punk?"

"We didn't give him a damn thing he wouldn't get the first day of discovery. And giving him the option to bring his man in shows good faith on our part."

"Think the money'll have an effect on him?"

"It's a wild card. He took Darby at his word, which is natural, any lawyer will give his client the benefit of the doubt. Now he's faced with the possibility his client conned him from the front end. Paul Rainey doesn't want to feel he's been suckered by a client he doesn't even like. If he's convinced Darby lied to him, then he's faced with either defending a man he knows is guilty and not getting paid for it or getting him the best deal he can."

"I don't think he'll buy it," she said.

"Maybe. What really got to him, what got his attention, was

Poppy Palmer running. That and the warrant. My guess is, he'll come back with a counteroffer."

"And . . . ?"

"We made him the best offer we're going to. If Rainey doesn't take it, Darby's all yours."

"Good!" Parver said staunchly. "I hope Rainey thumbs his nose at us. It will serve him right."

"If he does, we better find Poppy Palmer," Vail said. "She'll put the nail in his coffin."

19

Trial transcripts, autopsy reports, photographs, old police reports, and copies of book pages were all spread out on Martin Vail's large table. Naomi, Flaherty, and Harvey St. Claire stood in front of the big desk, studying what St. Claire called his "exhibits." Naomi and Dermott Flaherty stared mutely at the display, occasionally picking up a report or a photo and studying it, then slowly replacing it, obviously stunned by what St. Claire had laid out on the table.

"You make a good case, Harve. You ought to be a lawyer," Flaherty said.

"I don't make a very good impression in a courtroom. 'Cept in the witness stand. Hold m'own pretty good under oath."

"What's Abel say?" Naomi asked.

"He's concerned," said St. Claire.

"For Abel, that's verging on panic," Flaherty said with a chuckle.

"Am I wrong about this?" St. Claire asked. "Am I just being paranoid?"

"Paranoid! I hardly think so," said Naomi. "Why the hell didn't we know about this sooner?"

" 'Cause Gideon don't want the world t' know about it," said

St. Claire. "From what I gather, the town is run by old Fundamentalist farts. I imagine they all look like Abraham or Moses or John Brown. They don't want the world t' think Satanists are loose in their holy little village."

"Don't they care who did it?"

"Doesn't seem so. Been about six months, ain't happened again. Guess maybe they decided to shut it outta their minds. Pray it away on Sunday mornings."

"And they just wrote off Linda Balfour?"

"One way a puttin' it," said St. Claire.

"The first question that pops into my mind is, Who? And the second is, Why?" said Flaherty.

"Well, I can tell you who it ain't. Ain't Aaron Stampler." St. Claire dropped a wad of chewing tobacco in his silver cup. "He's still locked up in max security at Daisyville."

"That's Daisyland," Naomi corrected him.

"Just as stupid," St. Claire said.

Naomi looked up as Vail, Parver, and Stenner got off the elevator. "Here comes the one person who can answer these questions if anybody can," Naomi said, nodding toward Vail.

"What've we got here?" Vail asked as he entered the office.

They all looked at one another and then focused their attention on Harvey St. Claire. He smoothed out his mustache and got rid of the wad of tobacco in his cheek.

"Tell ya how it started out," he said. "I was runnin' the HITS network, thinkin' maybe we could turn up something outta town on them bodies in the city dump. Missin' persons, maybe a bank heist, drug gang. Playin' a hunch, okay? And Ben Meyer runs across this brutal murder down near the Kentucky border. Town called Gideon. Ever hear of it?"

"Not that I recall," Vail said.

"Anyway, uh, this town's run by some old religious jokers and they hushed it up. Wrote it off as Satanists. We got interested outta curiosity much as anything. The victim was a housewife. Happily married, nice solid husband. Year-old son. I thought what

I'd do, I'd read the autopsy report. The police chief brushed me off, but the town doctor, he's also the coroner, was a nice old guy, most cooperative."

St. Claire searched around the table and found Doc Field's autopsy, which Ben had entered into the computer and printed out, and read it out loud.

> "The victim, Linda Balfour, is a white female, age 26. The body is 53.5 inches in length and weighs 134 pounds and has blue eyes and light brown hair. She was dead upon my arrival at her home on Poplar Street, this city. The victim was stabbed, cut, and incised 56 times. There was evidence of cadaver spasm, trauma, and aero-embolism. There was significant exsanguination from stab wounds. The throat wound, which nearly decapitated Balfour, caused aero-embolism, which usually results in instantaneous death. Wounds in her hands and arms indicate a struggle before she was killed."

St. Claire looked up for a moment. "Beginning to sound a little familiar, Marty?"

"Where are you taking this, Harve?"

"Okay, now listen to this. It's from the M.E.'s testimony in Stampler's trial."

He read excerpts from William Danielson's description of the wounds that had killed Archbishop Richard Rushman ten years before:

> "*DANIELSON: Body trauma, aeroembolism, cadaveric spasm, exsanguination, that's loss of blood. All could have caused death ... The primary cause, I believe was the throat wound. ... It caused aeroembolism, which is the sudden exit of air from the lungs. This kind of wound is always fatal, in fact, death is usually instantaneous. ... And the wounds indicated a knowledge of surgical techniques.*"

Vail was beginning to react. He leaned forward in his chair, his cigarette smoldering, forgotten, between his fingers.

"Now listen t' the rest of Dr. Fields's report," St. Claire said, and finished reading the autopsy:

"There was also evidence of mutilation. Both the victim's nipples and the clitoris were amputated and placed in the victim's mouth. It appears that the wounds were accomplished by a person or persons with some surgical knowledge. Also the inscription C13.489 was printed with the victim's blood on the rear of the skull, 4.6 centimeters above the base of the skull and under the hairline. The weapon was determined to be a common carving knife with an eight-inch blade found on the premises and belonging to the victim . . ."

"She was also nine weeks pregnant," St. Claire added, almost as an afterthought.

Vail was staring into space. He did not say anything for almost a minute.

"Where's Stampler?" he finally asked.

"Up in Daisyland, still in maximum security," said Stenner. "Never had a visitor, never had a letter, never made a phone call."

"In ten years?"

"In ten years," Stenner said. "I talked to the head of security, Bascott and the other executives were in conference. He wouldn't tell me much, but he volunteered that."

"There's somethin' else," said St. Claire. "When I was finishing up the transcripts my eye caught somethin' I missed the first time 'round. Damn near jolted me outta m'chair when I saw it. It was when you was questionin' Stampler on the witness stand. Stampler says, 'My girlfriend, Linda, and I decided to live together . . .' I thought, Maybe it's just a coincidence—two women named Linda, so . . ." St. Claire selected one of the photos of Linda Balfour, a close-up of her head and shoulders, and handed it to Vail. "She look familiar?"

Vail studied the photograph for several seconds. "That's a horrible picture. I can't really—"

"I checked the records in Carbondale, where she and her husband got married. Maiden name's Linda Gellerman, from Akron, Ohio."

Vail looked up at St. Claire and his memory suddenly was jolted back ten years.

—

A tiny, waiflike creature, huddled in a yellow rain slicker, her fearful eyes peering up at him as she stood in the rain.

"Mr. Vail?" her tiny voice asked.

He took her inside, gave her a Coke, and asked her about her boyfriend, Aaron Stampler.

"You think Aaron killed the bishop?"

"Doesn't everybody?"

"Were you there, Linda?"

"Where?"

"At the bishop's the night he was killed?"

"Of course not!"

"Then how do you know Aaron did it?"

"Well, because he was hiding in the church with the knife and all . . ."

"How do you know it wasn't Peter or Billy Jordan?"

"You know about that?"

"About what?"

"Nothing."

"Linda, why did you come here?"

"'Cause I can't help Aaron and I want you to stop looking for me."

"Maybe you can help him."

"How?"

"I need you to testify."

"About what?"

"The Altar Boys."

She panicked, backing away from him like a cornered animal, then running for the door. Vail caught her arm as she reached for the doorknob.

"I won't do that! I'll never admit that! I'll lie. I'll tell them it isn't true."

"Linda, it may help for the jury to know what really went on. What the bishop made you do."

"Don't you understand? He didn't make us do anything! After a while it was fun. We liked it!"

She had turned and run out the door and vanished into the dark, rainswept night. He never saw her again until a moment before when he looked at the picture of the dowdy housewife, sprawled in her living room, covered with blood.

"Linda Gellerman," said Vail. "Aaron Stampler's girlfriend."

"I'm thinkin' maybe we got us a copycat on our hands here," St. Claire said.

"Except for one thing," Stenner added.

Vail finished the thought for him. "The Altar Boys."

Stenner nodded.

"Who the hell're the Altar Boys?" St. Claire asked. "They were never mentioned in the trial."

"That's right, they weren't," said Vail.

"But whoever killed Linda Gellerman knew about them. Had to," said Stenner.

"Who were they? What did they have to do with this?" St. Claire asked.

Vail snuffed out his cigarette and went to the urn for a cup of coffee.

"You have to understand, ten years ago, Archbishop Richard Rushman was known as the Saint of the Lakeview Drive," he began. "He wasn't liked, he was revered. He was also one of the most powerful men in the state. There was as much Richelieu in him as there was John the Baptist; as much Machiavelli as Billy Budd. But to the average person on the street, to your average juror? He was a man who awed.

"Aaron Stampler came here from a squalid little town in Kentucky. He was a true anachronism, a kid with a genius IQ and an illiterate mother and father, living in abject poverty in the coal-mining hills of western Kentucky. He had to sneak to his teacher's house to read books—his father wouldn't permit books in the house except for the Bible. His father also insisted that he work in the place he feared more than anything else in the world. The hole. Shaft number five—I can still remember him talking about it—the deep-pit mines. When he finally escaped that prison, he came here. Rushman met him, took him in at Savior House, which was a home for runaways and homeless kids. Stampler and the bishop grew very close.

"Then Aaron got himself a girlfriend. They decided to live together. And that's where the story started getting fuzzy. Jane Venable contended that the bishop was upset because these two were living in sin, so he threw them out. They were living down on the wharves in a terrible warehouse called the Hollows—it was demolished years ago. The girlfriend left Stampler, and in anger and despair he went to the church and carved up the bishop like a Christmas goose.

"Our story? Stampler left voluntarily. There was never any dispute between him and the bishop. He was in the library, thought he heard arguing up in the bishop's apartment, went up to check. When he looked into the bedroom he sensed that there was somebody else there. Then he blacked out, went into what's called a fugue state—he did it quite often, particularly under stress—and the next thing he knew, he was hiding in a confessional with the murder weapon, soaked with the bishop's blood. The girlfriend was Linda Gellerman."

"But that wasn't the real motive," said Stenner.

"No, there was another motive, much darker—both Venable and I knew about it—but neither of us used it in the trial."

"Which was?" Flaherty asked.

"The bishop was a pedophile. His victims were a group called the Altar Boys. The bishop would direct movies of the Altar Boys seducing a young lady. Then he'd turn off the camera and step in and do the girl, the boys, whatever suited him. Aaron Stampler was one of the Altar Boys. Linda was the girl."

"Why didn't that come out in the trial?" Parver asked.

"Too risky. And Venable and I agreed to destroy the tapes when the trial was over," said Vail.

"Why?"

"To protect the bishop's good name," Stenner said.

"Christ, a pedophile?" St. Claire said. "Why protect him?"

"You weren't there," Stenner offered. "He was loved by everybody. Raised millions for charity every year. Incredibly power-ful man."

"And he was dead," said Vail. "The tape we both had was very risky. The bishop did not appear on it, it was just his voice. Too risky for either Venable or me to introduce it. It could've been construed by the jury as a desperation move and the backlash might've lost the case. Besides, I didn't need it. Our case was that Stampler suffered multiple personality disorder—"

"Split personality?" said Flaherty.

"A misnomer, but yes. Like Sybil. His alter ego was a madman who called himself Roy. Stampler was this sweet, almost naïve backwoods kid. Roy was a psychotic killer. When Stampler be-came agitated or was abused in some way, Roy was triggered. He came out and did the dirty work. Stampler was in a fugue state and didn't know what was going on."

"So Roy was the other person in the room when the bishop was killed," St. Claire said.

Vail nodded. "Venable was cross-examining Aaron and she trig-gered Roy. He came out of the witness box like a skyrocket, tried to choke her right in the courtroom."

"You set her up, Martin," Stenner said.

"Did she say that?"

"I say it."

"How do you figure?"

"You knew from taping Aaron all those weeks."

"Knew what?" asked Parver.

"That hammering on those quotes in the books would cause the switch. You started in, then backed off the quotes. She took the bait, thought you were afraid to get into it, so she did."

"But you never bought it?"

Stenner shook his head.

"You gave Abel a real hard time on the witness stand over that there point. The fugue state 'n' everything," Harvey St. Claire said with a smile.

"I don't remember it all that well," Stenner said brusquely. "Ten years does tricks to your memory."

"How about these here Altar Boys?" St. Claire asked.

"There were five of them. Linda and one of them ran. Two others were killed. There were no witnesses to corroborate Rushman's voice, that's why neither of us would touch it in the courtroom."

"Killed?" Flaherty asked.

"By Stampler—Roy," Stenner said. "We all knew that, too. Venable figured she had Stampler, anyway, why risk trying him for three crimes when one would do."

"After he was put away, it became moot," Vail added. "Part of the plea bargain was that I turned him up for all three homicides. It was an inclusive sentence."

"There's one more thing," Harvey St. Claire said, interrupting Vail's reminiscence. "Found it in the bishop's library. His books're in a special collection over at th' Newberry. I didn't have any trouble when I got to page 489. The passage was marked for me."

"Was it recent?" Stenner asked. "What I mean is, was it marked recently?"

"I imagine Okimoto could tell us. Looked t' me like it'd been there a while."

"What was the message?" Vail asked.

"It's from *The Merchant of Venice*," said St. Claire:

> *"In law, what plea so tainted and corrupt*
> *But, being season'd with a gracious voice,*
> *Obscures the show of evil?"*

There was a minute or two of stone silence as Vail thought about the message. *What plea so tainted and corrupt,/But, being seasoned with a gracious voice,/Obscures the show of evil."*

It seemed obvious to Vail that the quote was directed at him. Was his defense of Stampler tainted? Corrupt? Did his defense obscure the show of evil? Was he just being paranoid? After the Stampler trial, Vail himself had considered the possibility that his clever tactics might have obscured the truth—what the Bard called "the show of evil." It had taunted him for months, forced him to appraise his career as a defense attorney, to ponder about the mobsters, drug dealers, cat burglars, and other miscreants who had been his stock-in-trade. In the past he had sometimes balanced the scales in his own mind—good versus evil, truth versus deceit—always tempered with the concept of reasonable doubt. But until now Vail had never given a moment's consideration to the question Shakespeare so eloquently posed to him: Had his voice been tainted and corrupt but seasoned with gracious and masterful conviction?

Thinking back, Vail realized that Stampler himself had raised the question in Vail's mind ten years before, as he was being led away to Daisyland; a devious comment, perhaps made in jest, that had goaded Vail for months. Eventually Vail had assumed the inevitable conclusion: It was his responsibility, as an officer of the court, to provide his client with the best defense possible, and that he always had done brilliantly. And so, eventually, Vail had discarded all these ideas as abstractions.

But not, as Vail now admitted to himself, until after they had influenced his decision to take the job as chief prosecutor.

Now, in a frightening déjà vu, Vail could make sense out of what was happening, for there was that one piece of the puzzle only he knew, a moment in time he had never shared with anyone, and never *could* share with anyone.

His thoughts were interrupted by the phone. Naomi stepped out of the office and answered it at her desk. She came back a moment later.

"It's for you, Harve. Buddy Harris at the IBI."

"What the hell's Buddy want?" St. Claire said, half aloud, as he left the office to take the call.

"Kind of an obscure message, that Shakespeare quote," Stenner said while St. Claire was gone.

"Yeah," Vail answered. "In the Rushman case, the messages always referred to the archbishop. Now who's he talking about?"

St. Claire returned to Vail's office, his face clouded by a frown.

"We got another one."

"What!" said Vail.   ·

"Where?" asked Stenner.

"Hilltown, Missouri. About thirty miles outside of St. Louis. A white male, age twenty-six. UPD man, delivering a package to a private home, was cut six ways to Sunday. Harris says St. Louis Homicide is handlin' the case and they're playin' it real tight. Don't wanna give up too much to the press yet. Buddy says he was talkin' to a cop in East St. Louis this mornin' about a drug case, the cop mentions they got a butcher job across the river. So Buddy calls the St. Louis PD and they didn't wanna talk about it. They finally told him this UPD delivery man got sliced and diced. Buddy says it sounds like a repeat of the Gideon case."

"Did he tell them about Balfour?"

"Nope. Didn't tell 'em anythin'. Just listened."

"Any name attached to this victim?"

"Ain't been released yet. Can't find a next a kin. Buddy says they're obviously riled up over it."

"Well, surprise, surprise!" said Naomi.

Vail was leaning back in his chair without moving. He stared at Stenner without blinking, deep in thought. Finally he said, "If Stampler's behind these killings, how does he *find* these people? Gideon, Illinois? Hilltown, Missouri? You can barely find these places on the map."

"And if he is involved, how the hell's he doin' it from maximum security at the State Hospital?" said St. Claire.

"Maybe Stampler isn't behind it," Stenner suggested. "Perhaps it is a copycat who found out about the Altar Boys."

"And waited ten years to move on it?" Vail said.

"Maybe he's lazy," Flaherty said with a smile.

Vail leaned forward, put his elbows on the desk, clenched his hands, and leaned his chin on his fists. He stared at St. Claire for several seconds.

"Harvey, I want you to grab the red-eye to St. Louis first thing in the morning and get everything you can from St. Louis Homicide."

"I can't, boss, I'm in court in the morning. The Quarrles case."

"Abel?"

"I got two depositions tomorrow."

"I'm between engagements," offered Flaherty.

"Okay, you're on. Naomi, book Dermott on the early-bird, arrange for a car at the airport. Dermott, call Buddy and get some names of people you can talk to."

"Right."

"Naomi, get me Bascott at Daisyland. I want him personally. I don't care if he's in a conference with God, I want him on the phone *now.*"

It took Naomi ten minutes to get the director of the state mental institution on the line. Vail had forgotten how disarmingly gentle his voice was.

"Mr. Vail," he said after the usual salutations, "Dr. Samuel Woodward has been handling the Stampler case for the past, oh, eight years now, I guess. Uh . . . Stampler . . . is his patient and I would prefer that you speak to him directly if you have any questions regarding—"

"What's Stampler's condition now?" Vail asked, interrupting Bascott.

"Once again, I prefer to—"

"Dr. Bascott, I have a problem down here and I need some questions answered. If Dr. Woodward is the man to talk to, then put him on the phone."

"He's on vacation, fishing up in Wisconsin. He'll be back tomorrow night. I'll have him call—"

"I'll be up there day after tomorrow, first thing," Vail said, and there was annoyance in his tone. "Please arrange for me to interview both Woodward and Stampler."

"Mr. Vail, you were, uh . . . Aaron's . . . lawyer. You haven't even been to visit him in ten years. I don't see that—"

"Day after tomorrow," Vail repeated. "I'll see him then." And he hung up. "Damn it," he said. "I'm getting the runaround from Bascott. Naomi, arrange for the county plane to fly me up to Daisyland at eight o'clock day after tomorrow."

"Done."

—

At six o'clock that night, Stenner appeared, as he always did, at Vail's office door.

"Ready to wrap it up?"

"Yeah," Vail said wearily. But before he could get up, the phone rang. It was Paul Rainey.

"I can't put my finger on Jim Darby," he said.

"What do you mean, you can't put your finger on him?"

"I was tied up in court all afternoon on a sentencing. Didn't have time to call until an hour or so ago. He's probably out with his pals. Give me until tomorrow morning, I'll have him there."

Vail hesitated for a few moments.

"I'm sure I can locate him, Marty, I've just been snowed under."

"Okay, Paul. Nine A.M. If he's not here by then, I'll have the sheriff issue a fugitive warrant on him."

"That's not necessary."

"Paul, I'm trying to be fair. He could be on his way to Rio for all I know."

"Hell, he doesn't know there's a warrant out on him. He's out raising hell somewhere. I'll have him there in the morning."

"You accepted service, he's your responsibility. Have you thought any more about our conversation at lunch?"

"I haven't even talked to him yet," Rainey said, but there was a note of urgency in his voice.

"See you in the morning," Vail said and cradled the phone. He looked up at Stenner. "We have a murder-one warrant out against James Darby and Rainey sounds a little panicky. If he doesn't deliver Darby by nine A.M., I want you to take two of your best men and a man from the sheriff's department, find Darby, and bring him in."

Stenner nodded, but he looked pensive.

"What's bothering you?" Vail asked.

"Poppy Palmer," Stenner said.

"What about her?"

"I was just thinking, maybe she panicked. Maybe . . ." He let the sentence hang ominously in the air.

"You have a morbid imagination, Abel."

"I've been a cop for almost twenty-five years," Stenner said. "It comes with the territory."

"What do you want to do?"

"Go out there and put some heat on, see if we can get a line on her. Darby's facing murder one and she's a key witness."

"How about your depositions tomorrow?"

"I'll work around them."

Vail thought for a moment and nodded. "Okay," he said. "She's all yours. Go find them both."

20

The St. Louis Homicide Division was almost devoid of people when Flaherty arrived at the downtown office, a stuffy room jammed with desks, telephones, file cabinets, and computers. Only two detectives were in the room: Oscar Gilanti, captain of the division, who was heading the investigation, and Sgt. Ed Nicholson, an old-timer who had the dignified demeanor and conservative look of an FBI agent.

The two detectives were more pleasant than Flaherty had expected. The captain was a short box of a man, bald except for a fringe of jet-black hair that curled around his ears. He had deep circles under his eyes, his cheeks were dark with the shadows of a two-day beard, and his suit looked like he had slept in it, which he probably had. His deep voice was raspy from lack of sleep.

"I gotta get back out to the scene," he growled to Flaherty. "I'm giving you Sergeant Nicholson here fer the day. Knows as much as anybody else about this mess. What was yer name again?"

"Dermott Flaherty."

"Okay, Dermott, you wanna go anywhere, see anything, Nick'll drive yuh. I pulled a package for yuh—pictures, preliminary reports, all that shit. Autopsy won't be up probably till tomorra. We can fax it to yuh, yuh need it."

"I can't thank you enough, Captain."

"Hell, you know anything we'd appreciate it. We can use all the help we can get on this one. Fuckin' nightmare."

"I can imagine."

"I'll be out at the scene, Nick. If Dermott here wants to come out, bring him along."

"Right."

The sergeant, obviously a man of habit, asked pleasantly if he had a weapon.

Flaherty smiled. "I'm an assistant D.A., Sergeant," he said. "Things haven't gotten *that* bad yet."

The cop chuckled. He was an old pro, tall, very straight-standing, with a tanned and leathery face, gentle, alert eyes, and blondish hair turning gray. Nicholson unlocked his desk drawer and took out his 9-mm H&K and slipped it into a holster on his belt. He also wore his badge pinned to his belt like an old western sheriff. He slid a thick file folder across the desk to Flaherty.

"You might take a look at this picture first, give you a point of reference. Hilltown's about thirty miles down the pike, off to the northeast of U.S. 44. The Spier place is a couple miles out of town, little frame house, one story, two bedrooms, kitchen, den, and big bathroom, that's about it. Sets back in the trees."

He had picked out an aerial photo showing the house at the end of a quarter mile of dirt road that wound through scrub pines and saw grass. Behind it, the road connected with another country road that ended at a lake.

"Calvin Spier and his wife—they own the place—are out in Las Vegas. Weren't due back until the middle of next week, but they're coming back now."

"Do the Spiers know him?" Flaherty asked.

"Spier says no. Want to go out to the scene? It's a thirty-minute drive"—he winked—"if I put on the flasher."

Flaherty nodded and said, "You're the boss."

The drive was pleasant despite a misting rain. Nicholson, a social creature, spoke in a quiet, authoritative voice, filling Flaherty in on the prologue to the killing while the young prosecutor made a cursory examination of the package. The pictures confirmed his suspicion that this killing was a repeat of the Balfour/Gellerman murder.

"Fellow owns a quick shop down the road from the road into the Spiers' place, lives behind it. He found him," Nicholson said. "Noticed the UPD truck through the trees when he got up yesterday morning. When it was still there at lunchtime, he strolled over to take a look. Front door was standing open. Then he heard the flies. Damn near had a heart attack when he saw that young guy in there all carved up like that. Plus he'd been dead about sixteen hours."

"What's the victim's name?" asked Flaherty.

"Alexander Lincoln," Nicholson answered. "They called him Lex."

Alex Lincoln, Flaherty thought. *The last of the Altar Boys.*

Except one. Aaron Stampler.

Rain dripped off the yellow crime ribbons that had been wrapped around a wide perimeter of the house when they got there. A sheriff's car was parked beside the driveway. A cop waved them through. Several police cars were parked single file as they approached the house.

"We're going to have to run for it," Nicholson said, turning up the collar of his suit coat. The two men got out of the car and ran through the rain to the small porch that spanned the front of the house. Several detectives in yellow rain slickers stood under the roof. They nodded as Nicholson and Flaherty ducked under the eaves.

"It's a bitch, Nick," one of the cops said. "This rain has washed out footprints, tire tracks, everything. The old man's a bear."

Nicholson and Flaherty stood just inside the front door for a few moments. A plainclothes detective was standing beside the door jotting a note to himself in a small notebook.

"Hi, Nick," he said. "What a mess, huh."

"That it is. Ray Jensen, this is Dermott Flaherty. He's a prosecutor with the Chicago D.A.'s office."

Jensen offered his hand. "What brings you out here?" he asked.

"We have a thing working up in Chicago. It's a long shot, but there could be a tie-in."

"Be a nice break for us if we could get some kind of a lead," said Jensen. "Right now we're sucking air."

A hallway led to the rear of the house. Flaherty could see white chalk lines marking where the victim's legs had protruded into the hall. He held a shot of the interior of the house taken from the front door out in front of him. Lincoln's legs could be seen protruding from the door halfway down the hall.

"The Spiers left a light on in the living room," said Jensen. "The rest of the place was dark. My guess is the killer called Lincoln back there to do his dirty work."

They walked past a living room that was cluttered with kewpie dolls, embroidered pillows, and dozens of photographs. The furniture was covered with plastic sheets. Flaherty smelled the acid-sweet odor of blood and death.

The death room was a small den with a fireplace. Sliding glass doors led from the room to an enclosed porch on the side of the house. Another door led into the kitchen, which dominated the rear of the place. There was blood everywhere: on the walls, the ceiling, the carpet. Flaherty found a full-length shot of the corpse. Lincoln lay on his side, his head askew. A terrible wound had almost severed his head. His mouth gaped open like that of a dead fish. The wounds were numerous and awesome. Lincoln's pants were pulled down around his knees and he had been emasculated. The results of the brutal amputation had been stuffed in his mouth.

Flaherty flipped through the pictures, found a close-up of the rear of Lincoln's head.

There it was: "R41.102." Flaherty showed no emotion. He kept flipping the photographs.

"How'd he get in? The killer, I mean?" he asked.

"Broke a window in back," Jensen said. "The way we figure it, he cased the place very carefully. Knew the back road to the lake would be abandoned this time of year, particularly after dark. He came in the back way, pulled on down to the house, and broke in through the sliding glass door leading from the little deck in the back. Here's what's interesting. It rained the night before, but there were no footprints in the house and the porch was hosed down so there were no footprints out there either. What I think, the perp took off his shoes when he came in. Then when he left he hosed off the deck so there weren't any out there, either. Probably used the hose to wash off the victim's blood, too. I mean, you look at the pictures of Lincoln, the perp had to be covered with blood."

"Yeah, somebody did some homework on this," Flaherty said, still flipping through the photographs. "Whoever set up the victim knew Spier and his wife were away. Little town like this—"

"Was in the *Post-Dispatch*," said Nicholson.

"What was?"

"About Spier and his wife going out to Vegas. A story in the people section. He drives a semi, won a trip for ten years' service without a citation or mishap."

"How about the package?"

"Mailed from over in East St. Louis, one of those wrap-and-send places," Jensen offered. "During lunch hour. Place was jammed, nobody remembers a damn thing about who posted it. Return name and address is a phony."

Flaherty looked at the receipt slip. On the line that read "sender" was the name M. Lafferty.

"Know an M. Lafferty?" the detective asked.

"Nope," Flaherty said. "The victim picked it up himself, huh?"

"Yeah. Was bellyaching about having to run over there after working hours and then drive down here and back after dark."

"What about this . . . Lex Lincoln? Anything on him?"

"Young guy, twenty-six, been workin' at UPD since he moved here from Minneapolis two years ago."

"Minneapolis? Anything there?"

"Nothing on him. No sheet. His boss—fellow named Josh Pringle—says he's a good worker, always on time, kind of a joker. No enemies we've uncovered so far. Big with the ladies—had two dates the night he was killed."

"Maybe they ganged up on him," Flaherty said with a smile.

The old pro laughed. "Way I heard it, they were both really torn up over it."

"Was anything taken?" Flaherty asked.

"Nothing from the house that we can determine," Jensen answered. "The Spiers will be able to tell us, but I think we can rule out robbery. This was an ambush. The only thing we know was taken was Lincoln's belt buckle."

"His belt buckle?"

"Yes. One of a kind—an American flag, embossed on brass," said Nicholson. "It was cut off his belt. There's one other thing. Look here at this photo, on the back of Lincoln's head, it's written in blood. R41.102. That mean anything to you?"

Before he could answer, Gilanti came back in the house, shaking rain off his coat. He stomped down the hall, his face bunched up in a scowl, talking aloud to himself as he approached Flaherty, Jensen, and Nicholson.

"We don't have a description of the perp, we don't have a description of the vehicle, we don't have shit. And whoever done this job's been on the run for eighteen to twenty goddamn hours." He stopped at the three men, looked down at the floor with disgust. "Hell, the son of a bitch could be halfway to New York by now."

Jensen said, "We're talking to everybody in town and in the area. We're checking all pass-through vehicles between seven and ten P.M. We're checking filling stations up and down 44. Looking for anybody suspicious."

"Christ, that's half the world. We'll be getting calls for the next year with that description."

"Maybe the M.E.'ll come up with something," said Nicholson. "Blood, fibers, DNA sample, something."

"Yeah, sure. And Little Bo Beep'll give us all a blow job if we're good boys. What we got is *nothing*! We don't know what or who the hell we're looking for or where he or she is going. Christ, the killer could be standing out there in the rain, looking across the ribbons, we wouldn't have a clue."

Then he looked at Flaherty and shrugged.

"Got any ideas, Dermott?"

Flaherty gave him a lazy smile. "I convict 'em, Captain, I'm not much at catching 'em."

"Well, sorry I disturbed you boys. Go back to whatever you were doin'." Gilanti moved away, then looked back at Flaherty. "You know anything, any *fuckin'* thing at all that'll help us, Dermott, I'll name my next kid after you, even if it's a girl."

"Thanks for your assistance, Captain."

"Yeah, sure," Gilanti said, and went out into the rain.

"What was in the box Lincoln delivered?" Flaherty asked Jensen.

"That's the sickest thing of all," said Jensen. "Just this, wrapped in a lot of tissue paper."

Flaherty looked at the object and a sudden chill rippled up his backbone.

———

Chief Hiram Young was just sitting down to his evening meal when the phone rang. "Damn," he grumbled under his breath as he snatched up the phone. "Abe Green's dog's probably raising cain in somebody's yard. Hello!"

"Chief Hiram Young?"

"Yes, sir," Young answered sternly.

"Sir, my name's Dermott Flaherty. I'm an assistant D.A. up in Chicago."

"I've already talked to your people. How many times I have to tell you—"

"Excuse me, sir. I just have one question."

"I'm just settin' down t' dinner."

"This will only take a minute. Was anything taken from the Balfour home when Linda Balfour was murdered?"

"I already told you people, robbery was not the motive."

"I'm not talking about robbery, Chief. I'm talking about some little insignificant thing. Nothing that would be important to anyone else."

There was a long pause. Young cradled the phone between his shoulder and jaw as he spread jam on a hot biscuit.

"Really wasn't anything," Young said.

"What was it?"

"A stuffed fish."

"You mean, like a fish mounted on the wall?"

"No, a little stuffed dolphin. It had ST. SIMONS ISLAND, GA. printed on the side. George bought it for Linda when they were on their honeymoon."

"Where was it? What I mean is, was it in the room where she was murdered?"

"Yes. On the mantelpiece."

"Same room as the murder?"

"That's what I just said."

"Thank you, sir. I appreciate your help. Goodbye."

Young slammed down the phone.

"Something wrong, honey?" his wife asked.

"Just some big-shot D.A. up in Chicago tryin' to mess in our business," he said, and returned to his dinner.

—

"Abel? I'm at the airport in St. Louis," Flaherty told Stenner. "Got to hurry, my plane's loading. I'll be there at seven-oh-five."

"I'll pick you up. Get anything?"

"A lot. I think we need to talk to Martin and Jane Venable tonight. It's the same perp, no question about it. Victim even has the symbol on the back of his head. Let me give it to you, maybe Harve can run over to the library and check it out. Got a pencil?"

"Yes."

"It's R41.102."

"R41.102," Stenner repeated. "We'll get on it right away."

"Good. See you at seven."

21

Jane Venable leaned over the spaghetti pot and, pursing her lips, sucked a tiny sample of the olio off a wooden spoon. *Pretty good*, she thought, and sprinkled a little more salt in it. She looked over at the table. Earlier in the day the florist had brought an enormous arrangement of flowers with a simple note: "These cannot compare to your beauty. Marty."

For the first time in years, Jane felt she was beginning to have a new life outside of her office. She had made a fortune, but it had cost her any semblance of a personal life. Now, in just a few days, that had changed. She stared at the flowers and wondered silently, *My God, am I falling in love with this man?* And just as quickly she dispelled the idea. *It's just a flirtation, don't make more of it than it is.*

"I didn't think you really cooked in this chef's fantasy," said Vail. "Where'd you learn to cook Italian spaghetti? You're not Italian."

"My mother was. Born in Florence. She was a translator at the Nuremberg trials when she was eighteen."

"Ahhh, so that's where that tough streak came from."

"My father was no slouch, either. He was a government attorney at the trials—that's where they met. And after that a federal prosecutor for fifteen years."

"What did he think when you quit prosecuting and went private?"

"He was all for it. He said ten years was enough unless I wanted to move up to attorney general or governor. I didn't need that kind of heat."

"Who does? There's damn little truth in politics."

"I don't know," she said. "When I was a prosecutor I honestly believed it was all about truth and justice and all that crap."

"I repeat, there's damn little truth in politics, Janie."

"You know what they say, truth is perception."

"No, truth is the *jury's* perception," Vail corrected.

"Does it ever bother you?" she asked. "About winning?"

"What do you mean?"

"Some people say we're both obsessed with winning."

"It's all point of view. Listen, when I was a young lawyer I defended a kid for ripping off a grocery store. The key piece of evidence was a felt hat. The prosecutor claimed my boy dropped it running out of the store. I tore up the prosecution, proved it couldn't be his hat, ate up the eyewitnesses, turned an open-and-shut case into a rout. After he was acquitted, the kid turns to me and says, 'Can I have my hat back now?' It bothered me so much that one night I was having dinner with a judge—who later became one of my best friends—and I told him what had happened. Know what he said? 'It wasn't your problem, it was the prosecutor's. Pass the butter, please.' "

She laughed softly. "So what's the lesson, Vail?"

Vail took a sip of wine and chuckled. "Nobody ever said life is fair—I guess that's the lesson, if there is one."

"That's a cynical response, Counselor."

"There are no guarantees. We give it the best we got no matter how good or bad the competition is. It isn't about winning anymore, it's about doing the best you can."

"I suppose we could practice euthanasia on all the bad lawyers in the world and try to even the playing field. That's the only way we'll ever approach true justice in the courtroom. Does it ever bother you, Martin? When you *know* the opposition is incompetent?"

"Nope, it makes the job that much easier. You're not going

through one of those guilt trips because you're successful, are you?"

"No," she said, but there was a hint of doubt in her tone.

"Janie, in the years you were a prosecutor, did you ever try someone you thought was innocent?"

She was shocked by the question. "Of course not!" she answered.

"Have you ever defended someone you thought was guilty?"

She hesitated for a long time. "I never ask," she said finally.

He held out his hands. "See, point of view. I rest my case." He lit a cigarette and leaned back in his chair. He watched her silently for a while.

"I think it's the Stoddard case," he said.

"What do you mean?"

"That's what all this yak-yak is about, the Stoddard case. You're having a problem."

"There's something wrong with the picture. Something doesn't make sense. This woman is forbidding me to defend her and I don't know why."

"We probably shouldn't even be discussing this. I'm sorry I brought it up."

"We both want to know what really happened that night in Delaney's penthouse, don't we?" she said.

"We know what happened."

A silence fell over the table, broken finally when Venable sighed. "You're right, we shouldn't be talking about it."

"I'll make a deal with you. When we're together, let's keep the law books on the shelf."

She smiled and raised her glass. "Sounds good to me," she said. She reached out with her other hand and stroked his cheek. He got up and moved to her side of the table and cupped her face in his hands, kissing her softly on the lips.

"How about dessert," she whispered between kisses.

"Later."

The phone rang.

"Let it ring," Jane said, her eyes closed, her tongue tapping his.

The machine came on. Vail recognized the familiar voice.

"Ms. Venable, this is Abel Stenner. Please forgive me for bothering you at home, but it's imperative we locate Martin Vail. . . ."

"Oh, Jesus," he moaned.

"When you get this message, if you know his whereabouts—"

"Talk about bringing the office home with you," she said.

Vail crossed to the corner of the kitchen counter and answered the portable phone. "Yes, Abel." He did not try to hide his exasperation.

"Hate to bother you, Martin, but Flaherty's back. We need to talk."

"What, *now*?"

"Yes, sir. And I think it's time to bring Jane Venable into it."

"Why?"

"You'll understand when we get there. I'd like to bring Harve and Dermott with me. I know it's an imposition, but it's very important."

"Just a minute." He held his hand over the mouthpiece. "I'm sorry to bring my business into your home, Janie, but Abel says he needs to talk to us both immediately."

"Both of us? What's the problem?"

He hesitated for a moment, then said, "It concerns Aaron Stampler."

"Oh my God," she said, her face registering a combination of curiosity and shock. Then: "Of course."

"Come on," Vail said, and hung up.

"What's this about, Martin?"

Vail told Jane about the Balfour and Missouri murders and their significance. She listened without a word, her eyes growing larger as he slowly described the details of the Balfour murder.

"It's the exact M.O. down to the bloody references on the backs of their heads. Harvey's getting the quotes from Rushman's books, which are now in the Newberry."

"How about Stampler?" was her first question.

"Still in max security Daisyland. As far as we know, he hasn't had any contact with the outside world for ten years."

"Is it a copycat killer?"

Vail shrugged. "Could be. A copycat killer could've discovered some of the quotes marked in those books. But *not* the part that Linda Gellerman played in the murders, that was never revealed in court. Did you ever show the tape to anyone?"

"Of course not. I erased it the day after the trial. How about you?"

"No. But the details *were* on the tapes Molly Arrington made during her interviews with Stampler."

"And where are they?"

"Probably in evidence storage at the warehouse."

"After all these years . . ." Jane said.

"Yeah." Vail nodded. "After all these years."

His face got very serious. "Listen, there's something I need to get off my chest. I've never told anybody this before. It's in the nature of client-lawyer confidentiality."

"What is it?" she asked, obviously concerned.

"Look, I spent a couple of months setting up the perfect defense for Stampler. Multiple personality disorder. Aaron was the innocent genius-boy, Roy was the evil twin doing the bad stuff. It worked. But that day, on the way out of the courtroom, Aaron—*Aaron*, not Roy, and I could tell the difference—Aaron turned to me with this funny, almost taunting, smile and said, 'Suppose there never was an Aaron.' And he laughed as they took him away to Daisyland."

"Oh, come on, it was probably his sick way of joking," she said with a shrug.

"Maybe. But what if he wasn't kidding? What if it was all a con job?"

"Come on, Martin, you were just lecturing me about having an attack of conscience. Did you think he was faking?"

"No. Nor did the psychiatrist, Molly Arrington."

"Then why worry about it? Besides, you can't tell anyone that. It *is* a confidential remark made by your client. You could be disbarred if you went public with it."

"What if he is directing these killings in some way?"

"That's pure hunch, Counselor. Based on incredibly circumstantial evidence. You need a lot more to go on than a chance remark, some circumstance, and an attack of conscience. Besides, you just told me he's in maximum security at Daisyland. Hasn't had any contact with the outside world in all these years. How could he do it?"

Vail shook his head. "I have no idea," he said.

"I just remembered something sweet, old Jack Yancey told me once. He said when he was a young lawyer he found out during the course of a murder trial that his client was guilty. He went to the judge and wanted to quit and the judge said no way, it would cause a mistrial and make a retrial impossible. Besides, it was confidential between Jack and his client. He was told to do the best he could and he did. He won the case, for a change, and his client took a hike."

"What did Yancey think about that?"

"All he said was 'Justice can't win every time.' So forget it, Counselor." She smiled and stroked his cheek.

Flaherty, St. Claire, and Stenner arrived a minute or so later, ending the conversation. They were properly apologetic.

"Good to see you again, Abel." Jane smiled and offered her hand. "It's been a long time."

"Read about you a lot," he said.

"This is Harve St. Claire and Dermott Flaherty," Vail said, completing the introductions. They moved the dishes off the dining room table and shoved the flowers back to make room for Flaherty's package.

"Nice flowers," Flaherty said, taking the reports and photographs from his shoulder bag. "Your birthday?"

Jane smiled. "Nope" was all she said.

"Have you filled Ms. Venable in, Marty?" Stenner asked.

"Up to Dermott leaving for St. Louis. What've you got?"

"Okay," Flaherty began. "First, there's no question in my mind that it's the same killer. Same M.O. as the Balfour kill." He spread some of the photos of Lincoln on the table. "Same variety of stab wounds, same mutilation we had with the male victims ten years ago. The messages on the backs of the heads . . ."

He hesitated for a moment and Vail looked at him and said, "Yeah? Go on."

"The victim was Alexander Lincoln."

Vail was surprised, although later he felt foolish that he hadn't guessed it sooner. "The last of the Altar Boys," he said.

"'Cept fer Aaron Stampler," St. Claire said.

"Could there be more than one person involved?" asked Jane.

"I think this answers that question," Flaherty answered. "This was in the box Alex Lincoln was delivering when he was murdered."

He handed a Polaroid photograph to Vail, who looked at it and whispered, "Jesus!" Jane took it from him and stared at it with disgust. It was a photograph of the bloody remains of Linda Balfour, her terrified eyes staring sightlessly at the ceiling.

"My God, who *is* this?" she asked.

"Linda Gellerman Balfour," said Flaherty. "Obviously taken immediately after the killer finished his work. You can actually see the blood spurting from the neck wound."

"So he or she *wants* us to know."

"That's right, ma'am. What we got here's a bona fidey serial killer at work."

"I want a twenty-four-hour guard on Jane starting right now," Vail said.

"Y'think he'll be after her?" St. Claire asked.

"Who the hell knows? He's cleaned out the Altar Boys, it seems logical he'll go after the principals in the trial next. I'll spend the night here for the time being. I can sleep in the guest room. That okay with you, Jane?" Vail's question was casual enough. Stenner didn't say a word. He leaned over and smelled the flowers, a move that did not go unnoticed by the rest of them.

"Whatever you feel is appropriate," Jane said innocently.

"It will certainly solve the logistical problem," said Stenner. "I can pick you both up in the morning and take you to work. We'll need two men assigned outside from nightfall until I come by in the morning, one in front, one in back."

"I'd suggest a man inside the house during the day, too, just in case the killer resorts to an invasion," said Flaherty.

"Good idea," Vail said.

"Might not hurt to have a man in your digs, too, Marty," added St. Claire. "Just in case this here killer decides to lay in wait there. Point is, it'd be nice to catch the son-bitch—excuse my French, ma'am—before he tries anything. Ambush him, so t'speak."

"Anybody else?" Vail asked.

"Shoat?" suggested Stenner.

"He's on the state supreme court now. Seems like a long shot," said Vail. "Warn him and let him take appropriate action if he chooses to."

"We may as well prepare ourselves," said Stenner. "Some people are going to think we're crazy."

"Let them," said Vail.

"How about the press?" asked Flaherty.

Vail scratched his jaw for a moment. "Just a matter of time before they put it all together. But let's not give them any help."

"Let's look at everything we know so far," Stenner said.

St. Claire looked at Jane and said, "The first message was the quote from *The Merchant of Venice*: And here's the latest message from the killer." He took out his notebook and flipped through the pages. "It's from *Hamlet*, first act, scene five:

> *"I could a tale unfold whose lightest word*
> *Would harrow up thy soul, freeze thy young blood,*
> *Make thy two eyes like stars start from their spheres,*
> *Thy knotted and combined locks to part,*
> *And each particular hair stand on end,*
> *Like quills upon the fearful porcupine."*

Nobody responded for a few moments, letting it sink in.

"Well, he's got classical taste, I'll say that for him," said Jane. "As I recall, ten years ago he quoted Hawthorne and Jefferson; now it's Shakespeare."

"He's already told some hair-raising tales," Vail said.

He suddenly remembered the tapes of Molly Arrington's interviews with Aaron/Roy. He was a storyteller, all right, in either persona. He remembered the angelic Aaron, describing an early experience in his peculiar Kentucky accent.

———

"When I was—like maybe seven r'eight?—we had this preacher, Josiah Shackles. Big, tall man, skinny as a pole with this long black beard down t'his chest and angry eyes—like the picture y'see in history books, y'know, of John Brown when they had him cornered at Harper's Ferry? Have you seen that picture, his eyes just piercin' through you? Reverend Shackles were like that. Fire in his eyes. He din't believe in redemption. You did one thing wrong, one thing! You told one simple lie, and you were hellbound. He'ud stare down at me, 'Look at me, boy,' he'd say, and his voice were like thunder, and I'd look up at him, was like lookin' up at a mountain, and he'ud slam his finger down hard toward th'ground and say, 'Yer goin' t'hell, boy!' And I believed't at th'time, I sure did. Reverend Shackles put that fear in me. Thair was no redemption r'forgiveness in Reverend Shackles' Bible."

———

Then Vail remembered something else, the images slowly seeping from his memory. It was the first time Roy had appeared during a taped interview with Molly Arrington. Aaron was off-camera and Molly was checking her notes. Suddenly she looked up. He remembered her telling him later that it had been as if all the air had been sucked out of the room. She gasped for breath. And then a shadow appeared on the wall behind her and a hand reached out and covered hers and a strange voice, a sibilant whisper, a hiss with an edge to it, an inch or two from her ear, said, "He'll lie to you." He was leaning forward, only a few inches from her face. But this was not Aaron. He had changed. He looked five years older. His features had become obdurate, arrogant, rigid; his eyes intense, almost feral, lighter in color, and glistening with desire; his lips seemed thicker and were curled back in a licentious smile. "Surprise," he whispered, and suddenly his hand swept down and grabbed her by the throat and squeezed, his fingers digging deeply into her flesh. "You can't scream, so don't even try." He smiled. "See this hand? I could twist this hand and break your neck. *Pop!* Just like that."

———

More chilling moments came back in a rush to Vail: Roy, finishing the Shackles story, no longer speaking in Aaron's curious west Kentucky patois, but in the flat, Chicago street accent of Roy, Aaron's psychopathic alter ego, although both were compelling storytellers.

"We were up at a place called East Gorge See. Highest place around there. It's this rock that sticks out over the ridge and it's straight down, maybe four hundred, five hundred feet, into East Gorge. You can see forever up there. Shackles used to go up there and he'd stand on the edge of the See, and he'd deliver sermons. Top of his fucking lungs, screaming about hellfire and damnation, and it would echo out and back, out and back. Over and over. He'd take Aaron up there all the time. That was the first time I ever came out. Up there. I had enough. He drags Aaron along, points down over the edge, tells him that's what it's gonna be like when he goes to hell, like falling off that cliff, and Aaron's petrified and then he grabs Aaron and shoves him down on his knees and starts going at him, like he was warming up before he started sermonizing. And when he started it was all that hate and hellfire and damnation, and all of it was aimed right at Aaron. So we ran off and hid in the woods watching him strutting around, talking to himself. Then he turns and walks back out to the cliff and he starts in again, yelling about how Aaron is hellbound, and how rotten he is. I sneaked down on him. Hell, it was easy. He was yelling so loud he didn't even hear me. I picked up this piece of busted tree limb and I walked up behind him, jammed it in the middle of his back, and shoved. He went right over. Wheee. I couldn't tell when he stopped sermonizing and started screaming, but I watched him hit on the incline at the bottom. I didn't want to miss that. He rolled down to the bottom and all this shale poured down on top of him—what was left of him. It was wild. All that shale buried him on the spot."

———

Vail should have known then, listening to that story. He should have known. . . .

And certainly later, when Roy had described the night Archbishop Richard Rushman was slaughtered.

———

"Aaron was by the door to the bedroom and then whoosh, *it's like the hand of God reaches down inside him and gives a giant tug and he turns inside out, and bingo, there I am. I had to take over at that point, he would have really screwed it up. I was thinking to myself, maybe this time he'll go through with it, but forget that. Not a chance. I hustled down the hall to the kitchen and checked the kitchen door. It was unlocked. I went outside on the landing and checked around and the place was deserted. I went back inside, took off my sneakers, and then got a Yoo-Hoo out of the refrigerator and drank it. My heart was beatin' so hard I thought it was going to break one of my ribs and the drink calmed me down. I opened the knife drawer and checked them out. The thick carving knife was perfect. Be like carving a turkey on Thanksgiving. I checked it and it was like a razor. I nicked my finger and sucked on it until the bleeding stopped. Then I went down the hall to the bedroom. He had the music way up.* Ode to Joy. *I could picture him standing in the bedroom directing that air orchestra of his. Shoulda been a goddamn orchestra conductor, maybe we never would've met him. That's just what he was doing. He had candles burning—cleaning the air, he called it— some kind of incense. His ring was lying on the table beside the bed. He always took his ring off before he took a shower. He left his watch on, I guess it was waterproof, but he took his ring off. Make sense out of that. So there he stood, the fucking saint of the city. His naked Holiness, conducting that imaginary band of angels. The music was building. I thought,* Now it's your turn. *So I went over and got the ring and put it on. His Excellency was out of it. Arms flailing around, eyes closed, unaware. I just walked up behind him and tapped him on the shoulder with the knife and he turns around and I thought his eyes were going to pop out of his head when he saw the knife. He got the message real fast.*

I held out the hand with the ring on it and pointed the knife at it and he begins to smile. So I jabbed the knife toward the carpet and that wiped the smile off his face. He got down on his knees and I wiggled that ring finger under his nose. The bishop slowly leaned forward to kiss the ring and I pulled away my hand and I swung that knife back with both hands and when he looked up, whack, I swung at his throat. I yelled 'Forgive me, Father!' but I was laughing in his face when I said it. He moved and I didn't catch him in the throat, the knife caught his shoulder and damn near chopped the whole thing off. He screamed and held out his hands. I don't know how he even raised up that one, but he did. I started chopping on him, but I kept hitting his hands and arms. Then I cut his throat switched and swung the knife up underhand right into his chest. It was a perfect hit. Didn't hit any ribs, just went right in to the hilt and he went, 'Oh,' like that, and he fell straight back and the knife pulled out of my hand. I had to put my foot on his chest to get it out. Then I took that big swipe at his neck. I couldn't stop. It was like free games on a pinball machine. Blood was flying everywhere. I know every cut I made, they were all perfect. Thirty-six stab wounds, twelve incised, seventeen cuts, and one beautiful amputation. I counted every one."

"Oh yeah," Vail sighed, half aloud, "Stampler certainly can tell some stories that will make—how did Shakespeare put it?—'each particular hair stand on end like the quills of a porcupine'?"

"Close enough," said St. Claire. "Question is, who's he talkin' to? Martin? Jane? I mean, who's this here serial killer leavin' messages fer, anyways?"

"Stampler was never a serial killer," said Stenner. He ticked off his points on his fingers. "He didn't pick his victims at random, he hid the crimes, he didn't collect what are known as totems—trophies from the scene of the murder."

Vail nodded in agreement. "When you look back at Stampler's killing spree, which lasted almost ten years, all the victims were individuals whom he thought had done him harm—and, arguably, they did. Shackles, the born-again madman, tossed over a cliff—the body was never found; his brother and ex-girlfriend, made to look like an accident; the hospital attendant in Louisville, cremated and the ashes thrown away."

"Then you have Rushman, Peter Holloway, and Billy Jordan," said Stenner. "That's when he started leaving symbols. Following a specific M.O."

"But he didn't hide the bodies and he didn't take totems," said Flaherty. "This new killer, he follows the M.O. to the letter, *but* he does remove items from the victim. Linda Balfour had a stuffed dolphin. It's missing. Same with Alex Lincoln's belt buckle. And the victims were meant to be found. So there are variables here."

"So what yer sayin', this here new fella *is* a serial killer," said St. Claire.

"Enjoys it," Stenner offered. "Gets off on the killing. Aaron, Roy, whichever, killed for personal reasons. Anger, revenge, getting even for past hurts. This new one, he's killing for motive *and* the joy of it."

"And Stampler's providing the motive," said Flaherty.

"You don't think Roy enjoyed it? He certainly enjoyed describing the murders," said Vail.

"But he had a specific motive fer everyone he killed," said St. Claire.

"These last two were specific victims," said Flaherty.

"Not *his* victims, Stampler's victims," said Jane.

"If Stampler's figgered out a way to trigger this here killer, what we got, we got a killer enjoys the killin' and Stampler providin' the victims," said St. Claire.

"Maybe it isn't that. Maybe it is a copycat killer. There was a composite tape of all Molly's interviews. It was the tape that was only shown in Shoat's chambers—to Jane and the judge."

"A moment I'm not likely to *ever* forget," she interjected.

"That tape is in evidence storage. I never got it out. Maybe somebody stumbled across it, maybe the tape is the trigger. The whole story's on that one tape."

St. Claire sighed. "Well, here I go back to the warehouse. Talk about the needle in the haystack."

"I'm guessing, sooner or later, Mr. X is going to start picking his own prey," Vail said.

"I don't know," said Jane. "Stampler could still have a few more victims on his list—you, me, Shoat. . . . Maybe that's our edge."

"What do you mean?" Flaherty asked.

"She means he's going to go after the other principals in the trial," Stenner answered softly. "Jane, Martin, Shoat . . ."

"Include yourself," Vail said to Stenner. "You were a powerful witness."

"Well, it isn't our case," said Stenner. "Gideon police are ignoring it. St. Louis has juris over the Lincoln murder."

"So the question is, who's he gonna hit next?" St. Claire said.

"And where?" said Flaherty.

"And how in God's name did he *find* these people?" Jane asked. "Gideon, Illinois? Wherever, Missouri? How did he track them down?"

"And if Stampler is involved, how the hell is he doing it?" Flaherty said.

"Hell, maybe we'll get lucky," said St. Claire hopefully. "Maybe St. Louis'll nail this nutcase 'fore he works his way back here. That's what we're all thinkin', ain't it? That he's comin' here?"

"I think we have to assume this killer is heading here," said Vail. "Maybe he's here already."

He felt Jane's hand brush against his. It was trembling and he took it gently in his and squeezed it reassuringly.

"I still remember that day in court when he came over the railing of the witness stand and grabbed me," she said. "It was those eyes. A moment before he grabbed me I looked into those eyes and . . ."

"And what?" Vail asked. "What did you see?"

"They turned red for just an instant. It was like . . . like they filled with blood. I've never seen such hate, such malevolence. I still dream about those eyes."

Suddenly Vail was no longer interested in the conversation. He stared into his coffee cup, thinking about Linda and Alex, about the Altar Boys and Bishop Rushman. All had been Stampler's friends and he had turned on them. Vail had been his friend during the trial and he was sure that this madness was being directed at him. He remembered Stampler's words again.

"Suppose there never was an Aaron."

Stampler hadn't been joking that day, Vail was more certain of that now than ever before. And if Stampler had been cool enough and smart enough to trick all of them before, he was smart enough to figure out how to orchestrate these murders from inside Daisyland. Vail was no longer concerned about *why* Stampler was doing it or whether he, Vail, was responsible in some way for the madness. Stampler had to be stopped. And as long as he was safely tucked away in the mental institution, they had to focus on his accomplice.

Catch the accomplice, turn him against Stampler, and end it once and for all. And the accomplice was near, Vail was certain of that.

He had run out of victims everywhere else.

22

Vail snatched up the car phone and punched out a number. Paul Rainey's smooth voice answered. "Paul Rainey speaking."

"It's Vail. Where is he, Paul?" Vail demanded.

"I, uh . . . I can't, uh . . ." Rainey stammered.

"You can't put your *finger* on him, right? Like you couldn't put your *finger* on him last night."

"It's no big deal, Marty, he doesn't know there's paper out on him. Probably fishing or hunting. He's been through a lot."

"So has his wife," Vail snapped back. "You're acting pretty damn cavalier for a guy with a murder-one warrant in his pocket and a client on the run."

"He's not on the *run*, damn it!"

"You accepted service, Paul. I'm putting out an APB on him."

"Another four hours, Marty. I'll have him there by noon."

"Four hours for what, a tutor session? What's it going to be? He was sexually abused by his mother and took it out on his wife, or he was afraid she was going to cut off his dick because he was running around with Poppy Palmer? The Menendez or the Bobbitt defense?"

"Damn you!"

"Get off it, Paul, don't pull that indignant shit on me, I've known you too long. We're going to find him. *And* Poppy Palmer while we're at it. And the deal's off. He's going to get the needle. Goodbye."

Vail hung up. He looked at St. Claire and Stenner. "Darby turned rabbit, I can tell. I could hear Rainey sweating over the phone."

St. Claire rubbed his hands together very slowly, stared out the window for a few seconds.

"I want a search warrant for the entire farm," Stenner said, keeping his eyes on the road. "We've checked airlines, buses, car rentals, trains. Nothing so far on the stripper."

"You think he off'd her, don'cha?" asked St. Claire. When Stenner nodded grimly, he said, "Well, it ain't like he's not up to the task."

"And he thinks he's off the hook," Stenner said.

"Unless Rainey's got 'im in tow, maybe workin' up a new yarn to get by the shot sequence."

Vail shook his head. "No, I don't think Rainey's up to anything. He accepted service of the warrant. If he hides Darby, he could be disbarred. The case isn't worth it to him. He's got to be thinking we have more than just the tape and he knows Darby hasn't a sou to his name. You two better get started as soon as you drop me at the airport."

"Yeah." St. Claire snickered. "It's almost eight-thirty. Day's half over."

———

He was totally bald with a tattoo of a lizard down the middle of his skull, its tongue arched down his forehead. The sleeves of a Hawaiian shirt were rolled up tightly against his health club biceps, from which other tattoos formed a tapestry of daggers, names, and pierced hearts down to his wrists. His pants were belted by a braided leather thong tied in a sailor's knot just below his belly button. In place of a toothpick, he had a ten-penny nail tucked in one corner of his mouth while a silver tooth gleamed from the other side. He was checking the stock behind the bar.

At ten in the morning, the bar smelled of stale cigarette smoke, old sweat, and spilled beer. A sliver of sunlight slanted through the front door, revealing an unswept floor littered with cigarette butts, wadded-up paper napkins, and dirt. Stenner held up his ID.

"I'm Major Stenner, Chicago D.A.'s office. This is Lieutenant St. Claire."

"Major. Lieutenant. A lotta weight fer two guys," the bartender answered with a lopsided grin.

"Is the manager around?"

"Lookin' at him. Mike Targis."

He shook hands as if he was trying to inflict pain on the two cops.

"Yer lookin' fer Poppy, I told you people all I know. She split day before yesterday, didn't even come by, called it in."

"What time was this?"

"I dunno, lessee . . . One, maybe, one-fifteen."

"She have any money coming?"

"Yeah. Three days, three bills."

"She sneezed off three C's, she was in that big a hurry?"

Targis shrugged. "Easy come . . ."

"Does she have a car?" Stenner asked.

"Whaddya think? She pulls down three, four K a month in tips, plus a hundred a day salary. She's my big attraction, gents. A red Mustang ragtop, last year's model."

"Know the tag number?"

Targis gave St. Claire a sucker look. "No, and I don't know the motor number either."

"Know where she lives?"

"Sure. Fairway Apartments, over near the golf course. Straight down 84 two miles. Can't miss it. This is about the Darby thing, right?"

"Do you know anything about it?" Stenner asked.

"Only what I read in the papers, if you can believe that."

"You don't?"

"What, that Calamity Jane–Wild Bill Hickok shootout? Shit."

"That's just a guess, right?"

"Oh, yeah, man."

"Did Poppy talk about it at all?"

"You kiddin'?" He leaned across the bar and lowered his voice even though they were the only people in the room. "She was scared shitless."

"Of what?"

"Everything. The cops. You guys. Big Jim."

"That's what you called Darby, Big Jim?"

"That's what Poppy called him. Everybody else picked up on it. A guy leaves a dollar tip after drinkin' for four hours? Big Jim, my ass. But who can figger women, y'know? Poppy's smart, got a figger'd give a statue a stiff, looks like Michelle . . . What's her name?"

"Pfeiffer?" said Stenner.

"No, the other one. Used to be a canary."

"Phillips," St. Claire said.

Targis jabbed a forefinger at him. "That's the one."

"Did she ever mention this sister of hers before?" Stenner asked.

"Uh, maybe once'r twice."

"So you didn't get the idea they were real close?"

"I didn't get any idea at all. I don't give a shit about her sister. I got enough trouble with my own family."

"Thanks, Mr. Targis," Stenner said, handing him a card. "If you think of something, give us a call."

"Is she on the lam or sompin'?"

"We just want to talk to her."

"I thought you already did."

"We forgot a coupla things. She happens to call in, give her that name and number, okay?"

"She ain't gonna call in. I been in this business almost twenty years, I know a goodbye call when I hear one and that call from her was definitely a goodbye call."

"Maybe she'll call about the three hundred you owe her."

He shook his head as he took out a towel, held it under the spigot, then twisted it damp and started cleaning the bar.

"It mattered, she'd a come by and got it. Had to drive right past the front door on her way to the interstate."

"That's what she told you, she was *driving* out to Texarkana?"

"Didn't say. I just figgered she drove down to O'Hare."

"Thanks."

"Sure. Come back later and have a drink. On the house."

"Thanks, Mike, you're a real gent."

On the way out the door, St. Claire said, "Targis is an ex-con."

"How do you know?"

"He's about ten years behind in his vernacular. Besides, I know everything, I even know who Michelle Phillips is."

"Mamas and the Papas," Stenner said, opening the car door. St. Claire stared at him with disbelief. "I wasn't always fifty, Harve."

They got in the car and headed back to Darby's farm to see how the search was going.

———

The chopper swerved off the main highway and swept down over the town of Daisyland. From the air, it was a modest village surrounded by old Victorian houses hidden among oak and elm trees. As the chopper headed north of town, the residential area became sparse and then quite suddenly the trees ended and the Stevenson Mental Health Institute appeared below them, a group of incompatible though pleasant-looking buildings separated from the town by tall, thick hedges and the brick wall that surrounded the place. Two new wings adjoined the older, rambling main structure of the hospital. Together they formed a quadrangle. Vail could see people moving about, like aphids on a large green leaf. Vail remembered one of the structures from his visits a decade earlier—a three-story building with a peaked atrium, its slanted sides constructed of large glass squares. Maximum security—Stampler's home for the past ten years.

Down below, in one of the buildings facing the quadrangle, a man watched the chopper *chunk-chunk-chunk* overhead. He was pleasant-looking, verging on handsome, and husky, his body tooled and hardened in the workout room, and he was dressed in the khaki pants and dark blue shirt of a guard. He had intense blue eyes with blondish hair trimmed just above the ears, was clean shaven, and smelled of bay rum aftershave lotion. There was just the trace of a smile on his full lips. He stood with his arms bent at the elbows, his fists under his chin, his fingers intertwined except for the two forefingers that formed a triangle that pressed against his mouth. His attention was pure, focused intently on the chopper. He watched it veer off and disappear beyond the trees. Finally he said, in a voice just above a whisper:

"Welcome, Mr. Vail."

And his smile broadened.

"You say something, Ray?" a voice said from the hall.

"No, Ralph, just hummin' to myself," he answered. His voice was like silk. He sat down at the worktable and went back to work.

As the chopper fluttered down on a large practice football field near the institution, a black, four-door Cadillac pulled down the service road and parked. The chopper settled lightly on the ground, its blade churning up dust devils that swirled around it.

"You could land on eggs, Sidney," Vail said, flipping off his safety belt and opening the door.

"You say that every time," the pilot answered.

The driver of the sedan was a trim man in his late thirties with an easy smile. He wore khaki pants and a dark blue shirt and did not look like a guard, which it turned out he was.

"I'm Tony," he said, opening the rear door. "I'm here to run you over to the Daisy."

"The Daisy? They call it the Daisy?"

"Yeah," Tony answered, holding the door for him. "Daisyland wasn't stupid enough."

Vail slid in and Tony slammed the door. The drive took five minutes. As they approached the sprawling complex, the large iron gates rolled back and Tony drove through and headed up a gravel road bordered on either side by knee-high winter shrubs. Vail felt vaguely uncomfortable. Perhaps subconsciously, he thought, he was afraid they would keep him there. Or, more likely, he did not look forward to seeing the unfortunate patients locked away from the world in the place cruelly known as the Daisy.

———

For Shana Parver, the objective of the deposition was to get as much information on the record as possible, enabling her to stand tough on a plea bargain. She was certain that Stoddard would never go to court and Venable would be maneuvering to get in the best position for a deal. She was partly right.

Jane Venable had to defend a client who did not want to be defended and maneuver into position for the best plea bargain she could get. Venable had to, at the very least, convince Edith Stoddard to let her continue to whittle away at and weaken Parver's case. Getting Stoddard to recant the confession was a big step. Now, hopefully, she could prevent Stoddard from incriminating herself during the Q and A with Parver.

They had a few minutes together before Shana Parver arrived. Edith Stoddard was brought to the interrogation room in the annex by a female guard who stood outside the door. Stoddard looked wan, almost gray, her mouth turned down at the corners, her eyes deeply circled. She was wearing a formless blue dress without a belt and white, low-cut tennis shoes. Her hair was haphazardly combed. Wisps of gray and black dangled from the sides and back.

"How are you this morning?" Venable asked.

"I'm not sure" was Stoddard's faint, enigmatic answer.

"This won't take long," said Venable. "Just a formality."

"When is it going to be over? When are you going to make whatever deal you're going to make?"

"This is part of it, Edith. I'd like to make a good, solid showing here today. It will help when we discuss your plea."

Stoddard shook her head in a helpless gesture.

"She's going to go big on the gun, Edith. I'm not going to ask you where you lost it or even *if* you lost it. When she asks about it—about losing the gun, I mean—be vague. Also she's going to bear down on where you were the night Delaney was killed. Just remember, the less Shana Parver knows, the better."

"Why can't you just tell her . . . why can't you do whatever it is you want to do? What do you call it?"

"Plea bargain."

"Just do it today. Get it *over* with, please."

"Please trust me. Let me set things up right."

"I just want it to end."

"I understand that, Edith. But let me do my job, too. Okay?"

Stoddard's shoulders sagged. She took several deep breaths.

"Good," Venable said. "You'll do just fine."

Shana Parver, dressed in a teal silk pantsuit, her black hair cascading down her shoulders, arrived a few minutes later with a stenographer, a tall, slender, pleasant-looking woman from the courthouse named Chorine Hempstead. There were pleasant "Good mornings" and offers of coffee from Hempstead, which everyone but Edith Stoddard gratefully accepted. She sat beside Jane Venable and across the table from Parver, her hands folded in front of her. She reminded Parver of a frightened bird.

Parver dropped a bulging shoulder bag on the floor, opened her briefcase, and took out a legal pad, a sheaf of notes, several pencils, and a small Sony tape recorder, all of which she placed on the table. Hempstead brought back the cups of coffee and sat at the end of the table with a shorthand tablet and waited.

"Are we ready?" Shana asked pleasantly, arranging in front of her her notes and those taken by Shock Johnson the day Stoddard had suddenly blurted out that she killed John Delaney.

"Let's get on with it," Venable said tersely.

"For the record," Parver began, "I would like to state that this is a formal interrogation of Mrs. Edith Stoddard, who is charged with first-degree murder in the death of Mr. John Farrell Delaney on February 10, 1994, in the city of Chicago. I am Shana Parver, representing the district attorney of Cook County. Also attending are Ms. Jane Venable, representing Mrs. Stoddard, and Chorine Hempstead, a clerk of the Cook County Court, who will transcribe this meeting. This interrogation is being conducted in the court-house annex, nine A.M., February 16, 1994. Mrs. Stoddard, do you have any objection to our tape-recording this meeting?"

Stoddard looked at Jane Venable.

"No objection," Venable said.

"Good. Please state your full name for the record."

"Edith Hobbs Stoddard."

"Are you married?"

"Yes."

"What is your husband's name?"

"Charles. Charles Stoddard."

"How long have you been married?"

"Twenty-six years."

"And where do you live?"

"At 1856 Magnolia."

"Do you have any children?"

"I have a daughter, Angelica."

"How old is she?"

"Twenty-one."

"Does she live at home?"

"She goes to the university. She lives in a dorm there, but she has a room at the house."

"Is that the University of Chicago or the University of Illinois?"

"Chicago. She's a junior."

"And you support her?"

"She has a small scholarship. It covers part of her tuition and her books and lab fees, but I—we—pay for her room and board and other necessities."

"How much does that run a month?"

"Five hundred dollars. We give her five hundred a month."

"And you have a full-time nurse for your husband?"

"Not a nurse. We have a housekeeper who attends to Charley, cooks meals, keeps the place clean."

"Do you have separate bedrooms, Mrs. Stoddard?"

"What's that got to do with anything?" Venable asked.

"A formality," Parver answered casually.

"We have adjoining bedrooms," Stoddard answered wearily. "I keep the door cracked at night in case he needs something."

"You work at Delaney Enterprises on Ashland, is that correct?"

"I did," Stoddard said with a touch of ire.

"And how long does—did—it take to get to work every day?"

"Thirty minutes or so. Depends on the traffic."

"You drive then?"

"Yes."

"How long did you work for Mr. Delaney?"

"Seventeen years."

"And you were his personal secretary?"

"Executive secretary was my title," she said proudly.

"And how long did you hold that position?"

"Nine years."

"In that position, did you have occasion or occasions to go to Mr. Delaney's apartment in the Lofts Apartments on Astor Street?"

"Yes."

"Frequently?"

"Yes. He liked to work there, away from the bustle of the office. I frequently took files, letters to sign, or took dictation over there."

"And did you have a key to that apartment?"

Venable started to object to the question, then thought better of it and kept quiet.

"Yes."

"Where is that key now?"

"I, uh, it's on my key ring with my other keys."

"And where are they?"

"The police took them when they arrested me."

"So the police have the key now?"

"Yes."

"Now, Mrs. Stoddard, I want to ask you about the gun. You do own a gun, do you not?"

"Yes."

"What caliber?"

"It's a .38."

"Make?"

"Smith and Weston."

"You mean Smith and Wesson?"

"I guess. Yes."

"Where did you acquire this gun?"

"The Sergeant York gun store on Wabash."

"Do you recall when you purchased it?"

"It was about a month ago. I don't remember the exact day."

"How much did you pay for the gun in question?"

"One hundred and thirty-five dollars."

"Why did you buy a gun?"

"For protection."

"Did you carry this gun with you all the time?"

Pause. "Yes."

"You seem uncertain, Mrs. Stoddard."

"I was. I was trying to remember if I ever left it home. I don't think I did."

"Where did you carry it?"

"I just told you, everywhere."

"No, I mean, where did you keep the gun when you were carrying it?"

"In my purse."

"And when you were at the office?"

"In my middle desk drawer on the left side. I locked it."

"And at night?"

"Under my mattress."

"In your bedroom?"

"Yes."

"Where is this weapon now?"

"I, uh, lost it."

"How? I mean, if you kept it in your purse and you locked it in the desk drawer and you kept it under the mattress at home, how did you manage to lose it? Is there a possibility that somebody stole the gun from your drawer at work?"

"I don't think . . . Maybe."

"So what happened to the gun?"

"I guess maybe . . . it must have fallen out of my purse."

"Was this after you shot Delaney?"

"Objection. Come on, Counselor, there's been no admission—"

"We have Mrs. Stoddard's confession—"

"Which she has recanted, as you well know. It was given under duress, she was emotionally disturbed at the time . . ."

"Did you lose the gun after Delaney was killed, Mrs. Stoddard?" Parver said, cutting off Venable's objection.

"I still don't like the question. I would prefer that you ask her when she lost it."

"All right, Mrs. Stoddard, when did you lose the gun in question?"

"I'm not sure. I first noticed it when I got home from work Thursday night."

"That was the night Delaney was killed, was it not?" Parver looked at Venable and raised an eyebrow.

"Yes," Mrs. Stoddard said.

"Now, Mrs. Stoddard, did you know anything about guns when you purchased this Smith and Wesson .38?"

"No."

"Did you take lessons?"

"Yes, that's right, I took lessons."

"To become proficient in its use, right?"

"Yes."

"And where did you take these lessons?"

"On Pershing Street, the Shooting Club."

"How proficient did you become, Mrs. Stoddard?"

"That's a relative question, Counselor. Would you rephrase, please?"

"Relative to what?" Parver demanded.

"Mrs. Stoddard has already stated that she knew nothing about guns. She has no point of reference for a comparison."

"Mrs. Stoddard, did you stop taking lessons?"

"Yes."

"Why?"

"The instructor told me I was good enough."

"Everything, right? Loading, cleaning it, shooting?"

"Yes."

"And you became good enough to discontinue the lessons, is that a fair statement?"

"I guess so."

"Did the instructor agree that you didn't need any further lessons?"

"Yes."

"And you purchased bullets for this weapon?"

"Yes."

"Do you know how many bullets you bought?"

"Two boxes."

"How many bullets in a box?"

"Fifty."

"And did you keep your gun loaded?"

"Yes."

"How many shells did it hold?"

"Six."

"And where do you keep the remaining shells?"

"On a shelf in my bedroom closet."

"Is that closet locked?"

"No. Why would I—"

Venable gently laid her hand over Stoddard's and shook her head, but Parver chose to ignore the comment. She opened her briefcase and took out a gray piece of paper that was folded over twice. She opened it up and laid it on the table in front of Stoddard.

"Mrs. Stoddard, this is a target we obtained from the Shooting Club. You left it behind the last day you were there and they saved it. They assumed you would be back in from time to time to practice and they thought you might like to keep it."

Venable looked down at the target, which was the customary black human silhouette on white background normally used in target ranges. There were six bullet holes, all tightly grouped in the area of the heart.

"Do you recognize the target, Mrs. Stoddard?"

"That could be anyone's target, Counselor," Venable snapped. "All targets look alike."

"They don't all have your client's name and the date written on the bottom," said Parver. She pointed to the two lines scribbled in one corner. "They did this to identify it for her."

"Then I guess it's mine," Stoddard said.

"That's from twenty-five yards, Mrs. Stoddard. You're pretty good."

Edith Stoddard didn't answer immediately. Finally she shrugged. "Most of the people at the range are that good."

"What kind of purse do you carry, Mrs. Stoddard?"

"It's a Louis Vuitton. Just a standard purse."

"That's the one about eight inches long and four or five inches deep, right?" Parver said, measuring out the general dimensions in the air with her hands.

"I guess."

"And what do you normally carry in it?"

"What's the relevance of this?" Venable asked.

"Bear with me, please," Parver said without changing her tone. She reached down to the floor and put her bulky leather bag on the desk. It was jammed with stuff. "This is my purse, Mrs. Stoddard," Parver said, and laughed. "As you can see, I've got everything in here but a set of the *Encyclopaedia Britannica*."

Edith Stoddard's face softened slightly and a smile flirted briefly with her lips.

"Was your purse jam-packed like mine?"

Stoddard chuckled. "I can't imagine having that much to carry in a purse."

"So your purse was fairly neat and uncluttered, would that be a fair assessment?"

"Yes. My wallet, checkbook, keys, Kleenex. Sometimes a paperback, if I was reading one. I sometimes read while eating lunch."

"Mrs. Stoddard, do you have any idea how much your gun weighed?" Parver said, checking through her notes.

"No."

Parver hesitated a moment, then turned a page. "One pound six ounces loaded," she said. "Enough to be noticeable when you were carrying it in that small, uncluttered purse, wouldn't you agree?"

"I . . . suppose so," Stoddard said cautiously.

"What I mean is, this gun was for your protection, isn't that what you said?"

"Yes."

"So wouldn't it be natural to be aware of the weight, know it was there in case of trouble?"

"Objection. She carried the gun for three weeks. More than enough time to become accustomed to the weight."

"Uh-huh. Now, Mrs. Stoddard, you say you put the gun in your desk drawer and locked it. Can you recall for me the last time you specifically remember putting the gun in that drawer?"

"Come on, Counselor, she was upset, distressed over—"

"Mrs. Stoddard, when were you were informed you were being retired?" Parver said, cutting off Venable.

"On Thursday."

"You had no idea before that?"

"There was nothing official."

"I didn't ask you that. Did you have any indication, prior to Thursday morning when Delaney replaced you, that you would be leaving?"

"There were rumors. There are always rumors."

"And when did you first hear these rumors?"

"You know how rumors are, you don't remember when you hear a thing. I don't even remember who said it."

"Had this been going on for a while? The rumors, I mean?"

"She just told you, Counselor, she doesn't know when they started," Venable said. "I'm going to intercede here. You're dealing in hearsay. Also it's immaterial—"

"On the contrary, Ms. Venable, it's quite material. Some of the other employees say it's been fairly common knowledge—that Delaney was planning to replace Edith, I mean—since just after Christmas. That's two months."

"I am advising my client not to answer any more questions related to what she may or may not have heard or when she may or may not have heard it or who she may or may not have heard it from. She's already told you, she heard it from Delaney last Thursday morning. That's when it became a fact of life for her."

"Mrs. Stoddard, on Thursday morning when Delaney told you he was replacing you, what was your immediate reaction?"

"I was, uh, I was shocked and, uh, I guess angry . . . upset, confused . . ."

"Confused?"

"I wanted to know why. All he said, all he *ever* said was, 'Edith, it's time for a change.' My whole life was . . . Everything was turned topsy-turvy in just a few minutes because it was . . . it was *time for a change.* Yes, I was upset and confused and angry. I was all those things!"

"When was the last time you saw Delaney?"

"He told me I would be paid for two weeks and I could have until Friday to clean out my things. I think the last time was when he left for lunch Thursday."

"The day he was killed?"

"Yes."

"And Friday was to be your last day?"

"Yes. I guess he thought my replacement could learn the job over the weekend and be ready to start Monday morning." She stopped for a moment and looked down at her hands, folded on the table in front of her. "Sorry, that was sarcastic of me. I'm sure she had been working with Mr. Delaney for weeks, maybe months."

"So now tell me, when was the last time you specifically remember locking the gun in your desk drawer?"

"I guess it was Wednesday."

"So Thursday you kept the gun in your purse, is that it?"

"Objection. She has already stated that she doesn't remember. She's guessing it was Wednesday."

"So you don't remember whether you had the gun Thursday or not?"

"That's what she said, Counselor."

"I just want to clarify, as closely as possible, when she lost the weapon."

"It was Thursday," Stoddard said suddenly. "I remember putting it in my purse Thursday when I left the house. I'm just hazy about what I did with it after that. It was a very upsetting day. People coming up, telling me they were sorry. That kind of thing."

"So let's recap for a minute. You bought the gun, took lessons, became proficient in its use"—Parver tapped the target lying on the table—"and carried it in your purse for protection. At the office you locked it in your desk drawer and at night you kept it under your mattress. The last time you remember seeing the gun was when you put it in your purse Thursday when you left for work. Then you got to the office and Delaney called you in and retired you. And you don't remember anything about the gun or its whereabouts after that. Is that correct?"

"Yes."

"Good. Now let's get to Thursday. Tell me in your own words what you did that day and evening—up until you went to bed that night."

"After Mr. Delaney told me, gave me the news, I went outside. There's a little picnic area behind the building. People eat lunch there, go outside to smoke, you know, a nice little place to take a break. And I sat outside for a while. I don't know how long. I think . . . I may have . . . I guess I cried. It was such a shock, finally realizing it was true, and I was trying to get my wits together—"

"Excuse me, Mrs. Stoddard, I'm sorry to interrupt, but you just said, 'It was such a shock, *finally realizing it was true.*' So you were aware of the rumors, weren't you?"

"Objection," Venable said sternly, "that's a conclusion on your part."

Parver's voice remained calm. "Not *my* conclusion, Counselor. She has admitted she heard the rumors—"

"She hasn't admitted a damn thing!"

Parver turned back to Edith Stoddard. "You had been hearing these rumors, had you not?"

"Don't answer that," Venable snapped.

"I . . . I . . ." Stoddard stammered.

"All right," Parver said softly, "we'll move on. You were saying you were trying to get your wits together?"

Stoddard, rattled, began dry-washing her hands. She licked her lips and said weakly: "Yes, uh, trying to, you know, I have a full-time housekeeper for Charley during the day and my daughter is going to the university and she lives at the school and, uh, I was . . . I don't know how long I sat out there. Some of the people came out and talked to me, told me they were sorry. Finally I just couldn't take it any longer, so I went back upstairs and got a box and started getting my things together. One of the women, Mr. Delaney asked one of the women to sit there, you know, when I gathered up my things, I guess so I wouldn't . . . wouldn't *steal* anything. I really didn't keep many personal things in the desk, anyway."

"Did you have anything in that middle desk drawer on the left? The one you kept locked?"

"No, there were mainly backup disks from the computer and some confidential files of Mr. Delaney's."

"But you did check it?"

"Yes."

"Was the gun in the drawer when you checked it?"

"I, uh . . ."

"We've been over this," Venable said. "She said she doesn't remember where the gun was."

"I realize that. But she was getting her personal things together and she checked that drawer, and certainly if the gun was in there she would have removed it since it was a personal item. Isn't that true, Mrs. Stoddard?"

"She says she doesn't remember!"

"Can she answer the question, please? Mrs. Stoddard, did you take *anything* out of the drawer of a personal nature?"

"She . . . doesn't . . . remember," Venable snapped.

"Well, what *did* you remove from the desk?"

"Some makeup. A Montblanc pen that was a Christmas gift. Uh, uh, some photographs of my family. A dictionary. I can't . . ."

Stoddard looked helplessly at Venable and started to shake her head. Her hands were trembling. Venable could see she was losing it, beginning to fall apart.

"Can we move on, Shana?" said Venable. "What she took from the desk is really immaterial. She was obviously distraught . . ."

Parver leaned back and turned off the tape recorder. "Would you like to take a break?" she asked.

"I want to get this over with," Edith Stoddard said in almost a whisper.

Parver pressed the record button again.

"I left the office early. At lunchtime. And I drove around a while. I drove into the city, to Grant Park, and sat by the fountain for the longest time."

"Was that the Great Lakes Fountain?"

"Buckingham."

"So you sat by Buckingham Fountain and just cleared your mind?"

"Tried to. I just stared out at the lake."

"Where did you park?"

"The indoor parking deck by the art institute."

"Is it possible someone could've broken into your car while you were over by the fountain?"

"Nobody broke into my car. It was locked and nobody broke into it."

"How long were you in the park?"

"I don't know. I got cold and left after a while. An hour, maybe."

"Then what?"

"I went over to the gift shop at the art institute and bought Angel a shoulder bag."

"Angel, that's what you call your daughter?"

She nodded. "It was one of those canvas bags to carry her books in. I remembered that hers was . . . it was pretty worn and she had mentioned she needed a new one and I went into the institute to get warm and I remembered that, so I went to the gift shop and bought it. Twelve dollars."

"It cost twelve dollars?"

"Uh-huh. And at four o'clock I went to the lab on Ellis Street—Angel has lab on Thursdays—and waited for her and we went across the street to the bookstore and had coffee and I gave her the canvas bag, and, uh . . . and then I, uh . . . I told her what happened and she was . . . she was so very . . . upset."

Stoddard's voice broke and she stared down at her lap.

Parver snapped off the recorder again, reached into her overstuffed bag, and slid a box of Kleenex across the table to her.

"Thank you."

She dabbed her eyes and blew her nose and then straightened her back and nodded. Parver started the recording machine.

"You see, she has this scholarship, but it's not enough to . . . She studies very hard, A average, and maybe she'd have to get a job and she got furious over that, so we left and I took her back to the house. She cried all the way home. It was very traumatic. So sad. She didn't want to see any of her friends. So I suggested that she spend the night at home."

"She has her own room?"

"Yes. I didn't tell my husband that night. He had a rather bad day and . . . Oh, what was the use? Why make the day worse for him? Our day lady had already fed him. We weren't hungry. He had already dozed off. So I took Alice up to the bus stop about five-thirty . . ."

"Alice is the housekeeper?"

"Yes. Alice Hightower. Been with us since the accident. And I went home. Angel had cried herself to sleep on her bed and I decided not to disturb her, so I went down to the living room and fixed myself a drink and turned on the TV, but I left the sound off. I was exhausted, too. And I guess I dozed off."

"What time was this?"

She shrugged. "Six or so. It was dark."

"And what time did you wake up?"

"I guess it was, I don't know, I didn't really notice, maybe ten, ten-thirty. Diane Sawyer was on the TV when I turned it off. I went upstairs and woke Angelica up and told her to get undressed and then I went to bed."

"So between, say, six and ten or ten-thirty, Charley was asleep in his room and Angelica was asleep in her room and you were asleep in the living room. Is that correct?"

Edith Stoddard nodded.

"And nobody saw you?"

"No."

"Nobody called? You know, to tell you they were sorry about your leaving?"

"No."

"Nobody called Angelica?"

"No."

Parver looked at Jane Venable, but she was busy taking notes on a yellow legal pad and did not look up.

"So your husband and your daughter can't account for your whereabouts during that period of time—between six and ten-thirty, I mean?"

Stoddard looked at her and her face clouded up. "Leave them out of this," she said, her voice suddenly becoming strident and stern. "They don't know anything, don't drag them through the mud!" She glared at Venable, her eyes watery, her lips trembling. "I told you—" she began, but Venable quickly cut her off.

"All right," Venable said. "That's enough for today. I'm advising my client to end this right now."

"I have a few more—"

Venable slapped her hand on the table and the sharp smack startled both Parver and Stoddard. "I said enough!" Venable said. "She told you about the gun and she told you where she was that night. That's all we've got to say for now."

"I just have one more question," Parver insisted, looking back at her notes.

"Make it quick and to the point," Venable said edgily.

"When did you first hear that Delaney was dead?" Parver asked softly.

Stoddard looked at her for several seconds, then said, "I heard it on the radio on my way to the office."

Bang! Parver's strategy had paid off. She turned to Shock Johnson's notes.

"I'd like to read something from Lieutenant Johnson's report of his first meeting with you at Delaney Enterprises last Friday, Mrs. Stoddard, and I'm quoting, 'Mrs. Stoddard, Delaney's executive secretary, was obviously very upset over the death of Delaney and was dressed in black and had a mourning ribbon on her sleeve.' Unquote.

"If you had just heard about Delaney's death on the way to your office, Mrs. Stoddard, why were you already dressed in mourning clothes?"

23

As Tony guided the Cadillac up to the main building of the Daisy, Vail saw a tall man sitting on a wooden bench beside the stairs to the administration office. He was filling a pipe, tapping the tobacco down with a small silver tool with a flat, circular tamper at the end of its stem. He seemed totally engrossed in the task, twisting the pipe between his fingers, stopping to study the tobacco, then packing it even tighter.

"That's the chief of staff, Dr. Samuel Woodward," Tony said. "Big muckety-muck. He's waiting to greet you officially."

"No band?" Vail said.

Tony laughed. "They only let them out on Fridays," he said.

As Vail got out of the car, Woodward stood. He was taller than Vail had guessed, six-three or four, and was dressed casually in dark brown corduroy pants, a pale blue button-down shirt, open at the collar, and a black alpaca cardigan, one of its side pockets bulging with a package of tobacco. He was a lean man with the gaunt, almost haunted face of a long-distance runner. His close-cropped, dark red hair receded on both sides to form a sharp widow's peak and he wore a beard that was also trimmed close to his face. He dropped the pipe tool in the other pocket of his cardigan and held out a hand with long, tapered, aesthetic-looking fingers.

"Mr. Vail," he said, "Dr. Sam Woodward. It's a pleasure. Sorry I wasn't here to take your call the other night."

"My pleasure," Vail said.

"It's such a pleasant day I thought we might stroll around the grounds and chat," he said in a soft, faraway voice that sounded like it was being piped in from someplace else. "No smoking inside the buildings. I quit cigarettes about six months ago and thought I'd taper off with a pipe. Instead of getting lung cancer, my tongue will probably rot out. You smoke?"

"I'm thinking about quitting."

"Ummm. Well, good luck. Ferocious habit."

He took out a small gold lighter and made a production of lighting his pipe. The sweet odor of aromatic tobacco drifted from its bowl. Vail lit a cigarette and tagged along with Woodward as he walked down the sidewalk that bounded the broad, manicured quadrangle formed by several buildings.

"I must say I'm curious as to why, after ten years, you should suddenly come back into Aaron Stampler's life," Woodward said. "You never even been to visit him."

"I don't make a practice of seeing any of my old clients when a case is over. It's a business relationship. It ends with the verdict."

"That's rather cold."

"How friendly are you with your patients, Doctor? Do you go to visit them after they're released?"

"Hmmph," he said, laughing gently. "You do go to the point, sir, and I like a man who goes to the point, says what he thinks, so to speak. That's rare in my business. Usually it takes years carving through all the angst to get to the baseline."

"I suppose so."

"So why are you here?"

"Curiosity."

"Really? Having second thoughts after all these years?"

"About what?"

"Come, come, sir. Now that you're a prosecutor, the shoe is on the other foot, so to speak. I have always found that all prosecutors think MPs are faking it."

"Hell, Doctor, he convinced me. I saved his life."

"And do you regret that now?"

The question took Vail by surprise and he thought about it for a moment before answering. "I don't . . . No."

"It is hard, isn't it? Accepting the absurdities of the mind."

"That's what you call it? Absurd?"

"Well, to the average person, yes. Absurd. Ludicrous. Preposterous. Crazy. It's very easy to label anything we don't understand or like or accept as fake or insane. Insanity is what I call a phrase of convenience, nothing more than a medical description. Multiple Personality Disorder, on the other hand, ah! Now there we have a recognized mental disease, defined in DSM 3, accepted by the profession, one of the true mysteries of the human condition."

"DSM 3, that's your bible, as I recall."

"True, sir, absolutely true. Catalogs and defines over three-hundred mental disorders. The *Gray's Anatomy* of the mind."

"Now that you've brought it up, what does DSM 3 say about faking it?"

Woodward stopped. He did not look at Vail; he stared straight ahead and took several puffs on his pipe.

"I assume, sir, this is in the realm of an academic question. By that I mean nonspecific."

"Of course. Generic."

They walked down the sidewalk and then Woodward led Vail out across a broad expanse of lawn bordered by the buildings. From one of the buildings, Vail heard a muffled scream, a howling that quickly changed to laughter and then died away. If Woodward heard it, he made no acknowledgment of the fact. There were several inmates in the quadrangle, one pacing frantically back and forth, waving his hands and screaming silently to himself; another standing against a tree, his face a few inches from the bole, talking intently in tongues; another strapped in a wheelchair, his mouth hanging askew, his eyes half open and unfocused, staring at infinity. It was hard for Vail to ignore these human aberrations. Woodward was right. As sympathetic as Vail felt toward these unfortunate souls, they did seem strange, absurd, and ludicrous and he felt embarrassed for thinking about it.

"It's acceptable to stare, Mr. Vail. Natural, in fact. They'll just stare back. You probably seem as bizarre to them as they seem to you."

He nodded to a patient, who was picking imaginary flowers, and she smiled and nodded back.

"As to your question—about faking multiples—I presume it could be done for a short period of time. I seriously doubt that it could be sustained for very long. Too much involved, you know. My God, changing one's entire posture, body language, voice, general appearance, personality, attitude, persona. Virtually impossible to pull off over a protracted time period."

"You said *virtually* impossible."

Woodward smiled condescendingly. "Hah! Forgot I was talking to a lawyer. Virtually impossible, yes, I did say that, didn't I? Well, sir, I suppose nothing is absolutely impossible anymore, technology being what it is. But I would say the chances of winning the lottery are far, far, *far* more likely than faking MPD."

"Is Aaron Stampler capable of doing it?"

Woodward stopped again, this time staring at Vail hard before he answered. "If he is, I wouldn't know it. Good lord, man, he was diagnosed as a dissociated multiple personality by your own psychiatrist. You were the one who uncovered this problem, Mr. Vail. Now ten years later you drop out of the sky and start raising questions. Questions that, in effect, could destroy eight years of hard work and incredible research? No, this man is not acting. This man is not faking it."

"I'm just asking, Doctor. We're just talking."

They strolled farther, Woodward puffing on his pipe, obviously deep in thought.

"Do you dream, Mr. Vail?" he said finally.

"Rarely."

"But you do dream?"

"Occasionally, yes."

"You're in another place, another dimension, and you wake up and suddenly you're in a totally different place"—he snapped his fingers—"just like that. Right?"

"Well, sometimes . . ."

"Instant displacement."

"You're saying dreams are a form of losing time, Doctor? That's what Aaron called it when he went into a fugue state and changed to Roy, losing time."

"It's a common expression used by anyone who suffers fugue events. Let me put it another way. Say you drift into a nap in the middle of a concert, next thing you know the concert's over, everybody's leaving the amphitheater. Would you call that losing time?"

"I'd call it boredom."

Dr. Samuel Woodward laughed. "That's because you're normal," he said. "Normal, of course, being a relative term. The point is, a fugue is losing time. Usually not for long, a few minutes. Five, I would say is average. It can occur over a period of years—its victims, understandably, are usually afraid to talk about it. Of course, everyone who experiences a fugue event isn't necessarily a multiple, you understand."

"How did you end up with Aaron?" Vail asked.

"That calls for a bit of biography, not that I want to bore you. I graduated from Harvard, interned at Bellevue, did my residency at Boston General, and then I was five years in psychiatric emergency at Philadelphia Memorial. I loved it. You saw everything, something new every day. That's when I first became fascinated by multiple personalities—MPs. From Philly, I went to the Menanger. And at Menanger I began to specialize in MPD. In fact, I've written several papers on the subject. When they offered me the position here, I jumped at it, and Aaron Stampler was one of the lures."

"What made him so different?"

"Everything, sir, everything. His background, his intelligence, the nature of his crimes, cause and effect. Absolutely fascinating case. I had read the reports prepared by Bascott, Ciaffo, and Solomon, as well as Dr. Arrington's summary. There were only two personalities involved. He hadn't splintered off into five, six, or a dozen, so it was a chance to deal with the disease on a relatively elementary level. A challenge. And—most important of all—he had not been treated. A lot of interrogation, therapy sessions, that sort of thing, but no attempt to treat the disease. Put it all together? Irresistible!"

He paused for a moment to relight his pipe, then: "I also read the trial transcript. Quite a legal feat, sir. The trial, I mean."

"I'm not sure whether that's meant to be a compliment or not."

"Oh yes, a compliment by all means. Back in those days, using the MPD defense was quite daring."

"It was a sticky problem—whether the jury would buy it or not. In court, the truth sometimes can be detrimental to the health of your client."

"Is that why you settled it in chambers?"

Vail suddenly felt cautious. The question triggered his paranoia for a second or two. *Did Woodward know Stampler had been faking it all along?* Vail wondered. Was he in on the game or had Stampler conned him, too? Vail quickly decided that Woodward had bought in to Stampler's malevolent trick.

"No," Vail answered. "The prosecutor triggered him. That's what put it into Judge Shoat's chambers."

They walked a little way in silence, then Woodward said, "Frequently, the initial reaction to multiple personality disorder is disbelief and rejection." He paused for a moment, then added, "And you're correct, sometimes the less the public knows about some things, the better."

"I've often wondered who really killed the bishop, Aaron or Roy," Vail said. "What I mean is, Aaron provided the motive, but Roy did the killing. Legally, a case could be made against Aaron for conspiracy to commit murder, possibly aiding and abetting."

"I disagree, sir, most heartily. They were two different separate and distinct personalities. Aaron didn't *consciously* conspire to kill the victims. In point of fact, he was as much a victim as the victims themselves."

Vail thought about that for a moment and nodded. "Good legal point," he said.

"From the beginning of his treatment, I had to deal with Aaron and Roy as two different people," Woodward said. "The same heart, different souls, if you believe in the soul."

"I believe in the conscience. I suppose they could be considered the same."

Woodward didn't respond to Vail's comment; he kept talking as if he was afraid he would lose his train of thought.

"What do you remember about the mind, Mr. Vail? About the superego and the id?"

"Not much. The superego is like the monitor of our morals. The id is where all those repressed desires go."

"Very succinct and relatively accurate, sir. When the wall between the id and the superego breaks down, the repressed desires become normal. Suddenly the idea of murder becomes normal. The mind is disordered—that's the disease—murder is just a symptom. In a manner of speaking, Roy was Aaron's id. Aaron repressed everything, Roy repressed nothing. If Aaron hated someone, Roy killed them."

"A very convenient arrangement when you think about it," said Vail.

"It's meant to be. That's one of the reasons human beings create other personalities, the pain becomes unbearable so they invent something to alleviate it. Look, Mr. Vail—"

"Call me Martin, please."

"Martin, I've been Aaron Stampler's shrink, confessor, friend, doctor—his only companion—for the last eight years. He was a classic mess when I came on board. Phobia, disassociation, alienation, religious disorientation, sexual disorientation, my God, sir, Aaron had them all! He feared the dark, hated authority, distrusted his elders, dismissed his peers, was sexually confused." Woodward stopped and shook his head. "Did you ever hear him talk about what he called the hole, the coal mine his father forced him into?"

Vail nodded. "The first time I ever interviewed him. Shaft number five, I'll never forget it. Creepy, crawling critters and demons."

"What was that?"

"Creepy, crawling critters and demons. That's what he told me was waiting for him at the bottom of the shaft. That I do remember quite vividly."

"That hole might very well be the symbol for everything in life that he dreaded. The dwelling place of his disobedient dreams. You see, when you look at Aaron, you see a madman. When I look at him, I see a person with a disease. And from the very first day I arrived, I regarded him as curable."

Vail looked at him incredulously.

"Why do you find that hard to believe? You saved his life."

"Couldn't let them kill the good guy just to get to the bad guy, Doctor."

"*Touché*," Woodward said with a laugh. Then his mood immediately became serious again. "In point of fact, my entire professional attitude changed because of Aaron Stampler. The belief that mental illness is a disease of the mind that can be treated with talk therapy was losing credibility when I started working with him. The new thing, the new kid on the block, was biological psychiatry."

"That's a mouthful," Vail said, just to keep his hand in.

"Well, you know what they say, we in the medical profession can't say hello in less than five syllables."

"And lawyers can't pronounce anything with more than one."

"Ha! Very good, sir, very good, indeed."

"You were talking about biological psychiatry."

"Yes. It theorizes that mental illness is caused by a chemical imbalance in the brain, that it can be medicated. So you had—still have—polarized viewpoints. Cure by talk or cure by pills. I was of the old school, a talker—old habits die hard, as they say—but I decided to go into the Stampler case with an open mind, to try everything and anything."

Woodward waved his arms around, clicked off numbers on his fingers, closed his eyes, lifted his eyebrows as he rambled on.

"The list seemed endless at times. Thorazine, Prozac, Xanax, Valium, Zoloft, Halcion. We have bezodiazepines, which are addictive, and Haldol to treat hallucinations and delusions. There are antipsychotic drugs and antidepressants and antianxiety drugs, and I tried them all, every damn one that I felt was applicable. I tried behavioral therapy, recreational therapy, occupational therapy. I tried shock treatments. . . ."

He stopped and lit his pipe again, each draw making a gurgling noise, and blew the smoke toward the blue sky.

"And I spent two hours a day, five days a week, for eight years with Aaron. Nobody, sir, *no*body knows him as I do."

Woodward began talking intimately about Aaron Stampler, a rambling discourse that brought back, in a rush, details that Vail had forgotten. Woodward described Stampler as a misplaced child who had grown into a gifted but frustrated young intellectual, his accomplishments scorned by a stern and relentless father determined that the boy follow him into the hell of the coal mines. His mother considered Aaron's education akin to devil's play; a boy to whom the strap and the insults of his parents had done little to discourage him from a bold and persistent quest for knowledge. That quest was abetted by a sympathetic schoolteacher, Rebecca, who saw in the lad a glimmering hope that occasionally there might be resurrection from a bitter life sentence in the emotionally barren and aesthetically vitiated Kentucky hamlet, and who ultimately seduced him. Aaron was a loner, attracted to both the professions and the arts, who had wanted—as do most young people at one time or another—to be lawyer, doctor, actor, and poet—but whose dreams were constantly thwarted by everyone except his mentor, Rebecca.

And Woodward talked about the schoolteacher who appeared to be Crikside's only beacon, a lighthouse of lore and wisdom in an otherwise bleak and tortured place; a woman whom some of the townsfolk regarded as a necessary evil; a woman who threatened the bigotry of their narrow and obdurate heritage, a notion possibly vindicated by Rebecca's "education" of Aaron Stampler. And finally he talked about the sexual liberation of Aaron

Stampler, first by Rebecca, then later in a perverse and tormenting way by the pedophile, Bishop Rushman.

"It's easy to understand how this could have happened, considering what we know about Aaron's childhood and teen years. The simplified assumption was that Aaron created Roy to assume the guilt and responsibility for acts that Aaron couldn't perform himself. He transferred his guilt to Roy. As I said, this is an oversimplification of a very complex problem. We're dealing with the human mind, remember. The science isn't as obvious as DNA or fingerprints, which are unequivocal."

"Look, Dr. Woodward, I wasn't in any way demeaning your—"

"I understand that. I just want *you* to understand that work with him isn't a twice-a-week gabfest. This young man has dominated my professional life. I'm not complaining, it has also been most rewarding. But just achieving transference with him took three years."

"Transference?" Vail said.

"A form of trust. When it works, the patient comes to regard the analyst as a figure from the past, a parent or a mentor, somebody they relate to. Trust is transferred from the mentor to the therapist."

"You just said Aaron transferred his guilt to Roy. Is this the same kind of thing?"

"Yes. He simply created his own avenger. There is a downside, there always is. It creates a subconscious fear that old injuries and insults will be repeated—what we call reexperiencing. Fear of reliving pain from children, friends, husbands, wives, just about anybody."

"So all the pain is transferred from past to present?"

"Everything. Pain, anger, frustration, unreasonable expectations. But it is important because it permits us to make connections between the past and the present. Drugs can ease the fear. And, of course, at times the pain."

"What's the ultimate objective, Doctor? What did you call it, the baseline?"

"Free association. Encouraging the subject to concentrate on inner experiences . . . thoughts, fantasies, feelings, pain. Hopefully creating an atmosphere in which the subject will say absolutely everything that comes to mind without fear of being censored or judged."

"How does that help you?" Vail said.

"Well, what you're getting is their mental topography, like a roadmap to their secrets. They remember things from the deep past—traumatic events, painful encounters—very clearly, reexperience the fears and feelings that go with them. And, we hope, learn to accept them. Doesn't always happen, of course. Ours is not a perfect science like mathematics, where two and two always equals four. No, no, sometimes when dealing with the human mind two and two equals eight or twelve. . . ."

"Or one?"

"Or one—or a half. In Aaron's case, remembering some of the horrible acts committed by Roy and learning to deal with the knowledge was the product of reexperiencing and free association."

"So you *have* made progress?"

Woodward stopped, knocked the dead embers from his pipe into a trash barrel, and stuffed the pipe in his cardigan pocket. "I would say so," he said. "I want you to meet someone. His name is Raymond Vulpes."

"Who's Raymond Vulpes?"

"The only other person alive who knows—as do I—every intimate detail of the lives of Aaron and Roy."

They walked across the yard to what was known as MaxSec. The first thing Vail noticed was that the windows had no bars, they were made of thick, bulletproof glass. It was an attractive-looking structure and obviously built to provide the most pleasant circumstances possible. Maximum security was at the end of a long, wide hallway that connected it to one of the wards in the newer wing. There was an office off to one side of the hall with a wire-mesh door and Woodward led Vail to it, took out a bunch of keys, unlocked the door, and entered. As Vail stepped through the doorway, he was instantly seized with an overwhelming sense of evil.

The air seemed suddenly to be sucked out of the room.

A wet, icy chill swept through it.

The hair bristled on the back of Vail's neck.

Gooseflesh rippled up his arms.

Sweat burst from the pores in his forehead—a frigid sweat, like water dribbling down the torso of a melting snowman.

He shivered spasmodically.

He unconsciously gasped for air.

And then it was over.

Vail was rooted in place for a moment, as if his legs had suddenly atrophied.

What was it? A rampant chimera let loose by his imagination?

A subconscious fear of the uncharted and unpredictable minds in this community of the deranged?

An omen of some kind?

He quickly regained his bearings, wondering if Woodward had had the same reaction. But it was obvious that Vail had been the only one who had experienced . . . whatever it was. They were in a fairly confined space, an electronic repair shop littered with TVs, VCRs, oscilloscopes, and computers lined up on workbenches and tables and further cramping the limited space.

A man in his mid to late twenties leaned over a worktable in a corner near the room's single window. A gooseneck lamp curved down beside his face, its light revealing the insides of a dismantled computer. He had the smooth, muscular build of a swimmer, dark blond hair, and pale eyes, and he was wearing the khaki pants and dark blue cotton shirt of a guard, the shirt's sleeves hitched halfway to his elbows. He looked up as Woodward and Vail entered the room and grinned, a wide, boyish grin, full of straight white teeth.

"Mr. Vail, I'm Raymond Vulpes," he said, sticking out his hand. "Can't tell you what a great thrill it is to meet you."

Vail took the hand and looked into Vulpes's face and in that moment realized that he was shaking hands with Aaron Stampler.

24

Caught off guard and shocked, Vail stepped back from Vulpes and turned to Woodward, who was leaning against a bench, smiling. For an instant he thought perhaps this was a perverse joke; that they were all mad and Woodward was the maddest one of all; that when Vail tried to leave, they would slam the doors and trap him inside with the other lunatics.

"I wanted you two to meet," Woodward said casually. "We're going to the visitor's suite, Raymond. I'll send Terry up for you in a few minutes."

"Fine, I have to finish changing a couple of chips in Landberg's machine."

"Excellent."

"See you then, Mr. Vail," Vulpes said, flashing another million-dollar grin as they left the repair room.

"What the hell's going on?" Vail asked as Woodward locked the door.

"Recognized him, eh?"

"Ten years hasn't changed him that much. He's a lot heavier and he seems to be in great shape."

"Works out an hour a day. Part of the regimen."

"What regimen? Is this some kind of bizarre joke?"

"Joke? Hardly. Relax, Martin, all in good time."

MaxSec was sealed from the hallway and the rest of the ward by a wall with a single, solid, sliding steel door. The security officer, a skinny young man named Harley, smiled as Woodward and Vail approached. He pushed a button under his desk. The heavy door slid open. Harley waved them in without bothering with the sign-in sheet.

The wide hallway continued inside the steel-guarded entrance. Light streamed in through the glass-paneled roof. The walls on both sides were lined with locked rooms. There was moaning behind one of the doors, but the hall itself was empty. Woodward led them into the first room on the right.

The room contained a small desk with two chairs, a padded wooden chair, a table and a TV, and a cot. The window was five feet above floor level. The entire space and everything in it—walls, furniture, and floor—was painted pure white.

Vail remembered the room. Except possibly for a slight rearrangement of the furniture, it had not changed in ten years.

"Is this, uh, what's his name again?"

"Raymond Vulpes."

"Is this his room?"

"No, no, this is the visitor's suite, as we jokingly call it."

"So they have visitors here."

"Yes. Patients in max are not permitted any visitors in their quarters, so we provide this homey little visitor's room. They're not permitted to associate with other patients, either."

"Can't they talk to each other?"

"No, sir. Sounds a bit medieval, I know. The reason, of course, is that they are in various stages of recovery. Social intercourse could be disastrous."

"I should think total isolation would be just as disastrous."

"There are people around," Woodward said with a shrug. "Therapists, security people, some staff. It's not solitary confinement. And they can spend an hour or two a day outside."

"They just can't communicate with each other?"

"Quite right."

"So Aaron hasn't had any communication with the outside world in ten years?"

"You mean Raymond."

"Raymond, Aaron," Vail said with annoyance.

"It's an important, even crucial distinction. Sit down, Martin. I hope that what I'm about to tell you will give you a sense of pride."

"Pride?"

"You had a part in it. Had it not been for you, Raymond would never have existed. The host would certainly have been dead by now, either by electrocution or terminal injection."

"Who *is* Vulpes?"

"Raymond is what is known as a resulting personality."

"A what?"

"Resulting personality. Roy was a resulting personality. Now Raymond is one."

"So Aaron's split into a third person?"

"Yes and no. He's certainly a third person. However, the others no longer exist. It's not a unique case, although it well might become one."

"How?"

"If we've stabilized Raymond. By that I mean he won't split again. They usually do."

"Where did Raymond come from and when?"

"He was created to mediate the problems between Roy and Aaron. He first appeared almost three years ago."

"Who created him?"

"Aaron was always the host."

"Another escape mechanism?"

"Not an escape. An alternative. Another form of transference. As I explained to you, transference is the conscious or subconscious mirroring of behavior patterns from one individual to another. This also applies to personae in a split personality. It's a form of denial. The schizoid places guilt on another individual, in this case, a new person—*voilà*, Raymond."

"Voilà." Vail said it with obvious distaste. "What if Roy had transferred to Raymond instead of Aaron?"

"It wouldn't have happened. Raymond didn't want that. Abhorrent behavior patterns can be mirrored only to individuals who would normally accept the transference."

"In other words, the receiver must be capable of such behavior to begin with?"

"Correct. Raymond doesn't need Roy, never did."

"And Aaron transferred to you, right?"

"Yes. That was a major breakthrough, I might add. It was not an easy transition. My strategy was to appeal to his need to be appreciated by his supervisors. That was what attracted him to Rushman. Aaron had transferred his need—as a child—for approval from his parents to the bishop. My problem, of course, was Rushman, who had betrayed that trust. Aaron didn't trust me for several years. The advantage, of course, is that Roy would come out, so I got to deal with both of them. Then when Raymond emerged, the transference was complete. Aaron and Roy eventually disappeared."

"And now you have Raymond, the perfect specimen."

Woodward was surprised by the remark. He nervously stroked his beard with both hands, then said, "There's no need for sarcasm, Martin. He'll be down in a minute. Talk to him before you judge him."

"I just mean it sounds like Raymond encompasses all the best of Aaron—his intelligence, his dreams, desires . . ."

"Exactly. Aaron always saw himself as an innocent victim. He had no control over Roy. He couldn't even communicate with him. I was the pipeline between them."

"There were two tapes. Do you know about them?"

"You mean the Altar Boys tapes?"

"You *do* know about that."

"Of course."

"Both the original and one copy were erased by mutual agreement with the prosecutor."

"Why?"

"To protect the Catholic church. Rushman was dead, the case was resolved. It wasn't necessary to drag all that up."

"That was very civilized of you two. I'm not sure it was in my patient's best interest."

"Why not? You could always get the information from the horse's mouth. I assume Roy went into detail about those events."

"That's true," Woodward agreed.

"Let's get back to Raymond. Where did the name come from?"

"That's what he called himself the first time he appeared. I said, 'Who are you?' and he said, 'I'm Raymond Vulpes.' "

"So Roy dominated Aaron and Raymond dominated Roy."

Woodward nodded. "Aaron never did confront either Roy or Raymond directly. As I said, I was the pipeline. But when Raymond appeared, I was able to bring both Raymond and Roy out. It was absolutely fascinating, watching them switch back and forth. They would interrupt each other, argue, an incredible clash of the two egos. And Raymond was as normal as you or I. His ego and id were all in the right places—he was totally in control. He completely frustrated Roy. Put him in his place. Roy was impotent in Raymond's presence."

"How about Aaron?"

"He stepped out of it and left Raymond to deal with Roy."

"How convenient."

"Understandable. Raymond isn't pained. Raymond didn't go through the agonies of reexperiencing; Aaron did. And what Aaron ultimately came to terms with—from all that pain— Raymond learned from him. Raymond could step back, study the clash between Aaron and Roy objectively, rationally. He accepted Aaron and Roy as one, not as a split personality. The horror that Aaron had to deal with did not infect Raymond. Raymond was capable of happiness. Raymond was, and is, everything Aaron wanted to be. So Raymond took over and ultimately destroyed Roy—and, incidentally, was perfectly happy to be rid of both of them."

"I'll bet," Vail snapped. "So you can't bring either one of them out anymore?"

"Precisely. For the past eighteen months, Raymond's been psychologically stable. No fugue events, no more appearances by either Aaron or Roy. In fact, for the last several months, Raymond
has rarely mentioned them. He's become far more interested in
the present and the future than the past."

"What you're telling me is that Raymond Vulpes is sane?"

"As sane as we are. In this case a very troubled teenager has
been replaced by a charming, educated, intelligent man. A
charming fellow with a genius level IQ and a remarkable memory. He's rational, well-adjusted, has a stunning spectrum of
interests. We're good friends, Raymond and I. We play chess
together, discuss movies and books—he reads incessantly, everything from textbooks, magazines, fiction, nonfiction, how-to
books. His thirst for information is unquenchable." Woodward
stopped and smiled.

Looking at Woodward's smug, self-satisfied grin, Vail's uneasiness toward him changed to contempt. When he talked about
Raymond, Woodward sounded like a modern Frankenstein who
had taken Aaron's skin and bones and fashioned them into a human being of his own design.

"My question was, has he had visitors, communication, letters,
phone calls, *anything* from the outside world?" Vail asked.

"Basically, no. We have had, in the past few months, visiting
doctors who have come to observe what we've done with him.
Always, of course, in concert with members of the staff. It's purely
academic. Q and A, no social involvement whatsoever."

"No phone calls?"

"Who would call him? He hasn't received a letter, not even a
postcard, in a decade."

"And he doesn't correspond with *anyone*?"

"To tell you the truth, Martin, I don't think there's anyone
Raymond *wants* to correspond with. Look at it this way: He knows
a great deal about his past, but not everything. He knows enough
to understand what happened to Aaron and why Roy appeared.
Some things don't interest him. I suppose in a way you could
compare Raymond to an amnesiac. He's learned enough about his

past to be comfortable with himself. He doesn't need or want to know any more."

Woodward stood up and walked to the door. "I'll send Max to get him," he said. "Excuse me for a minute."

Vail took out a cigarette and toyed with it. Everything Woodward said seemed perfectly logical. It was medically plausible, not even that uncommon. It all made perfect sense.

Sure it did, Vail thought. Here was a psychotic madman living comfortably in an insane asylum, where he has convinced all the doctors that he has been miraculously transformed into a real sweetheart named Raymond Vulpes, who was perfectly sane.

Talk about the inmates running the asylum.

Vail didn't believe a word of it. And he was prevented from discussing Aaron's remark after the trial by the rules of confidentiality.

A few minutes later, Max entered with Vulpes. He was still smiling, but his joviality had been replaced with a subtle caution.

"Anybody care for something to drink?" Max asked pleasantly.

"I'll have a Coke," Vulpes said. He was standing on the opposite side of the table facing Vail.

"Evian for me," Woodward said.

"Coke sounds good," Vail said. They sat down, Vail and Vulpes facing each other and Woodward at one end of the table, like the moderator on a talk show.

Vail did not know what to say. Congratulations on your new persona? Welcome to the world, Raymond? Whatever he said would be hypocritical at best.

"Well, you wanted to meet Raymond. Here he is," Woodward said proudly.

"You'll have to forgive me, Raymond," Vail said, "I'm a bit overwhelmed by miracles of science."

The smile faded from Woodward's face. Vulpes did not react at all. There was still a hint of the smile on his lips. His eyes bored into Vail.

"Most are," Vulpes said. "The doc is doing a book on me. Could win him a Pulitzer Prize, right, Sam?"

"Well, we'll see about that," Woodward said, feigning modesty.

"It seems strange to me," Vail said. "For instance, you just appeared. Don't you ever wonder who your mother was?"

Without hesitation Vulpes said, "My mother was Mnemosyne, goddess of memory and mother of the nine muses." Then he chuckled.

Woodward laughed. "Raymond has a wonderful sense of humor," he said, as if Vulpes was not in the room.

Vail said, "And you simply got rid of Roy?"

"Let's just say he had enough," Vulpes said. "He retired."

"So what did you learn from Roy and Aaron?"

"Well, Roy wasn't as intelligent as Aaron, but he was a hell of a lot smarter."

"You mean street-smart?"

"I mean he wasn't naïve."

"And Aaron was?"

"You know that."

"Do I?"

"The way you ambushed that prosecutor, what was her name?"

"Is that what Roy said? That I ambushed her?" Vail said without answering the question. Vulpes knew damn well what her name was.

"That's what *I* say."

"Really."

"I've read the trial transcripts. And Roy told me you played it just right. Started to ask about the symbols, then backed off. No wonder they called you a brilliant legal strategist."

"Did Aaron and Roy ever talk about killing the old preacher . . . uh, I can't think of his name, it's been ten years."

"Shackles."

"Shackles, right."

"Roy bragged about that one, all right. They really hated that old man."

"That's an understatement," Vail said.

Vulpes almost smiled and nodded. "Guess you're right about that. He was their first, you know."

"So I heard."

"Why, hell, Mr. Vail, you probably know more about the two of them than I do."

"Oh, I think not."

Their eyes met for just a second. Nothing. Not a blink, not a flinch. *It's the eyes,* Vail thought. *His eyes don't laugh when the rest of his face does. They never change. Ice-cold blue.*

"How about the others? Did he talk about them?"

"You mean his brother and Aaron's old girlfriend, Mary Lafferty?"

"I'd forgotten her name, too," Vail said.

Vulpes looked him directly in the eye. "Lafferty," he repeated, "Mary Lafferty."

"Oh yes," Vail said.

"Actually, Roy also talked about Peter Holloway and Billy Jordan," Vulpes said. "The Altar Boys."

Vail stared into Vulpes's barren eyes, devoid of everything but hate. Bile soured his throat as his mind darted back ten years to the night he had found the devastated remains of the two young men. The flashback was a collage of horrors: the dark, ominous, two-story lodge framed by the moon's reflection rippling on the lake; fingers of light probing an enormous den in the basement, a sweeping fireplace separating it into two rooms; a large raccoon racing past Vail followed by the rats, flushed by the light, squealing from behind a sofa; a hand rising up from behind the sofa, its fingers bent as if clawing the air, the flesh dark blue, almost black; the rest of the arm, a petrified limb stretched straight up, and then the naked, bloated torso; the face, or what was left of it, swollen beyond recognition, the eyes mere sockets, the cheeks, lips, and jaw gnawed and torn by furry night predators, the gaping mouth, a dark tunnel in an obscene facsimile of something once human; the throat sliced from side to side, further mutilated by the creatures that had feasted upon it; and the stabs, cuts, and incisions and the vast sea of petrified blood, black as tar, and the butchered groin. And the fossilized corpse next to it—a smaller version of the same.

I am responsible for this human ghoul, he thought. It took a moment for him to regain his composure and go on with the confrontation.

"So you discussed the Altar Boys," he said finally

"Of course, that's what it was all about, right?"

"It was all about a lot of things. How about Alex, did they discuss Alex with you?"

"Alex?"

"Lincoln. Alex Lincoln?"

"Lincoln." Not a glimmer when he spoke Lincoln's name. "You mean the other Altar Boy? I don't recall Roy ever said much about Lincoln."

If the eyes are a window to the soul, Vail thought, *Raymond has no soul.* Aaron may have passed on his IQ and his fantastic memory to Raymond Vulpes, and all that sweetness and light, but he hadn't passed on his soul because Aaron had had no soul to pass on.

"How about Linda? Did anyone talk about her?"

Vulpes stared out the window for a moment, then said, "Gellerman. Her name was Linda Gellerman. Aaron had a warm spot for her, even though she ran out on him."

"He said that, that she ran out on him?" Vail asked.

"Perhaps I'm paraphrasing," Vulpes said.

"Did Roy ever tell you the last thing he said to me?"

Vulpes stared at him blankly, then slowly shook his head. "I don't think he ever mentioned it. What was it about?"

"Nothing, really. An aimless remark. Kind of a joke."

"I'm always up for a good laugh."

"Some other time, maybe."

Vulpes's jaw tightened and he sat a little straighter. "Must've been pretty good for you to remember it after ten years."

"You know how it is, some things stick in your mind."

Woodward sensed the animosity growing between the two. "Raymond, tell Martin about your first trip downtown," he said.

This time it was Vail's jaw that tightened. He stared across the table at Vulpes and their eyes locked.

"You've been outside?" Vail asked, trying to sound indifferent.

"Just three times," Woodward interjected. "Under close supervision."

"When was this?"

"During the last two weeks," Vulpes said. His eyes were as expressionless as a snake's. "You don't know what it's like, to walk into an ice cream store and have your choice of twenty-eight different flavors and hot fudge covered with . . . with those little chocolate things."

What was wrong with that statement? Vail thought. Then he realized there had been no joy in his tone. No excitement, no animation. Vulpes was emotionless, making words, doing his best to create the perfect conundrum, a man so calm his equanimity invoked thoughts of the nightmare sleepwalker in *The Cabinet of Dr. Caligari*. Control. Raymond Vulpes had perfected control.

"Sprinkles," Vail said.

"Sprinkles," Vulpes repeated.

"That's what excited you about your first day of freedom in ten years, an ice cream with sprinkles?" Vail asked.

"Metaphorically. It's having the choice," Vulpes answered. "Here, it's chocolate or vanilla."

"Another metaphor," Vail said. "Black and white, like most choices in life when you carve away all the bullshit."

Their eyes never strayed. They sat three feet apart, their gazes locked in a hardball game of flinch. Black and white choices, Vail thought, and his mind leaped back to the last day of the trial. There was a clear black and white choice. Vail and his team had spent weeks struggling to prove that Aaron Stampler was really two personalities in one body: Aaron, the sweet kid from Crikside, Kentucky, who had suffered every imaginable kind of abuse; and Roy, the evil alter ego with an insatiable lust for murder and revenge. Vail had won for Stampler, rescued him from almost certain death in the electric chair or from a needle filled with terminal sleep. Venable, realizing she was beat, had agreed to the plea bargain: Aaron Stampler would be sent to Daisyland until such time as he was deemed cured and his evil psychological twin, Roy, was purged.

Vail had been elated with his victory. Then, on the way out of the courthouse, Stampler had turned to him, leering, and whispered: "Suppose there never was an Aaron." And laughed as they had led him away.

He wants me to know. He wants me to know but not be able to do anything about it. Just like that day after the trial. It was not enough that he had created the nightmare, he wanted to haunt me with it, knowing there was nothing I could do about it, nobody I could tell.

It had been their dark secret for ten years, a cruel umbilical that, even at this moment, bound them together.

Stampler had an insatiable ego. Vail understood that now. That was the game. The dare.

Stop me if you can. Catch me if you can.

Vail did not break the stare. "And what else did you do beside get a hot fudge sundae?" he asked.

"Went to a record store and bought a couple of CDs. Then we went to Data City, checked out the latest CD-ROMs. We went to Belk's and I bought a pair of jeans. My own choice, the color I wanted, the style I wanted. Two hours of freedom that first day, except, of course, Max was in my shadow all the time. And the next time and the next. Day before yesterday we went to the movies. It was astounding. That enormous screen. Digital sound. Instead of that tiny postage stamp of an image on my eleven-inch screen. Quite an experience."

"I'll bet," Vail said. Vail didn't ask what picture he saw although he knew Vulpes was dying to tell him. He was making conversation. He already knew what he had come to find out. The sooner he got out of there, the better.

"Where'd you get the money?" Vail asked, hoping to nick Vulpes's pride, to humiliate him just a little.

"I earned it," Vulpes answered calmly.

"Earned it?"

"Raymond has become a remarkably proficient electronics repairman. VCRs, TVs, computers . . ."

"Telephones?" Vail said, raising his eyebrows.

What passed for a smile toyed with Vulpes's lips. "The telephone company takes care of their own communications," he answered.

"Raymond earns seventy-five cents an hour repairing all our electronics equipment. So we let him branch out, repair equipment for people on the outside. They bring the stuff to the front desk—"

"I've got nine thousand and change in the bank," Vulpes interrupted in his silky tone. "The doc deposits it for me. They keep me busy."

"He's the best in the area. It's almost like a full-time job," Woodward said proudly.

And then Vulpes said, "Soon will be."

The comment froze Vail. Nothing in Vulpes's face changed, but the eyes twinkled for a moment.

"I don't understand," Vail said.

"Well, that's the real news," said Woodward. "In three more days, Raymond's on furlough."

"Furlough?" said Vail.

"Six weeks. He's got a job in an electronics repair place on Western—"

"He's coming to Chicago?" Vail interrupted.

"We have a halfway house there," said Woodward. "Full-time supervision, ten o'clock curfew, some group therapy—we think Raymond's ready for that now, right?"

"I'm sure I can handle it."

Vail felt as if an enormous hand were squeezing his chest. He modulated his breathing so as not to indicate it had suddenly become stifled. His hands became cold and he was sure the color had drained from his face. He took a sip of Coke.

"I'll bet you can," he finally managed to say.

"If it works out, I mean, if he makes it through those first weeks without incident, the board has elected to release him for good."

"Well, I guess congratulations are in order," Vail said.

"Maybe we can have lunch one day," said Vulpes. "After all,

you *are* responsible for my . . . well, for my very existence, aren't you?"

"Sounds like a splendid idea," Woodward chimed in.

"Maybe so."

"Well, what do you think, Mr. . . . Martin?" Woodward asked. "Does the news give you renewed belief in redemption and resurrection?"

"Resurrection?"

"Raymond, here, resurrected from the ashes, so to speak." Woodward said it with such anomalous pride that Vail was chilled again, not by Vulpes, this time by the egocentric doctor, a man so obviously dazzled by his own brilliance that he was blind to Vulpes's true nature. But then, ten years before, Vail had been just as pleased with himself for having saved Aaron Stampler from certain death.

Vail hardly heard the rest of the conversation. It was unimportant. He was just biding time until he could diplomatically get out of there.

"Well, I think that should be it for the day," Vail heard Woodward say. "I'm sure we all need to get back to work."

"Yes," Vail said, managing a meager smile.

Woodward went to the door and called out to Max. Vail got up and walked around the table until he was behind Vulpes. He leaned over and said, ever so softly, "Raymond?"

Vulpes didn't turn around. He stared straight ahead. "Yes?"

"Supposing there never was an Aaron?"

Raymond continued to look at the wall on the opposite side of the room. He smiled, but Vail could not see it.

He knows. He knows and there's not a thing he can do about it. I'm a free man and he can't stop that because nobody would believe him.

Half a minute passed before Vulpes turned around. He stood up, his face inches from Vail's. He was smiling, but suddenly, for just an instant, his eyes turned to stone. Hatred glittered in them and the irises turned bloodred.

Like the chill he had felt when he entered the repair room, it came and went in the blink of an eye, but it was enough to send an icicle straight into Vail's heart.

Venable was right. Now he had seen it. It was like looking into the mind of—whomever? Aaron, Roy, Raymond—and realizing that he was no different, no less malevolent and invidious, no less capable of *anything* than the youth Vail had saved from death ten years before. The only difference was, now he was older, more dangerous, and about to go free.

"There'll always be an Aaron in my heart," Vulpes said softly, tapping his chest. "Just as there will always be a Martin in there. I owe everything I am to the two of you." He said in his silken voice, smiling his sincerest smile, "Thank you."

———

Vulpes stood at the window and watched them walk back across the wide courtyard, Vail striding resolutely toward the entrance. He could guess what Vail was saying. He could almost hear his protest.

But he was wrong. Vail knew there was no percentage in arguing with Woodward. It was, as they say, a done deal and he was powerless to stop it.

"The press will have a field day with this," he told Woodward.

"The press won't know anything about it. The release order has been signed by a local judge who is very sympathetic to our work. Raymond Vulpes will be released. The press knows Aaron Stampler. They don't even know Raymond Vulpes exists."

For one fleeting moment, Vail toyed with the notion of bringing up the murders of Linda Balfour and Alex Lincoln, but he decided against it. It was only a matter of time before that news would come out. But Raymond had the perfect alibi. They would be chalked up as a copycat killing.

Perfect. Vulpes had thought of everything. He hadn't missed a note.

"I assume you'll honor the confidentiality of this meeting," Woodward said.

"Confidentiality?"

"Well, legally speaking, you're still his attorney."

Vail shook his head. "Conflict of interest," he answered sardonically. "As a prosecutor, I'd have to resign the job."

"Give the boy a chance," Woodward asked.

"He's not a boy anymore, Woodward," Vail said.

They shook hands and Vail walked to the car, where Tony waited beside the open door.

Tony drove him back to the football field and the pilot cranked up the chopper as he got out of the Cadillac and ran toward it. Vail ducked down under the blades, slid into the seat beside him, and snapped on his seat belt.

"Christ," the pilot said, "you look like you saw a ghost."

"I did," Vail said. "Let's get the hell out of here."

25

ARE YOU THERE, HYDRA?

YES, FOX.

YOU HAVE DONE EXCEPTIONALLY WELL. BEYOND
   EXPECTATIONS.

THANK YOU, FOX.

YOU HAVE STUDIED THE PLAN?

YES, FOX, THE BEAUTIFUL PLAN.

AND ARE YOU PREPARED?

YES, YES.

AND DO YOU HAVE THE MESSAGE?

YES, FOX.

EXCELLENT. ARE YOU EXCITED?

ALWAYS.

IT IS TIME, AGAIN.

THANK YOU. I DON'T LIKE THE WAITING.

HOW DO YOU FEEL TODAY?

I FEEL EXCEPTIONALLY ANXIOUS.

GOOD. YOU MUST BE MORE CAUTIOUS THAN EVER.

DOES HE KNOW?

YES. DO NOT CONCERN YOURSELF. IT IS AS WE EXPECTED.

I WILL BE CAUTIOUS.

GOOD. SOON, HYDRA.
YES, YES, YES!
UNTIL THEN . . .

26

Parver came into the office as dusk was ending. The last thin shafts of daylight pierced the windows, casting crimson streaks through the gloom of the office. It was empty except for Vail, who was sitting alone in his office. He was slumped in his chair, his legs stretched out stiffly in front of him, his elbows on the arms of his chair, the fingers of both hands entwined and resting on his chest. His desk lamp was the only illumination on the entire floor and he had pulled the expensive black, cantilevered light down so its beam was swallowed up by the dark wood of his table. He was staring into space.

She approached his office cautiously and rattled on the jamb with her fingers. He looked up, his eyes gleaming in the shadows.

"Ms. Parver," he said with a nod.

"You busy?" she asked.

He thought about that for a couple of seconds and said, "Yeah. I'm working real hard at being relaxed. I'm into sudden-death overtime at doing absolutely nothing."

"It can wait," she said, and started to leave.

"Too late," he said. "Come on in here and sit down. What's on your mind?"

"It's about the Stoddard case," she said, looking across the chaotic mess of his desk. She noticed, lying in front of him, a small tape recorder about the size of a credit card and perhaps half an inch thick attached to a fountain pen by a thread of wire.

"What about Stoddard?" Vail asked.

"I'm not sure, I think the case is still loose in places. Some of it, I don't . . . it doesn't quite . . ." She stopped, looking for the proper words.

"Make sense?" he offered.

"Yes. I know you want a perfect case."

"I don't expect perfection from us mortals," Vail said with a wry smile. "Perfection is a perfect sunrise on a clear day. A baby born whole and healthy. Mortals have nothing to do with it."

"Some people . . ." she said, and then aborted the sentence.

"Some people what?"

"It was a bad thought. I shouldn't have started—"

"Some people *what*, Parver?"

She took a deep breath and her cheeks puffed as she blew it out.

"Some people say you only go to court when you have a sure thing."

Vail thought about that for a few moments. "I suppose you might look at it that way," he said.

"How do you look at it?"

He took out a cigarette and twirled it between two fingers for a while. Finally he said, "What I expect is a case without any holes. I don't want to get halfway through a trial and discover we're prosecuting an innocent person. I want to *know* they're guilty—or forget it. If that's playing it safe, so be it. On the other hand, if we know, if we're absolutely, no-shit positive that the party is guilty, like Darby, I'll send them to hell or burn out my brain trying."

"Can we ever be that sure, Marty?" she asked.

"What do you mean?"

"I mean, if it's not absolutely open-and-shut, can we ever be sure?"

"We're sure about Darby."

"You're going to make a deal."

"Because we don't have a case yet. Even with old Mrs.

What'shername's fantastic auricle sense. Rainey will have the son of a bitch back on the street before the time changes. I told you at the time, better to get him off the street for twenty years than have him back at Poppy Palmer's bar with two hundred fifty K in the bank."

"Maybe that's what they're talking about."

"Who are 'they'? Who've you been talking to?"

She shrugged. "I swear I don't even remember. Some smart-ass young lawyer at the bar in Guido's."

"Did it bother you?"

"Made me mad," she said, her forehead gathering into seams.

"That's being bothered." He laughed and after a minute or so she joined him. "Who cares what those loudmouth suits think, anyway?" he said.

When their laughter had run its course, he fell quiet again. She looked across the desk at him and it occurred to her that she had never, since she had started working for him, seen him really blow up. When he was truly angry, he became the ultimate poker player. His face became a mask. He quieted up. Only his eyes showed anything. His eyes did the thinking. They became alert and feral. Otherwise, his attitude had always been typically Irish: either "Don't sweat the little ones" or "Don't get mad, get even."

His eyes were alert and feral right now.

"What's bugging you?" she asked, surprised that she had asked the question and concerned that perhaps she had crossed the line between business and personal things. He stared almost blankly across the desk, not at her, at some object on the other side of the room. He put the cigarette between his lips but did not light it.

"Stampler," he said after awhile.

"Stampler?"

"I saw him today."

"Why is he bugging you?"

"Because he's a liar. Because he's amoral and he knows it and he's comfortable with it. Because he's a psychopathic schemer and a killer and he's about to be set free *on our turf* and he already knows who he's going to kill and how and when. And he knows

I know he's going to do it and there's not a goddamn thing I can do to stop him."

Her eyebrows arched higher and higher as he spoke, and when he finished, she said, "Ooo-kaaay."

"Nobody else knows this yet," he said. "Keep it to yourself until I go public with it."

"Is that what the tape recorder was for? I mean, is that legal?"

He stared down at it and then back at her. "It's for reference," he said, and ended that part of the conversation.

"What are you going to do about him?" she asked.

"If I knew the answer to that, I wouldn't be sitting here in the dark. I'd be over at Janie's scarfing down homemade spaghetti and thinking about what a lovely evening it's going to get to be later on."

"Can I help?"

"Shana, you may have a short fuse and you may be hell on wheels in court, but this is not something you want to get involved in. This is not like looking at pictures of murder victims or going eyeball to eyeball with some drive-by shooter. This is devil's play and whatever innocence you still harbor will surely be destroyed if you come too close."

She did not answer and a silence fell on the room. After a while she squirmed in her chair and cleared her throat and started to get up, and he suddenly sat straight up in the chair and snapped his fingers so loudly it startled her.

"Okay," he said. "Thanks for listening to that. I'm going over to Jane Venable's now and try to forget all of this for a few hours. As for Edith Stoddard, you're right. As Jane says, there's something wrong with the picture. Figure out what it is. I'd like to know, too."

"Thanks," she said, rather flatly.

"It's your case, Parver. Was there anything substantial you wanted to discuss?"

"No, just needed to talk, I guess, and here you were."

"You want to talk some more?"

She smiled and shook her head. "Nope, and I'm sure you don't, either."

Vail stood up and stretched his arms. "Absolutely right," he said. "Come on, we'll share a cab. I'll buy."

"I'll pay my share," she said, somewhat defensively.

"Hey," Vail said, "you want to be that way about it, you can pay the whole damn tab."

———

Harvey St. Claire watched the day dying through the farmhouse window. Near the edge of a pine thicket half a mile away he saw the beams of flashlights begin to dance in the dusk. They had been at the search for Poppy Palmer six hours.

"They're not gonna find her, Abel."

"I know."

"So why're we wasting time out here?"

"I could be wrong."

Stenner had been seated at Darby's desk for two hours, painstakingly going through bills, mail, notebooks, everything he could find.

St. Claire swung a wooden chair around and sat backward on it. "No airline reservation. No cab ride. Her car's parked at the apartment—"

Stenner said, "He could've driven her down to O'Hare."

"No airline reservation," St. Claire repeated. "And no sister in Texarkana."

"To wherever she went."

"No airline reservation—"

"Paid cash, gave a phony name."

"Her photo's been flashed at every ticket counter at the airport. Nobody recognized her."

"Maybe she wore a wig."

"You're a very strange guy, Abel."

"I've worked for Martin Vail for ten years. You get to think that way after a while. It's the way he thinks. He hates surprises."

"So if she ain't here and she didn't leave, where the hell is she?"

Stenner did not answer. He continued his boring chore in silence.

"Sometimes I wish to hell I never heard of Miranda," St. Claire said. "Sometimes I yearn fer a little Texas justice."

"What is Texas justice?" Stenner said, and was almost immediately sorry he asked. He was carefully sorting through the stacks of opened mail on the desk. He had piled the day's delivery, unopened, on the opposite corner of the desk.

"Back when I was in the U.S. Marshal's, this was, hell, eighteen, twenty years ago," St. Claire started, "I got sent down to the Mexican border to sniff out a runner named Chulo Garciez, who had got himself busted for running illegals across the border and selling 'em to migrant farms. Two of my best friends were carryin' him up to San Antonio and what they didn't know, Chulo's girlfriend had smuggled him a watch spring in a candy bar. Was a Mars bar, I think, or maybe a Baby Ruth."

Stenner looked up at him dolefully for an instant and then went back to the mail.

St. Claire went on. "Chulo secrets this here spring in the back of his belt, knowing he would be cuffed behind his back in the backseat of the car, and he picks the cuffs with the spring, reaches over the front seat, hauls out Freddy Corello's .45, puts two in his head, and empties the other four into Charley Hinkle, who was driving, jumps over the seat, kicks Charley out, pulls onto the berm, kicks Freddy out, and heads back to the border in the government car. They find it about ten miles from Eagle Pass right on the border. So I go down to the Border Patrol station in Eagle Pass and that's where I met Harley Bohanan, who was about six-seven and weighed two-fifty and made John Wayne look like a midget. Carried an old-fashioned .44 low on his hip, like Wayne."

"Uh-huh."

"I tell my story to ol' Harley and he says he knows Garciez and he is one bad-ass Mex and maybe he can help me and he puts me up in this awful goddamn adobe motel outside a town with roaches as big as wharf rats and no air conditionin'. Has a damn ceiling fan so big it'd suck yer eyeballs out. You had to keep yer eyes closed when you laid down under it."

"Uh-huh."

"Two nights later Harley is bangin' on my door at four in the mornin' and we drive out toward Quemado and right there on the river in a little boxed canyon there's a dozen wannabe wetbacks, all shot in the back of the head, stripped clean, even had their gold teeth knocked out. Harley is snoopin' around and suddenly he says, 'One of 'em got away.' Sure enough, we pick up some barefoot tracks and we follow them for a couple hours and finally come on this illegal cowerin' in a little cave in the desert. Poor son-bitch dyin' a thirst."

"Uh-huh."

"He tells us they was set up by a federalee captain name a . . . hell, what was his name? . . . uh, Martino, Martinez, something like that, *and* a guy named Chulo, who was supposed to pick 'em up at the border and take 'em to find work on this side, only instead Chulo and the federalee started shootin' them. This fella just lucked out. Harley knows who this federalee is. That night we ford the Rio Grande—it's about a inch deep there—in his Jeep and the federalee is drinkin' in a cantina. We wait till he comes out and Harley grabs him like you'd grab a puppy by the back of the neck and throws him in the back of the Jeep and we drive back down to the river and he throws the Mex out into the river and then pulls down his pants. He pulls out that .44 and it don't have any front sight on it. Filed off. He goes into the chest on the back of the Jeep, takes out an old, dirty can of ten-weight motor oil, dips the muzzle of the .44 in the can, and then shoves this federalee down on the knees and bends him over and, as I stand here, swear t'God, sticks the muzzle of the pistol about an inch and a half up the federalee's ass and says, 'Where's Chulo? I count t'three and I don't know, I'm gonna blow your brains out the hard way.' "

"Uh-huh," Stenner said, still examining the mail.

"An hour later we're outside a cantina on the U.S. side. There's Chulo's truck and he's inside drinkin' beer and playin' with some little hot-stuff *señorita* and Harley pulls out a knife the size of Mount Everest and carves a hole outta the rear tire on the truck. I stroll into the bar and order a Corona and I say, in Mex, 'That truck out there's got a flat.' Chulo gets up and stomps out the door, me kinda amblin' behind him. He goes to the back a the truck and he's leaning over examinin' the damage and Harley steps around from behind it with his .44 drawn and says, 'Garciez, yer under arrest fer draft dodgin',' " and Chulo jumps up and makes th' mistake a reachin' under his arm and *kaBOOM*, ol' Harley blows a hole through that sorry son-bitch you could drive his truck through. And y' know what ol' Harley says? 'Costs twenty bucks a day to house a U.S. prisoner and Chulo was lookin' at twenty years. Hell, Harve, we just saved the taxpayers about a hundred grand.' That's what I mean by Texas justice."

Stenner still did not look up from the bills and letters.

"That was some long story just to explain two words," he said when St. Claire finished his epic.

"Thought you'd appreciate the details," St. Claire said. "Ain't like we're runnin' late for a ballgame or nothin'." He walked to a window, threw it open, and sent a long squirt of tobacco juice out on the lawn.

"You were Darby," Stenner said, "wanted to get lost for a week or two, where would you go, Harvey?"

"I dunno. Hawaii. One of the Caribbean islands?"

"Can't afford it. Insurance company has him on hold, bank account's almost empty. He's surely maxed out his credit cards. And he was still here yesterday, mail's open."

Stenner handed St. Claire two phone bills. "How about a little hunting trip?" he said. "Red Marsh Lodge, on the Pecatonica River about eighty miles from here. Called them twice last month and just a couple of days ago, last entry on the bill that came today."

He dialed the number.

"Red Marsh," answered a soft-spoken man with a slightly Swedish accent.

"Yes," Stenner said. "We're friends of Jim Darby's, Mr. James

Darby? We were supposed to go on this trip with him, but we thought we had to work. We got off early. Is he still there?"

"He's down riggin' out his boat. Take me a bit to get 'im back up here."

"No, we don't want to talk to him. We thought we'd drive on up and surprise him in the morning. Do you have a double open?"

"Sure do. Cabin eight, right next to him."

"He's in seven?"

"Nine."

"Good. Now don't tell him about the call, we want to surprise the hell out of him at breakfast."

"You'll have to get here mighty early then. He's takin' the boat out to the blind at four-thirty. Wants t'be there at first light. Most of the boys do."

"You have a boat rental open?"

"Sure do."

"Hold that for us, too. The name's Stenner. A. Stenner."

"Abe Stenner. Gotcha."

"Right, Abe Stenner." He hung up, looked at St. Claire, and almost smiled.

"We got him," he said.

———

Later that night, in bed, with Jane Venable nestled under his arm, one of her long legs thrown over one of his, and her breathing soft and steady in his ear, Vail thought how quickly and naturally their first furious lovemaking had turned into an untroubled, easy partnership. The passion was always sudden and furious and overwhelming, but there was also a sense of comfort when they were together. Perhaps it was because they were both in their forties and love—if that was what this was, neither of them had tampered with the word yet—was like finding some small treasure each of them had lost and both had given up hope of ever finding again. For the first time in years, Vail was thankful when the day was over, when he could flee the office and come to her and delight in her presence. He lay on his back, half smiling, and stared up through the darkness at the vaulted ceiling. But soon his thoughts began turning in on him and they drifted away from Jane Venable and back to Aaron Stampler—or Raymond Vulpes— or whoever the hell he was, and he thought: *Not this time, you son of a bitch. You did it to me once. That time was on me. This time it's on you.*

27

The fog was so cotton-thick as they neared the marshes guarding the river that Stenner was reduced to driving at twenty miles an hour. He leaned forward, eyes squinted, trying to discern the white line down the middle of the country road. He had missed the turnoff to the lodge in the soupy mist and they had had to double back, driving slowly along the blacktop road, flicking the lights between high and low so they could see through the earthbound clouds. Eventually they saw the sign, a small wooden square at the intersection of the main road and an unpaved lane that disappeared into the trees. They were running late, four-thirty having come and gone.

RED MARSH LODGE, it said in black letters on a mud-spattered white sign. A thick red arrow below the letters pointed down the dirt road. Even on low beam, the headlights turned the fog into a blinding mirror and they crept through the forest on the winding, rutted road for almost two miles before the rustic main building of the lodge suddenly jumped out at them through the haze.

Quarter to five.

Walt Sunderson, a heavyset Swede with a florid complexion and a thick red mustache that drooped down almost to his jaw, stepped out on the porch of the log cabin. He was dressed in overalls and a thick flannel shirt under a padded Arctic jacket.

"Abe Stenner?" he called out, the words sounding flat and without resonance in the thick gray condensation.

"Yes, sir," the detective said, getting out of the car.

"Just missed him," Sunderson said in the melodic cadence peculiar to the Swedish. "Darby hauled outta here ten, fifteen minutes ago. I got your boat ready, though, and a map of the marshes and blinds. Won't take you hardly any time at all to get rigged out. You can unpack when you get back. Don't even have to lock your car."

"That's right civilized," St. Claire said, shoving a wad of tobacco under his lip with his thumb.

"Got plenty hot coffee, you betcha, ready for you in a thermos. Hope you like it black?"

They both nodded. Although Stenner preferred a pinch or two of sugar in his, they were eager to get started. Stenner and St. Claire retrieved two shotguns in black leather cases from the trunk. St. Claire was wearing a fur-lined ammo vest, its slots filled with 12-gauge shotgun shells. Stenner stuffed another box of rounds in one of the pockets of his army field jacket while Sunderson got the quart thermos. He led them down a long, narrow floating dock.

"Careful, fellas, can't see a thing in this soup."

"Is it always this thick?" St. Claire asked.

"Not in the daytime."

The boat, a ten-foot, flat-bottomed skiff with a thirty HP motor riveted to the stern, lolled in the still water, barely distinguishable in the darkness and mist despite the heavy beam of a one-hundred-watt floodlight nearby. Sunderson checked the floor of the skiff and, scowling and muttering to himself, went to a small shed at the end of the dock. He came back with a coil of heavy rope looped over his shoulder.

"Could have sworn I put an anchor and chain in your boat last night," he said. "I'll hitch up this line for you. There's lots of trees and stumps out there, you won't have any trouble finding something to tie up to."

"That'll be fine," Stenner said, clambering aboard behind St. Claire, who had taken the stern and tiller. They set off into the windless, oppressive darkness, their faces and jackets dripping with condensation before they had traveled fifty yards.

"Kinda eerie," St. Claire said, following the beam of a small headlight mounted on the bow.

"Ah, 'death, to feel the fog in my throat, the mist in my face,' " Stenner said softly.

"Didn't know you was a poet, Abel." St. Claire chuckled.

"I'm not. Robert Browning was."

They fell silent and the boat moved slowly up the narrow creek, the motor gurgling behind them. Stenner held a small map trying to figure out where they were. Twenty minutes later Stenner could see another boat vaguely through the damp, shifting, strands of mist. It was tied to a fallen tree.

"Two of them," Stenner whispered as they approached the blind.

The two hunters were dressed in camouflage suits and had thrown their life jackets into the stern of the boat. Neither one was Darby. Rushes swished along the sides of the skiff as St. Claire guided it toward the blind. One of the men, who was tall and dissipated-looking, was taking a long pull from a gallon jug, holding it high in the crook of his arm and tilting his head back, letting the amber fluid run easily into his mouth. A large black lab with friendly eyes sat on the seat beside the other man and ruffed when he saw them coming through the fog.

"Morning," the man beside the dog said cheerfully. He was a short fellow, bordering on fat, with a jowly face that became almost cherubic when he smiled.

"Morning," Stenner said as St. Claire reversed the engine and angled in beside their boat. The drinker lowered the jug and wiped his mouth with the back of his hand.

"Care for a swig?" he asked, offering the bottle. "Homemade cider. It'll sure take the edge off this chill."

Stenner said, "Thanks, anyway." St. Claire reached out and took the jug and, holding up his elbow, expertly dropped it into the angle of his arm and took a long swig. He shuddered as he lowered the container and handed it back.

"Sure right about that," he said. "It warms ya right through to yer bones. Thanks."

"You seen another hunter out here this morning?" Stenner asked.

"You mean Jim Darby. He went on up to six. 'Bout half an hour ago."

"What's six?" Stenner asked.

"The blinds are numbered. On that map you got there. Old Walt hand-drew the sorry thing. Six is down the creek half a mile or so just before it dumps into the river. This is four here and that one over on the far side of the creek is five."

"How far away is six?" Stenner asked.

"Half-mile, maybe."

"Couldn't take more than ten minutes to go up there, could it?"

"More like five, even in the fog."

"Thanks."

"You friends of his?" one of them asked.

"Yeah," St. Claire said. "Thought we'd surprise him. Well, thanks for the help."

"Sure. Good hunting."

"Same to you."

St. Claire throttled up and angled the small boat back out into the creek and headed for the six blind. Five minutes later they picked out a small sign on a crooked post with a solitary 6 hand-painted on it. St. Claire turned into the tall river grass and cut the engine. The blind was empty.

"Hear that?" St. Claire said. Stenner listened keenly and through the fog could hear the low mutter of an engine. Then a dog started barking and a moment later they heard a muffled splash. The engine picked up a little speed and gradually got louder.

"Here he comes," Stenner whispered.

The sputtering sound of the motor moved slowly toward them and then the skiff emerged through the fog almost directly in front of them. Darby was hunched in the back of the skiff. He seemed preoccupied and did not see them until the dog, a spotted spaniel of some kind, started barking.

"Jesus," he said with surprise, and cut his motor. He had a 12-gauge shotgun turned down-side-up in his lap, snapping shells into the chamber. St. Claire eased a 9-mm Glock out of its shoulder holster and casually laid hand and gun on his thigh. As the other boat neared his, Darby squinted through the gauzy wisps of fog and suddenly recognized Stenner. He sat up, scowling, as he drew abreast of them. Stenner reached out and grabbed the gunwale of Darby's boat and pulled them together.

"Good morning, Mr. Darby," he said. He reached into his jacket pocket and took out the warrant. As he did, St. Claire raised up on one knee and held the pistol out at arm's length, pointing straight at Darby's face.

"Kindly put that scattergun down on the bottom of that skiff," he said with harsh authority.

"We have a warrant for your arrest, Mr. Darby," Stenner said, and held the warrant in front of his face.

Darby was obviously startled. Even in the fog and predawn gloom, they could see the color in his face drain from ruddy to pasty-white.

"That's no good up here," he snarled. The dog snarled menacingly in the front of the boat. "Shut up, Rags." The dog whined into silence.

"Sheriff'll be waiting when we get back t'camp," said St. Claire. "You wouldn't want to add unlawful flight to yer problems, now, would ya?"

"I'm not fleeing. Do I look like I'm fleeing to you? I got nothin' to flee about."

"This warrant charges you with first-degree murder in the death of your wife. You have a right to remain silent—"

"I know the drill," he hissed, and put the shotgun aside. "I heard it all before."

"I'd like you to turn around and put your hands behind your back, please," Stenner said formally. "I have to cuff you."

"I'm not going anywhere," Darby said.

"Procedure."

"Don't do that, please," he said. His tone had changed suddenly from arrogant to almost solicitous.

"I told you, it's procedure."

"Not behind my back, okay? Where would I go?"

"Don't give us any guff, son," St. Claire said.

"I'm asking you, please don't tie my hands behind my back," he begged. "I . . . I can't swim."

St. Claire looked at Stenner, who in turn looked at Darby, who was plainly terrified. The dog walked unsteadily back and started to growl again.

"I said, shut up!" Darby bellowed, and smacked the dog in the face. It yelped and curled up on the floor of the skiff. "Please," he pleaded.

"Cuff him in front, Harve," Stenner said in a flat, no-nonsense monotone. St. Claire holstered his pistol and moved up beside him.

"Thanks," Darby said, holding his hands out for St. Claire to shackle. Once cuffed, Darby laid on the bottom of the boat with his head barely visible over the side. The abused Rags crawled up beside him and licked his face.

"Dogs'll forgive anything," St. Claire said, shaking his head. He looked down at Darby. "What were ya doin' out there in the marsh?" he asked.

"Took a dump," Darby said sullenly.

"Helluva dump. Sounded like the *Titanic* goin' down." He swung the bow light around, letting its beam cut through the rising fog. Darby's boat had left a pathway through the water grass. "Lookee there," St. Claire said with a grin. "He left us a little trail t'foller."

He tied Darby's boat to the back of their skiff and headed back through the marsh grass. To the east, the rising sun bloodied the mist and cast long, dim shadows across the marsh. A snake glided past them, unconcerned, looking for breakfast, its head sticking up, perusing the terrain. Off in the still persistent fog, a bird squawked and they could hear its big wings flapping through the gray, awakening morning. Presently the path ended. The grass was folded down in a large circle. At one end, the skeletal fingers of a tree branch reached up out of the water.

"Think this here's the place," he told Stenner. "Why don't I tie down here and wait for you to take him back to the lodge and bring the sheriff and a coupla drag lines out here."

"Fair enough," Stenner answered, and swung the two boats together. "I'm coming over there," he told Darby. "Keep your dog in tow."

"He's all noise," Darby said. "What's this all about, anyway?"

"Poppy Palmer," Stenner said, and Darby's face turned the color of wet cement as Stenner stepped into his skiff.

"What're you talking about?" Darby whined. "She went to see her sister in Texarkana."

"She ain't got a sister in Texarkana."

"That ain't my fault!"

"Now there's a goddamn non sequitur for ya." St. Claire laughed.

"Back as fast as I can, Harve," Stenner said. "You'll be okay?"

St. Claire looked at him balefully and took a swig of coffee as the other skiff rumbled off through the grass and into the crimson morning.

———

Sun and wind had sent the fog swirling away and the morning had dawned bright and cold when St. Claire saw the thirty-foot powerboat cruising up the creek. He put two fingers in the corners of his mouth and whistled shrilly and waved. They turned into the marsh and slid quietly up to his boat. Stenner was standing beside the sheriff, a tall, bulky man in a dark blue jacket wearing a brown campaign hat with his badge pinned to the crown.

"Mornin', gentlemen," St. Claire said. "Thanks fer comin' by."

The sheriff's boat churned to a stop as he walked to the bow and, leaning over, took St. Claire's hand.

"Jake Broadstroke," he said in a voice that sounded like it came from his toes. "Sorry we took so long, had to round up a couple of divers. Hope you two know what you're talking about."

"Well, it's a hunch," St. Claire said. "But I got thirty years a hunches under m'belt and I ain't often wrong."

One of the divers, dressed in a black wet suit and a face mask, slipped over the side of the big boat. The water was waist-deep.

"Hell, Sheriff, I doubt we'll need the drag lines. Bottom's a little murky, but we oughtta be able to tread it out. Somebody hand me a light."

He took the waterproof lamp, adjusted his face mask, and went under, joined a minute or two later by the other diver. Everybody settled back and waited. Nobody said anything. The only sound was the wind rattling the reeds.

Half an hour crept by. The sheriff gnawed on the remnants of a cigar. St. Claire spat freely into the wind-rippled water. Stenner said nothing. All eyes gazed out over the reeds. Then the muddy swamp churned a bit and a woman's head suddenly broke the surface, rising up out of the water. Wet-dark hair streaked down over a bloated, blue-gray face, partially covering a gaping mouth filled with mud. Black links of chain were gnarled around her throat. Water dribbled from her glassy eyes and for just a moment or two she appeared to be weeping. Poppy Palmer had danced her last striptease.

"Ah, Jesus," St. Claire said.

"Yes," Stenner said, almost inaudibly. "I was hoping we were wrong, too."

28

Vail was behind the closed door of his office, a signal to the rest of the staff that he wanted to be left alone. Naomi called it "diving." It was as if Vail were underwater, in a different world, one without sound or distraction, one in which all the data and facts of the case were jumbled together. He sought to categorize them, to rearrange them into a logical chronology until they formed a picture that made sense to him. Like a legal jigsaw puzzle, the picture would eventually become clear even though some of the pieces were missing. Only one thing was on his mind: Aaron Stampler—or Raymond Vulpes—one and the same, unchanged, he was certain.

Vail had not yet broached the problem of Stampler/Vulpes with the staff and would not until he had analyzed his meeting with Vulpes and Woodward and formed a beginning strategy for dealing with the situation. He was wearing earphones, listening to the tape he had made of the interview with the psychiatrist and his "creation." He knew that somewhere in that tape Vulpes had revealed himself—purposely—to taunt Vail. Somewhere on that tape was a clue that Vail would recognize. Nothing incriminating, just Vulpes letting Vail know that he was still Aaron Stampler and that he had successfully scammed them all. If Vail knew anything, he knew that Stampler's ego would ultimately be his undoing.

He had been behind his closed door for hours when he got the call from Stenner. He and St. Claire would be in the office momentarily with details, but they wanted Vail to know that Darby was in custody and that they had discovered Poppy Palmer's body. Vail had to put Stampler/Vulpes aside for now and deal with the Darby case. Twenty minutes later Stenner and St. Claire blew into the office like a March wind.

My God, Vail thought, *did I just see Stenner smile?*

Vail waved Parver into his office and leaned back in his chair. "Okay," he said to his two chief investigators, "let's hear it."

"He spilled his guts," St. Claire said. "We had him pegged right on his wife's murder, Shana, the old lady's hearing was perfect. Thing is, Rainey never got hold of Darby, so he didn't know we were after his ass. He thought he was home free except for Poppy Palmer."

Stenner picked up the story: "Stretched his luck. Picked her up, told her he was taking her to the airport, drove to his barn, strangled her on the spot."

"Then the miserable son-bitch threw her in the trunk and drove around for the better part of a day with her body," St. Claire continued. "Spent the night in a motel outside Rockford, and this mornin' he wrapped her up in an anchor chain and dropped her in the marsh up along the Pecatonica."

"Congratulations," Vail said. "You two did a great job."

"We had some luck," said Stenner. "We were actually so close to him, we heard him drop her body in the water." He turned to Shana Parver. "But now you've got him." He held up two fingers. "Twice."

"Rainey was waitin' at county jail when we brought him down," said St. Claire. "Says he wants t'talk."

Vail laughed. "Sure he does. Well, the hell with Rainey, it's too late now." He turned to Shana Parver. "Okay, Shana, you got your way, Darby's all yours. I assume you'll want to max him out?"

She looked up and smiled, but there was little mirth in the grin. "Of course . . ." she said.

"You have a different idea?"

"No, sir!"

"Everything in order?" Vail asked Stenner. "About the arrest, I mean?"

"We served the warrant on him, Mirandized him, and used the sheriff in Stephenson County to locate the body."

Parver sat quietly in the corner, nibbling on the corner of one lip.

"What is it, Shana?" Vail asked.

"I can't help thinking if we had taken him down right after the deposition, Poppy Palmer'd still be alive."

"We didn't have anything to take him down *with* after the deposition," Vail answered, a bit annoyed. "Hell, by the time we got the warrant, she was already dead."

Parver did not reply to Vail's comment.

"Shana?"

"Yes, sir."

"If she hadn't lied to us, she'd still be alive."

"I know."

"There's no looking back on this. Tell Rainey for me the girl's blood is on his hands, not ours. If he had delivered his man to us when he said he would, Poppy Palmer would be alive today."

"I'll tell him that." She nodded.

"Good. No more plea bargains. You wanted to take him all the way? Do it. Take him all the way to the chair."

"Yes, sir."

———

St. Claire trudged through the chilly sunset to the records warehouse two blocks away. He had seen the sun rise and now was watching it set, but he was still too adrenalized to quit for the night. He decided to take a stab at finding the missing Stampler tapes among the mountains of records and files and boxes in the chaos that was the trial records warehouse. It would be impossible, he knew, but maybe he would get lucky twice in one day.

He walked wearily through the dim, two-story-high crisscross of corridors lined high with boxes and files and illuminated only by

green-shaded bulbs high above the walkways. He heard the muffled tones of Frank Sinatra singing "Come Fly with Me" echoing
from one of the corridors and the dim reflection of a light casting
long shadows into the main walkway. When he reached the corner and looked down the aisle, he saw a police sergeant seated in
a rocking chair under an old-fashioned floor lamp with a fringed
shade. He was listening to a small transistor radio with his feet
propped against a gray metal desk, gently rocking himself.

"Hi, there," St. Claire said, his voice reverberating down the
corridor.

The old cop jumped. "God*damn*," he said. "Scare a man half to
death."

"Sorry," said St. Claire, walking down the box-lined corridor.
"M'name's Harve St. Claire, D.A.'s office."

The cop lowered his feet and turned the radio volume down. A
handprinted sign on a doubled-over piece of white shirt-board
read c. FELSCHER, CUSTODIAN.

"Sgt. Claude Felscher at your service." He stuck out his hand.

He was a large, bulky man, overweight and rumpled, his uniform unpressed, his pants sagging under a beer belly, his tie askew
and not pulled tight enough to hide the missing top button on his
blue uniform shirt. A tangled fringe of gray hair curled over his
ears. He looked dusty and forgotten, like a fossil lost in the shad-
owy corner of a museum. Only his badge added an incongruous
touch to the gloomy scene. It was polished and it twinkled under
the dim bulb of the old lamp.

St. Claire wedged a healthy chew under his lip and offered the
plug to the old cop, who shook his head.

"How long've you been custodian here, Claude?"

"Hell, I been here since Cain knocked off Abel."

"Must be the loneliest job in town."

"Oh, I dunno," the old-timer said. "Look around you. I got all
these famous cases to keep me company. Remember Speck? Richard Speck?"

"Sure."

"Right over there in aisle 19. Gacy is down in 6. George Farley, killed twelve women, remember? Pickled them, kept them in jars in the basement? Over on 5. Even got a file on Dillinger, from when he was locked up after that bank robbery outside Gary. They had a touch of class about them, not like the bums these days. Drive-by shootings, easy store stickups, for Christ sake! World's really fucked up, Harve."

"I couldn't agree more. You remember the Rushman case?"

"The archbishop? Hell, that was like yesterday. That what you're looking for?"

St. Claire nodded. "State versus Aaron Stampler. Trial ended in late March."

"Anything specific?"

"Physical evidence."

"Aw, shit. Let me tell you about physical evidence. By the time it gets here, it's pretty well picked over. All we get is what hasn't been claimed. And it's not in any particular order. Look around you. I couldn't tell you how many cases are stored in here— thousands, hell, hundreds of thousands—a lot of it misplaced or misfiled."

"I was afraid of that. Thought maybe I'd luck out."

"Well, hell, don't give up so easy." The sergeant got a flashlight from a desk drawer and led St. Claire down through the caverns of records. The odor of mildew and damp paper stung St. Claire's nose. Felscher found the cardboard boxes filled with the Stampler records.

"I been down here before," St. Claire said. "Must've been your day off. There wasn't any evidence here, it's all paper."

"You're right," Felscher said, sliding several of the boxes out of their nesting places, checking them, and pushing them back. "What exactly are you after, anyway?"

"Some videotapes."

"Sorry. But you're welcome to look around the place." He swept his arm in a semicircle and laughed.

"Forget it. Thanks for your help, Claude." They shook hands and St. Claire started back down the dreary corridor of files.

"Don't feel too bad, Harve. They'd probably be pretty well deteriorated by now, anyway. This isn't exactly what you'd call a humidity-controlled facility."

"I didn't wanna look at 'em, I was hopin' to find out if they were disposed of. And to whom."

"Oh, now wait just a minute. Why didn't you say so? That's a little different story."

Felscher walked down the corridor to a series of bookshelves lined with long rows of canvas-bound ledgers identified by dates. He ran his forefinger along the spines.

"Let's see, September first to tenth, '82 . . . December . . . February . . . Here we go, March twentieth through thirtieth, 1983." Felscher pulled a mildewed and roach-gnawed ledger from the shelf. "These are the index ledgers. Not a lot of help when you're looking for something, but . . ."

He opened the book and carefully turned the pages, which were yellowed with age and faded, the entries handwritten by the clerk of the court.

"Got to be careful. These old books'll fall apart on you. Stampler, Stampler, yeah, that was some big case, all right. Wonder whatever happened to him?"

"Still in Daisyland."

"Good. The way he carved up the old bishop, they ought to keep him there forever."

"Yeah," St. Claire agreed.

"Okay, here we go, March twenty-third . . . State versus Aaron Stampler, murder in the first. Here's the inventory. Let's see, got some bloody clothes, shoes, a kitchen knife, couple of books, and a ring, they were returned to the cathedral out on Lakeview, 4/2/83. What d'ya know, Harve, you did get lucky. Here we go, twenty-three videotapes. They were released to a Dr. Molly Arrington, Winthrop, Indiana, 4/26/83."

"Well, I'll be damned," St. Claire said, and his heart jumped a beat. "She's got the whole damn tape library."

—

The office was abandoned except for Parver, who was sitting alone in her small office. The thick Darby file lay on the desk in front of her, but she had tired of looking at it and had pulled the Stoddard file. She really did not want to deal with either of them. She was tired and had no place to go but home, and so she sat alone in the big office, fighting off what was a mounting malaise. Behind her, the elevator door opened and Flaherty stepped off, carrying a battered old briefcase. He went to his office, threw the case on his desk, and only then noticed that Parver was still there. He ambled back to her cubbyhole and stood in the doorway with his hands stuffed in his pockets.

"Good news about Darby," he said. "I can hardly wait to hear your summation to the jury."

She looked up at him, her face bunched up as if she were in pain. "Did you hear about Poppy Palmer?"

"It's all over the afternoon editions," he said. "I hear Eckling is scorched. He's saying if his department had handled it, the girl never would have been killed."

"What do you expect? If he'd handled the case, Darby probably would have killed half the county before Eckling got his head far enough out of his ass to figure it out."

Flaherty whistled low through his teeth. "You okay?" he asked.

"Why?" she snapped back.

"Hey, excuse me, I should have knocked." He started to leave.

"Where are you going?" she demanded.

"I don't know, you seem a little . . ." He paused, searching for the right word. "Pensive?"

"Pensive?" She considered that and said, half smiling, "I guess I am a little pensive right now."

"Can I help?"

She stared up at him from behind her desk for a moment, then wheeled her chair back and stood up. "How'd you like to go over to Corchran's? I'll buy you a drink."

"No, I'll buy you a drink."

"Ah, one of those, huh? Tell you what, Flaherty, I'll toss you for it."

"You mean, like, throwing coins against the wall?"

"Uh-huh." She reached into her purse and took out two quarters, then handed him one. "Back in the computer room, there's no carpet on the floor."

"You sound like a pro."

"I have my days."

They walked back to the computer room and stood ten feet from the bare back wall.

"How do you do this?" he asked innocently.

"They don't pitch quarters in Boston?"

"I rarely had a quarter when I lived in Boston."

"You just pitch the coin. One who gets closest to the wall wins. Want a practice shot first?"

"Nah, let's just do it. Winner buys?"

"Winner buys."

"You go first, I'll see how it's done."

She leaned over, put one hand on her knee, held the coin between her thumb and forefinger, and scaled it side-hand. It hit the wall, bounced back three inches, and spun around several times before it dropped.

"Looks pretty good," he said.

"Not bad."

"Like this, huh," he said, assuming the same stance she had except that he used his left hand.

"You're a southpaw," she said. "I never noticed that before."

"You never noticed a lot about me, Parver," he answered.

The remark surprised her.

"Just kind of flip it, huh?"

"Uh-huh."

He leaned way over, held his hand at arm's length, and sighted down his arm, then tossed the coin overhand. It flipped through the air, twanged into the juncture of floor and wall, and died. There wasn't a quarter of an inch between the coin and the wall.

"What d'ya know," he said. "Beginner's luck."

Parver's eyes narrowed suspiciously. "You hustled me, Flaherty," she said through clenched teeth.

"Never!"

"I saw the way you did that. You definitely hustled me!"

He grinned, picked up the quarters, and handed them to her. "Shall we?"

They took a cab to Corchran's and went back to the Ladies Room. Steamroller gave them a gap-toothed smile and led them to a corner booth. He swept the table off with the damp rag stuck in his belt and looked at them with his good eye.

"Drinkin'? Eatin'?" he asked.

"We'll start with drinks and see what happens."

"Thwell, what'll it be?"

"Martini, very dry, straight up, no condiments," Parver said.

"Condi-what?"

"No fruit or vegetables," said Flaherty.

"Gotcha. Mithter Flaherty, the uthual?"

"Yep."

"On the way, sluggerth." Steamroller swaggered off toward the bar.

"Okay, Parver, what's eating you? Hell, you got everything you could want. You got Darby wired, you got Stoddard. Two capital cases. Want to give me one of them?"

"No, thank you very much," she said haughtily.

"So what's the problem?"

"It hit me for the first time today, when Marty asked me if I was ready to max out Darby."

"What do you want to do, throw the switch, too?"

Steamroller brought the drinks and set them on the table. She downed hers and ordered a second.

"That's not what I mean," she said, then squished up her face. "Damn! Martinis taste like ether or something."

"You never drank a martini before?"

"Nope. Usually drink Cuba Libres."

"Jesus, you dusted that off like it was a glass of milk. Those things are deadly."

"They come in a real small glass. Nothing to 'em. What were we talking about?"

"You had just said, uh, 'That's not what I mean,' after I said that thing about throwing the switch."

"Oh, yes, now I remember. The thing is, I've never tried a capital case, Flaherty."

"You getting stagefright?" Flaherty laughed. "Kickass Parver's getting weak knees? Come on, it's just another case—think of it as a misdemeanor."

"That's not what I mean. I'm not worried about winning, that's not it at all. I just . . . I never really thought about it before."

"What? What the hell're you talking about?"

"Asking for the death penalty."

"Ah, so that's it. Anticipating an attack of conscience, are you? Come on, this guy walked up to his wife and shot her in the face with a shotgun. And he choked the little dancer to death. Think about that, he was looking in her face while he was killing her."

"Stop it, Dermott."

"No. We're prosecutors, Shana. The last things standing between civilization and the jungle. We don't make the laws, we just uphold them, and the law says that if Darby's convicted of murder one, he's a wrap."

"I know all that, for God's sake," she said angrily. "I didn't come here to hear a rehash of Philosophy 101." She suddenly got up to leave.

He reached out and gently grabbed her arm. "Hey, I'm sorry," he said plaintively. "Sometimes I get too cynical for my own good. Old habits die hard. I promise, no more platitudes. Please . . . don't leave."

She looked down at him and smiled. "No more shit?"

"No more shit."

"Good." She sat back down and finished her second martini.

"Let me ask you something," he said. "If you were on a jury panel and they asked you if you were in favor of the death penalty, what would you say?"

"That's moot."

"Hell it is. Think about it for a minute." He turned back to his Coke. They were silent for a full minute before she answered.

"I'd say I'm not sure whether I am or not, but I wouldn't let that influence my judgment. It's the evidence that counts."

"Good. And would you go into court if you had doubts about the defendant's guilt?"

"God, you sound like Martin. He asked me the same thing the other night."

"It's what prosecutors fear more than anything else—convicting an innocent man."

"Or woman." She held a finger up to the waiter and dipped it toward her glass.

"Or woman. Point is, if you got 'em—and you've got Darby— then what's the dif? You do your job. How would you feel, knowing what you know about Darby, if he beat the rap? Suppose he walked?"

"Won't happen," she said defensively.

"I mean, supposing someone else was trying him and they blew the case?"

She thought for a moment, then decided to ignore the question. She suddenly changed the subject. "Then there's Edith Stoddard," she said.

"What about her?"

"Something's wrong there, Flaherty. She doesn't even want to put up a fight."

"That's her option. Not much to fight about. According to your preliminary report, she bought the gun, spent two weeks learning to use it, and then popped him—twice. One would've been enough. The second shot was malicious. That's murder one, hotshot. She's good as cooked."

"You'd send her to the chair?"

"Pretty open and shut. She obviously planned to waste him for at least two weeks. No sudden impulse, no temporary insanity, no imminent danger. She got pissed, planned it, and whacked him."

"She's so pitiful. There's something real . . . sad . . . about her."

"What's sad is she's looking twenty thousand volts in the eye. These things are not supposed to get personal, Shana."

"Well, it *is* personal, okay. I'm taking it very personal."

"Maybe you should let somebody else handle it."

"Not on your life, Irish. I'll do it and do it right."

"Hell, I wouldn't worry about it. Venable's handling the case. She hasn't tried a criminal case in ten years."

Parver finished her third martini and slid the glass to the edge of the table. "Think it's going to be a cakewalk, do you? Let me tell you, she's good. Ten years or not, she's good." She stopped and leaned across the table and said cautiously, "I think Marty's got a thing with her."

"Get outta here," he said with mock surprise, remembering the flowers on Venable's dining-room table.

Parver nodded emphatically and winked.

"Will wonders never cease," he said, and laughed.

The waiter brought her a new drink and took the empty away.

"That's your fourth martini," Flaherty said. "And I happen to know the bartender has a very heavy hand. It's none of my business, but I don't think you understand about martinis."

"Well, I may just get a li'l drunk tonight, Flaherty." She paused, took a sip, and then said, "Y'know, that's an awful long name. Fla-har-ty. That's almost three syl'bles. I'm going to call you Flay. Anyway, Flay, can you handle it, if I get a little snockered?"

He smiled at her. "I've never been drunk," he said, somewhat sheepishly.

"You're kidding?"

"Nope. Pot was my drug of choice."

"Pot's illegal."

"That's why I quit."

She held up her glass. "This isn't."

"That doesn't make a lot of sense, either."

"First time I tried grass, I sat in front of the oven in my friend's kitchen for an hour waiting for Johnny Carson to come on."

Flaherty laughed hard and nodded. "That must've been some good stuff."

"I dunno, never tried it again," she said, and realized her speech was getting a little slurred and Flaherty was suddenly transforming into twins. She closed one eye and focused across the table on his ruggedly handsome face. "How come you never asked m'out?"

"I just did."

"Uh-huh, six months later. I know you're not gay."

"Nope."

"And I, uh, I know I'm not *that* unesrable." She stopped and giggled. "Un-desir-able."

"Oh no," he said softly, and smiled.

"Well?"

"They don't have courses in the social graces on the streets of Boston—or in the state reformatory."

"You were *that* bad?"

"I was pretty bad."

"Wha's the worst thing y'ever did? Or maybe I shouldn't ask."

"Boosting cars."

"You stole cars?"

He nodded. "Me and my buddies."

"Can you do tha' thing they do in the movies, y'know, where they rip all th'wires out 'f the dashboard and make 'em spark and start th'car? Can you do that?" She closed one eye again and focused hard on him.

"You mean hot-wiring?" he said, nodding. "Sixty seconds, anything on wheels."

"Y'r kiddin'!"

"Nope."

"Wow. Why'd you quit?"

"I had a revelation. God appeared at the foot of my bed one night and told me if I kept it up I was gonna die young."

"And . . ."

"I took him seriously."

"She din't really," Parver said skeptically.

"She?"

"God."

"Oh." Flaherty smiled and made rings on the table with his wet glass. "In a way she did. One of my best friends went to the chair. He was robbing a grocery store and killed a cop. I mean, we were close, Ernie and I had done jobs together."

"That was his name, Ernie?"

"Ernie Holleran. There were five of us, hung out together, did stuff together. Ernie was one of us. But he did that thing and they maxed him out and the night they did it to him, we took the bus up to the state pen and we found this hill where you could see the prison and got two six-packs and sat there drinking and waiting until they did it. You can tell because when they throw the switch, the lights fade out, then they come back on. They do it twice, just to make sure. We sat there until the black Mariah left with him and we threw empty beer cans at the hearse and then we took the bus back home. That's the night God spoke to me. I decided I wasn't going out *that* way."

She was staring at him with one eye still closed, her mouth half open, mesmerized by his story.

"Know what?" she said after a while. "I'm not interstded, in-ter-ested, in social graces, Flay." She finished half her drink and slapped the glass back down on the table. "I'm in-ter-ested in scilnit, sincilat—"

"Scintillating?"

"Thank you . . . conversation, and, uh, and a beaut'ful man with lovely eyes and dark bl'ck hair and . . . sufer, sulper—"

"Superficial?"

"Than'you, su-per-fi-cial things like that. How come you always wear black, Flay? Why d'you have this Johnny Cash symrom . . . sidro . . . syn-drome."

He sighed and sipped his Coke and stared into her liquid eyes. "The truth?"

"What else is there?"

"I don't have any color sense. Don't know what goes with what. Long as I wear black, I'm safe."

"You really care about that, huh?"

He sat without comment for a minute, then nodded. "I guess I do," he said, and his cheeks began to color.

"Why, Couns'lor, I do b'lieve you're blushing," she said, and snickered. "You're somp'in else, Flay."

He laughed away the color. "And you're loaded."

"My embarr'sing you?"

"Never."

They stared across the table for a long moment, then she cast her eyes down. "Think we ... I ... could get outta here with't fallin' on m'face?"

"I'd never let you fall on your face, Hotshot."

"Ho'shot, s'cute, I like it."

"Want to go for it?"

"Go f'r th'gold." She snickered. "Jus' one min't."

"How about a cup of coffee?"

"Yuck!"

"Okay, we'll just sit here until you get it together."

"Ma'be Steamroller c'n get us a cab? Think?"

"Wait right here."

"Nooo, I'm gonna wait waaaay over there," she said, pointing across the room, and had a sudden fit of the giggles. The waiter got the cab and Flaherty helped her to her feet and put his arm under hers and pulled her against him.

"Make believe we're snuggling up, nobody'll pay any attention to us," he said, tilting her head against his shoulder and leading her toward the door.

"Sng'ling up, that what they call't in Boston?"

"Yeah," he said. They made it to the front door without incident, but as they walked outside a frigid blast of air swept off the river.

"Wow!" she said. "Wha' was'at?"

"Fresh air."

"I th'nk m'legs're goin'," she said, sagging as he led her to the cab. He slid her into the backseat.

"Flay?"

"Yeah?"

"Th'nks."

"For what?"

"List'nin' t'me."

"I'll listen to you anytime," he said, sliding in beside her.

"Really?"

"Sure."

"Th'n lissen caref'lly 'cause ... I'm gonna try t'remember ... what m'address is."

She got her address right on the third try and slid down in the seat and put her head on his shoulder and stared at him through her one eye and said, "Tell you secret, Mist' Flar'ty. I have cov'ted you from afar ev'since th' first time I saw you. That okay?"

He put his arm around her and drew her closer.

"I think it's great," he whispered, but did not tell her that he, too, had coveted her for just as long.

"Good," she murmured, and a moment later was sound asleep.

She lived in a second-floor apartment on the corner of West Eugenie and North Park, a two-story brick building with a pleasant nineteenth-century feel to it. Flaherty paid the cab driver and found her key in her purse and then got out, leaning into the backseat and gathering her up in his arms.

"Need some help?" the cabbie asked.

"Nah, she doesn't weigh more'n a nickel," Flaherty said, and carried her into the apartment building. He found her apartment without incident and, bracing one knee against the wall, balanced her against it while he opened the door, then carried her in and kicked it shut.

It was a bright, cheery one-bedroom, furnished with expensive and flawless taste and bright colors. Waterford and Wedgwood abounded and the furniture was warm and inviting. The kitchen, which was small but efficient, was separated from the main room by a small breakfast counter. The walls were covered with numbered prints by Miró, Matisse, and Degas. A single lamp glowed near the window. He carried her to the bedroom and flicked on the light switch with his elbow. It was a mess, the bed unmade, a dirty dish with the remains of a pizza on the nighttable, books piled haphazardly in the corner. He laid her on the bed and she stirred and gazed up sleepily.

"M'home?" she asked.

"Yep."

"You carried me up all those stairs?"

"Uh-huh."

"Sir Gagalad . . . oh, what'shisname. Tha's you. Glorious knight." She tried to sit up but flopped back on the feather mattress with her arms stretched out and sighed.

"Mouth's full a feathers," she said, and giggled softly.

"I'll get you some water."

"I'll try t'get undress'd while you're gone."

He went into the kitchen, found a pebbled glass in the cabinet, and drew ice cubes out of the icemaker in the refrigerator door. He poured cold water over them and swished the glass around a few times.

"How're you doing?" he called to her.

"Better'n 'spected."

"Let me know when you're in bed."

"Just any ol' time," she answered.

When he returned to the room, she was lying half under the covers, her clothes strewn on the floor. One leg was draped over the side of the bed. Her pantyhose hung forlornly from the leg.

"Almos' made it," she said. "That left leg was a real bitch." She wiggled the leg and laughed weakly. "Wow," she said. "You'er right 'bout martoonies."

He put the glass of water on the nighttable beside the bed and went to the window to close the blinds and suddenly a chill rippled across the back of his neck. He spread the blinds with his hands and scanned the street below.

Empty except for a single car parked across the street. It was also empty.

Paranoia, he thought. If the copycat killer was loose in Chicago, Shana Parver was certainly far down on his list. He closed the blinds.

"Flay?"

"Yeah." He looked at her and she turned her head toward him and peered through one half-open eye.

"Don' leave me, please. Don' wanna wake up lonesome in t'morning. 'Kay?"

"Okay."

"Wadda guy."

He walked over to the bed and helped her sit up and take a sip of water.

"Mmmm," she said, and fell back on the mattress. "Not gonna leave me?"

"No, I'm not going to leave you."

She smiled and immediately fell asleep again. Flaherty sat down on the bed and very carefully rolled the remaining leg of her pantyhose over her ankle and slipped it off her foot. He took her toes in his fingers and stroked them very gently.

God, he thought, *even her toes are gorgeous.*

———

In the backseat of the company limo, Jane Venable was already missing Martin. She had had a business meeting with her Japanese clients and Vail had decided he should spend at least an occasional night in his own apartment.

She was spoiled already. Spoiled by his attentiveness, spoiled by their passionate and inventive lovemaking, spoiled by just having him there. She stared out the window, watching the night lights streak by. When they stopped at a light, she suddenly sat up in her seat.

"Larry," she said, "pull over in front of the towers, please."

The driver pulled over and parked in front of the glittering shaft of glass and chrome. He jumped out and opened the door for her.

"I'll be back in a couple of minutes," she said, and hurried into the apartment building. The night manager sat behind a desk that looked like the cockpit of an SST. A closed-circuit video camera system permitted him to scan the halls of each of the thirty floors. He was slender, his face creased with age, his brown but graying hair combed straight back. He wore a blue blazer with a red carnation in its lapel and looked more like the deskman at an exclusive hotel than the inside doorman of an apartment building.

"May I help you?" he asked in a pseudo–cultured British accent, his eyes appraising the black limo.

Venable put on her most dazzling smile. "Hi," she said. "What's your name?"

"Victor," he said with a guarded smile.

"Well, Victor, I'm Jane Venable," she said, taking a sheet of paper from her purse and sliding it across the polished desk in front of him. "I'm an attorney. My client has been charged with the murder of John Delaney. I have a court order here permitting me access to the scene of the crime. I know this is a terrible imposition, but would you let me in?"

"What? Now? You want to inspect the premises *now*?"

She laid a folded fifty-dollar bill on the document.

"I just happened to be in the neighborhood. I doubt I'll be fifteen minutes."

He looked at the court order, cast another glance at the limo, then smiled at her as he palmed the fifty.

"How can I resist such a dazzling smile, Ms. Venable," he said. He opened a desk drawer, took out a ring of keys, and led her to the elevator.

"Terrible thing," he said as the elevator climbed to the thirtieth floor.

"Dreadful," she said, remembering that Delaney's death had probably been cause for celebrating all over the city. "Did you know him well?"

Victor raised an eyebrow and smiled. "He said 'Hello' coming in and 'Good evening' going out and gave me a bottle of scotch for Christmas. That's how well I knew Mr. Delaney."

"Was it good scotch?"

"Chivas."

"Nice."

They arrived at the thirtieth floor and Victor unlocked the door. The crime ribbons had been removed.

"Take your time, I'm on until two," Victor said. "The door will lock when you leave."

"You're a dream, Victor."

"Thank you, Ms. Venable." He left, pulling the door shut behind him.

A crazy notion, she thought, *coming here in the middle of the night.* But when she had looked through the car window and realized she was in front of the place—well, what the hell, she wasn't in any rush to get back to her empty condo anyway.

It had been years since Venable had visited the scene of a homicide and her adrenaline started pumping the instant she started down the hallway to the living room. She stood a few feet away from the black outline on the floor. It seemed to box in the wide, dark brown stain in the carpet.

She wasn't really looking for anything in particular; she felt it was her responsibility to Edith Stoddard to familiarize herself with the murder scene. She walked into the bedroom, noticed there were scratches on the spindles of the headboard. She stood in the bathroom. His toothbrush, a razor, and an Abercrombie & Fitch shaving bowl and brush were on one side of the marble-top sink and a bottle of bay rum aftershave lotion was on the other side. A towel hung unused on a gold rack near the shower.

She went into the kitchen, checked the refrigerator. Someone had emptied it out and cleaned it. There were canned foods in the small pantry. Delaney, it seemed, had a passion for LeSueur asparagus and Vienna sausages. She went back to the bedroom, checked through his desk and drawers, and found nothing of interest. She found an ashtray, carried it back to the bedroom, and sat down on the end of the bed facing the closet. She decided to have a cigarette before she left. Smoking was not permitted in company vehicles.

Stupid, she thought. *But at least I got this little junket out of the way.*

Did Edith Stoddard's sense of betrayal over losing her job really precipitate Delaney's death? she wondered anew. It was a persistent question in her mind. The other facts in the case seemed blatant, but the motive seemed so bland. But then she remembered reading about other cases not dissimilar, like the postman who lost his job, went back to the post office with an assault weapon, and killed nine people before turning it on himself. Perhaps it wasn't as bland as she thought.

Thinking about Edith Stoddard, she stared into the closet. From where she was sitting, she could see the entire area, which was adjacent to, and formed a small hallway into, the bathroom; a large closet, empty except for a suit, a couple of shirts on hangers, a bathrobe, a pair of leather slippers, and a pair of black loafers.

But something else caught her attention. As she stared at it, she realized that the closet was off balance. One side of the closet was deep, stretching to the wall, the other side was just wide enough to hang a suit. It was at least two feet narrower.

She stared at it for a full two minutes, her old instincts working, a combination of paranoia and nosiness that had made her the best prosecutor of her time.

"Why is that closet off center," she said aloud to herself.

She went into the bathroom and checked to see if there were shelves behind the wall, but the commode was located behind it and that wall was tiled. She went back into the bedroom, entered the closet, and turned on the light. *Only a woman would be curious about this odd bit of interior architecture,* she thought. *Only a woman would be concerned about the loss of that much closet space.* She rapped on the wall with her knuckles, thinking perhaps it was a riser, but the tapping was hollow.

A hollow space, two feet deep and five feet wide? A safe, perhaps? Secret files, something incriminating? Something she could use in court to taint the victim? She traced the seam where the two walls joined but found nothing. She stood at the juncture of the two walls and shoved against one of them.

It gave a little. She shoved harder. It bowed a little at the top.

The wall panel was not nailed; it was locked in the middle. She stepped back and once again scanned the seams, top, bottom, and sides. It was a door. Now she had to figure out how to open it.

She ran her fingertips around the doorsill and along the carpeting. Nothing.

She sighed and sat back down on the end of the bed and stared some more. She looked at the clothes rod. There were no clothes on the narrow side of the closet. She went back in, reached up, and jiggled the rod, then twisted it. The rod was threaded. She turned it four full turns before the whole end of the rod pulled away from the wall. She laid it on the floor and examined the receptacle. There was a button recessed in the threaded rod holder. She pushed it, heard a muffled *click,* and then the panel popped open an inch or two. A light blinked on inside the smaller closet. She swung it open.

Her breath came in a gasp. Her mouth gaped for a moment as she stared with shock and disbelief at its contents.

"My God," she whispered.

Then her eyes moved down to the floor of the secret compartment.

The gun.

29

Jane Venable arrived at Vail's office at exactly ten o'clock. The elevator doors parted and she stepped out, decked out in an emerald-green silk suit that made her red hair look like it was on fire. She had a tan Coach leather shoulder bag slung over one shoulder. She strode toward his office with the authority and assurance of a show horse prancing past the judges' stand. Everyone in the office suddenly found something to do that would put her directly in their line of sight. Every eye followed her to Naomi's desk.

"Hi," she said with a bright smile. "You must be Naomi. I'm Jane Venable." She thrust her hand out.

Vail came out of his office and greeted her, ignoring the momentary smirk Jane flashed at him, a look Naomi did not miss. *Marty*, she thought, *you're dead in the water.* Vail had included Venable in the special meeting because she was an integral part of the emerging Stampler crisis. They entered his office.

"Last night was the pits," she said, faking a big smile.

He smiled back. "I smoked a pack of cigarettes trying to go to sleep."

"That'll teach you to take a night off."

"We're being watched," he said, flicking his eyes toward the rest of the staff.

"I know. Isn't it fun?"

"Coffee?"

"Sure."

"I checked on you last night—to make sure your guardian angels were there," Vail said.

"I don't know what my neighbors think," she said. "One guy parks in front of the house all night and the other one parks on my terrace and cruises the grounds with a flashlight every hour on the hour."

"Just makes you even more mysterious than you already are."

"I don't know why I even brought it up, I've never met any of my neighbors." Her mood seemed to change suddenly when he turned his back to her to draw the coffee. He could see her reflection in the windowpane. She became less ebullient, more introspective, as if she had very quickly fallen into deep thought.

The Stoddard case was heavy on Venable's mind. The discovery of the secret compartment in Delaney's apartment presented her with a peculiar dilemma. As Stoddard's defender, she was not required to tell the prosecution what she had found. On the other hand, the gun was integral to the case and she could be accused of concealing evidence. Her decision had been not to touch anything. She had closed up the secret room and left; her argument would be that she had not been sure whose gun was in the closet. And she still had to deal with Edith Stoddard about her discovery. She decided to put the problem aside for the moment; obviously Vail's meeting would rule the agenda this morning. *Loosen up*, she told herself.

Vail poured a spoonful of sugar in her coffee cup. She quickly brightened again when he returned with her coffee. As she put the cup on the table in front of her, he said, "Something bothering you?"

"You haven't known me that long."

"How long?"

"Long enough to tell if something's got my goat."

"Ah! So something *has* got your goat," he said. He walked

around the table and sat down, tilting his chair back with one foot on the corner of the desk.

She leaned across the table and stared at him through half-closed eyes and said, with mock sarcasm, "I don't have a goat, Mr. District Attorney."

He laughed, and she asked, "Did you miss me?" looking as if she were asking the time of day.

"Nah, although it did occur to me that some corporate samurai warrior might steal your heart away at dinner last night."

She laughed at him. "You can't get rid of me that easily, Vail."

"I don't want to get rid of you at all."

They were keeping up the facade of two people casually making conversation, a pantomime for the staff, which was still working very hard to make it appear as if they were disinterested in the scene behind the glass partition.

"Good," she said, shaking her head so her hair flowed down over her shoulders.

He whistled very low in appreciation of her studied wiles. "You are a science unto yourself," he said.

"I suppose a good-morning kiss would stop traffic up here."

"It would probably stop traffic in Trafalgar Square."

"Pity."

"Let's let the Wild Bunch in and get started. I'm sure they're all sitting outside this fishbowl reading our lips. Besides, they're all dying to meet the legendary Jane Venable."

"Sure."

"Absolutely. They know all about you. They've all read the transcript of the Stampler trial."

"Well, that's just great!" she snapped. "The one trial where Mr. Wonderful whipped my ass and *that's* what they know about me?"

"Actually twice. I whipped your ass twice. Have you forgotten . . . ?"

"Just call them in, okay?" she said, cutting him off.

"I did miss you last night," he whispered as he walked past her.

"It was your decision."

"That's right, rub it in."

He opened the office door and waved at those of the staff who were in the office. They finished phone calls, put away files, and dribbled into the room over the next five minutes, each pleasantly greeting Venable, though regarding her with respectful suspicion since she was considered a potential threat in the courtroom. They drew coffee from the big urn, doctored it, grabbed a doughnut from the box provided by Naomi, and settled down, some in chairs, some on the floor, waiting expectantly. Vail rarely called an emergency staff meeting like this. Only Hazel Fleishman and Bucky Winslow were absent; both were in court.

The last to enter the room was Bobby Hartford, a tall, ramrod-straight black man from Mississippi whose father, Nate Hartford, a field rep for the NAACP, had been shot to death in front of Bobby. He'd been nine years old at the time. Now, at thirty-eight, Hartford was the oldest member of the Wild Bunch and its only married man (Fleishman was also married). He had about him an almost serene air despite his traumatic early years—Vail had never heard him raise his voice. He sat on the floor beside Flaherty.

"I asked Jane Venable here today because she's deeply involved in what we're about to discuss," Vail began. He turned to Venable. "This is what we call a brain scan. The rules are the same for all of us. If you have something to ask, clarify, or contribute, jump in anytime. You'll probably hear some challenges, some devil's advocacy, that's the way we do it here, okay?"

He paused to take a sip of coffee and light a cigarette, blowing the smoke at the exhaust fan.

"All right, here's the situation. I assume you've all read Dermott's report on the Balfour and Lincoln murders. You've also read the trial transcripts of the Stampler trial, so by now you are aware of the more than coincidental nexus of these crimes. And although the latest two killings are way out of our jurisdiction, we're going to become involved in this situation whether we like it or not. I'm convinced Stampler wanted me to know that he had conned us all—and he's still conning us. So when I went up to see him and his shrink, Dr. Woodward, I wired myself. Taped the conversations I had with them."

"Was that legal?" Hartford asked.

"We're not planning to use it in court."

"Not what I asked, Counselor," Hartford challenged.

Vail regarded him balefully for a few moments, then shook his head. "No, it wasn't." Then he grinned. "Want to leave the room when I play it?"

"Oh, hell, no," Hartford said with a laugh. "I just wanted to know where you're coming from."

There was a ripple of laughter in the room.

"Fear is where I'm coming from," Vail said seriously. "I fear this man. He is very dangerous. I hope I can convince you of that before this meeting's over. Before I play the tape, here's what we know. We know that Stampler hasn't had any contact with the outside world for ten years, no phone calls, no letters, no visitors. We know the killer is printing messages in code on the back of his victim's heads in blood, just as Stampler did. And the quotes are keyed to Rushman's old library books, which are now in the Newberry, just as Stampler's were. All those coincidences can reasonably be explained. Newspaper accounts, trial records, that sort of thing—none of that information is secret.

"But we also know that whoever killed Balfour and Lincoln was privy to information that could *only* have come from Stampler. What the public never knew was that Rushman was a pederast. He had a group called the Altar Boys—four boys and a girl—whom he directed in pornographic videos, then stepped in and took his pleasure with the girl or one of the boys, or all of them, whatever suited him. Stampler was one of the Altar Boys. He murdered two of them. But Alex Lincoln got away. So did Stampler's girlfriend, Linda, who was the young lady in the group. She later became Mrs. Linda Balfour. Now they're dead and the M.O. is exactly the same as the murders Stampler committed."

"There is one difference," Stenner interjected. "This killer takes trophies—little mementos of his tricks. He took a stuffed toy that belonged to Linda Balfour and Lincoln's belt buckle. My feeling is the copycat is a true serial killer."

"He also left a Polaroid shot of Linda Balfour's body when he killed Lincoln," Flaherty said, "so there would be no doubt he committed both crimes."

"None of the information about Rushman was ever revealed in the trial," Vail went on. "There were two tapes of one of the Altar Boys sessions. Jane and I each had one and we both erased them after the trial."

"Our theory is that Stampler is triggering this killer, but we don't know how he's doing it or how he originally made contact with the surrogate. I think somewhere in my conversation with Stampler he dropped a clue, something very subtle to let me know he's the real killer."

"Why?" Meyer asked.

"Because he's playing games with me. He's a psychopath. I think you better listen to the tape before you ask any more questions. Maybe I'm too close, maybe one of you will hear something I'm missing."

"Or maybe you're wrong," Flaherty said, half grinning. "Maybe he didn't plant a clue at all."

"You mean I'm paranoid, Dermott?"

"Something like that."

Vail shrugged and smiled. "Very possible. The question is, is my paranoia justified? You guys decide."

He punched the play button and the conversation with Woodward began. The group, including Venable, leaned forward, rapt in the conversation, zeroing in on every word as Woodward described his almost decade-long experience with Aaron Stampler. The revelation that Aaron Stampler had become Raymond Vulpes created the biggest buzz among the group. Then well into the interview between Vail and Stampler/Vulpes, Dermott Flaherty abruptly sat up and said, "Hold it! Stop it there."

Vail punched the stop button.

"Back it up a little and replay," Flaherty said.

Vail snapped the rewind button, let it run a few feet, and punched play.

vail: *Did Aaron and Roy ever talk about killing the old preacher . . . uh, I can't think of his name, it's been ten years.*
vulpes: *Shackles.*
vail: *Shackles, right.*
vulpes: *Roy bragged about that one, all right. They really hated that old man.*
vail: *That's an understatement.*
vulpes: *Guess you're right about that. He was their first, you know?*
vail: *So I heard.*
vulpes: *Why, hell, Mr. Vail, you probably know more about the two of them than I do.*
vail: *Oh, I think not. How about the others? Did he talk about them?*
vulpes: *You mean his brother and Aaron's old girlfriend, Mary Lafferty?*
vail: *I'd forgotten her name, too.*
vulpes: *Lafferty. Mary Lafferty.*

"There's your clue," Flaherty said. "He repeats Mary Lafferty's name three times. I never knew about Mary Lafferty, that's why I didn't catch it at the time. And I didn't include it in my report, so you never knew about it, Marty."

"Catch what? What are you talking about?" Venable asked.

"The name on the package that Lincoln was delivering when he was killed—the addressor was M. Lafferty. There's no way Stampler could know that, none of those details have been released to the press yet."

The revelation caused a flurry of conversation. St. Claire was the most excited.

"Ain't that enough to stall ol' Woodward in his tracks?" he asked. "I mean, doesn't that prove Vulpes or whoever the hell he is knew about these killings?"

"It makes no difference. I was Stampler's lawyer of record," Vail said. "I can't take any legal action against him, I can't even testify

against him in court. Anyway, all we have at this point is circumstantial evidence and hunches, and I guarantee, it would take a
lot more than that to stop Woodward. He regards Vulpes as his
personal medical victory and Vulpes knows it. But you're right
about the package, Dermott, Vuples thought I knew about the return address. It was his way of letting me know that he was at
least involved in the deaths of Alex Lincoln and Linda Balfour."

"There's something else," Jane Venable said. "Does the name
Vulpes ring anybody's bell?"

They all looked at one another and shook their heads.

"*Vulpes* is Latin—it's the genus for a fox."

"The craftiest of all creatures," Stenner intoned.

"Another goddamn message," St. Claire growled.

"Janie," said Vail, "I saw those red eyes you talked about—for
just the flash of a second, I saw pure hate. I saw murder. I saw the
damn four *horsemen* for an instant."

"Well, I've got a tidbit of information that should give us all a
chuckle at Mr. Vulpes's expense," said Naomi. "It's in the report
submitted to the judge who signed the order for Vulpes's furlough."

"How did you get that?" Vail asked.

"I went to a seminar once with the court clerk up there, she
faxed it to me," Naomi said, and winked. She flipped through
the pages. "Here it is, listed under the heading 'Miscellaneous.' "
She looked up. "Mr. Stampler, it seems is phobic."

"Phobic? What kind of phobia?" Vail asked.

"He's afraid of the dark," she said, and snickered.

"Afraid of the dark?" Parver said with disbelief. Flaherty broke
into a hearty laugh as thoughts of the madman, cowering in the
dark, flashed through his mind.

"Afraid of the dark," Naomi repeated. "He's had special permission to sleep with the lights on ever since he was admitted to
Daisyland."

"Is he still sleeping with the lights on?" asked Vail.

She nodded. "According to Doctors Woodward, Ciaffo, and
Bascott, who petitioned for his furlough, it's called a nonaggres-
sive phobic reaction. They attribute it to childhood traumas."

"According to Woodward, Raymond never went through reexperiencing; Aaron did," said Parver. "He says on the tape that Raymond doesn't suffer any of either Aaron's or Roy's psychological problems."

"So how come he picked up Stampler's phobia?" St. Claire asked.

"Because it's the one thing Stampler can't hide," Vail said.

"How could Woodward have missed it?" Naomi asked.

"Because he wanted to miss it," said Vail. "Woodward's already got a spot on his wall for the Nobel Prize in medicine."

"Or because he wasn't looking for it," suggested Venable, taking a more practical approach to the question. "Stampler had been sleeping with the lights on for years and Raymond just kept doing it. That miscellaneous note in the report was probably part of an earlier evaluation."

"Afraid of the dark," said Stenner. "Makes perfect sense—the thing Stampler feared most in life was the coal mines."

"And nothin' could be darker than the hole," said St. Claire.

"Except maybe Aaron Stampler's soul," said Jane Venable.

"I think I can answer one big question: I know how he tracked down Lincoln and Balfour," Bobby Hartford said quietly. "I'm going into my office and make a phone call. You guys can listen to it on Marty's speakerphone."

"Who are you calling?" asked Flaherty.

"Minnesota Department of Motor Vehicles."

Hartford went to his office and dialed the number. A high-pitched, somewhat comical, voice answered.

"DMV. Sergeant Colter speaking."

"Hey, Sergeant, this is Detective John Standish down in Chicago. How you doing?"

"Good, neighbor, what can I do you for?"

"We're looking for a witness in an old homicide case, dropped out of sight a couple of years ago. We just got a tip somebody saw him up in your neck of the woods. Can you run him through the computer for me?"

"Got a name?"

"Alexander Sanders Lincoln. White, male, twenty-six."

"Hang on a minute."

They could hear the keys of a computer board clicking in the background.

"You're out of luck, friend. We had him up until 1991, then his license expired. Wait a minute, there's an entry here—the Missouri DMV requested a citation report on him in November '91. He probably applied for a commercial driver's license. He was clean up here."

"Good, I'll try Missouri. Thanks, Sergeant. You've been a big help."

"Anytime."

Hartford hung up. He dialed another number.

"Illinois Department of Motor Vehicles, Officer Anderson. How may I help you?"

"Hi, Anderson, this is Detective John Standish, Chicago PD."

"Morning, Standish, what's the problem?"

"We've got an old warrant here, the statute's about to run out. Woman named Linda Gellerman, white, female, twenty-six. We got a tip she's back in Illinois. Run it through your computer, will you, see if she pops up."

"Gellerman? Two *l*'s?"

"Right."

Another pause, then: "Yeah. Linda Gellerman . . . married two years ago and had the license reissued in her married name. That's Linda Balfour, 102 Poplar Street, Gideon, Illinois."

"Hey, that was easy. I may take the rest of the day off."

Anderson laughed. "I should be so lucky."

"Thanks, brother. Come see us."

"Yes, sir. S'long."

Hartford hung up and returned to Vail's office. He snapped his fingers as he entered and sat back down on the floor.

"It's an old trick. Used to take down the license numbers of Ku Klux Klanners, find out who they were, and call 'em on the phone, tell them we were FBI and they better keep their noses clean," Hartford said. "Put the sweats on 'em for a while."

"Stampler could have done it from Daisyland if he had access to a phone," said Flaherty.

"He doesn't have access to a phone," Vail said.

"How about the repair shop?"

"No phone line."

"The killer coulda done it," St. Claire said.

"I got the chills when he talked about Linda Gellerman," Parver said. "Two years ago she thought she had her whole life ahead of her."

"She did," Naomi said. "She just didn't know how short it was going to be."

"You think he's been faking all along, Marty?" Flaherty asked.

"What do you believe, Abel?" Vail asked the stoic detective.

"I don't believe there was ever a Roy, never have. I believe Raymond Vulpes is a myth. Stampler was and is a clever, cold-blooded, psychopathic killer."

"Could you be a little more explicit?" Venable said with a smile. The group broke into nervous laughter, relieving the tension that had been building in the room.

"Hellacious trick, and I'd hate to have to prove it in court, but I agree with Abel," said Vail. "I think he's been pulling everyone's chain for the last ten years."

St. Claire said, "Everything that son-bitch does sends a message to us."

"Including his name—the Fox," said Hartford scornfully.

"Well, the new message is 'Catch me if you can,' " Vail said solemnly. "Because tomorrow morning Raymond Vulpes will be leaving Daisyland for six weeks. And he's coming here. Abel, I want two men on the Fox—around the clock—not too close, but close enough to videotape him. Let's see who he talks to, who he contacts, where he goes."

"That's kinda flirtin' with harassment, ain't it?" St. Claire asked casually, spitting into his baby cup.

"No," said Vail, just as casually. "Harassment is if we drag him into an alley and beat the living shit out of him."

Vail's response caught everyone off guard. They had never heard their boss so vitriolic, so openly angry.

"There's still the big question," said Flaherty. "How did he locate the serial killer and how does he trigger him?"

"There's somethin' we're all overlookin'," said St. Claire. "There were twenty-three other tapes admitted into evidence in the Stampler trial."

"Twenty-three other tapes?" Vail said.

"I remember that," Venable said. "Don't you remember, Marty? Judge Shoat wanted to review all the tapes Dr. Arrington made with Stampler to justify the agreement to send Stampler to Daisyland."

"Hell, I forgot all about it," said Vail. "I never got them back."

"Molly Arrington did," said St. Claire. "About a week after the trial ended. She's had 'em for ten years, if she kept 'em."

"Why wouldn't she?" Parver offered. "Seems to me they'd be great research material."

"Which brings up a point," suggested Venable. "Maybe you've been going about this problem backwards."

"What do you mean?" Stenner asked.

"Maybe Stampler didn't locate the serial killer," Venable answered. "Maybe the killer came to him."

30

"What say, Raymond?" Terry asked. "Want to go down to the commissary, eat with the inmates once before you leave?"

"I've gone ten years without eating with them," Vulpes answered, "why break my string now? I'll wait until we get downtown, have a hot fudge sundae and a hot dog."

Terry laughed. "You and your hot fudge sundaes. Gotta lock the door behind me. Y'know, rules."

"Sure. What's one more hour, more or less. Besides, I got to pack up my tools."

"Right. I'm proud of you, Raymond."

"Thanks, Terry. I'm going to miss you."

"Me, too." He laughed. "Hell, you're the only one I can talk to around here, gives me an answer that makes any sense. I'll bring you back a Coke."

"Thanks."

Terry pulled the gate closed behind him and key-locked it. Vulpes listened to his footsteps fade down the hallway. He opened one of the cabinets in the repair shop, took out a VCR, and put it on his worktable. He then took a small screwdriver and removed four screws from each side of the machine's cover and slid it off. He placed the cover on its side, so as to obscure the machine from the doorway.

He looked across the quadrangle at the purchasing office opposite his window. It was a small office run by three women. Two of them were standing in the doorway. The third, Verna Mableton, was pacing back and forth in front of the windows, talking on her portable phone. She waved the other two women on and they left. She sat on the corner of her desk and kept talking.

Vulpes watched her without any expression. Occasionally he glanced at the door to the repair shop.

Inside the VCR was a small, handmade computer. It was six inches long, four inches wide, and two inches deep and looked like a small keyboard with a tiny, oblong digital-readout screen above the keys. Beside it was a black box, three inches square and two inches deep. He took the two units out, laid them on the desk, and monitored the door while he attached the black box to the minicomputer with a two-inch piece of telephone wire.

Vulpes was proud of the minicomputer. It was basically a modem with a keyboard and he had made it from scratch. He was even prouder of the transmission box. He had waited patiently for more than a year until one of the purchasing department's computers had gone down. He suggested waiting until Saturday to repair it, when nobody was in the office. The guard had waited outside, sitting in the sun. Vulpes had dismantled the portable phone and sketched the circuitry. It had taken him five months, getting a piece at a time with his regular orders so they wouldn't become suspicious, to get the materials he needed. It took another four months to duplicate the radio phone in the purchasing office. Basically it was nothing more than a dialing device for the modem.

He looked back across the quad at the office. Verna stood up, nodded, and placed the portable phone on its stand. She took her purse and left the office. Vulpes turned the minicomputer on and typed MODEM. It hummed for a second and then ENTER appeared in the small screen. He typed in a phone number and waited. The numbers blinked out and after a few seconds the word CONTACT blinked three times. He began typing.

ARE YOU THERE, HYDRA?

YES, FOX, AS ALWAYS.

IT IS TIME.

OH, THANK YOU, FOX.

ARE YOU READY?

YES, FOX, ALWAYS READY.

HAVE YOU RESEARCHED THE LIST?

ALL FOUR OF THEM.

AND?

TAKE YOUR PICK.

EXCELLENT, AS USUAL, HYDRA.

THANK YOU, FOX. WHO SHALL IT BE?

DO YOU HAVE A CHOICE?

WHATEVER MAKES YOU HAPPY, FOX.

I THINK . . .

YES?

I THINK IT WILL BE TONIGHT.

OH, FOX, TONIGHT! THANK YOU. THANK YOU, FOX.

HYDRA?

YES, FOX.

YOU KNOW WHAT TO DO AFTER?

OH YES, FOX, I KNOW WHAT TO . . . SOMEONE COMING.

DO NUMBER THREE.

NUMBER THREE! YES, YES, FOX, YES! SOON . . .

Vulpes typed END on the screen and the screen blinked off. His heart was beating in his mouth. His penis was erect. He sat down, leaning forward so his face was hidden by the VCR cover. He was panting. And then suddenly he was released. He gasped, blew out a long breath, and finally sat up straight. He took several deep breaths and hummed very slowly to himself, reducing the tempo of his humming until it was a mere rattle in his throat. His heart slowed to normal. He sighed.

He disconnected the small box and removed the tray from his toolbox. He wrapped the minicomputer and the transmission box in lead foil and placed them in the bottom of the chest, covering them with tools.

There, it's over for now.

31

The pilot put the twin-engine plane down on a grass strip in a little town called Milford in southern Indiana. There was no Tony in a Cadillac to greet them, so Vail and St. Claire rented a car at the small airport and drove six miles south across the Flatrock River to the Justine Clinic. The hospital was a pleasant departure from the Daisy. It was shielded from the highway by a half-mile-deep stand of trees, at the end of a gravel road. As Vail and St. Claire burst out of the miniforest, Justine spread out before them, looking more like a collective farm than a mental hospital. A cluster of old brick buildings surrounded a small lake. A tall, brick silo stood alone and solitary, like a sentinel in the middle of the sprawling field that separated the facility from the woods. A tall chain-link fence behind the buildings on one side of the lake formed what appeared to be an enormous playground. Several children were hanging on a spinning whirligig, while a woman in a thick red jacket sat nearby reading a book. A boat dock with a tin-roofed boathouse at its end stretched out into the lake and a floating raft drifted forlornly about twenty yards from the shore. It was a pleasant-seeming place, unlike the cold, foreboding penal-colony atmosphere of the Daisy.

"Looks like a summer camp I went to once when I was a kid," St. Claire said.

"Somehow I never thought of you as a kid, Harve," Vail said.

"I was about nine. Damn, I hated it. We had to swim in this lake, musta been forty below. M'lips were blue the whole two weeks I was there." He paused to spit out the car window. "What's this guy's name again?"

"Lowenstein. Dr. Fred Lowenstein. He's the director."

"Sound like a nice guy?"

"He was very pleasant on the phone."

"And she wouldn't talk to you, huh?"

"Her secretary said she was in a meeting, so I asked for the director."

"He know what's goin' on?"

"Vaguely."

They pulled up to what appeared to be the main building, a sprawling brick barn of a place with a slate roof, and parked beside several other cars on a graveled oval in front of the structure. Gusts of wind whined off the lake and swirled into dancing dust monkeys as they got out of the car. A young boy in his early teens was hosing down a battered old pickup truck nearby.

"We're looking for Dr. Lowenstein," Vail said to him. "Is his office in here?" The boy nodded and watched them enter.

The lobby of the building was an enormous room with a soaring ceiling and a great open fireplace surrounded by faded, old, fluffy sofas and chairs. The receptionist, a chunky woman in her late forties with wispy blue-gray hair held up by bobby pins, sat behind a scarred maple desk angled to one side of the entrance. A Waterford drinking glass sat on one corner of her desk stuffed with a half-dozen straw flowers. Behind her, a large Audubon print of a cardinal hung slightly lopsided on the wall. The only thing modern in the entire room was the switchboard phone.

"Help you?" she asked pleasantly.

"Martin Vail to see Dr. Lowenstein. I have an appointment."

"From Chicago?"

"Right."

"Boy, didn't take you long t'get here," she said, lifting the phone receiver.

"The miracle of flight," St. Claire said, his eyes twinkling.

She looked at him over rimless glasses for a second, then: "Doc, your guests are here from the Windy City. Uh-huh, I mentioned that. It's the miracle of flight. 'Kay." She cradled the phone. "First door on the right," she said, motioning down a hall toward an open door and smiling impishly at St. Claire.

Lowenstein was a great moose of a man with burly shoulders and shaggy brown hair that swept over his ears and curled around the collar of a plaid shirt. The sleeves were turned up halfway to his elbows and his battered corduroy pants had shiny spots on the knees. He had a pleasant, ruddy face and warm brown eyes, and there was about him a pleasant, haphazard attitude unlike the measured mien of the pipe-smoking Woodward. He was sitting at a roll-top desk, leaning over a large yellow butterfly mounted on a white square of cardboard, studying it through a magnifying glass. A cup of tea sat forgotten among stacks of papers and pamphlets that cluttered the desktop. He looked up as Vail tapped on the door frame.

"Dr. Lowenstein? Martin Vail. This is Harve St. Claire."

"Well, you certainly didn't waste any time getting here," he said in a gruff rumble of a voice.

"We have a twin-engine Cessna available when the occasion demands," Vail said. "An hour beats driving for three hours."

"I would say." He put down the magnifying glass and offered a callused hand that engulfed Vail's.

"Pretty thing," St. Claire said, nodding to the mounted butterfly.

"Just a common monarch," Lowenstein said. "Found it on the windowsill this morning. Thought the kids might enjoy studying it. Can I get you anything? Tea, coffee?"

"No thanks," Vail said.

Lowenstein sat back at the desk and swept a large paw toward two wooden chairs.

"I appreciate your help on this, Doctor," said Vail. "I wouldn't have bothered you except that Molly wouldn't take my call."

"I understand the nature of your problem, Mr. Vail, but I don't know a hell of a lot about the Stampler case. It's my feeling that you and Molly need to address the problem. I'm also certain she would have refused a meeting if you had reached her by phone."

"Why?"

"Molly had a breakdown four years ago. A combination of exhaustion, depression, and alcohol. She was a patient here for a year and a half."

"I'm sorry, I had no idea . . ."

"She overcame the major problems. There were some side effects. She was agoraphobic for about a year. Lived on the grounds. Wouldn't leave. To her credit, she overcame that, too. Has a little house down the road. Bought herself a car. She's working mainly with children now, and quite successfully. Avoids pushing herself. She's a brilliant woman, as you know. Graduated *magna cum laude* from Indiana State. A very compassionate lady."

"I know that, sir," said Vail. "She did a remarkable job on the Stampler case."

"That's what I'm driving at. I think it left its scars."

"In what way?"

"I've never been quite sure. She was, uh, very subdued when she first came back. Didn't want to talk about the experience for a long time. In fact, never has except in the most clinical terms. It's certainly not an experience she cares to relive."

"Why did you invite us over if she won't speak to us?"

"Because your problem is serious. She's strong enough now to deal with it and put it behind her."

"Are you her therapist?"

"I have been. She is also a dear friend, has been for fifteen years. Her brother's problems contributed to the breakdown. Are you familiar with that?"

Vail nodded. "Delayed stress syndrome from Vietnam?"

"Yes. He's catatonic. Never has recovered. Pretty tough to deal with."

"This is certainly a pleasant atmosphere," Vail said. "If she had to suffer through that experience I can't think of a better place to do it. It's certainly a far cry from Daisyland."

"Thanks. We're not much for show here," he said.

"So Molly agreed to the meeting?"

"I told her it was a grave situation. No details. She trusts my judgment."

"Thanks." Vail and St. Claire stood to leave. Vail turned at the door. "By the way, Doctor, could you describe a psychopath for me? Not in heavy psychotalk, just the basics."

Lowenstein regarded Vail for a moment, slowly nodded. "Totally amoral, usually paranoid, harbors great rage—which he can successfully hide. Remember the boy in the Texas tower? Nobody knew how angry he was until he turned the town into a shooting gallery. Psychopaths also tend to consider others inferior, have contempt for their peers, and they're antisocial, pathological liars. Laws don't count to them."

"Homicidal?"

"Can be. Depends on the extent of the rage. They can also be charming, intelligent, witty, often socially desirable. Why?"

"I think Aaron Stampler fits the profile perfectly."

"A real charmer, eh?"

Vail nodded.

"Well, that's what keeps us in business, Mr. Vail," Lowenstein said, turning back to his butterfly. "Second door on the left. She's expecting you."

———

Dr. Molly Arrington's sitting room adjoined her office and was a study in simple elegance. It was a small room, cozy and inviting, dominated by a forest-green chesterfield sofa with overstuffed cushions and pillows. Two dark-oak Kennedy rocking chairs balanced the seating arrangement and a large antique coffee table held the group together. The walls were papered with a gray-and-white striped pattern. A shaggy blanket with a silly-looking, wall-eyed black and white cow knitted in its center was thrown over one arm of the sofa and there was a tube vase holding a single, enormous yellow daisy on one corner of the table. Soft light filtered through a single window, forming deep shadows in the corners of the room.

"Hello, Martin," she said, stepping out of the shadows, her voice just above a whisper. Vail was taken aback by Molly Arrington's appearance. She was smaller than Vail remembered, her once unblemished skin creased with the ridges of time and tragedy, her ash-brown hair streaked with gray and cropped close to her ears. Her pale blue eyes had an almost haunted look. It was obvious that a year and a half in the institution had taken a toll, and yet there was about her an aura of uncompromising stubbornness in the jut of her chin and the brace of her shoulders.

"Hi, Molly. Good to see you again."

"Ten years," she said. "Such a long time. You haven't changed a bit. Come in and sit down." She smiled at St. Claire. "I'm Molly."

"Harve St. Claire, Doctor. A real pleasure."

Vail sat on the sofa and St. Claire eased himself into one of the rockers and leaned back with a sigh.

"This place is delightful," Vail said. "Reminds me of a funky New England prep school. I can understand why you love it here."

"Fred calls it the campus," she said. "I lived out here for a while."

"He told us."

"I live in town now. Go shopping, go to the movies," she said with a rueful smile. "I'm not agoraphobic anymore."

"I'm sorry you were ill. I didn't know."

"Thanks. It was a strange experience, being one of them instead of one of us. Gave me a different perspective on life," she said, ending any further discussion of her hard times. She took an ashtray from a drawer and put it on the coffee table. "You may smoke in here," she said. She seemed so calm, Vail wondered if she was on some kind of tranquilizer.

"Whatever happened to Tommy Goodman?" she asked. "Is he still with you?"

"Tommy met a wine princess from Napa Valley, got married, and is now the vice president of her old man's wine company. He drives a Rolls and has a three-year-old son who looks like a ferret."

She laughed, a pleasant, loose kind of laugh, throwing her head back and closing her eyes.

"Tommy a mogul, hard to believe. And you?"

"I'm the district attorney."

"You're kidding."

"Afraid not. Harve, here, is one of my top investigators. He helped track down Pancho Villa."

"I ain't quite that old, ma'am." St. Claire chuckled.

"Naomi?"

"Still running the ship."

"I know about the Judge, he was a friend of my aunt's. How sad. He was such a gentleman. Always had that fresh carnation in his lapel."

"I miss him a lot," Vail said. "It's not as much fun anymore."

"What?"

For a moment, Vail seemed stumped by the question, then he said, "Everything, I guess."

She got up and walked across the room to a small refrigerator in the corner. "How about a Coke or some fruit juice?"

"Sure, I'll take a Coke."

"Same, ma'am," St. Claire said.

"Okay in the bottle?"

"Only way to drink 'em," St. Claire said with a smile.

She opened three bottles, carefully cleaned the tops of them with a paper towel, wrapped the bottles with linen napkins, and brought them back. She sat down and lit a cigarette.

"This involves Aaron Stampler, doesn't it? Your coming here?"

"Yes."

"Are they letting him out?"

"How'd you guess?"

"Well, it's been ten years. . . ."

"What's that mean?"

"They could have effected a cure in that time."

"There's no way to cure Stampler."

"You thought so ten years ago."

"I wanted to know that if he *was* cured, he would be freed, not sent to Rock Island to finish his sentence. But I never figured it would happen."

"What's the diagnosis?"

"Ever heard of a resulting personality?"

"Of course."

"His psychiatrist claims he has developed a new persona named Raymond Vulpes. Aaron and Roy, it seems, have gone to that great split-personality place in hell."

"That's pretty cynical, Martin. Don't you feel some sense of re-demption, knowing that you saved him?"

"No."

"Why, for heaven's sake?"

"Because I don't believe him. I don't believe there ever was a Roy and I think Raymond is a figment of Aaron's imagination, not his psyche—aided by Woodward's ego."

"Sam Woodward? He's his doctor?"

"Has been for almost ten years. You know Woodward?"

"Only by reputation."

"Which is . . . ?"

"Excellent. He's highly respected in the community. You think Aaron Stampler tricked Sam Woodward and you and me and the state psychiatrists, the prosecutor, the judge—"

"All of us. Yes, I believe that. I believe he's a raving psychopath and one helluva actor."

"That's impossible, Martin."

"You remember telling me the instant before Roy first appeared to you, the room got cold and you couldn't breathe? Do you re-member that?"

"Yes, I remember that quite well. I had never experienced any-thing quite like it."

"It happened to me when I walked into the room and met Stampler—or Vulpes—for the first time in ten years. It was like an omen. Like I was in the presence of tremendous evil. Nothing like that ever happened to me, either."

"Anticipation. You obviously have a vivid memory of my de-scription. You expected it and—"

"It happened before I saw him. I didn't even know he was in the room."

There was a pause, then she asked, "Did you have any sense of anxiety when you went up there?"

"I was uncomfortable."

"About seeing Aaron again?"

"That may have been a small part of it. Mainly, I don't like Daisyland."

"You're not supposed to like it, Martin. It's not like going to the theater."

"That's not what I mean. There's a . . . I don't know . . . a sense of hopelessness about the place."

He was leading her up to the reason they were there, trying to get the dialogue flowing easily, renewing her trust in him, and not doing too well.

He turned to St. Claire. "Harve, do you mind stepping outside for a minute?" The old-timer excused himself and left the room.

"What I'm about to tell you would normally violate the confidentiality between client and lawyer," Vail said, "but since you were his psychiatrist, I can tell you with immunity. You're also bound by confidentiality."

He told her about Aaron's last words to him after the trial.

"He wasn't kidding," Vail said as he finished. "I think his ego had to let me know."

"Why didn't you tell me at the time?"

"Why? Hell, it wouldn't have done a bit of good. Stampler could have stood on the courthouse steps five minutes after the trial and told the world he was sane and he killed those three people in cold blood and there's not a damn thing anyone could have done about it. He pleaded guilty to three murders and his sentence was passed and final. Nothing could have changed that, Molly, it's called double jeopardy."

"You also told me it was your job to find the holes and use them against the law so it would be changed."

"In a court of law. Don't you understand, we can't *get* Raymond Vulpes in court. You and I are both bound by the tenets of confidentiality. If I had gone to Judge Shoat and told him that I had made a mistake based on Stampler's comment, I could have been disbarred—and considering how Shoat despised me, probably would've been. So what possible good would have come from telling *you* what Stampler said? There wasn't a damn thing you could do about it, either."

"So now the time's come to free him and you want to keep him inside because of some remark he made ten years ago."

"It's a much more complex problem than that."

"Not *my* problem, Martin."

"That's right, but I need all the help I can get right now. Vulpes is going to walk. There's nothing I can do to stop him and Vulpes knows it. Woodward is convinced that Stampler and Roy no longer exist. He believes in Raymond Vulpes. And he's convinced the state board."

"It's uncomfortable to think about. I love medicine as much as you love the law. If this is true, I feel, I don't know, as if we both perverted our professions."

"Not you. You did your job."

"Not very well, I'm afraid."

"He faked us both out, Molly. But I wanted to be faked, I wanted to believe him because it was the one way to beat the case. Ironic, isn't it? The thing I fear most is prosecuting an innocent person, but I have to live with the fact that I am responsible for saving a guilty one."

"Then be practical about it. If there's nothing that can be done, put it behind you. It's not your business anymore."

"It's my business because *he* wants it that way."

"What do you mean, *he* wants it that way?"

Vail asked St. Claire to rejoin them. "What do you remember most about the murder of the bishop?" Vail asked.

"Most vividly? The pictures," she said. "They were ghastly."

"What else? How about the Altar Boys? Do you remember their names?"

"Afraid not. I remember he killed them."

"Not all. One got away. His name was Alex Lincoln. Do you remember Stampler's girlfriend?"

"Yes. I met her once. At that shelter . . ."

"Savior House. Her name was Linda Gellerman."

"She was very frightened. And she was pregnant. She was going to have an abortion, as I recall."

"That's right. She straightened her life out, married a nice guy two years ago, and had a little boy."

She smiled. "It's nice to hear a story with a happy ending."

"Unfortunately, the story doesn't end there. A few months ago somebody walked into her house one morning and chopped her to bits in front of her child."

"Oh . . ."

"Now somebody has done the same thing to Alex Lincoln. Exactly the same M.O. as the Stampler murders, including the genital mutilation and the symbols on the back of the head. We know the same person committed both murders—one in southern Illinois, the other one outside St. Louis. But Stampler's still in the maximum security wing and he hasn't had a letter or a visitor in almost ten years."

"But you think he's involved in some way?"

"Something like that."

"How could he be?"

"We don't know how and we don't know why. But I'm positive he's directing a copycat killer. We—Harve and I—think it may have something to do with transference."

"Transference? I don't understand."

"Isn't it true that transference sometimes causes the patient to have irrational expectations from the people they work and live with? That reexperiencing can cause problems?"

"It can. There are other reasons. People naturally seek approval from their parents or supervisors. Frustration of these expectations may evoke rage or other immature behavior patterns."

"Or worse?"

"Yes."

"And these tendencies wouldn't be immediately obvious to the psychiatrist, would they?"

"Usually the symptoms of abnormal behavior are what put the patient into treatment in the first place."

"I didn't ask you that."

"What are you suggesting?"

"That perhaps someone you were treating may have had mental problems far more severe than—"

Her cheeks began to color and her tone took on an edge. "You really don't think much of my ability, do you, Martin?"

"Of course I do!"

"You didn't even use me as a witness in the trial."

"You served your purpose, Molly. Hell, if it weren't for you . . ." He stopped, realizing where his thought was heading.

"If it weren't for me, you wouldn't be in this fix, is that what you were going to say?"

"No, no, no." He shook his head. "I'm responsible for the problem, nobody else."

"Then stop implying—"

"I'm not implying anything!"

"You're implying one of *my* patients is this killer of yours."

"No, we think it's *possible*, that's all. Do you still have the tapes you made with Stampler?"

"Yes, I do."

"Where are they?"

"Under lock and key."

"Where?"

"In my office."

"May we see them?"

"What are you trying to prove?"

"May we see them, please?"

She got up and opened the door to her private office. The walls were lined with oak book cabinets with glass doors. They were filled with reports, files, and near the end of one shelf the Stampler tapes, twenty-three of them, each in its own black box with the date on the spine. There were also several locked file cabinets.

"I also keep audiotapes of most of my interviews," she said with a touch of sarcasm. "They're in the locked files."

"Do you ever leave them open? You know, during the day when you're getting stuff out of them?"

"The tapes have never been out of this office."

"Have you ever discussed them with anyone?"

"I've discussed the case, in strictly medical terms."

"No details on, for instance, the Altar Boys?"

"Absolutely not. Never. They're confidential. And they're invaluable as a research tool." She stopped, her brow bunched up in a scowl. "You're questioning me as if I were on the witness stand and I resent it!"

"I'm trying to figure out how the copycat killer knew about Linda and Alex. The tapes are a very logical possibility. Did you ever mention anything about the motive for Rushman's murder to—"

"You know I couldn't do that even if I wanted to. I have a responsibility to my patient. You're asking me to violate confidentiality."

"Don't play games with me, Molly," Vail said, and anger was creeping into his tone. "This isn't about shrink-patient relationships, it's about slaughter. Not just murder—*slaughter!* Stampler is a mass murderer. Want a list? Shackles. His brother. Mary Lafferty, his old girlfriend. Some guy in Richmond, we don't even know his name, for God's sake. Rushman, Peter Holloway, Billy Jordan, Alex Lincoln, and poor little Linda Gellerman trying to make sense out of a screwed-up life in some little nowhere town. Count 'em up, lady, that's nine—that we *know* about! Don't tell me about confidentiality when there are two butchers on the loose."

"How dare you talk to me like that! How dare . . ."

"Molly, someone you treated or worked with may be a serial killer taking orders from Stampler. Think about it—both of them could be *your* clients. You want to protect them by invoking doctor-patient confidentiality?"

"You would, if they were your clients," she snapped back.

Vail hesitated for a moment. Suddenly he became calm, speaking just above a whisper. "Stampler *was* my client," he said. "I made a mistake. Now I'm trying to rectify it. We don't want details. We want names. We can check them out discreetly. We're not going to hurt or embarrass anyone, but we have to stop the killing."

She did not answer. Instead she got up and slunk back into the shadows of the room, becoming a fragile silhouette in the corner. St. Claire shifted uneasily in his chair, astounded by Vail's attack on Molly Arrington. He needed a chew. The silence in the room was unsettling. Then as suddenly as his temper had erupted, Vail became quiet. His shoulders sagged and he shook his head. The silent stalemate lasted a full five minutes. It was Molly who finally spoke.

"It's all supposition, anyway," she said feebly.

"I would have to disagree, ma'am," St. Claire said softly, finally breaking his silence. "I believe in my heart that the copycat killer came from here, just like I believe Stampler's makin' a fool of you like he's makin' a fool of us. I don't pretend t'understand why, I reckon you're the only one in this room could even make a stab at figgerin' that out. But there ain't any doubt in m'mind that he's a genuine, full-blown monster. He don't deserve an ounce of pity or sympathy or compassion. And whoever it is—doin' his biddin'?—is just as bad."

"How would you know?" she asked from the safety of her dark penumbra. "I mean, even if I gave you names, how would you know if one of them . . ." She let the sentence trail off.

"You'd just have t'trust us on that. Have to be somebody had access to your tapes. Somebody who may have even come here lookin' for 'em, who looked on Stampler as a hero."

"Somebody who was in a position to kill Linda Balfour and Alex Lincoln on the days they were murdered," Vail said.

"And you think Aaron Stampler turned this person into a serial killer?"

"Not at all. I think the potential was there, all Stampler did was capitalize on it. I think maybe, somehow, transference played a key role in this."

Molly stepped back out of the shadows and sat down on the rocker facing St. Claire and Vail. She said, "You keep bringing up transference."

"It's something Woodward said." Vail, who had taken notes of the audiotape, took out his notebook and flipped through the pages. "Here it is. He was talking about the downside of transference, how it creates a subconscious fear that old injuries and insults will be repeated. He said it's a double-edged sword, that the fear of reexperiencing all past injuries can turn the patient against the therapist. And then he said, and this is a quote, 'Abhorrent behavior patterns can be mirrored only to individuals who would normally accept the transference.' "

"That's true," she said. "Nobody can transmit abnormal moral standards to another unless the receiver is capable of such behavior to begin with."

"See, ma'am, what we think happened, and understand this here's a rank amateur talking, what we think is that this copycat killer was in therapy and reacted adversely to reexperiencing. So that person sought out Stampler for assurance, and Stampler was brilliant enough to become the killer's mentor."

"The killer transferred to Stampler?"

"Yes. And Stampler capitalized on the killer's instability," said Vail.

"We ain't sure just how the killer contacted Stampler, Doctor, we don't know at this point how that was accomplished, but that seems the likely scenario since Stampler wasn't in any position to contact anyone on the outside. What I mean, somebody came to him, he didn't go t'them."

"Why do you think that person was here?"

"'Cause of the tapes. The tapes are the one place the copycat coulda learned about Rushman and the Altar Boys. And about Linda." St. Claire paused for a minute, then said, "I just had a thought. S'posin' this person wasn't a full-time patient—"

"An outpatient?" Molly interrupted.

"Or maybe an employee. Somebody who was workin' here and who was also bein' treated for some kinda mental problem. Got into the files, studied Stampler . . . and then maybe left here—maybe got a job at Daisyland for a while . . ."

"And was proselytized by Stampler." Vail finished the sentence.

"It coulda happened. Ain't much else makes any sense."

"Is that possible, Molly?" Vail asked.

"Well, there's certainly no rule that says a patient always transfers to a doctor."

"So what we're lookin' for here is someone who is your basic psychopath and left here . . ."

"Or was on vacation or leave on the days when Balfour and Lincoln were killed," Vail added.

"You mean this person might still be here?"

"No, ma'am. We think—and once again we're guessin'—that the killer's in Chicago waitin' for Stampler—Vulpes—to get out."

"And he gets out today, Molly."

"We're also guessin' he's got a list of future victims."

"A list drawn up by Vulpes."

Vail put his briefcase on the couch beside him, opened it, and removed a large manila envelope. He took out three photographs. He handed her the photo of Linda Balfour's corpse, taken by the police. She looked at it in horror and turned her head as she handed it back to him.

"Alex Lincoln was a delivery man for UPD. He was lured to a house near St. Louis and killed. This photograph was in a box that Alex Lincoln was delivering. The real residents of the house were out of town at the time."

He handed her the Polaroid shot of Balfour. Her eyes widened as she realized it had been taken by the killer.

"My God."

"You're a psychiatrist, Molly," said Vail. "How do you figure this? The same M.O. as Stampler's murders. Messages in blood on the backs of both heads. References to Rushman's books, which are now in a private library. And the last surviving members of the Altar Boys. That information was never brought out in the trial. How did the killer even know about them?"

"Thing is, Dr. Arrington, we ain't askin' to look in no files or ask about specifics. What we need to find out is if there's a chance that a patient or an employee here coulda got a squint at those tapes, and if so, where we can locate that person now. Hell, could be a half-dozen or a dozen fits the bill. Our job'd be to narrow it down, find out if any of 'em coulda been in Gideon, Illinois, and St. Louis, Missouri, on the dates those two folks was killed. We sure ain't lookin' to drag a whole buncha folks in and have 'em psychologically evaluated, if that's what you're worried about."

"And you think this killer went from here to Daisyland?"

"Possibly," said Vail. "Maybe not directly from here, but ultimately managed to make contact with Stampler there."

"When would this killer have been here?"

"Not sure, ma'am. Could go way back, but the first killin' occurred last October, so my best guess is two, three years ago."

"How many people are on the grounds—staff and inmates?" Vail asked.

"Patients, not inmates, please."

"Sorry."

"Our patient list is held to three hundred fifty. There's a medical staff of twenty-two and another twenty in the kitchen, security, main office. About four hundred altogether."

"Big turnover?"

"On staff? Not really. It's a pleasant place to work, the wages are excellent."

"Patients?"

"I'm guessing—I would say the average stay would be two to three years. We have some long-termers and we have some who are gone in six months. Also about a third of them are children, three to twenty-one."

"Tell you what'd help, ma'am. If we could get us a list of the staff and patients for the past three years."

"We can't release the names of our patients. This is a private hospital, patients are guaranteed anonymity."

"How about a list of staff and anyone on staff who might have been undergoing treatment while they were employed here?" Vail suggested.

She thought about that for a bit, then excused herself and went toward her office. She stopped at the door and said, "I'm not playing prima donna. These people have very fragile egos. They need all the breaks they can get. It doesn't always have a happy ending, sometimes they end up back here—or someplace worse. We're not infallible, you know, it's not like treating mumps."

She went into the office and closed the door.

St. Claire leaned over and whispered, "You realize we could be chasin' the biggest wild goose in history."

"Got a better idea?" Vail whispered back.

"Hell, no, it was my idea to begin with."

They could hear her muffled voice as she spoke on the phone. Vail lit a cigarette. Ten minutes crept by before she came back. She sat down in the rocking chair.

"I'm not comfortable with this," she said. "I talked to Lowie— Fred—and our personnel director, Jean Frampton, and they agreed to give up the staff records. They left it up to me, whether to discuss staffers who were also outpatients. That's what I'm uncomfortable about. These people, when they reveal themselves to us, that's the ultimate in trust. To violate that . . ."

"I understand that, ma'am, and we certainly appreciate your feelings. Could I make one suggestion, please? If there are staffers who were patients, maybe we could discuss 'em in general terms, not necessarily by name, unless they become real strong candidates."

"We'll see."

"Fair 'nuff."

Thirty minutes later they had a computer printout of the staff members going back for the past five years. They spread the sheet on the coffee table and she began going down the list. It was divided into sections: Name, address, age, sex, education, qualifications, previous employment. There was also a check box marked References and another marked Photograph. There were fifty-five names on the list. Thirty-eight had been employed the entire three years. Six others had been there at least two years, four were relative newcomers, and seven had been terminated or had resigned.

"Let's start with them," St. Claire suggested.

Molly had a remarkable memory for all the staffers, knew their backgrounds and temperaments, how proficient they were. "When you see the same forty people every day for years, you get to know them very well," she explained. They went down the list, checking backgrounds, discussing each of the people as if he or she was a candidate for office. As the afternoon wore on, she became increasingly interested in the project, gradually cutting down the list, occasionally making a discreet phone call to clarify questions that arose. St. Claire was beginning to question his hunch, although not out loud. They finally eliminated all but three prospects, two women and a man.

"Jan Rider," said Molly. "She was an inpatient for several years, then lived in a halfway house as an outpatient for about six months. She was a housekeeper. Borderline psychotic. Delusionary, disassociated. Her neighbors had her committed when she went into the backyard stark naked and prayed to a tree. She believed it was the Virgin Mary."

"Do you know where she is now?"

"The state hospital in Ohio. She was one of our failures."

"Are you sure she's still there?"

"Yes."

"Next."

"Sidney Tribble. I'll tell you right off the top, he is from St. Louis and he went back there after he got his ticket. Tribble has a sister there, they're quite close. He's got a good job making an acceptable salary. No psychological recurrences so far."

"Why was he here?"

"Schizoid, paranoid, dissociative."

"Why was he committed?"

"Court order. His wife left him and he began to delude. Thought she and her new boyfriend were taunting him. He stabbed a man in a shopping mall, someone he didn't even know, he just picked up a pair of shears in a hardware department and attacked him."

"Did he kill him?"

She shook her head. "The wounds were relatively superficial.

The judge ordered confinement and treatment and his sister paid to have him committed here instead of the state hospital."

"How long was he here?"

"A year in treatment, a little over two years as an employee and an outpatient. He worked here as our electrician. Went back to St. Louis about a year ago."

St. Claire cast a glance at Vail, then made a note beside Tribble's name: "Possible."

"Okay, who's next?" Vail asked.

"Rene Hutchinson. She was also on the housecleaning staff. Very bright; in fact, she taught a class of ten-year-olds and was quite good at it, but she didn't want the responsibility. She worked as a housekeeper, then later she assisted in the infirmary. Pretty woman, kind of raw-boned. Pioneer stock."

"How old was she?"

"Late thirties."

"What was her problem?"

"She wasn't my patient," Molly said. "I would prefer you ask Dr. Salzman. He treated her."

"Think he'll talk to us?"

"We'll find out," she said, and went to the phone.

———

Orin Salzman was a small man with a graying Vandyke beard and neatly cropped black hair. His shoulders were stooped and rounded as if weighted by the burden of his patients. He wore a black turtleneck sweater, khaki pants, and a tweed jacket with leather patches on the elbows and seemed a bit put out at being interrupted. He appeared at Molly's door, hands stuffed in his pockets, staring at them through thick tortoiseshell glasses. Molly offered him a drink, which he declined.

"What's this about?" he asked in a stern tone, leaning against the doorjamb.

Molly introduced Vail and St. Claire and explained the situation briefly, without going into too many details. Salzman was superficially familiar with the Stampler case, which helped.

"They're interested in Rene Hutchinson's case," Molly said.

"You know I can't divulge my work with Rene," he said.

"Look, Doctor," St. Claire said, "we ain't lookin' to cause this Hutchinson woman any grief. But we gotta check all these people out. If we ask anythin' that you feel is privileged, jest say so, we'll back off."

"Hmm," he said. He slowly eased himself into the room and sat on the opposite end of the couch from Vail. "So I gather you're looking for people with psychopathic tendencies, that it?"

"Kinda."

He drummed his fingers on the coffee table for a few moments, then said, "Well, if Molly says okay, I'm willing to listen."

"What can you tell us—off the top—about her?" Vail asked.

"Her father was an army man, sergeant as I recall. She was born out west somewhere, lived all over the world. Left home when she was fairly young. Went to college for two years, University of Colorado. Very bright woman with an extremely fragile psyche."

"Did you ever figure out why?"

"Not really. She had suffered a nervous breakdown before she came here, which she concealed from us when she applied for the job. It came out after she'd been here about two years. She was working the night clean-up staff here and going to school in the daytime, got exhausted and almost had a relapse. Then she was arrested for shoplifting."

"What'd she steal?"

"Something inconsequential, a cheap purse as I remember. Kleptomania is often a cry for attention."

"And how long was she here?"

"She worked here about three years. She was in therapy for the last six months of her employment, mainly to mend a damaged ego and shaky self-image and build back her strength."

"What's her background."

"Well, she wasn't particularly anxious to discuss her past."

"Isn't that why she came to you?"

"She came to me because she had to. The judge ordered her to get psychiatric help."

"For how long?"

"Six months."

"Did she resent these sessions with you?"

"No. She was in pain, and believe me, mental disorders are as painful as your pain would be if you broke a leg. It's not the kind of pain you can take an aspirin for or rub away, and you can't take antibiotics to cure it, but the hurt is very real to those who are suffering."

"How did she deal with her past?"

"She didn't. I never did really connect with her. The reexperiencing process is the most painful of all. It requires the individual to deal with their darkest side, examine motives and actions they'd rather forget."

"And Rene resisted it?"

"Wasn't really interested. I strongly suspect she was sexually abused by her father although she never admitted that. She did tell me once that her father was physically and mentally abusive, but that's as far as she took it."

"So she was uncooperative?"

"No, she was friendly and talkative, she just didn't want to deal with the past, and six months wasn't enough time to earn her trust."

"You liked her, then?"

"I didn't dislike her. She was a patient I saw for three hours a week. We never got beyond her shielding, which is not uncommon at all."

"Did you ever consider her dangerous?"

"No—well, to herself, perhaps, when she first came to me. She was verging on manic-depression, there's always a danger of suicide in depression cases. But I never considered her capable of purposely hurting someone else."

"So you feel she was cured?"

"Let's just say we stopped the problem before it got too bad. She was never an inpatient, she just met with me for three hours a week and I had her on some antidepressant medication."

"Worked at night, you say?" asked Vail.

He nodded. "Five nights a week for four hours and eight hours on the weekends. She was the night housekeeping staff, cleaned the offices and meeting rooms."

"So she would have had access to keys to the offices, for clean-up purposes?" said Vail.

"Uh-huh . . ."

"You say she was goin' t'school. Remember what she was studyin'?"

"Data processing. The wave of the future, she called it."

"Where was that, here in Winthrop?" Vail asked.

Salzman chuckled. "Obviously you've never seen Winthrop. It's about the size of your hand. She commuted to Shelbyville, about fifteen miles up the Indy highway. Drove an old Pontiac Firebird."

"Do you know where she went when she left here?"

"Sorry. We lost track of her after she left. You might check with Jean in Personnel on the off-chance somebody asked for a reference." Molly excused herself and went into her office. They could hear her talking to someone on the phone.

"One more thing," said St. Claire to Salzman. "Did ya ever get any indication that Rene Hutchinson might have been psychotic, or have psychotic tendencies?"

"No, but that doesn't mean she wasn't. Psychopaths are consummate liars, among other things. She was aloof and could be very guarded at times. And she had mood swings, but then, who doesn't."

"Anything else you can think of?"

"Well, no, not really. She was excellent with young people, particularly in the eight-to-fifteen age range. They seemed to relate to her, if that means anything."

"Did she ever mention Aaron Stampler or a fella named Vulpes? Raymond Vulpes?" St. Claire asked.

"Not that I recall."

Vail gave Salzman his card. "If you think of anything else, would you give me a call?" he asked.

Salzman lifted his glasses, propping them on his forehead as he studied the card. "D.A., huh? What's your interest in Stampler?"

"I defended him," said Vail. "Before I became a prosecutor."

"Huh," said the psychiatrist, lowering his glasses. "That's kind of a sticky wicket, isn't it?"

"I think you could say that," said Vail with a smile.

"Well, tell Molly I'll see her later. Will you two be around for a while?"

"No, we'll be leaving shortly. Thanks for your help."

"Not much help, I'm afraid, but it was nice to see you," Salzman said, and left the office.

When Molly came back, she said, "I have a little information for you. Jean says she got a request for a recommendation for Rene about two months after she left. It was from City General Hospital in Terre Haute. I just talked to the personnel director there. He says she worked there for four months, left around the first of the year. They've had no further contact with her."

"So she was there at the time of the Balfour kill," said St. Claire.

"And it was just a nervous breakdown, she didn't show signs of any other mental problems?" Vail said.

"Maybe," said St. Claire, "she was an adroit liar, as Dr. Lowenstein would say."

"You really think she was psychotic?" Molly asked.

"I'm askin' you, ma'am," St. Claire said, and smiled.

Molly lit another cigarette, considered his question carefully before she answered. "If she was, Orin didn't detect it," she said finally.

"Where did she come from before she worked here?" Vail asked.

"Accordin' to her record on this sheet, she came here from Regional General Hospital in Dayton, Ohio. General housekeeping," St. Claire answered, checking the computer printout. "You also got a picture of her, if that's what this here checkmark means."

"I'll have Jean pull it," Molly said.

"May I show you something?" St. Claire said. He led them into her office. "Got a coupla bobby pins?" he asked Molly.

She laughed. "Afraid I don't use them."

"How about paperclips. I need two."

He took the two paperclips she gave him and straightened them out, then inserted them into the bookcase lock. Working with both hands, he moved the two wires around until he felt the tumblers in the lock. He twisted both clips and the door clicked open. It took about thirty seconds. He reached in, took out one of the tape boxes, and removed the tape, then put the empty box back. He turned to Molly and handed her the tape.

"When's the last time ya looked at one of these, Doctor?"

"I have no idea," Molly answered. "I haven't looked at them since I got my ticket. Four years, maybe longer."

"She was workin' at night, had a key to the office, came in, popped the lock, took a tape, maybe two or three, returned them the next night. Nothin' to it. You never woulda known the dif, 'less a'course you happened to check the particular box she borrowed. That's if it was Hutchinson, a'course."

"You think she knew how to pick a lock?"

"No big secret, ma'am. I mean, it ain't some inside cop thing. I read it in one of those books, y'know the kind? *101 Things You Always Wanted to Know How to Do But Nobody'd Tell You* kinda books? Point is, she coulda got into the tapes, she was missin' for two months before she applied for work in Terre Haute, and she had mental problems. Nobody else here fits the bill except Tribble."

They returned to the sitting room. The personnel director had sent 3 × 5 color mug shots of Rene Hutchinson and Tribble to the office. Molly handed them to Vail and then turned over the photograph of Linda Balfour's body, which was lying facedown on the table. She stared down at it.

"You think a woman is capable of this?" she asked.

"Ma'am," said St. Claire, "I think a woman can do anything a man can do but sire a child—and I ain't even too sure 'bout that anymore."

32

Angelica Stoddard was short and favored her mother. She had a trim, tight body, good posture, and blue eyes so pale she almost looked blind—a striking young woman in an extra-large sweater that hung down halfway to the knees of her bleached-out jeans. She wore jogging shoes with white sweat socks that sagged over the tops and a black felt hat over ash-blond hair. The hat was pulled down almost to her ears. She looked somber and walked quickly with her head down. Venable fell in beside her. Angelica paid no attention at first but finally turned and looked up at Venable.

"Hi," said Venable, "I'm Jane Venable. I'm your mother's lawyer. Can we go somewhere and talk for a few minutes?"

"Not here," the young woman answered in a whisper, looking around furtively.

"Anywhere you say."

"Anywhere but here," Angelica said.

Venable had her car drive them to a coffee shop off campus. They found a table in the back of the small café. Angelica ordered cappuccino and Venable had black coffee.

"Why did you come to the school?" Angelica Stoddard said. "Why didn't you call first?"

"I tried, but I couldn't get through."

Angelica's shoulders sagged. "Oh, yeah, it's a hall phone," she said, shaking her head. "It's always busy. I'm sorry I said that, but I . . . I'm so embarrassed by all this. I know it's wrong, but I can't help it."

"It's okay, Angelica. It's absolutely understandable, you don't have to apologize to me."

"What do you want?"

"I need your help."

"To do what?"

"I want you to come with me to see your mother."

The young woman looked shocked. "I can't do that," she said urgently, but still speaking almost in a whisper. "She absolutely forbids me to—"

"Angelica, she must put up a fight."

"You don't know my mother. Once she makes up her mind . . ."

"Look, for God's sake, she's not deciding what kind of car to buy, her life is on the line here."

"What can I do?"

"Tell her to defend herself."

"She won't listen to me, and she won't change her mind. I know her, Ms. Venable. I talked to her. They let her call me. She kept saying, 'This is the only way.' "

"You've got to go with me to see her and back me up."

"She'd kill me!" Angelica said, then quickly added, "Figuratively speaking, I mean."

"Angelica . . . do they call you Angel?" The young student nodded. "Angel, you tell her you and your dad need her. She can't just stand by and get maxed out by the state. If she'll put up a fight we can win this case. Do you want her to spend the next twenty years in state prison?"

"No! Oh no. Oh God, what's happening to us?" Angelica shook her head and started to cry.

"Trust me," Venable said. "Just do exactly what I tell you to do and trust me."

———

Vail had secured wiretapping permits for the pay phone in the hall outside Vulpes's door and in his room. The two electronics experts in the investigative department had set up a listening and watching post in an empty loft across the street from the halfway house. One of them, Bob Morris, had graduated from electronics school and had attended the FBI academy. His partner, Reggie Solomon, was a classic nerd, who was interested only in the mysteries of electronic surveillance. A second team comprised of Randy Dobson, a young, lean detective who wore baggy khakis and an Atlanta Braves T-shirt under a leather jacket, and Kirby Grosso, a tallish, raw-boned woman wearing a jogging outfit—the two best shadows on the D.A.'s investigative staff—was on standby in a car a block away. Grosso had a Hi8 video camera secreted in her athletic bag so she could videotape Vulpes without being detected.

They watched Terry bring Vulpes to the halfway house and help him carry his belongings to the second-floor room. Vulpes had a large old-fashioned leather suitcase, a stereo, TV, and VCR, his tool chest and two large cardboard boxes of books and tapes. They listened on the monitor when Vulpes entered his room, and Morris, using a 500-mm telephoto lens, videotaped him through the open window of the room. They heard the supervisor running down the rules and regulations, the most important of which was a 10 P.M. curfew that was strictly enforced. The supervisor, whose name was David Schmidt, had a pleasant, reassuring voice.

"You'll do just fine, Raymond," he said as he left the room.

"Thanks," Vulpes answered. A few moments later he appeared at the window of his room. He leaned on the sill and looked up and down the street. He closed his eyes and took a deep breath of fresh air.

Actually, Vulpes was studying the terrain. He was certain the phone and his room were bugged, just as he was certain that he was being observed from somewhere in the old building across the street. Excellent. Vail had taken the bait.

Then he closed the window, pulled down the shade, and turned on his CD player. In the loft across the street, the sounds of a Judas Priest album roared into Solomon's earphones and he pulled them off.

"Well, shit," Morris said. "There goes our sound and picture." He snatched up his portable phone and punched out the number of the chase car.

Grosso answered. "Yeeees?" she said pleasantly.

"This is Bird Watch. Got Fox in his den, shades drawn, music drowning out our sound. Suggest you cover the back door."

"Way ahead of you, Bird Watch. Got it in view."

"See ya."

"Over and out."

Morris and Solomon settled back to watch and wait.

"You sure he can't see in here?" Solomon said.

"Not with his shades drawn."

"How about when the shades are up?"

"Not unless he's Superman."

"What are we on this guy about, anyway?"

"I dunno," said Morris. "All I know, Stenner said he's dangerous, whatever the hell that means."

———

Vulpes stood in the middle of his room and surveyed his surroundings. It was large enough to include a bed, dresser, night table, and lamp. On the opposite side of the room was a small loveseat covered with a blanket and an easy chair with a battered coffee table between them. Against the wall was a table large enough to hold his TV. He lifted the blanket on the loveseat. Gray duct tape held a large rip together.

What the hell, he thought, *it's just for the night.* He kept the volume on his CD player as loud as he felt was safe. He moved the small night table to the wall beside the door. He unpacked his minicomputer, set it up on the table, and plugged it in. He went into the hall with a small tape recorder, lifted the receiver off the phone, and taped the sound as he dropped a quarter into the slot. When he got a dial tone, he dialed the Time of Day and then hung up. He went back to his room. The halfway house was almost empty, everyone was at work at that time of day. He looked at his watch.

Ten minutes. He had ten minutes. He had to take the chance.

He went back to the hall, unscrewed the cover of the phone, found the external line into the phone, and unplugged it. If the phone was tapped they wouldn't even know it was momentarily out of service. He worked quickly. He detached four colored wires leading to the small magnet in the phone and attached one wire to the "in" screws of the radio component he had made at Daisyland then the others to the "out" side. The component successfully acted as a conduit between the external line and the line of the phone. He plugged the external line back in and quickly slipped the cover back and screwed it into place. He stepped back into his room and closed the door.

It had taken seven minutes.

He opened his suitcase and removed a city map from a pocket in the top of the bag and spread it out on the bed. There were four crosses marked in red on the map. He smiled and refolded the map and put it back in its pocket.

He was ready.

———

Stoddard looked gray, her mouth slack and her eyes swollen from lack of sleep. Her gray-black hair was straggly and had not been combed for several days. The female guard, a slender black woman with her hair pulled back and held by a barrette, led her out of the cell and toward the visitor's room.

"Listen, I heard you talking to your daughter on the phone," the guard said. "Sorry about that, I was standing there and couldn't help overhearing you. I heard you tell her not to come, but she's here."

"What!"

"Ma'am, I got a daughter and a son and if I was in your shoes, they'd come whether I liked it or not. Stop here a minute."

They stopped at the check-in desk while the guard unlocked a drawer and removed her purse.

"I got some powder and lipstick and a comb in here and a little mirror," she said. "Why don't you do a little repair job on your face. Make both of you feel good."

"I don't want her to be here."

"Well, she is, honey, so give her a break." The guard handed her a small compact, a mirror, and a comb. Edith took them haltingly, stared in the tiny mirror, and shuddered. She started to dab her face with powder.

"Here," the guard said, taking the compact, "let me do that." She started working on Stoddard's face.

"What's your name?" Stoddard asked.

"Cheryl Williams," the guard answered. "Used to work in a beauty parlor before I decided to become a cop."

She powdered the pallor away, put a thin line of lipstick on Stoddard's lips, and combed her straggly hair back, then took off her own barrette and, pulling Stoddard's hair tight, slipped it on. She stepped back and admired her work.

"There," she said. "You put a smile on and she'll leave here a lot happier than when she came." She held the mirror up so Stoddard could check herself out. Stoddard smiled for the first time in days.

"Thank you," she said.

"Sure. Tell her the food's good. They seem to worry a lot about that."

When Edith Stoddard entered the small visitor's cell and saw Venable and Angelica, she stopped cold, her shackled arms dropping stiffly in front of her and her eyes blazing with fury.

"I told you, I didn't want her . . ." she started, but she didn't finish the sentence. Angelica, overwhelmed at the sight of her mother in the drab prison clothes and handcuffs, rushed to her and wrapped her arms around her.

"Oh, Mama!" she sobbed. "I love you. Please listen to Ms. Venable. We need you, Mama. I need you." She clung to Edith

Stoddard, her shoulders shaking as tears suddenly flooded her face.

Stoddard looked at Jane Venable, her face clouded with anger, but finally her eyes closed and her lips trembled and tears crept from her closed eyes.

"Oh, Angel," she said in a shaky voice. "I love you so much."

"Then please, *please* listen to Ms. Venable. Please do as she says. Please trust her."

Stoddard pushed her daughter away and fixed a hard stare at her.

"Now, Angie, you listen to me. I *know* what I'm doing. You trust *me*."

"I want you to come home," the young woman sobbed.

"Well, that's not going to happen, dear. You must adjust to that. You're going to have to spend a little more time with Dad and keep his spirits up."

Angelica suddenly pulled back from her. "And who keeps *my* spirits up, Mom? You just sit here and do nothing. You let them write about you in the papers and everybody at school says you must be guilty because—"

"I *am* guilty, Angie. Get it through that thick little head of yours. Let me handle this."

"Fine," her daughter spat at her. "Handle it then. And the hell with the rest of us." She whirled around and banged on the door. The guard opened it and she left the room.

Edith Stoddard sank into a chair. "Why did you do that? What possible reason could you have for doing that to both of us?" she asked Venable.

"Edith, look at me."

The older woman slowly raised her eyes, eyes filled with anger.

"I found the room, Edith."

Stoddard said nothing. The expression in her eyes changed from anger to fear.

"I found the room in the closet, you know the room I'm talking about."

Stoddard said nothing.

"How long did Delaney keep you in this kind of bondage?"

"It wasn't like that."

"Oh, come on! I saw the handcuffs, the leather straps, the whips, the corsets, the garter belts. How long were you in sexual bondage to Delaney?"

Stoddard turned away from Venable.

"Do they have to know?"

"Who? Vail? Parver? The police? It's significant evidence in a murder investigation, I can be disbarred if I don't report it. And even if I didn't tell them, somebody's going to tumble across that closet just like I did, carpenters or painters redoing the room. How did this start, Edith? Did he make you do these things in order to keep your job?"

"They don't have to know," she said, turning to Venable and pleading. "They don't have to know you found out."

"What about the gun?"

"The gun? Oh yes, the gun . . ."

"Would you like me to throw it in the lake? Hell, Edith, I'm your lawyer, not your accomplice."

Stoddard slumped in her chair. "Why didn't you mind your own business?"

"This *is* my business. What do you fear, Edith? Are you worried about what your husband and daughter will think? You were a bonded slave, for God's sake. You think I can't make hay out of that? We can beat this rap, Edith."

"Never!" Edith Stoddard glared at her angrily. Venable stared back at her just as hard.

"If you think I'm going to let the state put you away for twenty years to life, you're out of your mind. I have a responsibility to you and the court." She sat down facing Stoddard and reached for her cuffed hands, but Stoddard pulled them away. "Edith, listen to me. Even if we don't go all the way to trial, I'll be able to bargain very strongly in your favor with this information. Martin Vail is a very smart lawyer. He'll see the possibilities, too. But I must tell them, do you understand that?"

"Not if I fire you."

"Even if you fired me, I'd have to give up this knowledge."

"So the whole world will know . . ."

"The police and the district attorney will know. And, yes, it will make the press—there will be a police report. So what do you have to lose? Let me fight the good fight, Edith. I don't want you to go to jail at all."

Stoddard stared at her for several long moments, then said, "You don't understand. At first it was humiliating, but then . . ."

"Yes?"

"But then I began to look forward to it. I wasn't a slave. I began to look forward to the times I'd go over there and he'd come out of that closet in that garter belt and hand me the handcuffs and I would hook his hands over his head to the headboard and do whatever I wanted to him."

"You don't have to tell me this, Edith—"

"I *want* to tell you," Stoddard said, cutting her off. "Don't you understand, I haven't had sex with my husband for more than ten years. *Ten years!* There were no other men, I didn't cheat on him. I . . . I just considered . . . it . . . part of my job. One of my *duties*. And when it was over, I whipped him. *I* whipped *him.* 'You bad boy,' I'd say, and I'd take the whip and he would bend over and I would give him several hard lashes across his backside. It was like getting even for all the humiliation. You understand what I'm saying, Ms. Venable? I *enjoyed* it. What do you think the prosecutors are going to think about that?"

"The prosecutor will never know," Venable said emphatically. "You don't have to tell them *anything*. We will bargain this out. You will never testify."

Edith Stoddard stood slowly and walked to the door and tapped on it. Officer Williams opened it. As she left, Stoddard turned to Jane and said, "You betrayed me, Ms. Venable."

———

Rudi Hines had manipulated the clean-up schedule so as to arrive at the billing office in City Hospital at five minutes to three. The billing office worked from six-thirty to two-thirty on weekends and usually everyone was out of there before three o'clock. Nobody ever worked overtime. But on this day the manager of the department, Herman Laverne, was still in the office on the phone. Hines immediately panicked but decided to go ahead with the usual procedure.

God, get out of here before three.

Laverne looked up as Hines shuffled in. Hines, wearing coveralls, was slightly built with short red hair under a Red Sox cap turned backward. The bucket was on wheels and Hines directed it into the office with the mop. It rattled past Laverne, who cupped his hand over the mouthpiece of the phone.

"I'll be outta here in a minute," he said.

Hines nodded, went to the back of the room, and began mopping the floor, all the while watching the screen of one of the three computers in the back of the room. That particular computer had a modem and was left on all night to receive bills, order confirmations, or messages. The clock on the wall crept closer to three o'clock and Laverne was still yapping on the phone.

———

At exactly three o'clock, Vulpes typed FONCOM into his minicomputer and immediately got the dial tone of the hall phone. He held the tape recorder up to the small mike built into the machine and pressed play. The sound of a quarter dropping into the phone slot played into the mike and from there to the phone. In an instant he had a dial tone. He dialed 555–7478. It rang once and then the word CONNECT flashed on the screen. He typed DIRCOM into his machine and the screen went blank.

———

Across the street Morris heard the phone operate, heard the coin drop, and then heard the dial tone.

"He's on the horn again," Morris said. He turned on the monitor. Solomon put the paperback novel he was reading aside. They listened to Vulpes dial. The phone rang once and as soon as it was answered, there was a hum on the line.

"What the hell's that?" Solomon said.

"Sounds like he got a bad connection."

"Can't you do something with all that stuff you got, you know, get it on another frequency or something?"

"What do you mean, another frequency? We got a bug in the damn phone. He dialed wrong or got a bad connection."

In his room, Vulpes began talking to the computer on the other end of the line as soon as his screen went blank.

———

At City Hospital, Laverne was about to leave the billing office when he heard the computer beep.

"What's that?" he said, half aloud, and walked back to the computer. Rudi Hines stood back against the wall, eyes staring at the screen, terrified, squeezing the mop handle with both hands.

HYDRA. FOX IS FREE. The message appeared on the screen.

"What the hell is this?" Laverne said. "Hydra? Fox? Some hackers must be screwing around."

HYDRA?

"This is ridiculous," Laverne snapped.

HYDRA?

Laverne leaned over the keyboard and typed: WHO THE HELL IS HYDRA? AND WHO ARE YOU?

In his room, Vulpes immediately typed DISCON and the program returned to READY. He sat and stared at the computer for several seconds. Someone must have come in and seen the computer screen. Vulpes would not try again. Everything was ready. If Hydra was there, the message was clear. Vulpes was free. That was the only reason for the call.

Across the street in the loft, Solomon was getting nervous.

"Why isn't he hanging up?"

"Maybe he's stupid," Morris said.

"What's he doing, sitting over there listening to a dead line?"

"I don't know what the hell he's—"

The line suddenly went dead.

"There. Stupid schmuck finally figured it out," Solomon said. He picked up his paperback and started reading again.

In his room, Vulpes unplugged the minicomputer, put it back in the toolbox, and returned the night table to its place. He looked at his watch.

Three-ten. Time to go.

And at the hospital Laverne muttered, "Just some crazy kid hackers," as he headed out the door. And to Hines: "Be sure the door locks behind you when you finish up."

Hines nodded and watched Laverne go. Hines sighed with relief. It was all right, Laverne was annoyed but not concerned by the message from Fox. Fox was free, that was all that mattered. The clock on the wall said 3:12.

Only six more hours.

———

Ten minutes later Vulpes left the halfway house. Morris dialed Grosso.

"Present," she said.

"Fox is out of the den. Heading toward the Loop."

"Keep me on the line," she said. Morris watched the corner. The gray Mustang drifted into sight, turned, and drove past the listening post. A block away Vulpes climbed the stairs to the elevated train stop.

"He's taking the el," Grosso said a moment later on the phone. "We're on foot. Call traffic and tell 'em not to bust our car. We'll contact Icicle as soon as he lights somewhere."

"Rodge. Over and out," Morris answered.

———

Grosso and Dobson followed Vulpes to a three-story open-atrium mall in the downtown section. Vulpes seemed to be in no hurry. Grosso stayed half a city block behind Vulpes while Dobson tracked him from the opposite side of the atrium. Occasionally Grosso would enter a store and snoop around while Dobson kept

Vulpes in view. Dobson stopped occasionally and window-shopped, watching Vulpes in the reflection of the store window. When Grosso was back on track, Dobson would enter a store. They both wore beepers and each had dialed in the other's number. If either of them lost Vulpes or got in trouble, they would simply push the send button and immediately beep the other. They were a good team: cautious, savvy, alert.

Vulpes strolled the first floor of the mall, engrossed in window-shopping, occasionally stopping and watching the shoppers. The mall was crowded. Winter sales. Vulpes went to the second floor of the mall, entered an ice cream store, and came out with a hot fudge sundae piled high with whipped cream and sprinkles. He sat on a bench and ate it slowly, savoring every bite. He went to a record store and bought two CDs, then went to a men's clothing store, where he bought a black turtleneck sweater. He rented a copy of *Sleepless in Seattle* from the video rental store, then went to a one-dollar movie theater in the mall and bought a ticket for *Schindler's List*. He got a hot dog and a Coke at one of the food counters that surrounded the entrance to the theater and sat at a small table eating. Dobson and Grosso rendezvoused out of his line of sight.

"Shit, I saw that picture," Dobson complained. "It's three hours long!"

"Well, you're about to see it again," Grosso answered. "And don't talk about the movie while it's on. I hate people who tell me what's going to happen."

When Vulpes finished eating, he checked his watch and went into the theater.

"I'll get the tickets, you get the popcorn," Grosso said.

"I'm getting the short end of that deal," Dobson complained.

"For a change," Grosso answered, and headed for the ticket window.

———

Stenner was waiting at the county airport when Vail and St. Claire landed from their trip to the Justine Clinic.

"I brought Jane with me," Stenner said, adding, almost as an apology, "Didn't want to leave her by herself."

"How about the house guard?" Vail asked.

Stenner looked at his watch. "Just coming on now."

He opened the back door of the car and Jane peered out. Vail smiled when he saw her. The tension that had ridged his face with hard lines seemed to ease a bit.

"You okay?" he asked, climbing in beside her.

"Of course. Hey, Mr. D.A., I wanted to come, okay?"

"I'm a little stressed out. Sorry," he said. "Let's swing by the office on the way home, Abel."

She wrapped both arms around one of his arms. "You can relax. Your bad boy is sitting in the movies as we speak."

"The movies?"

"Our two best tails are baby-sitting him through *Schindler's List*," Stenner said, driving away from the airport. "If he stays for the whole show, they'll be getting out about now."

"And he has to be in by ten," said Venable. "That's a little over an hour from now."

"What did he do before the movie?"

"Went shopping, rented a movie, ate some ice cream."

"Him and his damn ice cream," said Vail. "How about phone calls?"

"Morris says nothing significant."

"Get him on the phone," Vail said.

"Y'know, if he is tied in with our copycat, the old Fox could be bidin' his time," St. Claire said, tapping out the number on the car phone. "Makes us wait until we get a little lax, then hit."

"That's why we're not going to get lax, Harve," Vail said.

"Here's Morris," St. Claire answered, stretching the cord and handing the phone back to Vail.

"This is Martin Vail, Bobby. Who did Vulpes call?"

"Only made two calls, Mr. Vail. He called and got the time and then he made a call and got a bad connection. That's it. Then he left."

"Thanks," Vail said with disgust, cradling the receiver. "He only made two calls and one of them was a bad connection."

"We drew a bad connection at Daisyland, too," said Stenner. "They have an enormous cleaning staff and a fairly regular turnover. Over eight hundred patients. Delivery people, visiting firemen, a constant flow of traffic. Trying to go back two years?" He shook his head. "Impossible."

"So the only leads we got left are Hutchinson and Tribble. Both of 'em as long as a shot gets," St. Claire grumbled.

"Flaherty ran both of them through the state payroll computer after you called," said Stenner. "There's no record either of them ever worked at Daisyland. St. Louis isn't doing any better. Flaherty talked to his pal, Sergeant Nicholson, this afternoon. They haven't got the first clue. Not a fingerprint, no blood samples, nobody saw anything, nobody heard anything."

"We're dealin' with a real pro here, Marty," St. Claire said.

"No, we're dealing with Stampler. He's calling every turn."

"Maybe you're puttin' too much emphasis on Stampler," St. Claire said. "Maybe it is just a copycat killer, saw the tapes in Arrington's office, knew how it was done, found out about the bishop's library . . ."

"It's Stampler," Vail said flatly. "I saw him, I talked to him. He's running it and he's going to keep running it."

"So we just wait, that it?" Stenner said.

"That's it. Everybody on the staff covered?"

"Yes, sir," said Stenner. "They're either under surveillance or with their families. Flaherty's keeping an eye on Shana—a task he seems to be enjoying, as does she, I might add."

"Y'know, I don't like to bring this up," said St. Claire, "but it's gonna get right costly—all this surveillance, I mean, if we gotta keep it up for long."

Vail glared at the back of his head.

"You got a better idea, Harve?"

"I don't even have an idea half as good."

———

Grosso and Dobson sat two rows apart in the back of the theater so they could keep Vulpes in view and get out quickly when he got up to leave. He sat through the entire picture. He stood up as the credits rolled and Grosso and Dobson slipped out.

Outside, Grosso grabbed for her cigarettes.

"Three hours without a smoke," she said. "I'm having a seizure. You better get lost."

"Too late," Dobson said. Grosso turned and was face-to-face with Vulpes. His eyes were like stones.

"Excuse me," he said, "can I trouble you for a light?" He put a cigarette between his lips.

"Sure."

"Did you enjoy the film?"

"It's a great picture," she said calmly.

He smiled. "Thanks for the light," he said, and walked off toward the mall exit.

"He made us," Grosso growled to Dobson.

"How? Man, we were practically invisible."

"I don't know how, but he made us. Not only that, but he wants us to know it. Shit, we're off the detail."

"Well, he's probably on his way home. Let's tuck him in and let the electronics wizards take over. Stenner will decide what to do with us."

"He's going to pull us off the case, Randy."

"What case? Is this a case? Hell, nobody knows why we're even following this guy."

"Stenner says he's dangerous."

"That's it? We're following him because he's dangerous? Half the people in the city are dangerous, for Christ sakes."

"He's spooky-looking," Grosso said. "Did ya see those eyes?"

"Oh, we're following him because he's spooky-looking and dangerous. I feel much better."

On the train heading back to his room, Vulpes checked his watch. Eight-thirty. He smiled. Hydra would strike in half an hour.

The game he had been waiting ten years to play was about to begin.

33

In the hazy light of an almost full moon, gargoyles and harpies and strange mythical creatures lurked in the spires of the Gothic buildings forming one of the University of Chicago's many quadrangles. Staring up at them, Naomi Chance felt a sudden thrust of fear, as if they were harbingers of doom. The medieval beasts seemed to be taunting her. She quickly shook it off and turned up the collar of her coat against the brisk wind that funneled between the buildings, assaulting her as she left the library and started across the quad toward the parking lot a block away. The monthly meeting of the Association of Legal Secretaries had been particularly dull, but she had presided with her usual élan and kept the proceedings moving as briskly as possible.

As she approached 57th Street, she saw the glow of a cigarette among the trees and shrubs near the street. A moment later the butt arced to the ground. A man was huddled in the shadows, his hands buried in his pockets. A car was parked by the curb ten or twelve feet away.

She gripped the small can of Mace she always kept handy in her pocket and subconsciously quickened her pace. Normally, she would not have noticed him, but tonight was different. Tonight she saw omens everywhere. *Hell,* she thought, *everybody's jumpy because of Stampler's release.* As she approached the figure huddled in the bushes, she gripped the Mace even tighter and steered a course away from the bushes and trees. But before she got to the street, a voice said, "Naomi Chance."

"Who's that?" she demanded when he said it, increasing the pace.

"Hold up a minute, please."

She glared into the darkness as a large, bulky man moved away from the shrubs. He was tall and muscular, a powerful black man, his features obscured by the dark.

"What the hell do you want?" Naomi demanded, and took her hand out of her pocket. "Keep your distance, this is a can of Mace."

"Whoa," the big man said, and stopped in his tracks, fumbling in his coat pocket. "Man, they warned me you were rough and ready," he said in a deep voice, and laughed. He held out his hand and flipped open his wallet. A gold badge twinkled in the streetlights.

"Detective Zack Lyde, Chicago PD," he said. "My boss, Shock Johnson, loaned us out to the D.A. and the D.A. says keep an eye on you. So that's just what my partner and I are doin', Ms. Chance, keepin' an eye on you."

Naomi's breath came out in a rush. "You scared the shit out of me, son," she said.

"I'll tell you, that can of Mace gave my pulse a little kick, too. Look, why not let us drive you home? We need to clear your apartment when we get there and then just kinda, you know . . ."

"Keep an eye on me?" she said, finishing the sentence for him.

"Yeah," he said, chuckling, in his deep, gruff voice. "My pard and I can follow your car. I'd feel a lot better that way."

"Why don't you just drive with me and let your pard follow us," she suggested.

"Fair enough," Lyde said. As they walked toward his unmarked police car, Naomi saw Judge Harry Shoat leaving the library after his weekly graduate-school seminar. His driver trotted up to him as Shoat started down the walk.

"How about Judge Shoat over there? Watching him, too?" Naomi asked.

"Hell, he just laughed at us," Lyde said. "Says Mr. Vail looks for spooks under his bed before he goes to sleep."

"You mean you don't?" she said with a grin, and followed her protector to the car to fill his partner in on the plan.

———

A block away Jefferson Hicks, a city patrolman assigned as Shoat's driver and bodyguard, rushed up to him and took his briefcase.

"How'd it go, Your Honor?" he asked.

"Excellent, as always," Shoat said, exuding self-assurance. "Although for the life of me, I don't see how some of those oafs ever hope to pass the bar."

"Yes, sir," said the driver.

Hicks had a black belt in karate and had attended a special course in antiterrorism. He had been assigned to Shoat for four months, ever since an irate taxpayer, who felt he had been treated unjustly in court, had shot and nearly killed one of Shoat's peers. Hicks belonged to the city; the sedan belonged to the judge.

Once inside the four-door Mercedes, Shoat reached into the pocket in back of the shotgun seat, took out a bottle of Napoleon brandy and a snifter, and poured himself a drink. He savored the brandy, swirling the snifter around, sniffing the aroma and gauging his sips so the drink would last the thirty minutes it took to get to his condominium in the Edgewater district.

"I got another call from the D.A.'s office while you were in lecturing," Hicks said. "About that Stampler guy."

"Vail!" Shoat snapped with disdain. Before he became a state supreme court judge, back when he was known as Hanging Harry Shoat, the ultraconservative jurist was a "max-out" judge known for meting out harsh sentences, often tainted with racism. An impatient and humorless perfectionist, he dispensed justice with a callous disregard for the situations or circumstances of defendants and had been passed over three times for the supreme court before his impressive knowledge of the law and precedents had made it impossible to snub him further.

He huddled down in the backseat, a stern man with a razor-slim mustache and black hair tinted to hide its gray streaks. He and Vail had gone to the mat many times in the courtroom. Shoat still harbored resentment toward the man who defied convention and challenged the law with consistent fervor. Even as a prosecutor Vail had an arrogant attitude about authority that rankled the jurist. Now that he had changed sides, Vail was slandering his own client, implying the man should not be freed, even though the state's leading psychiatrists had approved the release.

"Wants it both ways," Shoat muttered, taking a sip of brandy, remembering with distaste how Vail had ambushed Venable in the Stampler trial. "The hell with Vail," he said aloud.

"Yes, sir," Hicks agreed.

"He's baaack," Morris said as Vulpes entered the house. He trained the video camera on the open window and waited until he saw Vulpes enter the room before he started shooting.

"Been shopping," Solomon said, watching through binoculars. He saw Vulpes dump out the contents of two shopping bags on the bed. "Got himself a couple CDs, looks like a sweater."

"He's got a videotape, too," Morris said, squinting into the eyepiece. "Looks like . . . *Sleeping* . . ."

"*Sleepless in Seattle,*" Solomon said. "That's a funny picture."

"I hope it *sounds* funny because we're probably gonna have to listen to it."

"Got some pretty good music in it. It's got Jimmy Durante singing 'As Time Goes By.' "

"Who's Jimmy Durante?"

"He's an old-time movie actor. Big nose. Voice like a gravel grinder. You'll hear."

"He's putting the tape in the VCR," Solomon said.

"I can see that, Solomon, I don't need a play-by-play."

Vulpes started to get undressed, then almost as an afterthought he went to the window and closed the blind.

"Well, shit," said Morris. "We're back on ear-time."

They could hear Vulpes whistling softly, moving around the

room, heard the bed groan as he lay down on it, then they heard the TV turn on, followed by a preview at the beginning of the tape.

Morris turned off the camera and leaned back in his chair.

"What a way to make a living," Solomon said. "Listening to movies you can't see."

—

In his room, Vulpes quickly switched to the black turtleneck after pulling down the shade. He took a small tape recorder from the tool chest and put it on the night table. He had made the audiotape while still at Daisyland, playing the movie through several times, stopping it at any funny spots and taping his laughter, timing it perfectly. He even sang along with Durante.

Vulpes waited until the film started and on a precise cut he pressed the play button of the audio recorder. The movie and the tape, now perfectly in sync, were about two hours long. He set the TV so it would turn off at eleven. The audio recorder would turn itself off. With luck, nobody would know he was gone until morning.

He opened the door to his room and looked down the stairs. He could hear Schmidt moving around in the kitchen. He went down the stairs.

"Hi, Raymond," Schmidt said.

"Hi. Thought I'd get a Coke."

"Sure. Well, I'm packing it in," said Schmidt. "Lock the door after me, will you?"

"Sure. Good night."

"You're gonna be happy here, Raymond. I'm sure of it," said Schmidt.

Vulpes smiled and nodded. "Already love it," he said.

At nine-fifteen Morris saw Schmidt leave the halfway house, huddled in his plaid lumber jacket. Five minutes later the lights on the first floor of the halfway house blinked out. And five minutes after that Vulpes slid open the side window in the kitchen, slipped over the sill, and dropped silently into the shrubs beside the house.

—

Stenner had never seen Vail this edgy. He had double-checked everyone in the Wild Bunch to make sure they were protected. He was jumpy about Naomi going to the meeting at the University of Chicago until he was assured she was in capable hands. And he insisted that Parver, Flaherty, and Meyer, who lived alone, stay together for the night.

"Why don't I take you home," Stenner said to Vail. "Vulpes is tucked in watching a movie on TV."

"I have a nudge," said Vail. "The kind of nudge Harvey gets. And you, too, only you call it instinct."

"I got a nudge, too," said St. Claire. "Had it ever since we got to the office."

"What kind of nudge, Harve?" Flaherty asked.

St. Claire said, with a touch of annoyance, "How many times I gotta tell ya, Dermott, if I knew, it wouldn't be a nudge, it'd be a reality."

"Last time you had one of your nudges, you turned up the Linda Balfour case," Stenner said.

"The last time you had a nudge, we turned over Poppy Palmer," St. Claire countered.

"I agree with Abel, let's go home," Venable said to Vail. "But I want to talk to you for a minute before we leave."

Surprised at how serious she seemed, Vail led her into his office and closed the door.

"Something got your goat?" he joked.

"I have to tell you something," she said. "And this isn't about Aaron Stampler."

"So . . . tell."

"I went to Delaney's apartment. Out of a sense of duty, I suppose. Wanted to experience the scene of the crime. And I discovered something. There's a hidden compartment built into the closet in the bedroom."

"What kind of compartment?"

"It's about two feet deep and five feet long. It's a hiding place for Delaney's toys."

"What kind of toys?"

"Whips, handcuffs, garter belts—"

"*What?*"

"And a .38-caliber Smith & Wesson. It's on the floor. Looks like it was just thrown there. I didn't touch any of it."

"The gun is in this room?"

Venable nodded. "I assume it's the murder weapon."

"How did you find it?"

"Probably only a woman would have noticed it—women are very conscious of closet space. I was sitting on the bed, staring at the closet, and I realized that it's lopsided. I mean, there's a lot more room on one side than the other. So I snooped around and couldn't figure out why. And I snooped around some more and felt the door give. And I kept snooping. To open it, you unscrew the hanging rod and take it out. There's a button recessed in the fixture it screws into."

"That's very sneaky, Venable. You want a job?"

"I have a job—defending Edith Stoddard."

"If this is going to be a bargaining session I'd like to bring Shana in on it, it's her case."

"We're not going to bargain, Marty. We're going to trial."

"Janie, you probably turned up the murder weapon. That's all we need to burn this lady."

"She was a victim for almost ten years, Martin. He degraded her and she took it so she could keep her job. Then he tossed her over for a younger model and ruined her life. I can make that add up to a walk."

"On what grounds?"

"Name it. How about the McNaghten Rule. Namely that Stoddard was laboring under such a defect of reason, caused by the circumstances, that she didn't know the nature and quality of the act she was committing. Then we have the concept of irresistible impulse—she was so distressed she couldn't control her actions. Or how about temporary insanity? She was degraded and humiliated and finally thrown away like a piece of garbage."

"Save your closing statement for the jury," he said. He lit two cigarettes and handed her one. "And you're forgetting we have premeditation. And I thought Stoddard was determined to cop a plea?"

"I never was."

"She's the client."

"And I'm an officer of the court charged with giving my client the best advice and defense possible. That's what I'm going to do. You want to settle for involuntary manslaughter?"

Vail laughed. "I can't do that, I'd be disbarred for incompetence. Either she's not guilty or she's guilty of *some*thing."

"Then I guess it's Parver and me," she said. "Unless you're going to step in."

"I don't step in on my prosecutor's cases," he said. "I'll send St. Claire and Parver over to investigate the secret room. Then maybe you and Parver can have a sit-down."

"What do you think she'll do?"

"Go for the jugular."

"Trained her well, huh?"

"Didn't have to, it comes naturally with her. Thanks for telling me."

"You wouldn't have told me?"

"Sure. But it still had to give you some bad moments, considering the options, I mean."

"There weren't any options and you know it."

"Ain't ethics hell?" He grinned.

"Yeah, ain't they," she said, and after a moment, "You never cease to amaze me, Mr. Vail." She was obviously relieved.

"Why? Did you expect me to throw a temper tantrum?"

"I know some men who would."

"Look, we'll both do what we have to do, Janie. Hell, in a way, I got you into this."

"In a *way*?" she said, raising her eyebrows. They both laughed.

St. Claire tapped on the door and Vail waved him into the office.

"I just figured out what my nudge is," he said. "Something you said about Vulpes's phone calls strikes me as odd."

"What's that?"

"You said he made a phone call and got a bad connection?"

"That's what Morris told me."

"Well, if he got a bad connection, how come he didn't try the call again?"

Vail stared across the room at him, then looked at Venable.

"He's right," she said. "It's not like he didn't have time to dial again. If I made a call and got a bad connection—"

"You'd either call the operator or try again, right?" St. Claire finished the sentence.

—

Hicks entered Shoat's elegant two-bedroom condo first. He flicked on the lights and walked down the short entrance hall to the living room. He put Shoat's briefcase on his desk. Shoat had bought the condo after his wife died, preferring to get rid of the old house near Loyola University with its painful memories. The two-bedroom condo near the lake was convenient, was in a proper neighborhood, and was on the ground floor. It suited his purpose perfectly. It had a small deck at the rear that was secluded by a high redwood fence. He enjoyed sitting on this rustic terrace, reading cases and writing out his opinions in longhand. Hicks pulled back the thin, white cotton drapes, flicked on the lights, and slid open the door, checking the deck then closing the door and pulling the drapes closed again. He checked the living room, the master and guest bedrooms and baths, all the closets, and the small sitting room the judge used as an office.

"All clear," he told his boss.

"Very good, Hicks," the judge said. "Don't know what I'd do without you."

"Look, you want I should maybe spend the night in the guest room what with all this hoopla over . . . ?"

"Don't be silly," Shoat said, waving him off. "I'm going to get in bed and watch Court TV for an hour or so. I'll be sound asleep by ten."

"Right, sir. Seven o'clock in the morning?"

"As usual."

He followed Hicks to the door, putting on the night chain and twisting the dead bolt after letting his bodyguard out. He made himself a scotch and water, turned off the lights, and went into the bedroom.

Shoat was fastidious in his nightly ritual. He set out his clothes for the next day, placed his scotch and water on the night table, brushed his teeth and scrubbed his face, and changed into scarlet silk pajamas. He folded his silk bathrobe carefully over a chair within arm's reach of the bed, lined up his slippers side by side exactly where he expected his feet to hit the floor when he arose, piled three goose-down pillows, and fluffed them up just right before finally turning down the covers and slipping sideways between the flannel sheets so as not to wrinkle them. He propped himself up and pulled the feather comforter up under his chin and turned on the television, flicking the remote control to the Court TV channel. Settling down, he sipped his drink and watched with the sound turned low. Within minutes, he was trying to keep awake. He finished the drink and clicked off the TV.

He was dozing when suddenly the room seemed to be flooded with cold air. He lay in bed, staring sleepily into the dark. It got colder.

Then he thought he heard something. The sound seemed to be coming from the living room, although he was sleepy and confused in the dark.

"Hicks, is that you?" he called out, thinking perhaps his bodyguard had come back for something and was at the front door. He waited and listened.

There it was again. Was someone talking outside the condo?

Disoriented in the dark, he groped for the lamp and instead grabbed his bathrobe. He stumbled out of bed in the dark, his feet padding the floor of the darkened room in search of his slippers. The room was frigid and he gave up on the slippers and floundered his way toward the living room.

A frosty draft sighed past him as he reached the bedroom door.

He looked across the room. The door to the terrace had blown open. The white cotton curtains, flapping and twisting in the wind, looked like apparitions in the ghostly moonlight.

Damn! he thought. *Hicks forgot to lock the door to the terrace.*

He started toward the door. Then he heard a voice.

"Order. Order in the court." And a gavel smacking against wood.

The voice seemed to come from the dervish curtains, swirling in the wind. He stepped closer, squinting his eyes to get a clearer look. And then he saw something, a vague shape hidden within the gossamer panels. Shoat was suddenly hypnotized with fear. The shape slowly materialized into a dark form that seemed to emerge from within the whirling folds. It moved toward him. Shoat's mouth turned to sand. His feet would not move.

"W-w-who's that?" he stammered.

The figure, silhouetted by the moonlight against the shimmering drapes, raised its hand. There was a click and the same voice, the same husky whisper he had heard a moment before, said:

"The prince who keeps the world in awe;
The judge whose dictates fix the law;
The rich, the poor, the great, the small,
Are levelled—death confounds them all."

There was a slight pause, then: "Greetings from Daisyland, Judge."

"Oh, my God!" the judge shrieked. He turned and rushed toward a table near the door, pulled open a drawer, thrust his hand in, and felt the cold steel of his .32-caliber pistol. But before he could pull it from its hiding place, he felt a hand grab his hair and his head was snapped back.

Shoat felt only a slight burning sensation when the knife sliced through his throat. But when he opened his mouth to scream, all he heard was a rush of air from beneath his chin. And then the taste of salt flooded his mouth.

When the pain struck, it was too late for Shoat to feel it.

34

It was easy to trace the phone number. Morris had attached a digital readout to the monitor and had the number listed in his log. Stenner made one phone call and got the rest of the information.

"City Hospital," he said. "The last three digits, 4–7–8, is the office extension. He was calling the billing department."

"Why in hell was he calling the billing department at City Hospital?" Vail wondered aloud.

"And why'd he get a bad connection?" asked St. Claire.

Meyer, the computer expert, had been sitting in the corner listening to the discussion. He turned to his computer and entered the modem program, then brought up the menu. He dialed the phone number, 555–7478, and listened to it ring as he watched his computer screen. The screen went blank for a moment, then the word CONNECT flashed on and another menu appeared across the top of the screen.

"There's your answer," he said. "He was calling a modem line. Vulpes was talking to a computer."

"With what?" Parver asked.

"Yeah. Where'd he get a computer?" St. Claire asked.

"I don't know, but that's what the call was all about, that's the hum on the line," said Meyer. "If he stayed on for ninety seconds and he's a computer expert, he knew exactly what he was doing."

"Maybe we ought to roust him and ask him," said Flaherty.

"On what grounds?" Vail said. "He's a free man. If he does have a computer, it's understandable. It's his business. But if he's using it to trigger the copycat, then we got him."

He dialed Morris.

"Yes, sir?"

"This is Martin, Bobby. What's Vulpes up to right now?"

"He's watchin' a video. *Sleepless in Seattle.*"

"You're sure he's there?"

"We can hear him laughing. Few minutes ago he was singin 'As Time Goes By' with Jimmy Durante."

"Is the back door covered?"

"Sure."

"You stay on top of this guy, Bobby. He makes any phone calls or does anything out of the ordinary, call the office immediately."

"Absolutely."

Vail hung up. "He's in his room watching a video, they can hear him on the room tap."

He paced his office for a few moments. "All right, here's what we're going to do," he said. "Harve and Ben, come with me. We'll check out the billing department at the hospital. Shana and Dermott, stay here in the office and monitor the phones. And call Naomi right now just to make sure she's protected. Anything happens? Any calls from Morris or anybody else, call me on the portable. Abel, I want you to take Jane home and stay with her, and I mean in the house with her until I get back. I don't trust anyone else but you to protect her. And I want the house guard to patrol the entire perimeter. Any questions? Good. Let's get on with it."

—

The emergency ward at City Hospital looked like a battle zone. Three ambulances were parked at the entrance, one with its red light still blinking. Once inside, Vail, Meyer, and St. Claire were greeted with a rush of noise and motion. An aide raced by pushing a young woman on a gurney. Her face was covered by an oxygen mask and IVs were protruding from both arms. Her eyes were half open and her head wobbled back and forth with the movement of the stretcher. A young doctor was racing along beside it, shouting orders to a nurse who held open the door to the OR preparation station.

"I got a compound fracture of the lower leg, possible head injuries. I need a CAT scan before we go to OR."

"We're ready for her," the nurse yelled back.

Another doctor dashed from the receiving room, his gown streaked with blood, and headed up the hall.

"Excuse me," Vail said, but the M.D. waved him off. "Not now," he said, and ran off toward the operating room.

Vail looked through the door of Receiving and saw a nurse pull a sheet over a body. Two feet away, a team of doctors and nurses worked frantically to prepare another victim for treatment. A nurse burst out of the room carrying a clipboard.

"Excuse me," Vail said. "We're trying to find the night superintendent."

"Down the hall, elevator to the first floor, third door on your left, Mrs. Wilonski," she said without looking at them or slowing down.

"Thanks," Vail said.

They found the night superintendent's station and a nurse paged Eve Wilonski, the super on duty, then raced off, advising them to stay put.

"If you don't, she'll never find you," she said.

"Doesn't anybody around here *walk*?" Meyer asked.

The elevator door swung open and a short, square woman in a rigidly starched uniform marched toward them. Her stern face wore the ferocious expression of a bulldog.

"Gentlemen, I'm Eve Wilonski, night super. Sorry I'm in a rush right now, we've got a mess in Emergency."

"We came up that way. I'm Martin Vail, acting D.A."

"Yes, sir, I recognized you from pictures in the paper."

"These are two of my associates, Ben Meyer and Harve St. Claire."

"Gentlemen," she said with a nod.

"What happened?"

"Three-car pileup on LaSalle," she said. "Three dead, six trying to stay alive. A drive-by on the south side with a dead three-year-old and her mother hanging on by her fingernails. We got two heart attacks and they just brought one in for the psych ward who was standing on the marquee of the Chicago Theater peeing on people walking by on the sidewalk. That's in the last forty minutes and it isn't even eleven o'clock yet. It's just warming up out there."

"Sorry to bother you when things are so crazy," said Vail.

"It's always crazy down there," she said casually. "Do we have a problem with the district attorney's office, too?"

"No, we do. I need to take a look at your billing office and also find out if anyone was in there at three o'clock this afternoon."

"That office closes at two-thirty on weekends," she said.

"I know. But we have reason to believe that someone was in there at three. It's imperative we know who that person was."

"Maybe a cleaning person, somebody like that?" St. Claire suggested.

"That's quite possible," she said. "If it's an emergency, I can call Mr. Laverne at home. He's the billing supervisor. Someone could have been working overtime."

"That would help a lot," Vail said.

"May I ask what this is about?"

"A hacker," Meyer said casually. "We have reason to believe someone may be hacking into your billing computer. The consequences could be serious."

"Oh, my God," she said. She flipped through a staff telephone directory, her finger tracking down the rows of staffers and stopping at Laverne's name. She dialed the number and waited for what seemed an eternity.

"He's not home," St. Claire moaned.

"Mr. Laverne?" she said suddenly. "I'm sorry to bother you at home, this is Eve Wilonski. I have the district attorney here. He'd like to speak to you." She handed the phone to Vail.

"Mr. Laverne, this is Martin Vail."

"Yes, Mr. Vail."

"Mr. Laverne, we're checking on a computer problem and we need to know if anyone in your department worked overtime today."

"I did."

"You did? Were you there at three o'clock?"

"Yes, sir, I was talking to a pharmaceutical company on the West Coast."

"Was anyone else in the room at the time?"

"Uh, yes. Hines, I think is the name. Cleans up. Is this about the hacker?"

His question surprised Vail. "You know about that?"

"I was there when the message came across the modem line."

"What message?"

"Well, it was crazy. Something about a fox and someone named Hydra."

"Hydra? Do you remember exactly what the message said?"

"Let's see. First it said 'Hydra, Fox is free.' Then it repeated the name Hydra a couple of times. Then I jumped in and asked who Hydra was and who was on-line and the connection went dead."

"And you say Hines was in there at the time?"

"Yes. Came in while I was on the phone."

"Thank you, Mr. Laverne. You've been a great help."

"It was a hacker, right?"

"Yes. We're investigating it."

"I knew it. Too nutty to be anything else. You people always work this late at night?"

"When it's something this important. Thanks, Mr. Laverne. Goodbye." He cradled the phone. "Do you know someone in clean-up named Hines?"

"Yes, Rudi Hines."

"Show Ms. Wilonski the picture of Tribble," Vail said to St. Claire.

Harvey took a flat wallet out of his pocket and removed the photograph of Tribble supplied by the Justine Clinic.

"Is this Rudi Hines?" Vail asked.

She looked at the photograph and shook her head. "No, this is a man. Rudi Hines is a woman."

Her answer stopped conversation for a moment. Vail looked at St. Claire. "Show her the other one," he said. St. Claire showed her the photo of Rene Hutchinson. She studied it for a moment and then slowly nodded. "Yes, her hair's darker and much shorter, but that's Rudi."

"Can we take a look at the billing office?"

"Of course." She took a ring of keys out of a drawer and led them down a maze of hallways to a fairly large room with several desks and a bank of computers at the rear. The screens faced away from the door. Meyer walked straight back to them and stopped short.

"Christ, look at this," he said. They all crowded around the screen and read the message:

> *Very Clever . . .*
> *The prince who keeps the world in awe;*
> *The judge whose dictates fix the law;*
> *The rich, the poor, the great, the small,*
> *Are levelled—death confounds them all.*
>
> > *Hydra*

"I don't know what the hell it is, but it'll be in one of Rushman's books, that's for damn sure," St. Claire said.

"What's it mean?" Eve Wilonski asked. "Who is Hydra?"

"Greek mythology, ma'am," St. Claire answered. "Hydra was a demon with two heads. Every time Ulysses cut one of 'em off, she grew two more in its place."

"Or maybe grew a new name whenever things got hot?" suggested Vail.

"Maybe," agreed St. Claire.

"He's telling us something, Harve. Everything he does sends a

message—names, quotes, *everything*. He's taunting us." Vail read it
again and then a chill rippled through him. He repeated the second line aloud: " *'The judge whose dictates fix the law.'* "

"Shoat?"

"What other judge could it be? I'll get Shock Johnson on the
portable."

St. Claire turned back to Eve Wilonski. "Tell you what the message really means, ma'am. It means we need an address on this
here Rudi Hines ASAP," he said.

———

Stenner parked the car in front of Venable's house and opened the
door for her. As they approached the front door, he drew his gun.
Venable was surprised. Stenner always seemed so totally in control, it was hard to imagine him armed. He took her gently by the
arm, stepped in front of her at the door, and held out his hand for
the key. She gave it to him and he unlocked the door, then swung
it open with his foot. He moved cautiously into the foyer, then
moved quickly and professionally through the first floor, checking
the living room, kitchen, guest bedroom, and all the closets.

"We're clear down here," he said. The outside guard was sitting
on the terrace with his back to the door. He was wearing earphones and listening to a Walkman.

"I could have walked out there and pulled the chair out from
under him, he wouldn't know the difference," Stenner said, walking to the door of the terrace. "I want him to stay in here with
you while I check the second floor."

He opened the door and tapped the house guard on the shoulder. The man pulled off the earphones.

He stood up and turned around.

His face wore a hideous grin.

It was a moment or two before Stenner, with a shock, recognized the grinning face of Aaron Stampler.

By then it was too late.

"Welcome home," Stampler hissed. The knife slashed the air as
he swung it underhanded. It pierced Stenner just over his belt, its

deadly point angled upward, slicing toward his heart. The two men stumbled back into the living room and crashed into the wall.

Gasping, Stenner grabbed Stampler's wrist to keep him from withdrawing the blade. Stampler, his face inches away from Stenner's, curled his lips in a leer. He shoved his other hand into Stenner's coat pocket, felt his car keys, and grabbed them.

As they burst back into the room, Venable fell back against the wall. She gaped with horror when she saw the knife buried in Stenner's side. Then rage took over. She grabbed a heavy brass lamp from an end table and charged Stampler, swinging it like a club. It smashed the ridge of his jaw and split it open. Stenner slid from his grasp and fell at their feet, the knife still embedded in his side.

Stampler roared with pain. He grabbed the lamp and with his other hand hit Venable on the jaw. The blow knocked her backward against the other wall. Stampler grabbed the lamp with both hands and swung it overhanded.

She felt the heavy metal hit her cheek, felt the bones crush and a searing pain in her eye. Blood flooded down into her mouth. Her legs gave out and she fell to the floor, looking up at the enraged killer through one eye.

Stampler turned to get the knife, but Stenner had rolled over. It was under him. The madman ran around the corner into the kitchen, grabbed a dish towel, and pressed it against the wound in his jaw. He pulled open a drawer, dumped its contents on the floor. He pulled out another and another and finally found the knife drawer. He snatched up a vicious-looking boning knife and raced back into the living room. But as he did, Stenner rolled over and, with great effort, slid his 9-mm pistol across the hardwood floor to Venable. She grabbed it as Stampler rushed into the room from the kitchen. Half conscious and in pain, she swung the gun up and fired. It tore a corner off the kitchen cabinet. Stampler dove into the living room, scrambling for cover. She fired again and again. He skittered along behind a sofa. A shot ripped into it, bursting through the other side in a cloud of cotton and foam rubber. Stampler grabbed a chair. Hunched over, he ran toward a window, shoved the chair through it, dove through the shower of glass, and ran toward Stenner's car.

Inside, Venable rolled over on her stomach. She stared through her good eye at Stenner, who had the knife in his hand. He went limp and the knife slipped out of his grasp. He fell forward.

Outside, she heard Stenner's car start and roar away.

"Abel . . ." Venable moaned, and passed out.

35

When Shock Johnson arrived at Judge Harry Shoat's condominium, three patrol cars were already there. The six patrolmen had searched the grounds around the perimeter of the two-story building, but on Johnson's instructions had not attempted to enter the condo.

"We knocked on the door and tried him on the phone," said a sergeant who had taken charge of the small force. "No answer from inside and no answer on the phone."

"Shit," Johnson grumbled. He tucked his hands in his rear pockets and stared at the house.

"What's the layout, Sergeant?" he asked, without taking his eyes off the condo.

"One-floor condominium. The people upstairs are wintering in Georgia, so he's the only one in the building right now. There's a terrace with a six-foot fence around there on the side, windows in back and on that side. The place is dark and his car's in the garage."

"Where the hell's his goddamn bodyguard? What's his name?"

"Hicks, sir. I called him. The judge dismissed him, told him to go home. Hicks drives his car here every morning and they travel in the judge's Mercedes, that's why it's in the garage."

"Wasn't Shoat warned?"

"Hicks said he laughed at Vail."

"Christ. Eckling's gonna have me for lunch when he gets back from Atlanta."

"The chief's in Atlanta?"

"Yeah, at some lawmen's convention. Free drinks and food is what that's about." He looked around, pointed to a young, athletic patrolman. "What's your name, son?" he asked.

"Jackowitz, sir."

"Take that fence and see if you can see anything through the terrace door. I don't wanna go kickin' in anythin' until I'm sure he's in there."

"Yes, sir."

"Take a walkie-talkie and be cautious."

Jackowitz took the fence like a pro, jumping up and grabbing the top slat, chinning himself, and swinging first one leg then the other over the top. He dropped down onto the terrace.

Johnson waited.

The walkie-talkie crackled to life.

"Terrace door's unlocked, sir," Jackowitz reported.

"Oh, shit," Johnson moaned. "You got a flashlight?"

"Yes, sir."

"Take a look inside, but be careful."

"Going in."

There was a minute or two of silence, then: "Oh, sweet Jesus, Lieutenant, I ain't believing this. I'm opening the front door."

Johnson walked to the entrance and a moment later the front lights flickered on and the door swung open and Jackowitz stared out at them. Even in the dim light he was pale and swallowing hard.

"I been on the force twelve years, sir, I never seen anything the likes of this."

Johnson walked into the foyer and turned into the living room. Shoat was lying in the middle of the room, naked, his arms folded across his chest as if he had been laid out by a funeral director. The destruction of the body was profound, from the wounds on his torso, legs, and arms, to the emasculation of his private parts.

There was blood everywhere. Johnson stared at the scene for a full two minutes, the muscles in his jaw twitching.

Finally he said, "Where the hell's his head?" to nobody in particular.

"Good question," Jackowitz answered in a hoarse whisper.

—

Vulpes held the towel hard against his jaw to stem the bleeding. It was already beginning to swell and pain was etched into the side of his face. He had the city map on his lap marked with the route from the halfway house to Venable's place and back to Hydra's apartment. He watched his speed. He had to ditch Stenner's car fast, forced to assume that Venable had called in the report and his situation had suddenly became desperate.

What shitty luck, he thought. First, Stenner had brought her home instead of Vail. And then the bitch had screwed everything up. That was twice she had tried to kill him. Once in court, where she tried to send him to the chair, and again tonight.

Okay, so he had gotten Stenner instead of Vail. And he had smashed the bitch up good, maybe scrambled her brains. Poetic justice. As his own brain raced, he momentarily forgot the pain in his jaw.

He was cautious when he got to Hydra's apartment. He drove past it. The street looked safe. He parked at the opposite end of the street. Too bad Hydra didn't have a phone; he could have called her, told her to split, to follow him until he could find a good spot to ditch the car. He would have to take a chance, go up to her place and get her out of there.

As he got out of the car, he saw the police car. It was a block away and it cruised in quietly, parking perpendicular to the street he was on. Two cops got out, strolled to the corner, and crossed to Hydra's apartment building. They looked around, went in the front door.

They're on to her, he thought. *How the* hell *did they get on to her?* He decided he had to abandon Hydra. But she knew the plan. He didn't think she would talk, though she was now so far over the edge he couldn't be sure. He got back in, pulled the door shut, and started the car. Then he saw the two policemen come around the side of the house and return to their car.

He sat in Stenner's darkened sedan. Maybe they were just answering a disturbance call. Maybe it was just a coincidence and they would leave. He decided to give them a few minutes.

—

Meyer drove the car to the row-house apartment south of Garfield Park. Vail sat in the backseat, twirling an unlit cigarette between his fingers. St. Claire turned in the shotgun seat and looked back at him.

"What about Vulpes?" he asked. "We got enough to pull him in?"

"For talking to a computer? We need the woman, then we'll decide. We're still not positive she's the copycat."

"He's not going anywhere," said Meyer. "He's home singing duets with Jimmy Durante."

"Okay," said St. Claire.

"You disagree?" Vail asked.

"Nope, just thinkin' out loud."

"You got another nudge?" asked Meyer.

"Kinda."

"What's a kinda nudge?" Meyer asked.

"It's just, you know, a kinda nudge. Ain't a full-fledged nudge yet."

"Your nudges make me nervous, Harve," Vail said.

"Why?"

"Because most of the time they turn out to be harbingers of doom."

"Can't help it, just happens."

"I'm not knocking it, I'm just saying they make me nervous."

The police car was parked a block away from Rudi Hines's apartment. The driver was an old-timer named John Bohane. His partner, Richard Luscati, was a rookie, two months on the job.

"Lieutenant Johnson said we should wait here for you, Mr. Vail, so as not to rile anybody up. We did walk down there and look around."

"And . . . ?"

"Her car's parked around back in an alley. Hood's warm. And there's a lot of blood on the front seat."

"Uh-oh," St. Claire said.

"You think she's in there then?" Vail asked.

"Yes, sir, I do."

"Okay, let's do this cautiously. This lady should be considered armed and dangerous."

"Right."

Meyer pulled the car in front of the patrol car and parked. The five men walked up the quiet, deserted street to the converted row house.

"That's her apartment," Bohane said, pointing to the corner of the second floor.

"There a back door?" St. Claire asked.

"Uh-huh."

"Whyn't you two go in the back, we'll take the front, just in case she decides to take a drive."

"Right."

The two patrolmen disappeared quietly down the paved walk that separated the two houses. Vail, St. Claire, and Meyer walked quietly to the front door.

Vulpes watched as the second car pulled up beside the police car. He couldn't see what was going on. Then the new arrival pulled over to the curb in front of the patrol car and three men got out. The cops joined them. They started across the street toward the apartment building. As they passed under the street light, he recognized Vail.

His pulse throbbed in his jaw, increasing the pain, but he ignored it. He was overwhelmed with hatred. There was Vail, a block away, and he could do nothing about it.

Damn you, damn you, Vail! You figured it out faster than I gave you credit for.

Well, perhaps the police did not know about the attack on Stenner and Venable yet. Stenner was surely dead, Venable was out cold, so probably Stenner's car wasn't hot yet.

Maybe I hurt that bitch more than I thought. He laughed thinking about it. Still, he had to ditch the car in a hurry.

It was too late to help Hydra. Hopefully she was so far over the edge, she wouldn't give away the rest of the plan. *Too bad,* he thought. It was such a perfect plan and she had carried it out flawlessly until now. But Venable had screwed him up and now Vail had beat him to her.

He had to get away from there, lift another car and ditch Stenner's. He checked the map and found a group of high-rise apartments. *Perfect,* he thought. He had to find a parking lot and heist another car.

Goodbye, Hydra. Sorry it didn't work out.

He wheeled the car into a U-turn and headed for North River.

———

"Lemme go first," St. Claire said, arcing a wad of chewing tobacco into the grass.

"How come you go first?" Meyer asked.

"'Cause I got the gun," St. Claire said. He drew a .357 Magnum from under his coat and led the way inside. A poorly lit hallway was swallowed up by darkness and a flight of stairs on one side led to the second floor. A moment later the two patrolmen emerged from the other end of the hall.

"We're clear," Bohane said. "Her car's still back there." The patrolmen led the way, followed by St. Claire, Meyer, and Vail. Bohane knocked on the door.

"Ms. Hines?" he called out.

Inside the apartment Rudi Hines was in the bathroom. She

stood naked in front of the sink, scrubbing her hands, the water pouring off her hands tinged with red. When she heard the rap on the door, she hurriedly threw on a cotton housecoat and stepped from the bathroom into the living room.

It was sparsely furnished. A sofa with its springs sagging to the floor, a round kitchen table with two chairs, two easy chairs in the same disrepair as the sofa. The only light came from the 60-watt bulb in a floor lamp near the door.

"Is it you?" she cried eagerly.

She heard the muffled reply. "Ms. Hines, it's the police. We need to talk to you. It's about your car."

She went back into the bathroom and emerged a moment later with a large carving knife clutched in one hand. She backed into a dark corner of the room.

"Look, ma'am," St. Claire said, standing near the door. "We don't wanna have to bust up your door. Just open up and talk to us for a minute."

"Go away."

In the hall, St. Claire looked at Vail and shrugged. He turned to Bohane. "Waste it," he ordered.

The two cops drew their revolvers. Bohane stepped back and slammed his foot into the door an inch or two from the knob. It burst open. Somewhere down the hall a door opened and a dim face peered out.

"Go back inside," Vail said. "And stay there."

The face disappeared and the door closed.

The two patrolmen jumped inside the room, Bohane first, Luscati covering him, then St. Claire behind them. St. Claire saw her first, standing in the shadows.

"Lemme do the talking," he said softly, and to her, "Now why'd you make us go and do that?"

"What do you want?" she said. She saw Vail enter the room. Her eyes blazed in the dim light.

"I know who you are," she hissed.

"Ms. Hines, I'm Martin Vail, acting district attor—"

"I *know* who you are. Why aren't you out there?"

"Out where?"

"What do you *want*?"

"Ma'am, do you also go under the name Rene Hutchinson?" St. Claire asked.

She backed farther into the corner, her eyes peering at them from the darkness. She lurked in the shadows, but Vail could see one hand in the spilled light from the lamp. It was still covered with dried blood.

" *'Vengeance with its sacred light shines upon you.' Sophocles,"* she whispered.

"Miss Hines, do you also go by the name—"

"I am Hydra," she said. She held the knife tight at her side, within the folds of the housecoat.

"Do you know Aaron Stampler?"

"There's no such person."

"Do you know Raymond Vulpes?"

" *'Revenge is sweeter than flowing honey.' Homer."*

"Do you know the Fox?" St. Claire said, cutting her off.

" *'Punishment is justice for the unjust.' "*

"Listen here, ma'am . . ."

She glared from the darkness at Vail. "What are you *doing* here?" she demanded.

"Where should I be?" Vail asked.

"With her."

"With who?"

" *'To die is a debt we must all pay.' "*

The two patrolmen looked at each other quizzically. Meyer looked around the room. On a table near the door he saw a small tape recorder. It was caked with blood.

"Look here, ma'am, we know you're Rene Hutchinson. Wouldn't you like to tell us where Fox is?" He took a step toward her. "We need to talk to you and Fox."

"I taught him everything he knows," she whispered suddenly and with pride.

"What was that?" St. Claire asked.

"I taught him everything he knows."

Meyer moved sideways to the table. He took out a pencil and punched the play button of the recorder.

"Stop that!" she shrieked.

"Order. Order in the courtroom." The hollow sound of a gavel rapping. Then:

> *"The prince who keeps the world in awe;*
> *The judge whose dictates fix the law;*
> *The rich, the poor, the great, the small,*
> *Are levelled; death confounds them all.*
> *Greetings from Daisyland, Judge."*

Vail immediately recognized the voice on the tape. It was Vulpes.

"Miss Hutchin—" St. Claire started to say, but the woman suddenly charged out of the darkness. She rushed straight toward Vail. The knife glittered in her hand.

St. Claire moved quickly in front of him, aiming his gun at Hydra as she charged.

"Hold it!" he ordered, but she didn't stop.

The rookie cop panicked and shot her in the chest.

She screamed. The knife twirled from her hand and she was knocked backward, landing flat on her back on the floor. She lay there, gasping for breath, staring at the ceiling.

"Thank you," she whispered. "Thank you . . ."

The rookie lost it. He stared down at her in horror. "Oh God! Oh sweet God, why didn't you stop when I told you?" he screamed at her.

"Shut up, Ritch. Call the medics."

"She charged us with a knife," the rookie babbled. "I didn't . . . didn't . . ."

His cheeks suddenly ballooned. He clasped his hand over his nose and mouth and raced to the bathroom.

"I got eighteen years in, never fired my gun except on the range," Bohane said disgustedly. "He's on the street two months and shoots a woman." He shook his head. "I'll call an ambulance."

"Use this," Vail said, handing him the portable phone. The cop dialed 911.

St. Claire kneeled down beside Hydra.

"Rene Hutchinson?" he asked.

"I am Hydra," she said faintly.

"Who named you that?"

"Fox. Fox knows everything. But I taught him everything he knows."

St. Claire's "kinda" nudge suddenly became a reality. He was remembering some notes he had read among the files on Stampler. Notes that Tommy Goodman had written ten years before after his return from a trip to Kentucky, to do background on Stampler.

"How did you meet him?" St. Claire asked Hydra.

"I have known him forever."

"You're Rebecca, aren't you?"

"I am . . . Hydra."

"Before that. You were Rebecca?"

Her voice faded to a whisper. "Taught him every . . . thing he knows," she said.

"Jesus, you're his teacher, ain't ya?"

She didn't answer.

"When did you first contact him, Rebecca?"

For just an instant her memory streaked back to the young boy with the brutal strap marks on his buttocks who sat in the corner of her living room, devouring her books and the passages *she* had marked for *him*; to a time when it had been just the two of them, alone in the sanctuary of her house, sheltered from the brutal world around them as they made love in front of the fire. Then, suddenly, the moment dissolved into a clear, hot, white light.

As St. Claire stared at her, her eyes suddenly crossed slightly. Life blinked out of them and they turned to stone. St. Claire held his fingers against her throat, but he knew there would be no pulse.

"She was Stampler's schoolteacher, Marty," said St. Claire. "I remembered readin' the notes Goodman wrote when he came back from Kentucky. It's the last entry in the report. She told him, 'I taught Aaron everything he knows.' She was as crazy as he is."

"He isn't crazy, Harve. He's a cold-blooded killer, that's all he ever was. Call Morris. Tell him to go across the street and take the son of a bitch down."

"My pleasure."

The rookie staggered to the doorway of the bathroom, wiping his lips with a washcloth.

"Mr. Vail, there's something in here for Major Stenner."

Vail went into the bathroom. There was a box addressed to Stenner sitting in the bathtub. Below the name was scrawled:

> *What are fears but voices airy,*
> *whispering harm where harm is not.*
> *And deluding the unwary,*
> *until the fatal bolt is shot.*

Vail opened the box and stared into the face of Harry Shoat.

36

Morris and Solomon banged on the door of the halfway house until a young man with long hair tied back in a ponytail stumbled down the stairs and cracked open the door.

"Huh?" he said.

Morris showed him his ID. "Police, open up," he said.

"Police!" the young man said in a panic.

"We're just checking on the new man," Morris said as he and Solomon brushed past him and went up the stairs. Through the door, they heard Vulpes's raspy voice singing a duet with Durante.

"Make someone happy . . ."

"Open up, police!" Morris demanded. He tried the door. It was unlocked. The titles of the movie were rolling as they burst into the room. Morris froze when he saw the tape recorder.

"Make just someone happy . . ."

Solomon stared bleakly into the empty room. "Shit, he bluffed us out, Bobby," he moaned.

Vail was just leaving Rebecca Hutchinson's apartment when the phone rang. He listened while Morris babbled on the other end. His mind raced ahead of the conversation.

"Get the Chicago PD over there right now and give them a full report," he said. "I'll be back at the office."

The question now: Where was Vulpes?

Shock Johnson answered that question with more bad news.

"Where are you?" the police lieutenant asked.

"In the car heading back to my office," Vail answered.

"Go straight to the hospital, Marty. Stampler got Jane Venable and Abel. They're alive but just barely. Should be arriving in Emergency about now. He killed our house guard."

"Goddamn! God*damn* him!" Vail cried. "What happened?" he asked Johnson.

"He killed our man and jumped Abel and Jane when they arrived at her house. She got a couple of shots off and sent him packing in Stenner's car. That's all she told us before she passed out. Some neighbors heard the shots and called it in. We have an APB out on him now, but our pictures are all ten years old."

"Get your artist to put twenty pounds and ten years on him and get it to the media. Also I suggest a five-state alarm. If he breaks out of Chicago, God knows how long it may take to track him down."

"Done. I heard about what happened with the woman. We found the rest of Shoat out at his place. She must've been doing Shoat while Stampler was doing his dirty work at Venable's house."

"Stampler faked my people out," said Vail. "Sneaked out of the halfway house."

"Christ, what the *hell's* goin' on, Marty?"

"Stampler is what's going on. He's on the loose and who knows *what* he's got in mind."

"What do we tell the press?"

"You tell them the truth, Shock. How's Eckling reacting to all this?"

"He's at a convention in Atlanta. I haven't talked to him yet."

"Well, we've got three dead people, including a cop and a judge, two people in the hospital, and a mass murderer on the loose. You better break the news before he sees it on TV."

"See you at the hospital."

"Yeah." Vail hung up.

Meyer, not a cowboy behind the wheel by any means, took off like an antic teenager, threading through traffic with his hand on the horn.

"Doesn't this car have a siren?" Vail yelled.

"No, sir."

"Harvey, get a damn siren put on this thing tomorrow!"

"Yes, sir. What'd he say about Abel?"

"They're both hanging on, whatever the hell that means."

Ten minutes later Meyer screeched into the emergency parking lot and pulled up against a brick wall near the entrance. Vail was out of the car before Meyer set the brakes, taking the steps to the loading dock two at a time and pushing open the swinging doors, startling the short, chubby nurse with round eyes and heart-shaped lips who was sitting at the receiving desk.

"I'm Martin Vail. Any report on Jane Venable or Abel Stenner?"

"They're both in the OR," the nurse said. "That's all I can tell you at this time."

"I'm the D.A. These people are on my staff. Can't you do a little better than that? How bad are they?"

"You'll have to wait until the doctors come out," she answered apologetically. "I really don't know anything. I'm sorry."

Meyer and St. Claire joined him a moment later. Vail paced the hall, staring at the operating-room doors. The nurse, obviously accustomed to relatives and friends of emergency victims in the halls, leaned across the desk and in a half-whisper said to St. Claire, "There's a visitors' room down the hall. Coffee machine, soft chairs, a TV. I'll call you soon as I—"

"Thank ya, ma'am. I don't think he's gonna leave this hall till he knows something."

"That could be a while."

"I know th' man real good. He ain't movin' till he knows the score. What's happening?"

"They took them into prep about fifteen minutes ago. I expect they're both in surgery by now."

"Thanks."

Vail leaned against the wall and stared up at a clock over the operating-room doors. It was eleven-twenty. Stampler had been free less than twelve hours.

———

Aaron Stampler lurked in the darkness, watching the gate. He was on the first-floor landing of a six-story deck that provided private parking for tenants in the attached apartment building. The gate was activated by a card similar to a credit card. Stampler had lucked on to the building after dumping Stenner's car. It was nearly midnight. He reasoned that anyone coming in now was probably in for the evening and would not miss his or her car until morning. It was a perfect setup for him.

He had passed up a car with two couples in it. It seemed risky to him. He decided to wait. Ten minutes passed and a two-door BMW pulled up to the gate. In it was a man and he was by himself. Perfect.

As the car drove past and started up the ramp to the second floor, Stampler ran up the stairs. He peered through the door. He was in luck. The BMW was pulling into a parking space in a dark corner. Stampler threw the bloody towel into a waste can, ran across the lighted section of the deck, and ducked behind a row of cars, then crept down the row toward the parked car. The driver got out. He lowered the driver's seat and leaned into the back of the car, taking out a leather satchel. He put it on the ground and locked the car door.

Stampler was hunched behind the car next to his. He waited until the driver passed him, then he moved like an animal, soundlessly, taking two long steps, and grabbed the man's head with both hands, one under his chin, the other on the back of his head. He snapped the driver's neck like a breadstick. The man sagged as Stampler caught him under the arms and dragged him back to the car.

Down below, he heard the gate open and a car drive through. Stampler looked around frantically. The driver's satchel was sitting in the middle of the driveway. He quickly opened the trunk of the car, rolled the driver's body inside, then ran and picked up the satchel. He unlocked the door of the BMW just as the car approached the second-floor deck. Stampler jumped in and lay across the front seat just as the car circled onto the second floor. The car's lights swept past the windshield, then continued on up the ramp.

Stampler sat up and studied the instrument panel of the car. Until tonight he had not driven an automobile in ten years. The car had everything: a tape and CD player, cruise control, heat, air, and a telephone. He opened the leather satchel. The first thing he saw was the stethoscope.

He had killed a doctor.

He rooted through the satchel, found bandages and hydrogen peroxide. He had to duck down twice as other cars entered the parking facility. He finished cleaning his wound. His jaw was already swollen and beginning to discolor. He covered the gash with a thin bandage. There were several kinds of painkillers, but Stampler ignored them. He had to stay alert.

He got out of the car, opened the trunk, retrieved the dead man's wallet, and got back in the car. He searched through the wallet. One hundred and eighty-seven dollars and several credit cards. Not bad. The man's name was Steven Rifkin. According to his ID, he was a staff doctor at the University Medical Center. Under "person to notify in case of an accident": his mother.

God, am I in luck, thought Stampler. *He lives alone. Nobody's waiting up for him.* If his luck held, it could be late morning before the doctor was missed.

Stampler took two maps from his inside pocket, stretched them out on the seat next to the city map, and found his location. With his finger, he traced a route to Interstate 80. He felt suddenly secure. Once he got on the interstate, he could get lost in traffic. He looked at the dashboard clock: 11:25. He started the car and left the parking lot.

—

As Stampler was making his way toward the interstate, Shock Johnson arrived at the emergency room, looking harried and unhappy.

"We got two TV stations and a radio reporter outside," he said. "They're at Shoat's place and at the Hutchinson woman's apartment. They're on this story like ants on honey. What's the news here?"

"No news yet," Vail said, and began pacing the hallway outside the operating rooms again.

"I called Eckling," Johnson went on, falling in beside Vail. "He's doing barrel rolls over this. He's taking the red-eye back here. Gets in at six. He says to stall the press."

"How the hell can you stall the press? We need the media now. We have to put the heat on Stampler."

"We found Stenner's car parked in a dead-end alley off Wabash."

"He's going to lift another set of wheels, bank on it," said Vail. "He's too smart to stay around here."

"I talked to the state police. They've alerted Wisconsin, Iowa, Indiana, Ohio, and Missouri. I got Cal Murphy updating the photo. We should have it on HITS in another two, three hours."

A youthful doctor with his hair askew and his gown blood-splattered came out of the OR. He fell against the wall, pulled down his face mask, and pinched exhaustion from his eyes. He dug under the robe and took out a cigarette. Vail walked over to him and offered a light.

"Thanks," the doctor said, drawing in the smoke and blowing it toward the ceiling with a sigh. He stared at Vail, his eyes etched with weariness.

"You're the D.A., aren't you?" he said.

"Yes, Martin Vail. This is Lieutenant Johnson, Chicago PD."

"You here about Venable and Stenner?"

Vail nodded. "What can you tell us?"

"Stenner's still on the table in three. It may be a while before we know anything. He has a deep stab wound, entered here—" he pointed to his side just under his rib cage—"angled up toward his heart. It's a rough one."

"Is he going to make it?"

"It's a toss-up. He's on the edge."

"How about Jane?"

"She's going to live, but she took a terrible blow to the right cheek. The bones in her face are crushed and we pulled a bone splinter from her right eye. She may lose it. She also has a concussion. She's in for the long haul, constructive surgery, cosmetic work. What happened to her?"

"The same madman that stabbed Stenner hit her with something," said Johnson. "We're not sure yet, probably a brass lamp."

"Christ, what're people coming to?" he said, as much to himself as to Vail and Johnson. "I've got to go outside, we're not supposed to smoke in here."

"Can I see her?"

"Wait until they take her out of Recovery, okay? It's a madhouse in there right now. Probably an hour or so."

"Thanks."

"Sure."

Eve Wilonski, the night supervisor, came striding down the hall, her face looking like an angry bulldog's.

"Well, Mr. Vail, you're becoming a fixture around here," she growled.

"I hardly have any choice," Vail answered, and there was anger in his tone.

"Is all this related in some way to your earlier visit?" she asked, her voice softening.

"Unfortunately. I'm afraid we're going to be around here for a while," Vail said. "Sorry if we're screwing things up."

"It's the press, sir," she said. "They're making a nuisance of themselves."

Vail looked at Shock Johnson.

"I guess it's time to make an official statement," he said, then turned to Mrs. Wilonski. "Is there someplace we can hold a quick press conference without turning the hospital inside out?"

"We have a press room on the first floor," she said. "It's all yours."

———

Five miles away Stampler guided the stolen BMW onto Interstate 80. It was fairly crowded with people returning from dinner and the theater. He maneuvered into the fast-moving outside lane. It was eleven thirty-five. With a self-satisfied smile, he headed east.

37

The driving was going well, a breeze, in fact. Stampler had figured out the cruise control and set it on 70, a safe speed according to Rebecca. Hold it to 70, be sure to use your turn indicator when you pass, do not drive erratically, she had told him. It's like swimming, she had told him. You never forget how. Don't worry.

Worry? He never worried. Worry was destructive. He remembered a quote from Emerson. *"What fears you endured, from evils that never arrived."* Worry sapped his strength, fear drained his energy. Together they were destructive forces, distractions he could not afford.

He turned his thoughts to Daisyland, to Max and Woodward, patronizing him, telling him how "well" he was doing. Panderers. Treating him like a child. His grip on the steering wheel tightened until his knuckles almost glowed in the dark. God, would he like to see their faces now.

The news was coming on and he turned up the radio.

"Good morning, this is Jerry Quinn with the two A.M. edition of the news. Updating the hottest story of the hour, in a bizarre murder case that is still unfolding, Supreme Court Judge Harry Shoat was brutally murdered in his Lakeshore condominium earlier tonight and his killer, a deranged woman, was shot and killed while resisting arrest less than an hour later. During a hastily called press conference at midnight, Lt. Shock Johnson of the Chicago Police Homicide Division told reporters Shoat was brutally murdered about 9 P.M.

"According to Johnson, Shoat's body was mutilated and he was beheaded. His head was found an hour later in the apartment of Rebecca Hutchinson at 3215 Grace Avenue. Ms. Hutchinson was killed when she attacked one of the arresting officers with the same knife she allegedly used to kill Judge Shoat.

"Acting District Attorney Martin Vail, who joined Johnson at the press conference, said that his office has issued a murder warrant against Raymond Vulpes, aka Aaron Stampler, of a central city address. The warrant will charge Vulpes/Stampler with the murder of police officer John Rischel and the attempted murders of attorney Jane Venable and special officer Maj. Abel Stenner.

"Vail said these attacks took place at approximately the same time Shoat was killed by Hutchinson. Vail identified Vulpes as Aaron Stampler, confessed killer of Bishop Richard Rushman. Vail said Stampler was released from the state mental institution at Daisyland earlier in the day. Stampler has been a patient at Daisyland since the Rushman murder ten years ago. Ironically, Vail defended Stampler in the Rushman murder trial before becoming chief prosecutor of the district attorney's office.

"Vail said Stampler will also be charged with one count of murder and two counts of attempted murder and mayhem in the attacks on well-known attorney Jane Venable and Maj. Abel Stenner, head of the D.A.'s Special Investigation Squad, both of whom also figured prominently in the Rushman case. Here is a portion of acting D.A. Vail's statement."

"We have reason to believe that Aaron Stampler, during the past several years, communicated by computer with Ms. Hutchinson, who was his teacher in grammar school. We also believe Stampler abetted Ms. Hutchinson in two other murders. The murder of Mrs. Linda Balfour at her home in Gideon, Illinois, last October, and Alex Lincoln, a UPD delivery person, in Hilltown,

Missouri, a few weeks ago. In both cases, the M.O. was exactly the same as was used in the Rushman murder. Stampler also attacked attorney Jane Venable and detective Abel Stenner at Ms. Venable's home. Both are in critical condition in the Intensive Care Unit of City Hospital but are expected to survive."

"Police have issued a five-state alarm for Stampler and will have an updated photograph of him in about an hour. Stampler is twenty-nine years old, five-nine, weighs one hundred and fifty pounds, and has blue eyes and blond hair. According to Ms. Venable, she struck Vulpes during the attack and he has a severe laceration on the left side of his jaw. Police said Stampler should be considered armed and extremely dangerous—"

Stampler snapped the radio off.

"Son of a bitch," he said aloud. "Son of a bitch!" *They killed Rebecca! How did Vail track her down? What had gone wrong?* He slammed a fist into the steering wheel. His eyes glittered with hatred. Venable and Stenner, who sat on the witness stand and told the court that Stampler was faking it, had survived.

Well, he'd show them. Get-even time. *Get-fucking-even time!*

He passed the sign on the edge of the interstate: SHELBYVILLE, NEXT EXIT.

This time there wouldn't be any mistakes.

He pulled into a sprawling truck-stop complex and parked in a dark area off to the side of the restaurant. He checked his map and stuffed it in his pocket, then went through the doctor's satchel again. He opened a flat leather case and his eyes gleamed. It was a set of scalpels. He took out the largest one, tapped his thumb on the blade, and drew a drop of blood. He sucked it off and slipped the razor-sharp tool in his breast pocket. He also took a hypodermic needle, a vial of morphine, and a large roll of adhesive tape from the bag. He got out of the car and locked it. He looked around. Nobody was near him. He hastily opened the trunk and threw the doctor's satchel on top of Rifkin's body. He slammed the trunk shut and walked off into the darkness.

———

Vail sat next to Jane Venable in the ICU. The entire right side of her face was swathed in bandages. IVs protruded from both arms, the narrow tubes, like snakes, curling up to bottles attached to the back of her bed. Behind her, machines beeped and hummed as they measured her life signs. An oxygen mask covered her mouth and nose. Her limp hand, which he clutched between both of his, seemed cold and lifeless.

He watched the clock on the wall. It was nearly 2:30 A.M. Stenner had been in surgery for more than four hours. An hour earlier, one of the doctors had stepped briefly into the hall.

"We're doing everything we can," the weary surgeon had told Vail. "He's a lucky man. The point of that knife missed his heart by a quarter of an inch. If it had nicked the aorta he would have bled to death before the medics got to him."

"But he's going to make it, right?" Vail said, almost pleadingly.

"It's touch and go. He's still opened up, we're having to do a lot of microsurgery. But he's strong, in excellent physical condition, that's going to help."

Since then the tortured minutes had crawled by.

Outside the ICU the entire staff had gathered at the hospital, monitoring phone calls in a small office Mrs. Wilonski had hastily cleared out for them. But in the outside world there was nothing but silence. Stampler had simply vanished into the night. Was he holed up somewhere in the city? Had he stolen another car? Vail was overwhelmed with anxiety, guilt, and hatred toward the man who had so successfully conned them all and was now on a madhouse killing spree.

He felt a slight pressure from Jane's hand and looked over at her. Her lips moved under the oxygen mask.

"Take it off," her lips said.

"Can't do that, Janie."

"Just a minute," the lips said.

"Okay, just for a minute." Vail reached over and slid the face mask down to her chin. She squeezed his hand again.

"Hi," Vail said.

"Abel?" she asked, her speech blurred by drugs.

"He's carved up pretty badly, but they think he's going to make it."

"Sav'd m'life, Marty."

"And you saved his."

"D'you catch Stampler?"

"Not yet. Just a matter of time. I can't stay long. I'm not even supposed to be in here."

"Pull rank, you're th' D.A. . . . 'm I all smashed up, Marty?"

"Nah. I know a good body shop, they'll knock the dents out in no time."

She smiled up at him.

"'Fraid m' goin' t'sleep again."

"Sleep well, my dear. I'll be here when you wake up."

"Marty?"

"Yeah?"

"Kiss me?"

He leaned over and gently touched her lips with his.

"I love you."

"And I love you, Janie."

And she drifted off again.

———

She was in a deep, deep sleep, dreaming the dream she always dreamed: She was walking through dense fog, hearing the voices but never quite seeing the faces that went with them, those harpy songs that taunted her, luring her deeper and deeper into the mist. *Help me, help me, help me,* the voices cried until the sense of futility overwhelmed even her dreams, until suddenly she stepped into the hole and fell through the clouds, tumbling toward oblivion until she awakened with a start.

This time as she moved through the cottony mist, her feet froze in place and the haze blazed into light just before she fell. She awoke with a start. The bed-table light was on and her feet were tied to the foot of the bed. She tried to reach down and untie them, but her hands, too, were tied. She tried to scream, but her mouth was bound with tape. Fear turned sour in her mouth.

She looked around and saw, a few inches from her face, a scalpel.

Its blade twinkled as it was twisted in the light's beam. Her eyes gradually refocused on the face behind the scalpel's edge.

"Hi, Miss Molly," he said in the innocent Appalachian accent he had discarded years before. " 'Member me?"

She recognized Stampler immediately. Time had not changed him that much. Molly Arrington's heart was pounding in her throat, her temples, her wrists. She was having trouble breathing through her nose. Behind him, she saw the open window, the curtains wafting lazily in the draft. She peered at him in terror, but then just as quickly—as she adjusted to waking up—she grew calm. Questions assaulted her mind. *How did he get here? What was he doing?*

"Listen to me," he said, and his voice was cold, calculating, without accent or tone. "I'm going to take that tape off your mouth, but if you scream, if you talk above a whisper, I'll make an incision right here"—he put the point of the blade against her throat—"and cut out your vocal cords. It won't kill you, unless maybe you drown in your own blood, but it will be almighty painful. Do we have an understanding?"

She slowly nodded.

He picked a corner of the tape up with the tip of his little finger and then ripped it off. It tore her lips. Tears flushed her eyes, but she did not scream.

"That's good, that's very, very good," he said. "I always did admire your spunk. I suppose you have some questions?"

She did not answer but instead stared down in shock at him. He was stark naked and erect, sitting in a chair beside the bed.

"Cat got your tongue?" He chuckled. He moved the scalpel to the neckline of her silk nightshirt and drew the sharp blade slowly down the length of the shirt. It spread open in the wake of the incision until he had split it all the way to her knees. He took the knife and flipped first one side of the shirt, then the other, aside.

"There," he said, staring lasciviously at her naked body. "Now we're even."

Still not a sound from her.

"Can't you even say hello?"

She did not look at him. She stared at the ceiling.

"Talk to me!" he roared.

She turned her head slowly toward him.

"Martin was right," she said.

"Oh, *Martin was right. Martin was right,*" he mimicked her. "Martin was *finally* right, you should say. And only because I let him know. I gave him the clues and he *finally* figured it all out."

"That's what he said."

"Bright boy. Well, Doc, I don't have much time. Got a lot to do before I'm on my way. Got to be waiting when he comes."

"Comes where?"

He just smiled.

She did not ask again.

He held the scalpel up again and regarded it with sensual pleasure. "Know what I like about knives, Doctor? I like the way they feel. I like their power. People have a visceral fear of knives. And they're so efficient. All you have to do . . ."—he slashed the scalpel through the air—". . . is that. *Swish*, and it's all over. Exsanguination. Instant rigor mortis. *Instant!* All the air rushes out of the lungs. It's such a . . . a pure sound. *Whoosh.* Ten, fifteen seconds and it's all over. And this? This is a masterpiece. A scalpel. The ultimate blade. So beautiful."

"It's nice to know you killed them first, before you—"

"Oh, she can talk. Before I what? Before I cleansed them? Before I blooded them?"

"So that's what you did. Cleansed them," she said with sarcasm.

"Oh, we're going to push it, are we?"

"Push what?" she answered wearily. "I don't doubt for a minute you're going to kill me."

"I might surprise you."

"You can't surprise me anymore," she said.

He stood up and began to stroke himself. His lips were twitching around a sickening leer.

"You always wanted it, didn't you? Huh? Wanted me to throw you down on the floor of that cell and fuck your brains out."

"You're delusionary."

The smile vanished. The eyes went dead.

"Rebecca was right. Rebecca was always right. She was right about my brother and Mary. *Get rid of them,* she told me. *Get rid of the hate.* She was there when I stuffed the towels in the car window. And when they were cold and stiff, we did it in the front seat, right in front of them. *Now you're even,* she said. *Now you can forget them.* Just like I forgot Shackles and Rushman and Peter and Billy. Just like I finally could forget Linda and that creepy little coward, Alex Lincoln. She told me you were in the pit, too, that you were just as nuts as the rest of us. You know what it's like, don't you? To be smarter than all of them, listen to them pampering, pandering, so *righteous.* So fucking proud of themselves playing God. And they were all wrong. All of you were *wrong.* That's the best part of it all. Now everybody will know, the whole *world* will know."

"I was wrong," Molly said. "You're not delusionary, you're demonic."

"Demonic," he sneered, raising his eyebrows. "Demonic," he repeated, savoring the word. "I like that. Is that a medical term?"

"You want to kill the people that kept you alive."

"Alive. You call ten years in bedlam *alive*?"

"Would you have preferred the electric chair?"

"I would have preferred freedom. He played games with me."

"He did the best he—"

"He *fucked* me to protect that miserable faggot Rushman. He had the tape. Not a woman on that jury would have found me guilty if they had seen the tape. Christ, after that he had plenty of room for reasonable doubt. A second person in the room, temporary insanity, irresistible impulse. But nooo, he had to play the clever boy, protecting Rushman's good name, sucking that prosecutor into his game. And you went along with it."

"You tricked yourself. *You* provided the multiple personality defense. . . ."

"I didn't know you two would use it to sell me out. I knew when he came up to see me in Daisyland the other day he was going to try and ruin me. Hell, he would have looked like a fool if he tried to stop me from leaving, but he was too smart for that. We had the perfect plan, Hydra and me. Hydra got Shoat and I was supposed to get Venable. I could have been back in the room with a perfect alibi. I could've laughed at Vail. I could've got them all—Venable, Shoat, Stenner, you—all but Vail. I would've let him live in his own hell. Then that *bitch*, Venable, screwed me up. Look at my face. She did that!"

Molly said nothing. She stared at him in disgust as he straddled her, resting on his knees.

"He should've pleaded temporary insanity. I could have walked out of there free and clear."

"That's ridiculous, he couldn't—"

"*Don't speak to me like that!*"

"I'm sorry."

"You're not sorry. You're patronizing me. You should know better."

She shut up and stared at the ceiling again.

"Vail was so fucking clever, playing all those little legal games of his in court, dicking around with that insufferable Shoat. Jesus, *I* could have done better."

No answer.

"Ten years of drugs and shock treatments, egomaniac doctors, panderers, panderers, they were all fucking *panderers*."

He turned to the night table and put the scalpel down. He picked up a hypodermic needle, stared at its point. He picked up the vial of morphine, inserted the needle into it, working the plunger until it was full of the deadly painkiller.

"Well, now, Mr. Vail understands what it's like to hate enough to kill. And it's going to get worse." He settled down on her and held the needle in front of her face. "One hundred CCs, Doc. Permanent sleep, like the shot they give you when they put you away like a dog. I'll give it to you a little bit at a time, so the pain won't be so bad. *A cc here, a cc there, here a cc, there a cc...*" he sang.

He had lost it, she realized. Disassociated. Calm replaced by rage. Whatever he was going to do, he would do, she knew that now. She closed her eyes and waited with an eerie calm for the inevitable. She hardly felt the needle when it pierced her arm.

38

An exhausted young surgeon walked out of operating room three. He was surprisingly young, a tall, lean man with his long black hair tucked up under his green surgical cap. His surgical gown and shoe mittens were blood-splattered. His eyes were bloodshot. He pulled off his face mask and breathed a sigh of relief. Vail approached him.

"Doctor? I'm Martin Vail. Any news?"

The young doctor smiled and held out a large hand with long, delicate fingers. "It's a pleasure, Mr. Vail. I'm Alex Rosenbloom. Your man Stenner is one tough cookie."

"He's going to make it, then?"

Rosenbloom nodded. "But an hour ago I wouldn't have bet on it. We almost lost him twice."

"Thank you, sir. Thank you very much."

The young doctor slapped Vail on the shoulder. "I'm thankful I didn't have to bring bad news out," he said. "Look, I know you've been very patient. They're taking him into Recovery now. You can stick your head in for just a minute."

"Thanks. There are a lot of us here that thank you."

"I heard the whole D.A.'s staff is here," Rosenbloom said. "He must be a very special person."

"Yes, he is."

Vail entered the small recovery room. Stenner seemed frighteningly tiny and frail. He looked gray and vulnerable with his arms attached to a half-dozen IV tubes and various machines beeping and humming beside his bed. Vail took his hand.

"Welcome back," he said softly.

Stenner groaned.

"Can you hear me, Abel?"

Stenner's eyes opened a hair and he stared, unfocused, at his friend. He blinked his eyes once.

"You're going to be okay, my friend. And so is Janie. Thank you. Thank you."

Stenner slowly blinked his eyes again.

"We've got Stampler in our sights," Vail lied. "Just a matter of time."

Under the oxygen mask, he saw Stenner's lips form the word "Good." Then his hand slipped out of Vail's and he fell asleep.

———

Vail stood by the window, staring out at the first red signs of dawn. It was nearing 5 A.M. and everyone was exhausted. But the crisis seemed to be over. Both Stenner and Venable were holding their own and for that Vail was grateful. He gathered the troops together.

"I think it's safe to call it a night—or morning," he said with an attempt at a smile. "I'd like to work in shifts, keep somebody here around the clock. Naomi, work up a schedule, okay? I'm going to hang in here for a while longer."

"I ain't goin' nowheres," St. Claire said emphatically.

"Me either," Meyer joined in.

"Look, we all need to get some rest," Naomi said, taking command. "Let's not forget we still have an office to run."

"I'm going outside and have a cigarette," Vail said. He went down the long hallway and out on the emergency dock. There was very little activity. The chaos of the night before had been replaced by an eerie calm. He lit up and watched the sky begin to brighten. Parver and Flaherty joined him.

"I hate to bring this up," Parver said, "but Stoddard is up for arraignment tomorrow. What're we going to do?"

"Postpone it until we see how Jane is doing. Hell, I don't want
to deal with that right now."

"I'm sorry," she answered. "I'll take care of it."

"You're still having mixed feelings about Stoddard, aren't you?"

She thought for a minute and nodded. "After finding that stuff
in that closet room, I . . ." She hesitated for a moment, then finished the sentence. "Don't worry, I'll handle it properly."

"I know you will." He smiled at Flaherty, who stood quietly by,
holding her hand. "You two take care of each other. Time has a
bad habit of running out when you least expect it."

"Yes, sir."

"Better go home and get some shut-eye."

The emergency doors swung open and St. Claire peered out.

"I think we got us a break," he said.

———

Buddy Harris was on the phone. The state police officer had been
up all night, fielding false alarms and the usual nut calls that result from an APB. It seemed everybody in the city of Chicago had
seen Stampler during the long night.

"But I think we got a live one," he told Vail. "I just got a call
from the Indiana HP. They think they've tumbled on a stolen car
with Illinois plates and an MD's tag. Probably wouldn't have noticed it for hours except the dumb bastard parked in a handicapped space next to a diner. It was spotted by a waitress a little
after two A.M., so it's been parked there for a couple of hours.
They ran the registration. It's owned by a Dr. Steven Rifkin.
There's no answer at his house, so I called the University Medical
Center. They say he checked out of there about ten-thirty last
night. Apparently he had a really hard day and was going straight
home to bed."

"You say Indiana has the car?"

"Yeah. In a place outside Indianapolis called Shelbyville."

Vail thought for a moment. The name struck a chord. Then he

remembered the shrink at the Justine Clinic telling him Rene Hutchinson had taken computer lessons in Shelbyville.

"Jesus, Buddy, that's only a few miles from the Justine Clinic. My God! He's going after Molly Arrington. Call the Indiana patrol, tell them to get an address on a Dr. Molly Arrington in Winthrop and get over there on the double. I'm going out to the airport and fly down there."

"Hell, that isn't necessary, Marty, they got—"

"I'll call you from the airport. Just get on it, Buddy."

Vail turned to Naomi. "Call Hawk Permar and tell him we need the chopper. There's going to be three of us and we're going about thirty miles southeast of Indianapolis, a town called Winthrop. If he starts bitching, tell him I'll personally throw in a two-hundred-dollar bonus."

"Three passengers?" St. Claire said.

"You, me, and Flaherty. We're going down there to find that son of a bitch and bring him back."

—

They were airborne, swinging south from the airport and following Interstate 65 toward Indianapolis. The pilot, Matt Permar, who had earned the nickname Hawk flying choppers in Vietnam, was grumbling about not getting enough sleep as he followed the interstate straight toward Indianapolis. A chunky, good-humored man, he was an excellent pilot who loved to gripe—a hangover from his army days.

"What'ya mumblin' about?" St. Claire asked.

"Cockamamie D.A., never does anything at *normal* hours. It's always the middle of the night or dawn. Always spur of the moment—"

"Blah, blah, blah," said Vail. "You can always say no."

"You pay too well," Hawk answered.

"Then stop bellyaching," Vail said.

"Bellyaching is good. Bellyaching is normal. I love to bellyache. If I didn't bellyache, I'd be a fruitcake by now."

"Ain't nobody ever told ya, Hawk. You *are* a fruitcake," St. Claire said, and stuffed a wad of tobacco under his lip.

The gripe session was cut short by the squawk of the radio. It was Harris, who was still on duty.

"I got some bad news from Winthrop, Marty," he said, his voice getting hoarse from lack of sleep.

"I'm prepared for that. Lay it on me."

"Molly Arrington's dead, Martin. Spread-eagled on her bed, body mutilated, probably was raped. The weirdest thing about it is, he pumped her full of enough morphine to kill her even if he hadn't cut her up. He also printed in blood on her torso the words 'I'm waiting.' Does any of that make sense to you?"

Vail was thinking about Molly. Gentle Molly, who had never hurt a soul in her life. "Nothing that bastard does makes any sense," he said angrily.

"He stole her car, probably been on the road at least two, maybe three hours. There's nothing you can do there, Marty. The creep could be anywhere."

Vail did not answer immediately. He thought about the message. *"I'm waiting."* And then suddenly it did make sense. There was only one place Stampler *could* go. He couldn't go back to Chicago and by now the whole country knew the story. He would go back to where it had started. Vail grabbed the sectional map and traced a path with his finger south from Shelbyville. His finger finally found what he was looking for.

"I know where to find him," he said. "We'll pass on Winthrop. Head for Crikside, Kentucky."

"Huh?" Hawk said.

"Where?" Harris said.

"Crikside, spelling C-r-i-k-s-i-d-e. Call the Kentucky HP and fill them in. Hold on a minute." He made an arch with his thumb and forefinger and measured the distance south of Indianapolis.

"About one hundred and seventy-five miles and we're still one hundred miles from Indianapolis. How about it, Matt, how long?"

"What, two hundred and seventy-five miles? Hour and a half, maybe two. What's the weather like down there?"

"Who cares?" said Vail.

"I care!" Hawk hunched down in his seat and shoved the throttles forward. "I know the weather's for shit," he said.

"Just keep flying south toward Louisville."

"You really think that's where the son-bitch's headin'?" St. Claire said.

"There's no place else left for him to go," Vail said. "He had this thing planned out perfectly. He sneaked out of the halfway house. His plan was to kill Jane and me while Rebecca killed Shoat. She sneaks back to her place, he sneaks back into the halfway house, and we would be his alibi."

"How about Rebecca takin' off Shoat's head?"

"She collected trophies, remember?" said Flaherty. "It's what serial killers do, just like hunters collect antlers or animal heads. That was her trophy, Harve. She was going to send it to Abel, the way she left the photo of Linda Balfour when she killed Alex Lincoln."

"Stampler only made one mistake," said Vail.

"The call to the hospital," said Flaherty.

"Right," agreed Vail. "And he underestimated Jane Venable. When he couldn't kill her, he was on the run, his plan was blown. His face is on every TV station in the country by now. My guess is, he's playing head games with me now."

"And he killed Molly Arrington—" Flaherty started to say.

"To goad me. He's finished and he knows it." Vail finished the sentence. "He's going to make catching him as tough as he can. Let's say he snatched the doctor's car at eleven, eleven-thirty. That put him in Shelbyville at around two A.M., about the time a waitress spotted the car parked in a handicapped zone. Winthrop's just outside the outskirts of Shelbyville. He could've walked to Arrington's house from there in, say, half an hour. That puts him at Arrington's at between two-thirty and three. An hour to do his dirty work and get out with her car. From there to Louisville is about a hundred miles, say another two hours."

"So he was in Louisville maybe half an hour ago," Hawk calculated.

"It's another one hundred and twenty miles to Crikside. If he gets through in the weather he could be in Crikside, say, two and a half, three hours from now. With luck we may just catch him while he's still on the road."

"We gotta stop and refuel," Hawk said.

"Do it in Louisville," said Vail.

"Mind if I ask a question?" Flaherty said.

"What's that?" Vail answered.

"We don't even have a warrant for Stampler. Is this legal?"

"I'm making a citizen's arrest," said Vail.

"Citizen's arrest?"

"That's right. I'm arresting him for stealing Molly Arrington's car. We'll charge him with the rest of his sins when we get him back to Chicago."

"Citizen's arrest." St. Claire laughed. "You sound like Barney Fife."

"Sounds like kidnapping to me," grumbled Hawk.

"Well, keep that notion to yourself," Vail said.

The radio squawked to life again. Harris's calm voice reported the latest developments. "We've alerted the Kentucky state cops and the sheriff of the county, but they got traffic problems down there. They got themselves a spring snowstorm and a lot of traffic problems."

"A snowstorm! I knew it. I *knew* it!" Hawk howled.

"Just keep flying," said Vail.

"They aren't all steamed up over the possibility that he *might* have killed a woman and he *might* be on his way to Crikside," Harris continued. "They said they'll get somebody over to check it out by noon or one o'clock."

"Shit," Vail snapped.

"I got some more bad news," Harris went on. "Indiana HP popped the trunk on that car. The doctor's body was inside. Broken neck."

"That makes three so far he's personally killed," Vail said bitterly.

"One other thing. Arrington's car is a '93 black Camaro two-door, license: J32 576. Got that?"

"Got it."

"And be careful, you're flying into the Cumberland Mountains down there. Good luck."

"Thanks for the help, Buddy. Over and out."

"Snow and mountains," Hawk groaned. "Two of my favorite things. All we need now's a little ground fire to make this a dream vacation."

39

The chopper swung over the low ridge and dropped down closer to the road. Snow flurries splattered against the windshield. Below them the two-lane blacktop was still discernible although the snow was beginning to cover it. They had seen only three cars in the last twenty minutes. Hawk's gaze jumped from window to windshield as he roared two hundred feet over the rugged terrain. Beside him, Vail was navigating from a roadmap. They were following the state road that led to Crikside. Behind them, St. Claire and Flaherty also scanned the road, Flaherty with a pair of binoculars. Hawk glanced at the clock.

Nine twenty-two.

"How am I doing?" he yelled.

"We're about ten miles from the place. It's just over that next ridge."

"I can't even see the next ridge," Hawk said.

"It's eight or nine miles ahead. He can't be far ahead of us, not with the road conditions the way they are."

"I thought we'd pick him up before this," Hawk answered. "He must be driving like a madman—*if* he's coming here."

"He's coming here," Vail answered with finality. "He just stopped off in Winthrop long enough to satisfy his blood lust, claim another victim."

"I think we missed him," Hawk said.

"We ain't missed him," said St. Claire. "Marty's right, been right all along."

"You having one of your nudges?" Flaherty asked without taking his eyes off the road.

"This ain't a nudge, it's a reality," Vail said, imitating St. Claire's gruff voice. Their laughter eased the tension.

Flaherty leaned forward, the binoculars tapping the side window. "I got some tracks," he said.

"Where?" the others asked, almost in unison.

"Right under us. They're blowing off the road, but there's a car somewhere in front of us. Can we get lower?"

"This thing don't do well underground," Hawk answered. But he dropped down another fifty feet.

"See anything?" Flaherty asked Vail.

"I can't see that far up the road. I'm not sure how close we are to that ridge. Maybe we ought to gain a little altitude. I can't tell exactly where we are on this map."

"There it is," said Flaherty.

They peered down in front of the chopper. Through the rushing snowflakes a car was visible racing through the storm.

Flaherty said, "It's black . . . I can't tell the make, but it's a two-door."

"Gotta be the son-bitch," St. Claire said. He stuffed a fresh wad of tobacco into his cheek.

"We're coming up on that ridge," Hawk said. "We could be a couple hundred feet short." He pulled back on the throttle, easing the chopper's speed.

"You're right on top of him," said Vail. "Slow her down a little more."

Hawk cut the power a little more. He was heading for the ridge at about fifty miles an hour.

—

Below them, Stampler heard the unmistakable sound of a helicopter. He looked out the car window. It was no more than a hundred feet above him. To his right was another ridge, thick with pine trees. Ahead of him he saw a turnoff. A faded sign said:

KC&M

HILLSIDE DIVISION

Stampler hit the brakes and almost lost it. The car skittered across the road, showered up snow as it ripped through a low drift, and then swung back on the road. He got the car under control and turned into the road. A wooden horse was stretched across the entrance. Stampler tore through it, showering bits of wood into the trees. The macadam road was pitted by disuse and bad weather. He was having trouble keeping the sedan on the road. But he was climbing up the side of the ridge, forcing the chopper to gain altitude.

But it didn't. He could hear it, *chung, chung, chung, chung* over his head. The car skewed beneath him, its wheels spinning helplessly on the snow-packed road. He lost control, slammed on the brakes, and sent the car into a wild spin. It teetered on the edge of a ditch, then spun out the other way and plunged off the road. Stampler saw the trees hurtling toward him, crossed his arms over the steering wheel, and put his head against them as the car swiped one tree and crashed into the one beyond it. The hood flew up and shattered the windshield. Stampler's arms took the brunt of the blow. Numbly, he felt for the door handle, pulled it back, and tumbled out of the car. Small whirlwinds of snow spun around him and he looked up. The chopper was fifty feet over his head. He dove into the trees and started running.

———

Hawk looked around at the forest that encroached on him. Tree limbs reached treacherously out over the road.

"I'm not sure I've got enough room to put down here," he yelled. "But it's a helluva lot safer than trying to follow him up this damn mountain."

He lowered the helicopter slowly to the ground. The rotors thrashed at the trees limbs, snapping them off, scattered the debris into the air. Hawk eased it down, felt the skids hit the ground and settle in.

"Okay, we're down," he said, and Vail, Flaherty, and St. Claire scrambled out. Vail vaulted the ditch and took off after Stampler, with Flaherty close behind. St. Claire wasn't as lucky. He slipped on the muddy bank and fell, twisting his ankle.

"KeeRIST!" he yelled. Vail turned, raced back to him.

"Just get goin'," St. Claire said. "It ain't broke. Here, take this."

He pulled the .357 from under his arm and handed it to Vail. When Vail hesitated, St. Claire said, "Hell, you might not use the damn thing, but it's one helluva good scare card."

Vail took the gun and ran off into the forest.

———

Stampler stumbled out into a clearing, gasping for breath, clutching at the pain in his side. He was in front of the shambles of a wooden office building, boarded up and rotting. He stared around at the snowy landscape. His gaze settled on the muscular steel framework of an elevator. It was vaguely familiar, the relic, now idle and rusted. A large sign said:

CLOSED

TRESPASSERS WILL BE PROSECUTED

KENTUCKY COAL AND MINING COMPANY

Even obscured by snow, the place began to take on an air of familiarity. Memories began nibbling at his mind and with them a gnawing sense of apprehension. In his mind, he heard the sound of the elevator clinking and groaning as it lowered men into the guts of the earth. Blackened faces and haunted eyes filtered through his flashback like demons in a nightmare.

He remembered awakening on his ninth birthday, seeing the hard hat with the ominous lamp on the front perched on the chair beside his bed, and the fear that went with his "present." He remembered shrinking down on the bed, trying to keep from crying, knowing that on this day he was going down into the hole, that fearful pit, for the first time; being so terrified, he threw up on the way there; and the boss man standing right where he was standing now in front of the office, looking down at him, grinning, telling him today he was going to become a man.

"Stampler!"

Stampler turned and, there, across the snowy clearing, stood Vail. Perhaps fifty yards away, on the opposite side of the clearing. From the corner of his eye he saw another man emerge from the forest, a younger man, who joined Vail. They stood and waited for him.

Stampler started across the clearing, past the ghostly silhouette of the elevator shaft, heading for the opposite side of the clearing, the snow squeaking underfoot as he made his way across a low mound that separated him from his nemesis.

"Stampler!"

Vail raised his hand. He was aiming a gun at him. The other one, the younger one, also had a pistol, but he stood with his gun hand lowered at his side.

The ground seemed to groan underfoot.

Vail aimed the gun over Stampler's head and fired a shot. Its thunder echoed through the trees and snow showered down from the limbs. Stampler stopped, glared across the white expanse at Vail.

"You wouldn't shoot an unarmed man, would you, Counselor?"

"Don't kid yourself."

Stampler leered at him. "Know what it's like, now, don't you, Marty? Blood for blood. We're not that different, you and me."

Vail did not answer. He pondered the question, thinking about the carnage of the last twelve hours; about Abel and Jane fighting for their lives; about Shoat and Dr. Rifkin and a good cop and poor Molly Arrington, innocents all, sacrificed on Stampler's altar of vengeance. And about Rebecca, who had planted the seeds of Stampler's hate and also had the blood of Alex and Linda on her hands. Five people dead, three in just half a day, and two gravely injured. And of all his targets only Vail had escaped the madman's wrath.

Stampler slipped back into his Crikside accent for a moment. "Now, yuh know what I main, Marty. Feel it, don't yuh? A hurtin' in the chest. Yer stomach's on fire. Head feels like it's in a vise and somebody's squaizin' it tighter and tighter. Got a hard-on waitin' fer it t' happen. You feel it, don't yuh, Marty? The urge to kill."

Vail's finger tightened on the trigger.

"Or maybe I shouldn't call you Marty? Too familiar. How about *Mr.* Vail? Or *Mr.* Counselor? *Mr.* Prosecutor? *Martin?* Oh, help me, Martin," he jibed, slipping easily from one accent to the other. "Ah'm so scairt and confused. I lost time, Martin, and Ah jest *know* sompin' terrible has happened. Plaise help me, suh."

Hate ate up Vail's insides, assaulted his head, gnawed at his heart. Stampler was right, he wanted to squeeze the trigger, watch the bullet rip into his chest. He wanted to watch Stampler die.

"Marty?" Flaherty said behind him.

"Stay out of it, Dermott."

"Let me go bring him in. You're making me nervous."

"How 'bout it, *Martin*? Can yuh help me, suh?" Stampler began to laugh. "I'm goan turn 'round now, I'm jes' gonna walk away from you. Go ahead, shoot an unarmed man in the back. That's what you want to do, isn't it?"

"He's pushing you, Marty."

Vail felt the cold trigger against his finger. His fist tightened a little more.

"I know what he's doing," Vail said.

"I'm going out there and get him."

"Stay right there, Dermott, can't you read the sign?"

The sign, weather-scarred and leaning sideways in the drifting snow, said:

DANGER   UNSAFE   DANGER
This mine shaft has been sealed
No admittance to this area
DANGER   UNSAFE   DANGER

And behind it the mound in the snow was the cover that had been placed over the shaft years before. Vail called out to Stampler. "Put your hands behind your head and walk toward me."

Stampler walked away from them. "Ah'm leavin now, Martin." He laughed harder. "Catch me if you can."

"You're standing right over mine shaft five, Stampler," Vail called to him. "The hole. Remember the hole?" He pointed to an old sign lying near the shed: KC&M MINE NUMBER FIVE.

Stampler hesitated. He looked back at Vail and Flaherty, then at the rusting elevator mount. The groaning, clinking, awful sound it used to make rang again in his ears. He looked down at his feet and his gaze pierced the snow and boards and plummeted into the darkness. He saw twelve men—eleven men and a boy—suspended under the steel mount, being lowered from the land of the living into that pit of pure darkness; men, old long before their years, bent over and stooped from chopping away at walls of coal; saw the light at the top of the shaft as it shrank, growing smaller and smaller until he couldn't see it anymore; dropped into air that smelled of bad eggs, with his mouth so dry his tongue stuck to his teeth. Dropping down into hell. A pitch-black hell.

"What's with him?" said Flaherty. "He's just staring at the ground."

The boards under Stampler's feet whimpered and sagged ever so slightly. Stampler stared at his feet. Snow cascaded between the boards. His jaw began throbbing as his pulse increased. He took a step forward. The ancient boards, ruined by years of bad weather and neglect, groaned as Stampler's weight tortured them. The platform sagged even more. He stopped—afraid to move ahead and afraid to stay in place. He took a giant step, put his foot down gently, leaned forward, and swung the other leg beside it. There was a crack under his feet. It sounded like a rifle shot as the board underfoot broke.

"Oh, Jesus," Stampler said to himself. He started to run and with each step the rotted platform collapsed underfoot, disintegrating behind him as he dashed madly toward the trees. Then his leg crashed through the platform and he fell forward, felt the platform behind him start to fall away. He started to crawl and it cracked again. This time the platform began disappearing from under him. He leaned forward, reaching out, trying to find something to grab. His fingers burst through the snow, dug into the rotten wood. He pulled himself forward and another section broke away. He looked over his shoulder. Behind him, like an enormous, obscene black mouth, the hole kept spreading.

"Aw, Jesus!" he screamed. He started to fall and he dug his fingernails deeper into the wood. His weight pulled at the nails, but they began to slide, and splinters, like needles, pierced his fingertips, jutted under his fingernails, and punctured the quick. He was too terrified to cry out in pain. He was scrambling for his life as the decayed platform disintegrated completely around him.

The last boards gave way.

Stampler looked back for an instant. His eyes locked on to Vail's. His fingers scratched across the disintegrating platform and he vanished into the black maw.

He did not scream. He did not utter a sound. He plunged soundlessly down, down, down.

It was a very long time before they heard the dull, faraway thump; the faint clatter of wood slats as they plunged down behind him. Then it was deathly still except for the wind rattling the dead limbs of the trees.

"God almighty," Flaherty whispered.

"Save your prayers for somebody who deserves them," Vail said. He turned and walked away from the gaping hole in the snow.

—

They followed the road back to the chopper, which was waiting with its rotors idling. Vail and Flaherty helped St. Claire into the helicopter and climbed aboard behind him.

"Where's Stampler?" he asked.

"Where he belongs," Vail answered. "In hell."

The chopper lifted off and climbed toward the top of the ridge. Vail watched mine shaft five pass below them. He stared down at the black circle surrounded by fresh snow. It looked like the bull's-eye of a target. He watched it until the chopper swept over the top of the ridge and he could no longer see Aaron Stampler's grave.

EPILOGUE

The mixed aromas of ether, antiseptics, and disinfectant permeated the silent hallways of the hospital. Doctors and nurses consulted in hushed conversation at doorways. Visitors wandered to and from rooms, some smiling and encouraged, others teary-eyed and wan as they struggled to comprehend bad news. Elation and melancholy walked hand-in-hand, and the atmosphere was charged with emotion. Nothing seemed commonplace in these corridors where strangers were drawn together by the common bonds of disease, misfortune, and mishap.

Vail avoided everyone, speaking briefly when forced to, merely nodding to those he recognized as regulars or staff. He rushed to the hospital at the end of each day, first checking on Jane and Abel, then eating tasteless food in the cafeteria or standing outside the emergency door to grab a smoke.

Martin Vail had always detested hospitals because they reminded him of the blackest and most agonizing days of his past. They evoked images, in sharp and painful focus, of his mother as they put her in an ambulance and carried her out of his life forever; of the intensive care unit where his father lay dead from a coronary; of the pale blue room in which he said farewell to Ma Cat, the grandmother who had raised him, as she lay dying of cancer. Ironically, those images now had been replaced by relief and thanksgiving and by the sheer joy of knowing that Jane Venable and Abel Stenner had been saved by the surgeons, nurses, and attendants in the emergency room at Chicago General.

A few days after the demise of Stampler, Jack Yancey died as the result of his stroke, and Vail officially became the district attorney. Dr. Samuel Woodward, under fire for his role in the release of Stampler, held a press conference and, bolstered by half a dozen colleagues, weaseled out of the situation with long-winded psychobabble.

During the weeks that followed, Vail kept a nightly vigil between the hospital rooms of Jane Venable and Abel Stenner, sleeping in the chair in Venable's room and going home only to shower and change clothes on his way to work. Sometimes he sat beside Jane's bed, holding her hand for an hour at a time, convinced that he was to blame for her pain and suffering, as well as Stenner's.

Stenner was making a remarkable recovery. By the end of the third week he was taking short walks down the halls with the help of a walker. Jane, who faced several weeks of torturous facial reconstruction, seemed in good spirits despite the painful injuries and the loss of her eye. Weak but ebullient, her face swathed in bandages from her forehead to her jaw and bruises tainting her nose and throat, she was indomitable. It was Jane who bolstered Vail's spirits during the long nights in the hospital as he fought with his conscience.

"Boy," she said one night, "I'll bet Aaron Stampler's sitting down in hell, laughing his buns off about now."

"What do you mean?"

"Because he's still getting to you, darling. He's reaching out of his grave and pulling your chain. He conned everyone, Marty. Everybody bought his lie, why should you be any different?"

"Because I helped manufacture the lie."

"He *conned* you, Marty. Admit it and forget it. Stampler isn't worth five minutes of bad time. You're a great lawyer. You did exactly what the law prescribes, you gave Stampler the best possible defense. You beat me fair and square, and believe me, I've thought a lot about the way you sandbagged me in the years since the trial. It was perfect. It was textbook stuff. The fact that the son of a bitch was guilty is beside the point."

"Beside the point?"

"Marty, how many lawyers do you know who ask their clients whether they're guilty or not?"

"What's that got to do with anything? It's immaterial."

"No, it's practical. If the client did it, he'll lie to you, so why bother to ask? You presume innocence and gather evidence to support that assumption, which you did brilliantly."

"You're talking like a college professor."

"And you're acting like a student. I remember a quote from an article about you—years ago," Venable said. "I don't remember the exact words, but in essence you said the only way for the law to remain strong is if we constantly attack its weaknesses."

"You have a good memory."

"Don't you still feel that way?"

"It doesn't have a damn thing to do with the courtroom. It has to do with acting. The courtroom has become the theater of the absurd. Which lawyer gives the best performance? How good is the judge? How gullible is the jury? The truth gets lost in the shuffle."

"Reality is what the jury perceives as truth. You also said that."

"Well, I was young and brash in those . . . do you remember everything you read?"

"Just the stuff I agree with." She tried to laugh but it was painful. "Sure, it's theater. Sure, it's the best man—or woman—wins. And yes, it's all about swaying the jury. So what? Those are the rules. And you're hellaciously good at pushing the rules to the limit no matter what side you're on." She paused a moment and winked her good eye. "It's one of the reasons I love you," she said.

"I can't even begin to list all the reasons I love you, Janie," he said. He leaned over and kissed her gently on the mouth.

"Don't go away," she whispered. "Kiss me some more. Unless you'd like to lock the door and slide in beside me."

"You're under sedation," he whispered back.

"It wore off."

—

Characteristically, when he brought up the subject with Stenner, the detective's response was short and direct.

"You made a mistake ten years ago. You think you're infallible, Marty?"

—

But the subject of Stampler could not be ignored.

St. Claire and Naomi had stayed on the phone for the first week or so, sorting through police records in Colorado, San Francisco, and Kentucky and putting together a background profile on Rebecca, a sorrowful and sordid story in itself. Gradually the saga of Rebecca and Aaron Stampler began to make sense.

Harvey St. Claire, with his baby cup in hand and a wad of tobacco in his cheek, settled back in a chair on his nightly visit to Abel and gave him all the details.

"We've managed to trace her back as far as high school. That was Denver, 1965," he began. "Her mother died when she was twelve, her father was regular Air Force. An NCO, rose up through the ranks, ultimately made captain. He was killed in a burglary in their apartment in early 1965. She vanished right after that. Accordin' to a retired homicide detective named Ashcraft, she was a suspect—there were reports of sexual and physical abuse by the old man—but they couldn't make anythin' stick. The murder was never solved."

"How was he killed?" Stenner mumbled.

"Stabbed to death."

"Not usually a burglar's choice of weapons."

St. Claire nodded. "It was a messy job. I got the feelin' talkin' to Ashcraft that they deep-sixed the investigation because everyone assumed Rebecca did him but they couldn't put a case together. Anyway, she popped up on the computer in San Francisco two years later—a dope bust in the Haight-Ashbury. Paid a menial fine, seventy-five bucks. Nothin' else until she accepted a teachin' job in Crikside in 1970. Stampler was in the first grade then—that's when she became his teacher and later mentor and finally lover."

"When was Stampler born?" asked Stenner.

"Sixty-five, coincidentally the same year Rebecca's father was killed and she took a hike. We went back over Tommy Goodman's notes from his meetin' with her—he went down there and talked to her when Vail was preparin' Stampler's defense. She mentioned some drug problems to him and there was somethin' about living in a commune in New Mexico for awhile and teaching kids there, but we couldn't put that together, most of those communes appeared and disappeared like sand gnats back in the late eighties. And there's no further arrest records on her—that we could uncover—so she's literally a cipher until she showed up in Crikside. What attracted her to the job was they didn't ask for references. I assume Crikside was beggin' and not too choosy. The state has no employment or health records on her, and social security didn't turn up anythin' on her until she went to work teachin' school. Apparently they needed a teacher so bad they overlooked certain fundamentals, like a teaching certificate and a background check. The locals say she was a good teacher."

"Depends on what she was teaching," Stenner said.

"Well, she sure taught Stampler a few tricks you don't normally learn in school, like Murder 101. Anyway, she taught there until 1991, then she just left. Boarded up this little house she owns one weekend and vanished into the night, just like in Denver. But interestingly enough, she paid her taxes every year by money order, so the house is still in her name."

"I missed the last act," said Stenner. "You think that's where Stampler was heading when you caught up with him?"

"He was ten miles from her house when we nailed him. You tell me."

———

As the weeks drifted by, the subject of Aaron Stampler took a backseat to the Edith Stoddard case. When Vail was not there,

Venable stared at the blank TV screen or out the window, thinking about the night she discovered the hidden closet in Delaney's apartment, about the paraphernalia. About the gun. And she wondered whether Edith Stoddard was a victim or a willing participant in the bizarre sexual games Delaney obviously liked to play. If Stoddard contended that she was victimized by the dead man, Venable could build a strong case in her favor.

She sent notes to Stoddard, advising her not to discuss the case with *anyone* until Venable was back on her feet and able to resume her duties. Stoddard never answered the notes and refused to recant the confession she made to Shock Johnson.

———

Shana Parver, with the assistance of Dermott Flaherty, continued to construct the Murder One case against Edith Stoddard, whose arraignment had been postponed for a month because Jane Venable was in the hospital. Parver was the strategist, Flaherty the pragmatist.

"Venable will use the insanity defense," Flaherty guessed.

"It's still premeditated murder," Shana snapped back.

"But extenuated. Venable will argue that she was a sexual victim of Delany. That he kept her in sexual bondage. That her job was at stake. And then he cut her loose and she was mentally unstable because of her daughter and husband."

"We still have her confession," Parver countered.

"Which Venable will get thrown out. She was distraught, scared, anguished . . ."

"Oh blah, blah, blah," Parver said.

Flaherty laughed. "C'mon," he said. "I'll buy you dinner."

"No, I'll buy you dinner. I'm the primary on this case. And don't let me order a martini."

"Oh, I don't know," he laughed. "You get very lovable when you're loaded."

She cast a dubious glance at him. "I don't have to be loaded to be lovable, Flay," she said.

Trees trembled before a warm spring breeze as Vail drove along Lakeshore Drive. He stopped and bought several bunches of spring flowers from a street vendor before entering the hospital. Jane was sitting up in bed and Stenner, who could now get around with the help of a cane, was sitting across the room.

"I got my walking papers today," Stenner said. "They're going to parole me an hour early so I can come to court in the morning."

"Nothing to see," Vail said. "We're going to ask for a continuance of the arraignment until Jane's well enough to go to court."

"That was thoughtful of you," Venable said. "Do I see signs of a crack in your armor?"

"It was Shana's idea," Vail said with a smile. "And I don't see so much as a blemish in her armor."

"She's a tough little cookie, Marty," Jane said. "You taught her well."

"I didn't teach her anything," Vail laughed. "She was born tough. Wait'll she gets John Wayne Darcy in court."

"How about Edith Stoddard?" Jane asked.

"That's between the two of you. I'm not involved in that one, thank God."

"You're involved in everything that goes on in the D.A.'s office, Marty. Who are you trying to kid?"

"I didn't come here to talk business," Vail said. He handed her the bouquet of spring flowers. "I came to tamper with your affections."

"You can tamper with my affections anytime," she said and took the dead flowers from a vase on the table beside the bed and dropped them in the wastebasket. Vail took the vase to the sink in the corner and filled it with fresh water.

"I think I'll go back to my room and spend a little time," Stenner said. "Been there four weeks. Be like leaving home. Good night."

"I'll drop by and tuck you in," Vail said.

"My nurse takes care of that," Stenner responded brusquely, walking as jauntily as he could from the room.

"I'm jealous of Abel," Venable said. "He's going home and I have two more operations to go."

Vail sat down beside her and ran a finger gently down the bandage on her face. "A few more weeks and it will all be behind us," he said gently.

He stood up and walked to the window.

"Still have Stampler on your mind, don't you?" she said softly.

"You know," he said, "there was a moment there . . . there was a moment when . . . when it was a catharsis. For a minute or two I had the power of life and death over him. I had him in my sights. God knows, I wanted to kill him. I wanted to shoot him over and over again. A bullet for every one he butchered. The trigger had an eighth of an inch to go and I knew what he wanted, Janie, I knew he *wanted* me to put him down, to pull me down to his level. Then I saw the sign and eased off and let the devil have him."

"Well, it's over, my dear." She said and patted the bed beside her.

Maybe, he thought. *And maybe it will never be over.*

———

The next morning, Shana Parver and Dermott Flaherty sat at the prosecutor's table, prepared to ask for another continuance of the arraignment of Edith Stoddard. Vail, Naomi, and St. Claire, accompanied by Abel Stenner, sat beside them in the first row. Edith Stoddard's daughter, Angelica, sat on the opposite side of the courtroom, nervously awaiting the hearing to start. She kept staring back at the entrance to the courtroom.

At exactly 9 A.M., Judge Thelma McElroy, a handsome black woman whose glittering, intelligent eyes hid behind round, wire-rimmed glasses, entered the room. A fair judge, she was known for her stern, no-nonsense approach to the law.

Edith Stoddard was led into the courtroom and took a seat at the defense table. She was drawn and thin. It was obvious her weeks in jail had worn her down. She folded her hands on the table and stared down at them.

A moment later there was a rumble from the rear of the courtroom. Vail turned to see what the commotion was about.

Jane Venable entered in a wheelchair. She was resplendent in an emerald green silk business suit, her red hair pulled back in a tight bun, a black patch over her eye, the side of her face covered with a fresh bandage.

She wheeled down the center aisle, cast her good eye at Vail, smiled, and winked as she headed for the defendant's table. Vail could not conceal his surprise. Shana Parver was even more surprised. She looked back at Vail, who just raised his eyebrows and shrugged.

"What the hell . . ." he mumbled under his breath.

"I think we're in trouble," Stenner said.

"We were in trouble when she took the case," Vail answered.

Judge McElroy lowered her head and peered over her glasses at Venable.

"Well, Ms. Venable, this is a surprise. Welcome back."

"Thank you, your honor," Venable said.

"Are we ready to proceed?" the judge asked.

"Quite," Venable answered.

"We were prepared to seek a postponement because of Ms. Venable's injuries, your honor . . ."

"That won't be necessary," Venable interrupted. "The defendant is prepared to answer the charges."

"The State is ready, your honor," Shana Parver stammered as Flaherty dug into his briefcase and began pulling out files.

The judge looked down at her agenda sheet.

"This is an arraignment, correct?"

"Yes," Parver answered.

"Any motions before we proceed?"

"Your honor," Venable began, "if it please the court, the defense asks that we be permitted to introduce one witness for the defense."

"Before we even start?" the judge said.

"We will seek bond for the defendant, Edith Stoddard, your honor. She has been incarcerated for almost two months without relief. We would seek permission for a character witness to appear in her behalf."

"Your honor . . ." Parver began, but the judge raised her hand and cut her off.

"Just one minute, counselor," she said, and to Venable, "who is this witness, Ms. Venable?"

"Her daughter, Angelica, your honor."

"Your honor, this is highly irregular," Parver snapped back. "This is an arraignment. We are prepared to present grand jury findings supporting the state's contention that Mrs. Stoddard committed the offense of first-degree murder. There can be no bond."

"Your honor, there are extenuating circumstances in this case," Venable countered. "My client has no previous criminal record. She was a valued executive secretary for years and has supported a daughter in college as well as a husband who is a paraplegic. Certainly the court and the prosecution can not object to hearing her daughter's plea. Fifteen minutes, your honor, that's all we ask."

Judge McElroy leaned back in her chair and took off her glasses.

"I assume the defense is prepared to enter a plea," she said, staring down at Venable.

"Yes, your honor."

"And you want to introduce this witness *before* the prosecution makes its presentments?"

"I think it would be appropriate to do it now," Venable answered.

"Huh," McElroy said. She picked up a pencil and tapped the point on a pad for several seconds. "Well, I agree with the prosecution. It certainly is an unusual departure from normal procedure. On the other hand, I do not wish this court to appear without compassion. Ms. Parver, I'm going to overrule your objection. Keep in mind there is no jury here. The question of bail rests with my discretion."

Although she was angry, Parver realized it would be foolish to stir the judge's wrath this early in the game.

"Yes, your honor," Parver said.

"Thank you. Alright, the defense may call its witness," she said.

"Defense calls Angelica Stoddard."

———

Angelica Stoddard was pale and nervous. Her hands were shaking as she took the oath and sat down in the witness box. Her eyes were fixed on Venable as she wheeled her chair to the front of the courtroom. Edith Stoddard stared suspiciously at Venable.

"Just relax," Venable said softly. "I know you're nervous but this will only take a few minutes. Give your name, please."

"Angelica Stoddard."

"How old are you, Angelica?"

"Twenty-one."

"And where do you reside?"

"In Chalmers Dormitory. I attend Chicago University."

"And how long have you been attending college?"

"Three years."

"What kind of grades do you make, Angelica?"

"I have a 3.6 going into my senior year."

"An A-student?"

"Well, yes. I've made a couple of B's, but mostly A's."

"You have a scholarship, do you not?"

"Yes. It pays tuition and books."

"And who pays your room and board?"

"My mother."

"Mrs. Edith Stoddard?"

"Yes."

"What is your father's name?"

"Charles. Charles Stoddard."

"Is your father employed?"

"No. My father is paralyzed from the neck down."

"And he lives with your mother?"

"Yes."

"*So*, your mother is the sole support of both you and your father, is that correct?"

"Yes."

"And until recently, she worked at Delaney Enterprises?"

"Yes. Mister Delaney fired her."

"Who takes care of your father during the day?"

"We have *had* a nurse who was also our housekeeper. She came at eight in the morning and left at five."

"So your mother takes care of him from five on?"

"Yes. Except when she has to . . . had to, work at night. Once or twice a week I went to the house when she had to work after five."

"So you both take care of him."

"Yes, but mainly my mom watches . . . watched over him."

"And have things changed since your mother's arrest?"

"Yes. Our nurse quit. The insurance wasn't enough to cover her wages anyway."

"And do you take care of your father now?"

"Yes. I dropped out of school and moved back to the house."

"So when your mother lost her job, it changed your lifestyle radically, is that true?"

"Yes."

"And this happened when your mother was arrested?"

Angelica nodded and stared down at her lap. "Doctor Saperstein—he's my father doctor—says we should put him in a nursing home." She began to cry and dabbed at her eyes with a tissue.

"Can you afford that? I mean, if your insurance doesn't cover the nurse, how could you afford a nursing home?"

"I will . . . would get a job. Sell the house . . ."

She stopped for a moment, stared down again, and seemed to gather her composure. Then she looked up and her expression had changed from sorrow to anger.

"It's so unfair . . ." she said, then hesitated for a moment and looking straight at Edith Stoddard, her voice stronger and her eyes flashing, she said. "It's unfair because my mother didn't kill Delaney, I did! She confessed to protect me!"

The judge was jolted back in her chair. Venable seemed shocked. Edith Stoddard leaped to her feet.

"That's a lie," she yelled. "She's trying to protect me! I killed Delaney, I confessed to killing Delaney. The police have my confession on record. Stop this now!"

"No, you stop it, Mama," Angelica yelled back. "I was the one he kept in bondage. Since I was eighteen. He held your job over my head. He threatened me . . ."

The courtroom was in bedlam. Parver was on her feet.

"Objection, your honor, *objection!*"

Venable stammered: "Your honor, I had no idea . . ."

Naomi turned to Vail. "Holy shit!" she whispered. But Vail did not answer. He stared at Venable with absolute awe.

"It's true," Angelica Stoddard screamed. "I went there that night to plead with him to give her job back and he forced me to . . ."

"Objection, your honor," Parver yelled.

McElroy slammed her gavel several times. "Quiet in this courtroom," she demanded, her eyes flashing with rage. "Quiet, NOW! Counselors—in my chambers, this minute. This court is in recess."

"Excuse me, your honor, may we have ten minutes before you meet with the attorneys?" Parver asked.

Judge McElroy still flushed with ire, glanced at Venable. "Alright, allll-*right,*" she snapped. "Fifteen minutes, ladies. Then I'll see you both in chambers."

She fled the bench.

Vail looked across the room at Venable, who held her hands out at her side as if to say, "I'm just as confused as you are." He smiled at her and shook his head.

—

Vail led Parver, Naomi, St. Claire, Stenner, and Flaherty into a small holding office beside the courtroom.

"Okay, Shana," Vail said after pulling the door shut, "now what're you going to do? Punt or play?"

She looked him straight in the eyes and said, "I'll be damned if I know. I can't even figure out what the options are."

"Do you think Venable planned this, or is she just as surprised as we are?" Naomi asked.

"I don't think she planned it," Vail said. "But I think there's a chance she knew it was going to happen."

"Shock defense," Flaherty said.

"Theater of the law," Vail answered.

"You should know," Stenner said. "You pulled the same kind of stunt on Jane ten years ago."

"Maybe so, Abel," Shana agreed, "but who do we deal with? What's your gut feeling? Which one of them did it?"

Stenner made a practical decision. "The mother did it. The other way is too convoluted."

"I say the mother," Flaherty said. "But I think the daughter was involved with Delaney, just as she said she was on the stand, and the mother killed him to set her free. All this can come out in discovery. I say we postpone the arraignment and go back to the drawing board."

"The daughter did it and the mother's covering for her," St. Claire said. "I don't care how convoluted it is."

"I think Angelica did it," Parver agreed.

"I think Edith did it for a lot of reasons," Naomi said.

"They're both giving the same story, both say the other one knew nothing about it, they have the same motive, the same opportunity, and neither one of them has an alibi," Stenner said.

"That's ridiculous," said St. Claire. "We got Stoddard's fingerprints all over the weapon."

Vail stared at the ceiling. "Why wouldn't Stoddard's fingerprints be all over the weapon, it's her gun?" he asked of nobody in particular.

"How about the bullets?" Flaherty asked.

"Same story," Vail said. "It's her gun. Naturally, she loaded it."

"And the daughter?" asked Flaherty. "How about her prints?"

"She'll say she wore gloves," Shana said. "If she wants to stick with her story."

"Indict 'em both, see if we can break one of 'em down before we get to court," suggested St. Claire.

Vail laughed. "Oh sure, I can see that. What do you think the grand jury will say if we go back in there and tell 'em we want to indict two people because we're not sure which one committed the crime?"

"I think it's a setup," said Stenner. "Either they were in it together or they're confusing the issue now."

"Can we crack one story?" said Flaherty. "Find a chink in Edith Stoddard's story and see if the daughter stays with the wrong yarn?"

Shana Parver shifted uneasily in her chair. She stared down at the floor but said nothing.

"Okay, Parver," Vail said. "What's bugging you? Out with it."

"I think . . ." she started, hesitated for a moment, then went on. "I think he deserved what he got no matter who shot him."

That quieted the room down. They all looked at each other, then back at Shana.

"Let me ask you all something," said Vail. "Do any of you think Edith Stoddard would willingly have become involved in Delaney's sex games?"

"Why?" Shana asked.

"Because that may be the key to this whole mess," Vail said. "Delaney shined to the daughter and dazzled her. Look, she's a kid, all of a sudden she's getting attention from her mother's boss who is a big shot in town. He lures her in, the next thing you know he's playing kinky sex games with her. She doesn't tell anybody, certainly not her mother. Delaney was naked when he was hit. Supposing he was with the daughter and Edith Stoddard came in and caught them. She goes off the wall, pulls the gun, and drops Delaney. Then she hustles Angelica out of there, dumps the gun, and splits. The next day during Johnson's interrogation, she realizes she can't buffalo the pros so she cops to the crime, says she lost it because Delaney got rid of her, and hopes it will end there. That way she protects her husband and her daughter."

"Pretty good scenario," Stenner said.

"Except we know the truth," said Flaherty.

"Do we?" St. Claire offered. "All we know is that Delaney was one sick son of a bitch and whoever whacked him knew about his closet full of goodies. Either way, he comes off in court as a greaseball and the ladies get the sympathy."

"Gonna be hard to get a unanimous decision on this," Naomi said. "If half the jurors are women, they'll hang that jury up forever."

"I think Naomi's right," Vail said. "The question here is, what do *we* want. Do we want to put Edith or Angelica Stoddard away for the rest of their lives?"

"Compassion?" Stenner said, eyeing Vail.

"Expedience," Flaherty offered. "I say make the best deal we can, otherwise she may walk."

"Shana?" Vail said. "It's your call."

"First-degree manslaughter. Ten to twenty."

"Venable won't buy it," said Vail. "She'll take her chances with the jury."

"You're overlooking Edith Stoddard," said Shana. "She doesn't want to go to trial. She sure as hell doesn't want what happened in the courtroom this morning to be repeated. Her whole thing now is to protect her daughter and her husband."

"You think she'll go for manslaughter one?" Naomi asked.

"I think Janie wants her client to walk out of this courtroom a free woman," said Vail.

"So?" Shana said.

"So, I think it's time to make a deal," Vail said.

"And I think no matter what happens, justice is going to get another swift kick in the ass," Stenner said.

It was the first time anyone in the room ever saw him smile.

———

"What the hell are you pulling, Ms. Venable?" Judge McElroy asked, scowling across her desk at Venable.

"I swear, I had no idea she was going to say that," Venable answered. "She asked if she could be a character witness, to help her mother get bail."

"I certainly hope so. I don't take kindly to lawyers who try to

turn my courtroom into a carnival." Judge McElroy glared at her
for a few seconds more.

"You have my word," Venable replied firmly.

"Alright," McElroy said. "What are we going to do about this
mess?"

"I think that's up to Ms. Venable," Shana answered immediately.

"Me?" Venable said.

"Yes," Parver said. "You can't defend them both. That means
Angelica will have to get her own lawyer. Are you prepared in
your defense to lay this off on Angelica Stoddard?"

"What do you mean?" Venable answered, her voice getting
edgy.

"That's the only way you can walk Edith out of here," said
Parver. "Either we assume Edith Stoddard is guilty and try to work
something out, or you're going to have to convince your client
that you should go after her own daughter. Only one of them's
guilty."

"Then we'll go to the jury," Venable snapped.

"And wash all that dirty laundry in front of the press?" Shana
answered. "I don't think so. We still have a confession, counselor.
Your client hasn't recanted that yet."

"No jury in the world will convict Edith Stoddard," Venable said.

"That isn't the point, is it?" Shana said.

"What is the point?"

"We have a clear case of premeditated murder. We have a powerful civic leader who has a lot of friends in high places. The only
way to break that down is to drag Edith through the mud, too.
Think about it."

McElroy leaned back in her chair, making a pyramid of her fingertips and leaning her chin on them. She smothered a smile. This
Parver child was slick and tough, she thought. Inwardly, she admired both women. She stood finally.

"If you two will excuse me," she said, "I'm going to step outside
for a few minutes. I would like to think that when I get back we
can resolve this problem."

She left the room.

"Okay, what are you offering?" Venable said.

"Manslaughter one. Ten to twenty. She could be out in six or seven years."

"Not a chance. I'd be betraying my client. We'll take second degree. Five to ten."

"I can't do that."

"What does Martin want?"

"This is my case, not his."

"He didn't make a recommendation?"

"Nope."

Venable smiled. "What a guy," she said.

"We agree on that," Shana said, and finally smiled too.

"So—what's the answer, Shana? We can wrap it up here and now."

"Your way?"

"Hell, girl, you got me into this in the first place," Venable said with a smile. "I was perfectly happy sitting up in platinum city making a fortune. I think the question is, do you really want to go to trial on this?"

Shana Parver did not answer immediately. She stared at the ceiling, as Vail often did, thinking. Finally she said, "How about a compromise? Plead her guilty to first-degree manslaughter if the judge will agree to five to twenty. She could be out in three years."

"Minimum security prison?"

"I have no problem with that."

Venable smiled and stuck out her hand.

"Deal," she said. "You're a helluva lawyer, Shana."

"Look who's talking."

———

A few days after the arraignment, the governor of Kentucky ordered the state patrol to recover Stampler's body from mine shaft number five. Spring rains had washed away the snow, leaving behind a muddy oasis in the forest with the gaping hole, like a bull's-eye, in the center of the timbers that covered the old elevator shaft. A small crowd of Crikside residents stood on the periphery, watching with anticipation the way crowds will, although there was nothing much to see but a small crane with lights and a video camera that was lowered into the bowels of the Kentucky mountainside, and a half dozen state troopers staring at the video monitor.

The mine shaft was empty.

ABOUT THE AUTHOR

WILLIAM DIEHL is the author of six previous bestsellers: *Sharky's Machine, Chameleon, Hooligans, Thai Horse, 27,* and *Primal Fear.* He lives on St. Simons Island, Georgia, with his wife, Virginia Gunn, and daughter, Temple. He is Distinguished Visiting Writer at Georgia Southern University and is working on his eighth novel.